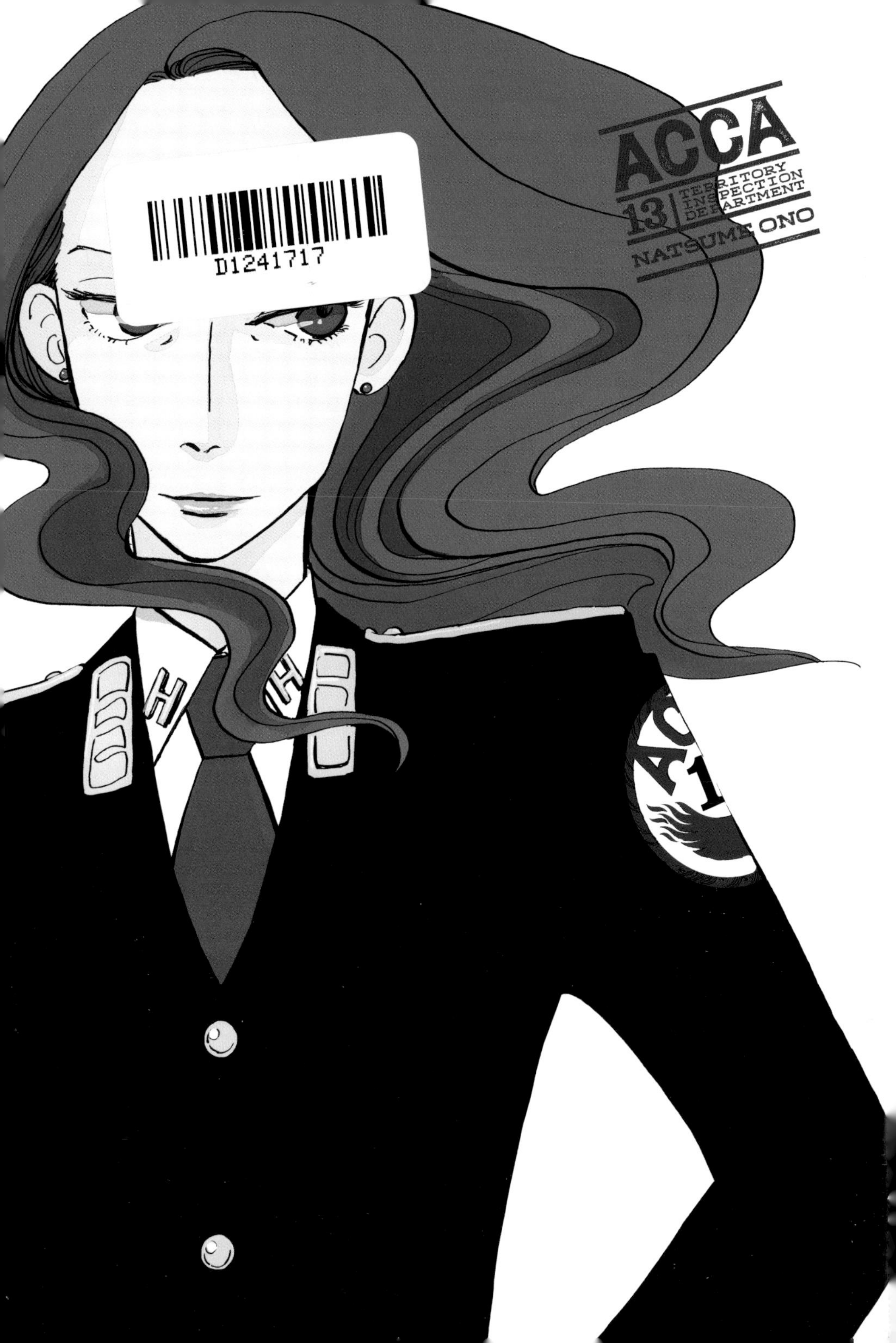
ACCA
13
TERRITORY INSPECTION DEPARTMENT
NATSUME ONO

ACCA 13 TERRITORY INSPECTION DEPARTMENT 4

CONTENTS

ACCA
13 Terr Insp Dept
Natsume Ono

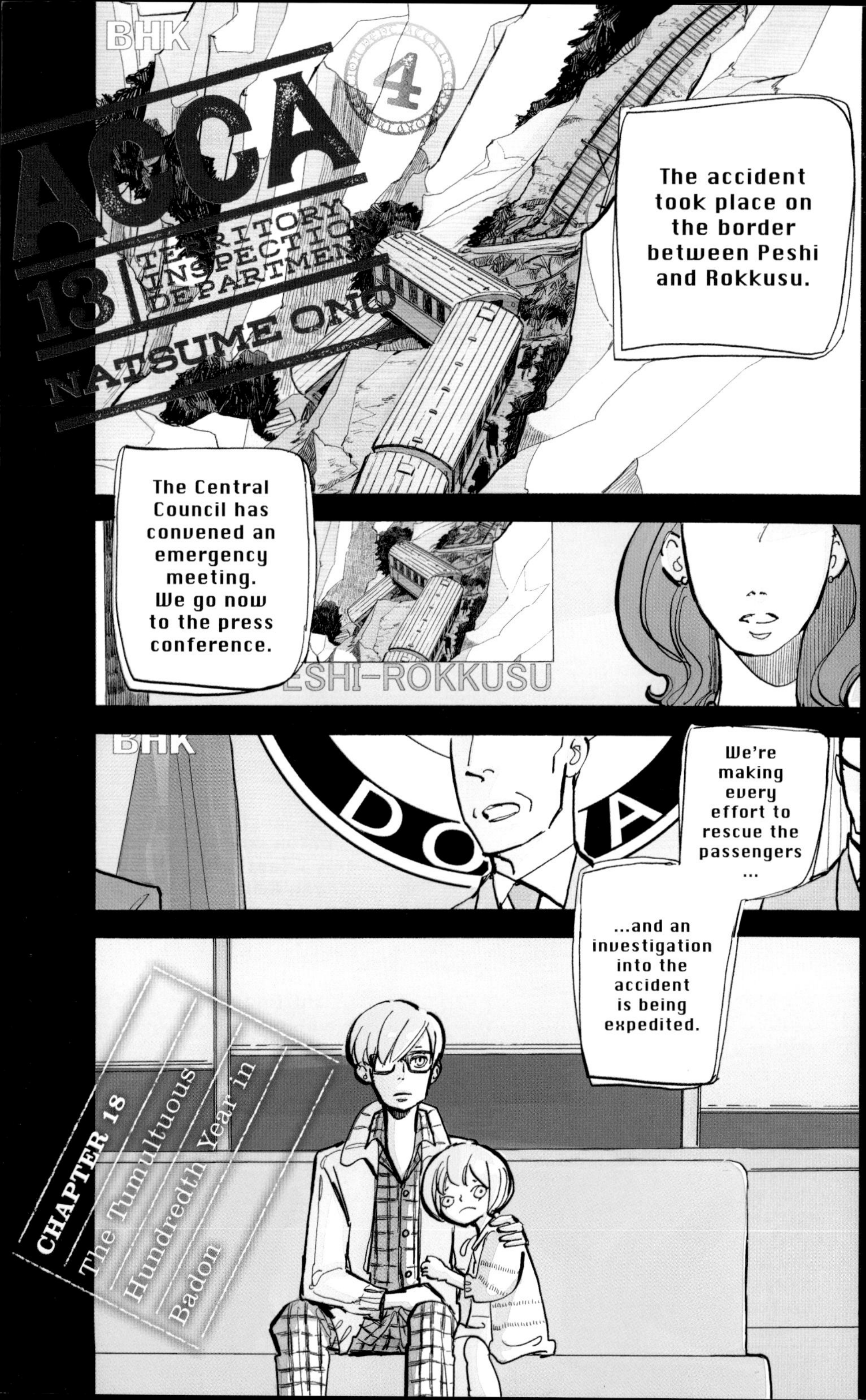
BHK
ACCA
13
NATSUME ONO
The accident took place on the border between Peshi and Rokkusu.
ESHI-ROKKUSU
The Central Council has convened an emergency meeting. We go now to the press conference.
BHK
We're making every effort to rescue the passengers...
...and an investigation into the accident is being expedited.
CHAPTER 18
The Tumultuous Hundredth Year in Badon

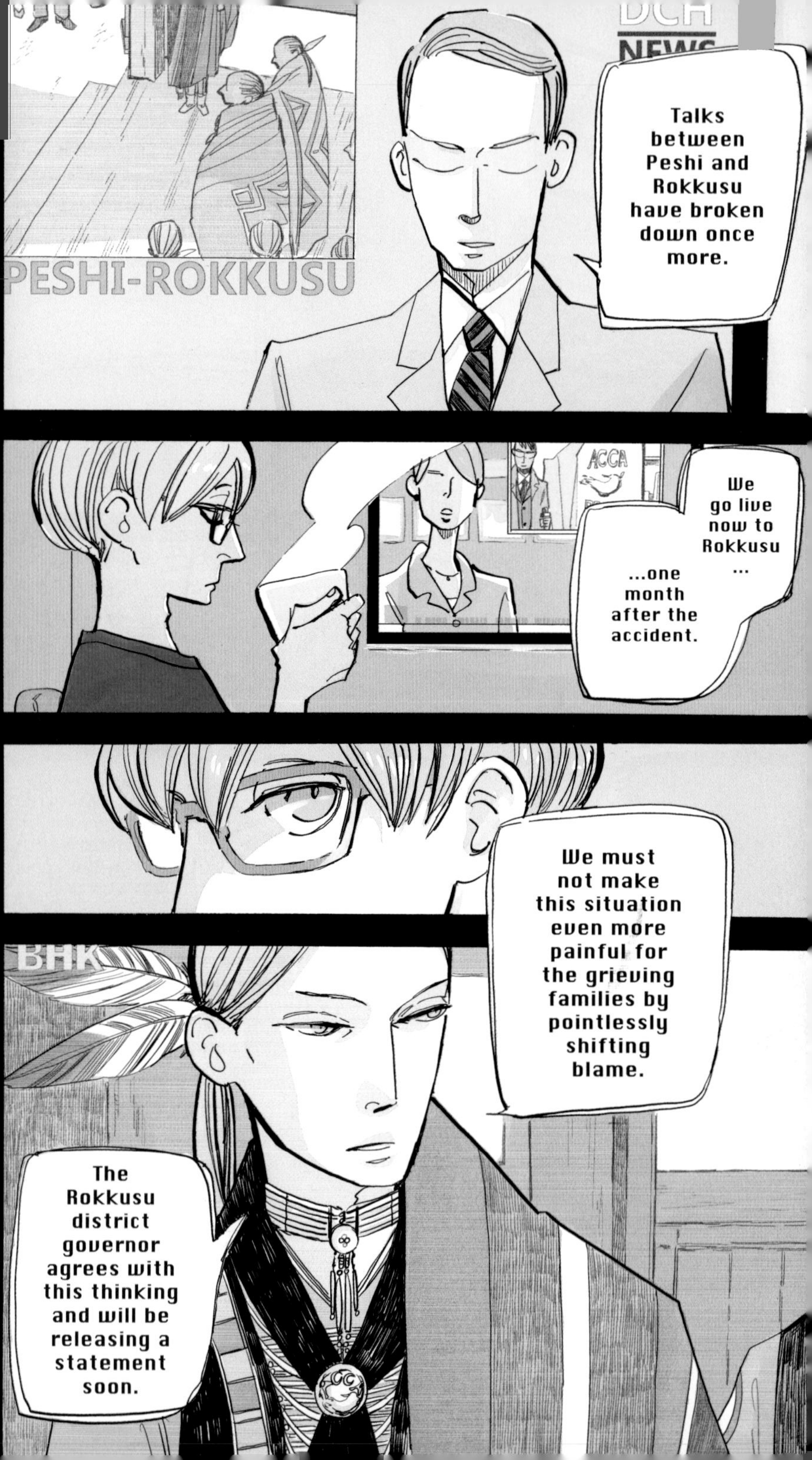
DCH NEWS
Talks between Peshi and Rokkusu have broken down once more.
PESHI-ROKKUSU
We go live now to Rokkusu ...
...one month after the accident.
ACCA
We must not make this situation even more painful for the grieving families by pointlessly shifting blame.
BHK
The Rokkusu district governor agrees with this thinking and will be releasing a statement soon.

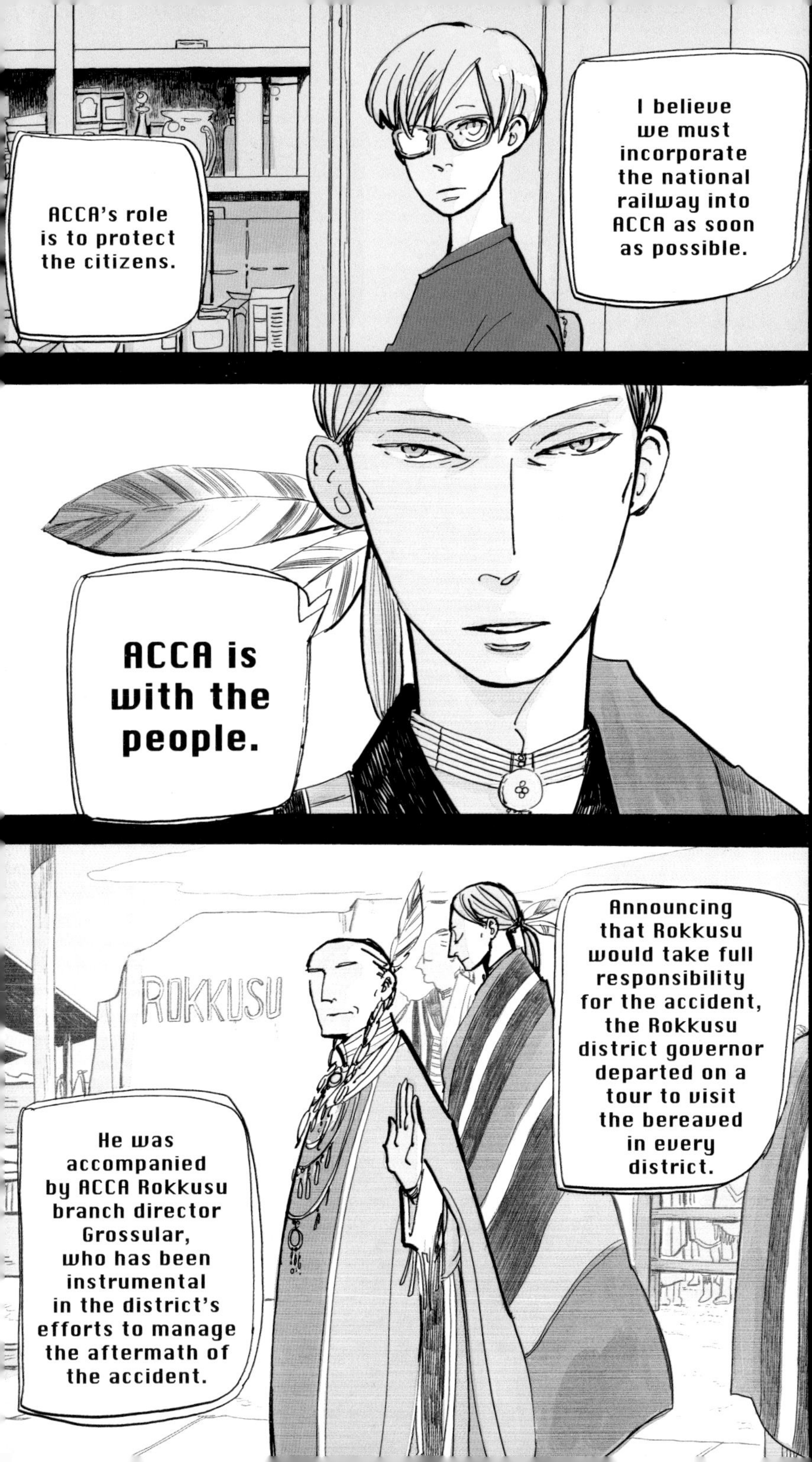
I believe we must incorporate the national railway into ACCA as soon as possible.
ACCA's role is to protect the citizens.
ACCA is with the people.
Announcing that Rokkusu would take full responsibility for the accident, the Rokkusu district governor departed on a tour to visit the bereaved in every district.
ROKKUSU
He was accompanied by ACCA Rokkusu branch director Grossular, who has been instrumental in the district's efforts to manage the aftermath of the accident.

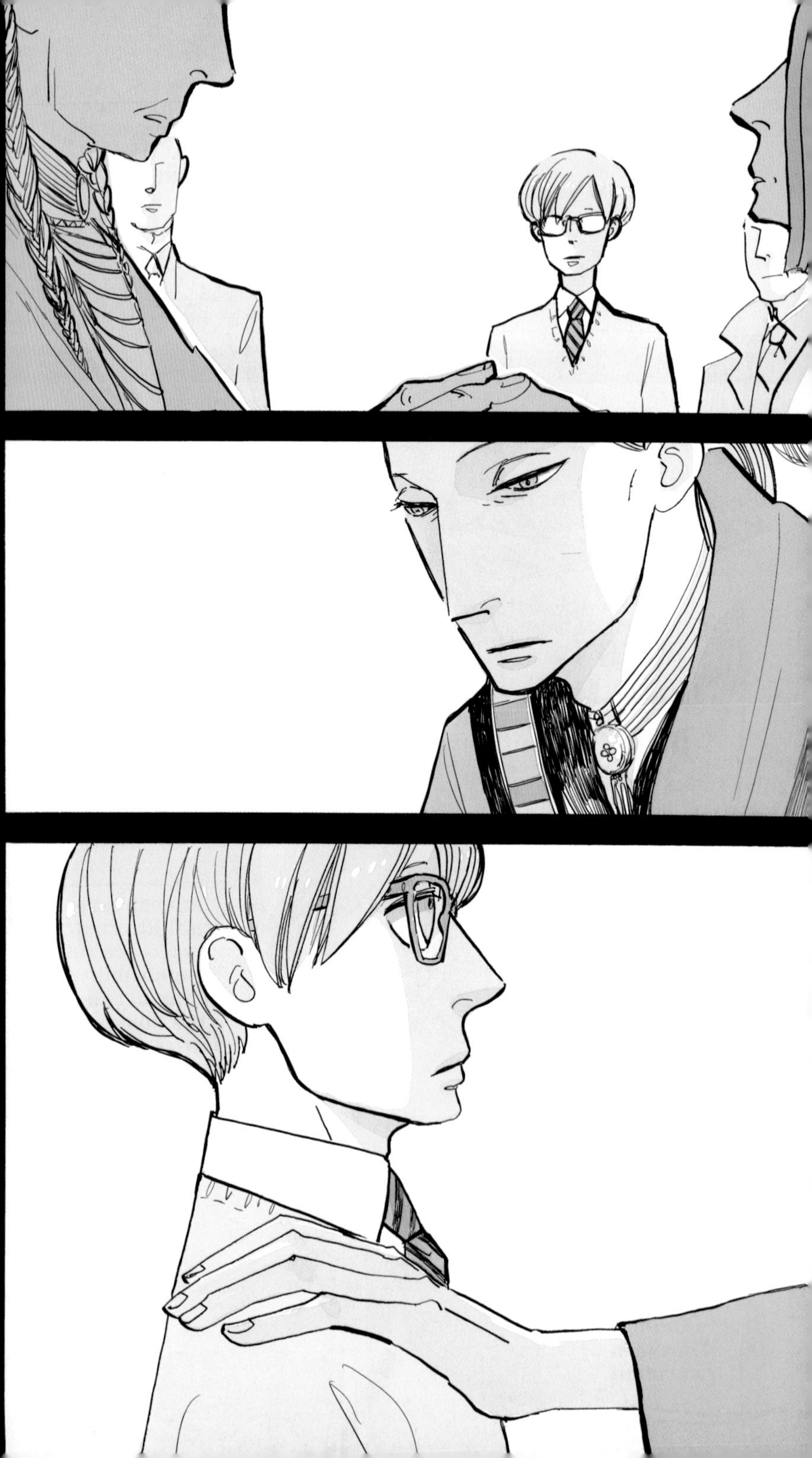

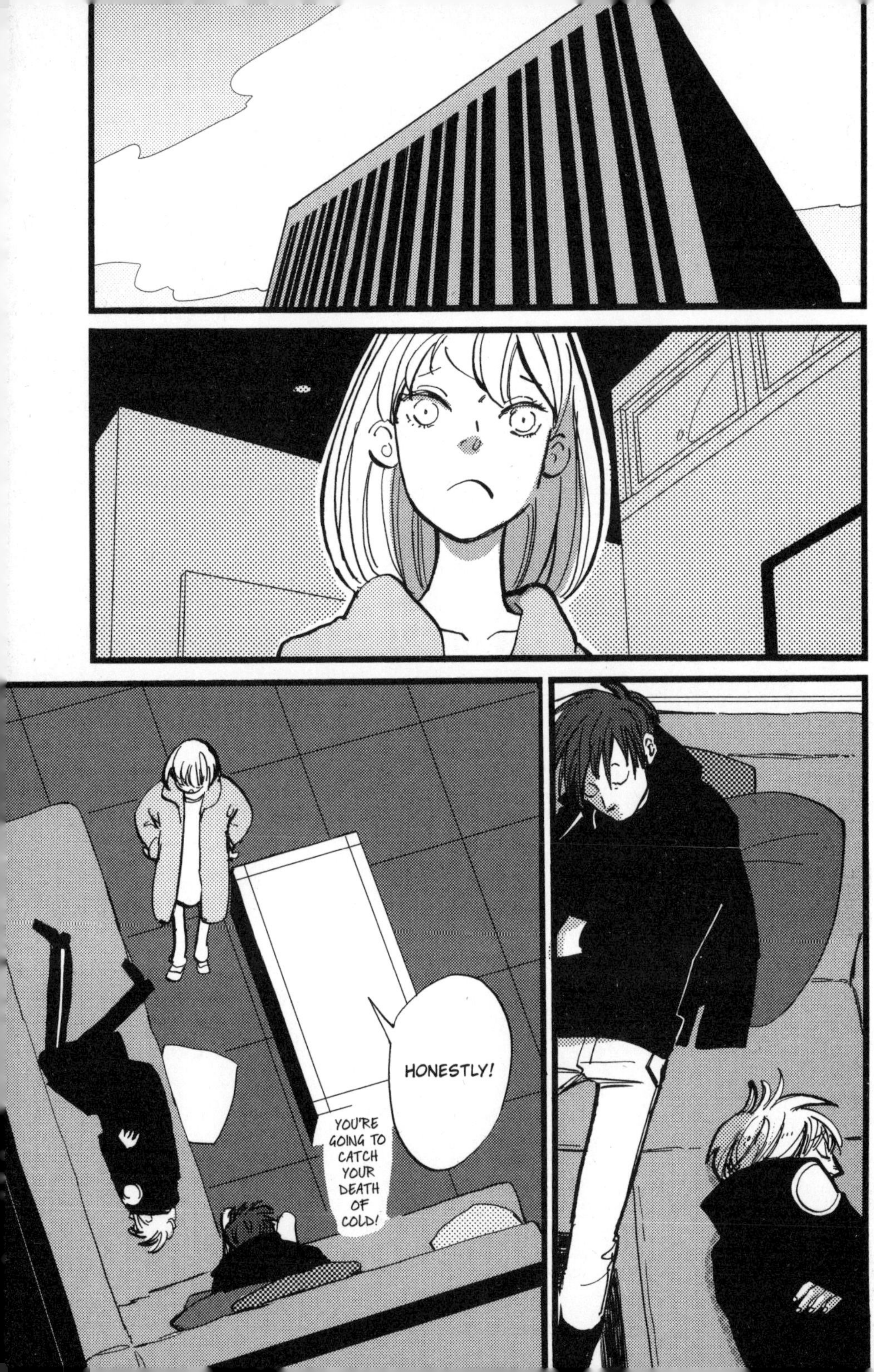
HONESTLY!
YOU'RE GOING TO CATCH YOUR DEATH OF COLD!

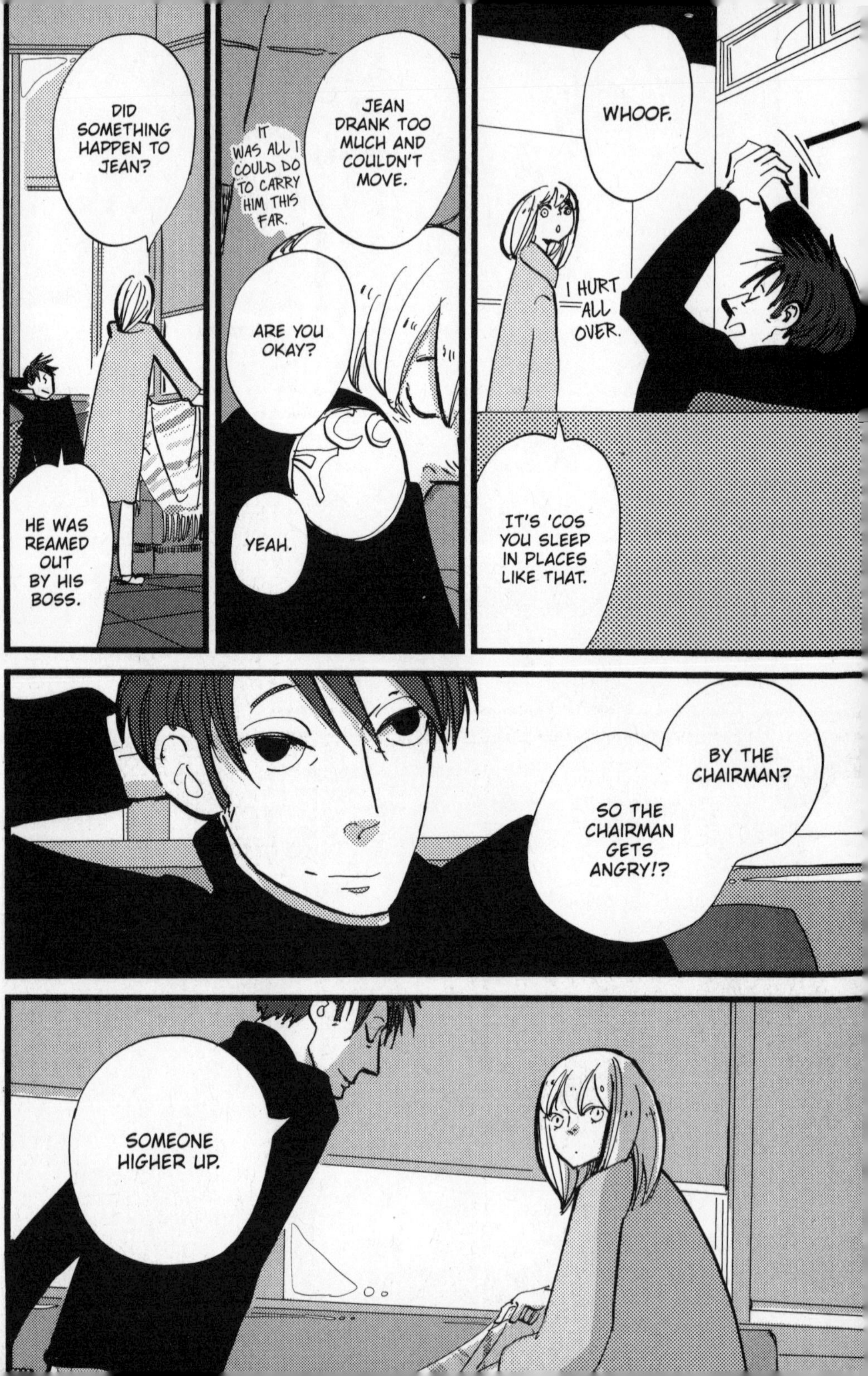
WHOOF.
I HURT ALL OVER.
IT'S 'COS YOU SLEEP IN PLACES LIKE THAT.
JEAN DRANK TOO MUCH AND COULDN'T MOVE.
IT WAS ALL I COULD DO TO CARRY HIM THIS FAR.
ARE YOU OKAY?
YEAH.
DID SOMETHING HAPPEN TO JEAN?
HE WAS REAMED OUT BY HIS BOSS.
BY THE CHAIRMAN?
SO THE CHAIRMAN GETS ANGRY!?
SOMEONE HIGHER UP.

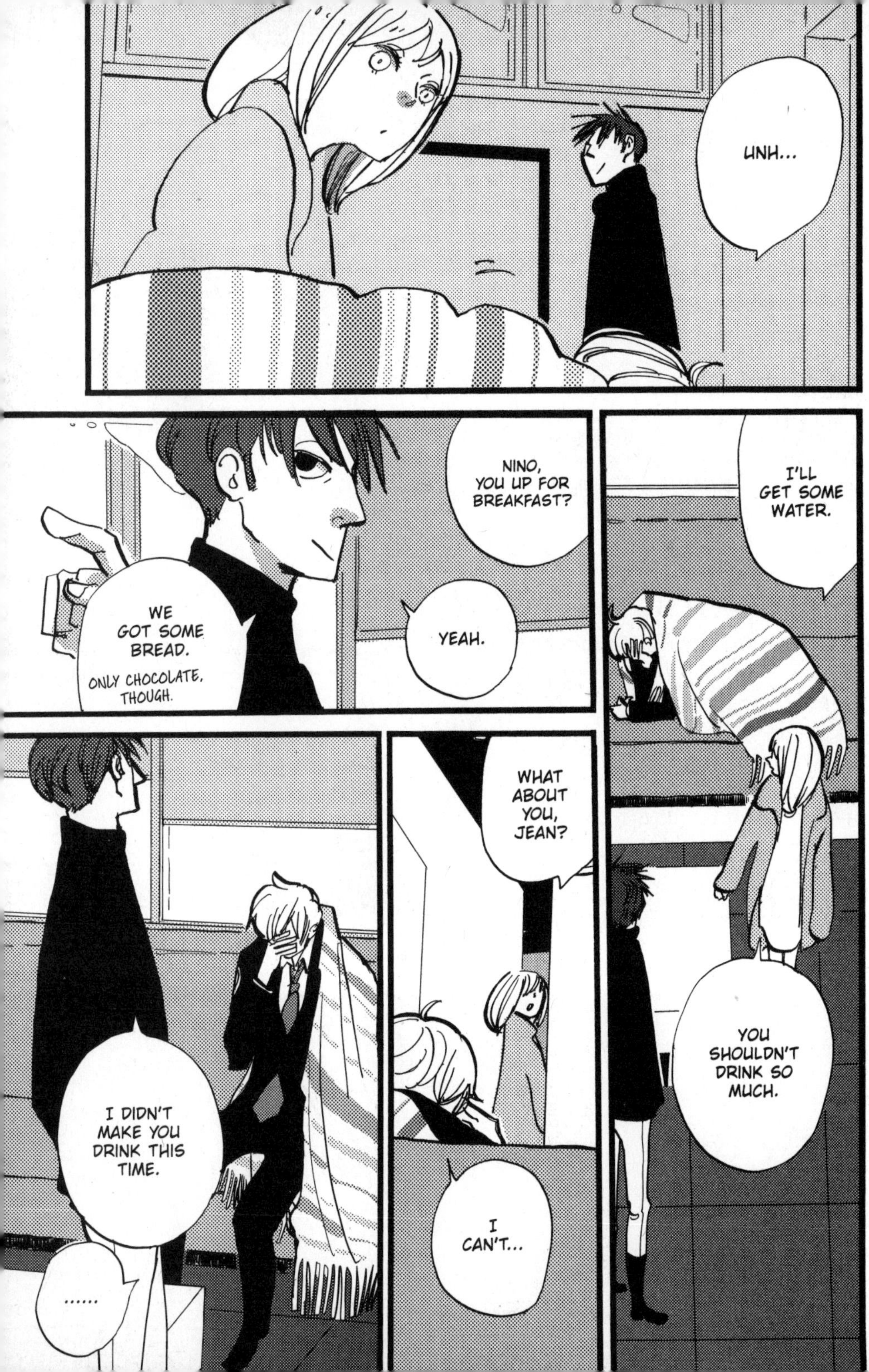
UNH...
I'LL GET SOME WATER.
NINO, YOU UP FOR BREAKFAST?
WE GOT SOME BREAD.
ONLY CHOCOLATE, THOUGH.
YEAH.
YOU SHOULDN'T DRINK SO MUCH.
WHAT ABOUT YOU, JEAN?
I CAN'T...
I DIDN'T MAKE YOU DRINK THIS TIME.
......

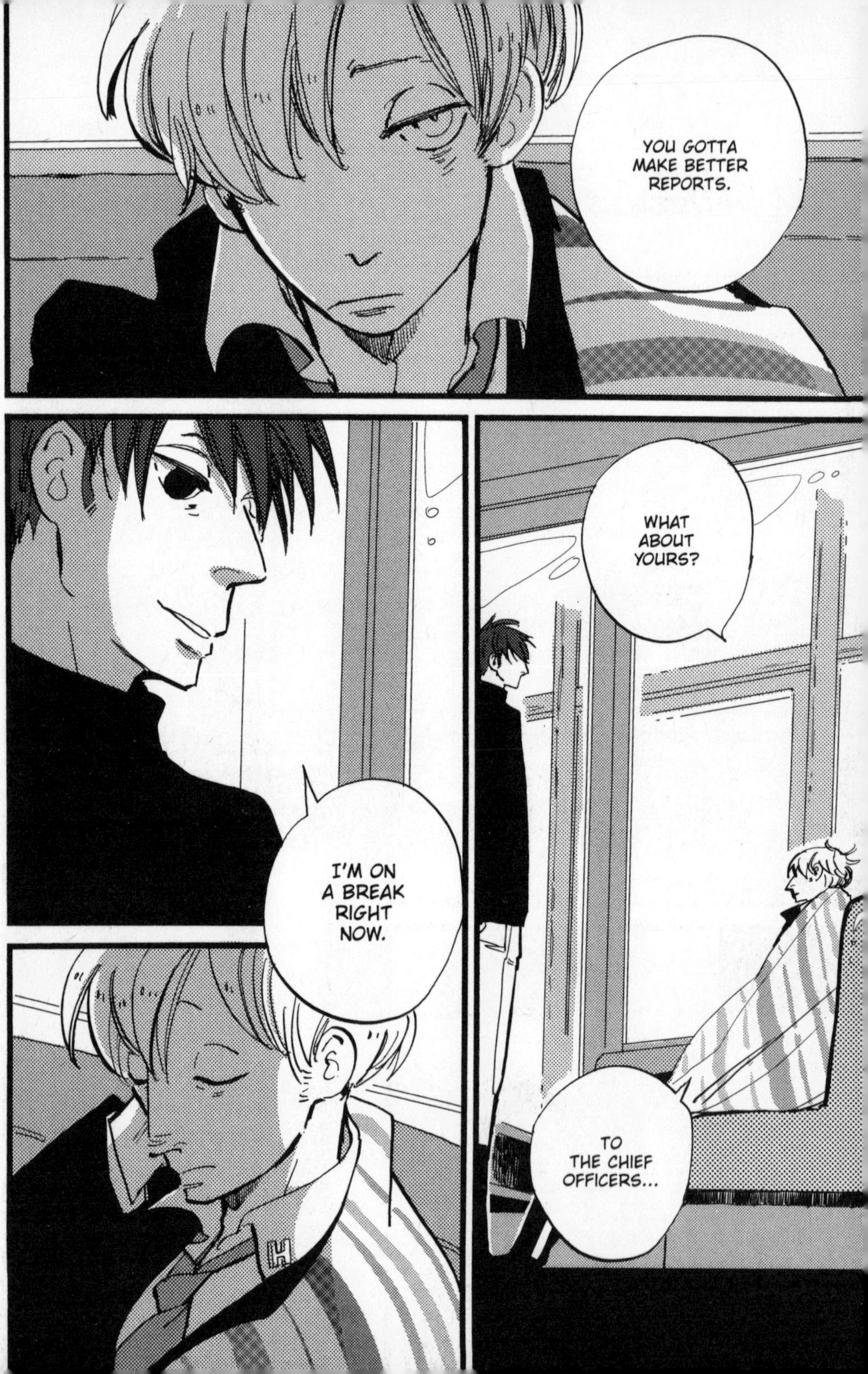
YOU GOTTA MAKE BETTER REPORTS.
WHAT ABOUT YOURS?
TO THE CHIEF OFFICERS...
I'M ON A BREAK RIGHT NOW.

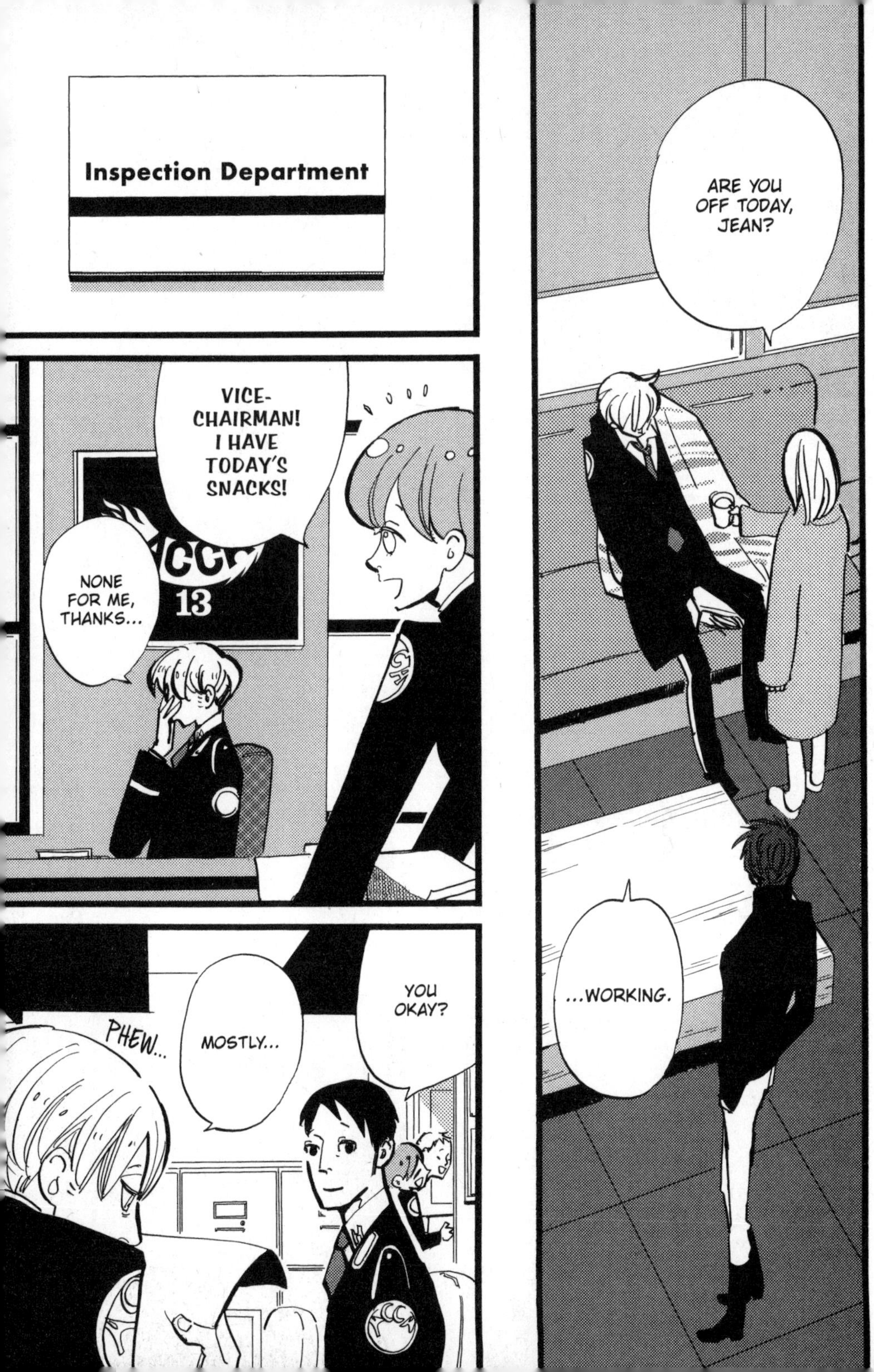
ARE YOU OFF TODAY, JEAN?
...WORKING.
Inspection Department
VICE-CHAIRMAN! I HAVE TODAY'S SNACKS!
NONE FOR ME, THANKS...
YOU OKAY?
MOSTLY...
PHEW...

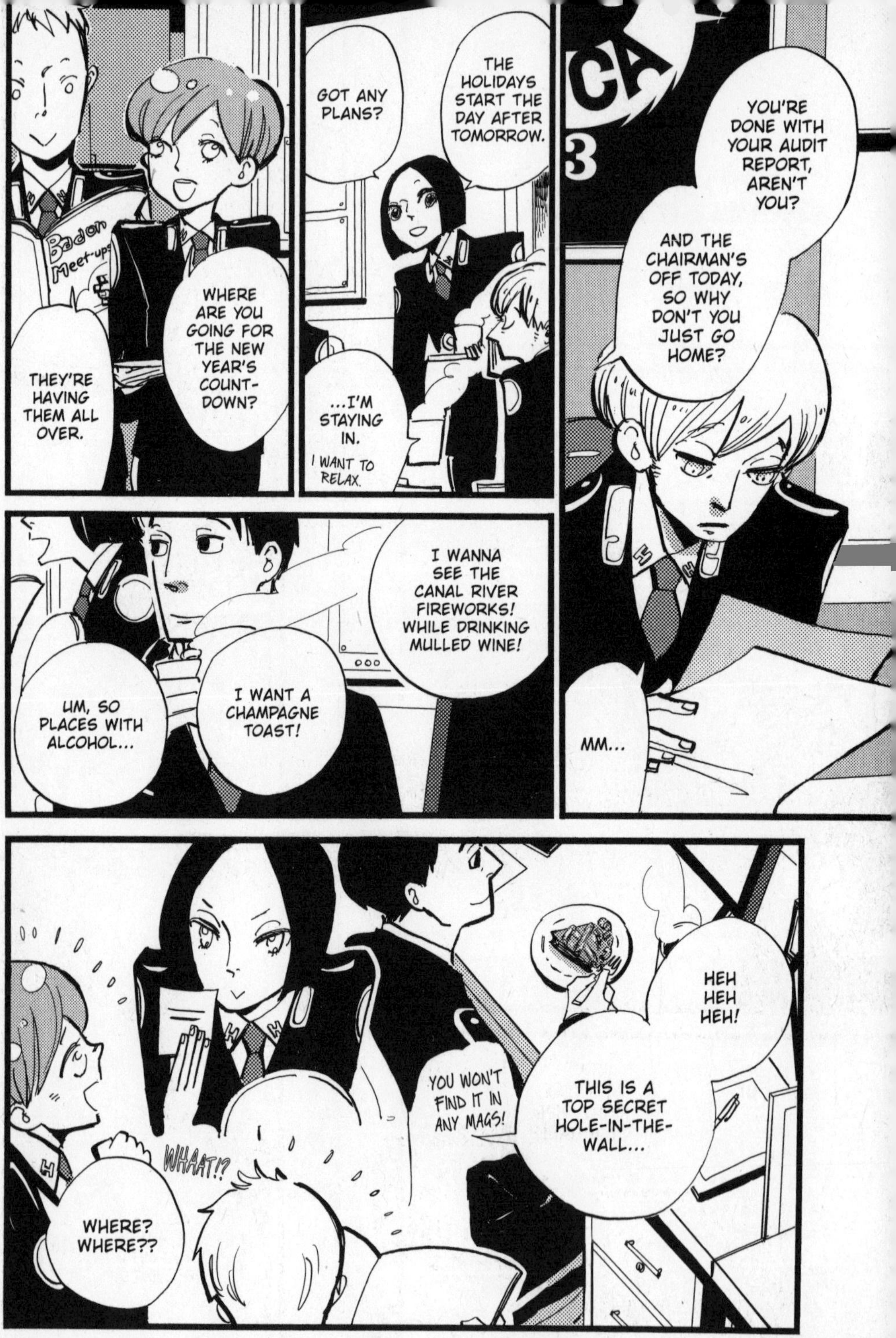
YOU'RE DONE WITH YOUR AUDIT REPORT, AREN'T YOU?
AND THE CHAIRMAN'S OFF TODAY, SO WHY DON'T YOU JUST GO HOME?
MM...
THE HOLIDAYS START THE DAY AFTER TOMORROW.
GOT ANY PLANS?
...I'M STAYING IN.
I WANT TO RELAX.
WHERE ARE YOU GOING FOR THE NEW YEAR'S COUNT-DOWN?
THEY'RE HAVING THEM ALL OVER.
I WANNA SEE THE CANAL RIVER FIREWORKS! WHILE DRINKING MULLED WINE!
I WANT A CHAMPAGNE TOAST!
UM, SO PLACES WITH ALCOHOL...
HEH HEH HEH!
THIS IS A TOP SECRET HOLE-IN-THE-WALL...
YOU WON'T FIND IT IN ANY MAGS!
WHAAT!?
WHERE? WHERE??

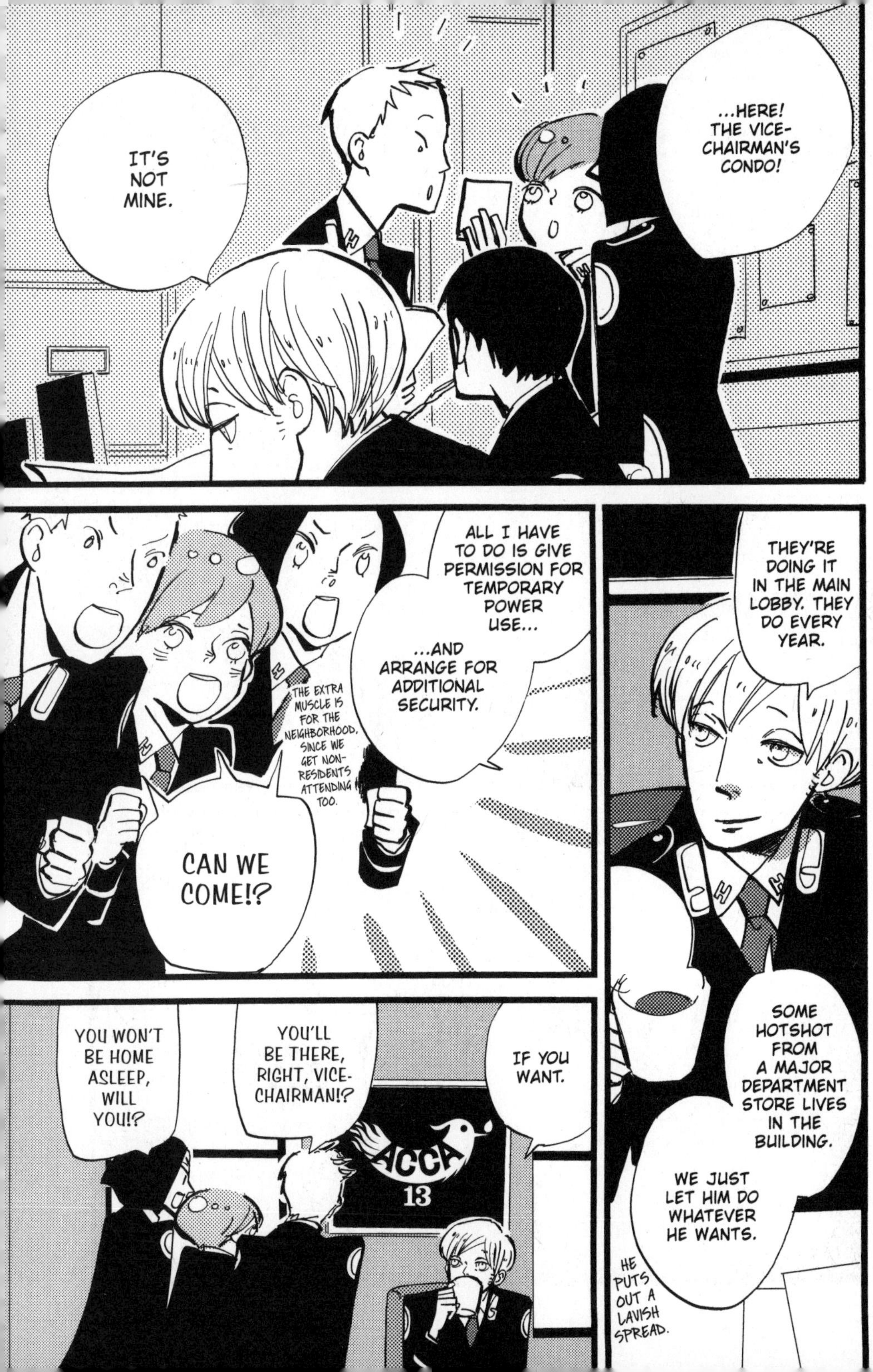
...HERE! THE VICE-CHAIRMAN'S CONDO!
IT'S NOT MINE.
THEY'RE DOING IT IN THE MAIN LOBBY. THEY DO EVERY YEAR.
SOME HOTSHOT FROM A MAJOR DEPARTMENT STORE LIVES IN THE BUILDING.
WE JUST LET HIM DO WHATEVER HE WANTS.
HE PUTS OUT A LAVISH SPREAD.
ALL I HAVE TO DO IS GIVE PERMISSION FOR TEMPORARY POWER USE...
...AND ARRANGE FOR ADDITIONAL SECURITY.
THE EXTRA MUSCLE IS FOR THE NEIGHBORHOOD, SINCE WE GET NON-RESIDENTS ATTENDING TOO.
CAN WE COME!?
IF YOU WANT.
YOU'LL BE THERE, RIGHT, VICE-CHAIRMAN!?
YOU WON'T BE HOME ASLEEP, WILL YOU!?
ACCA
13

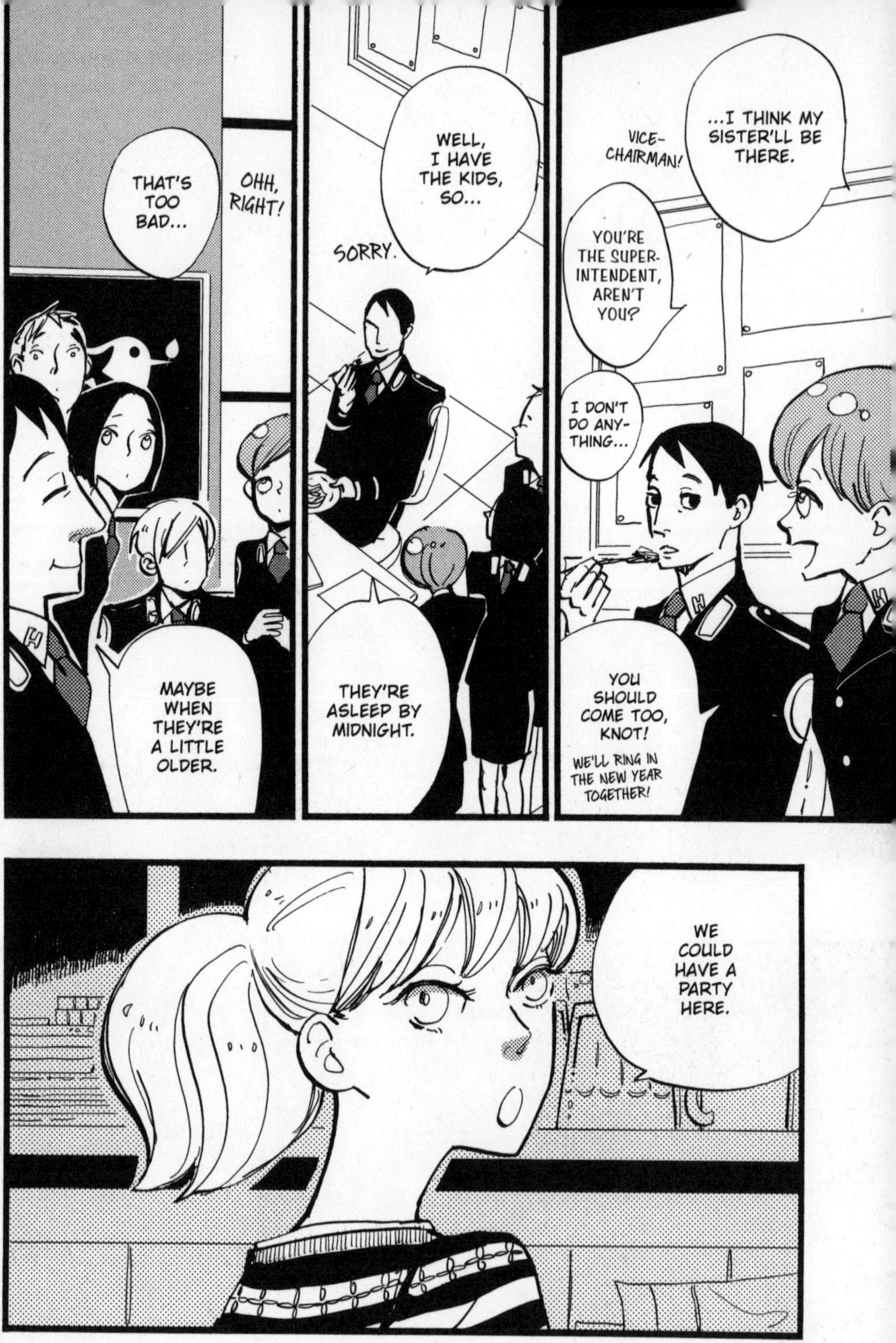
...I THINK MY SISTER'LL BE THERE.
VICE-CHAIRMAN!
YOU'RE THE SUPER-INTENDENT, AREN'T YOU?
I DON'T DO ANYTHING...
YOU SHOULD COME TOO, KNOT!
WE'LL RING IN THE NEW YEAR TOGETHER!
WELL, I HAVE THE KIDS, SO...
SORRY.
THEY'RE ASLEEP BY MIDNIGHT.
OHH, RIGHT!
THAT'S TOO BAD...
MAYBE WHEN THEY'RE A LITTLE OLDER.
WE COULD HAVE A PARTY HERE.

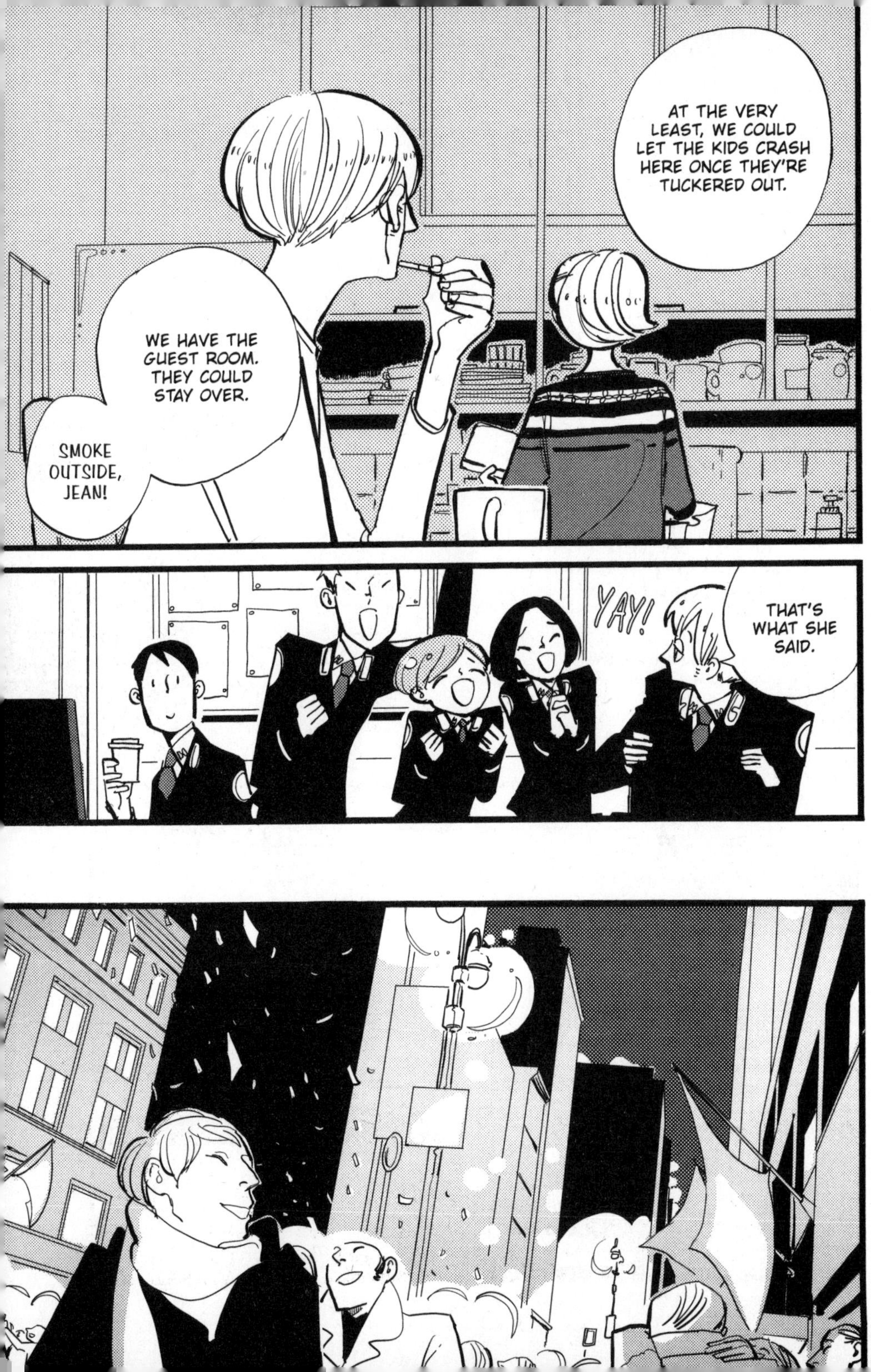
AT THE VERY LEAST, WE COULD LET THE KIDS CRASH HERE ONCE THEY'RE TUCKERED OUT.
WE HAVE THE GUEST ROOM. THEY COULD STAY OVER.
SMOKE OUTSIDE, JEAN!
THAT'S WHAT SHE SAID.
YAY!

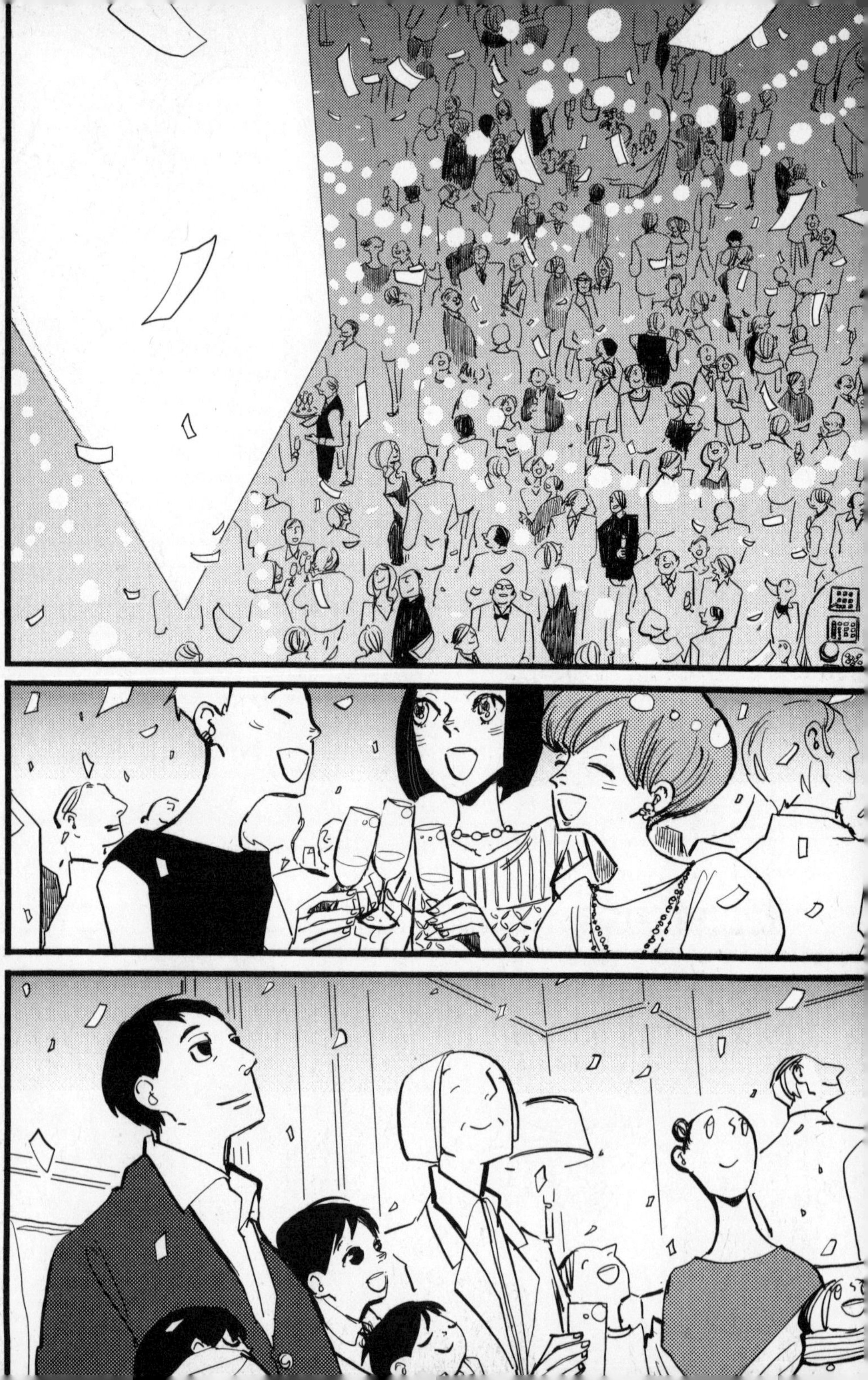

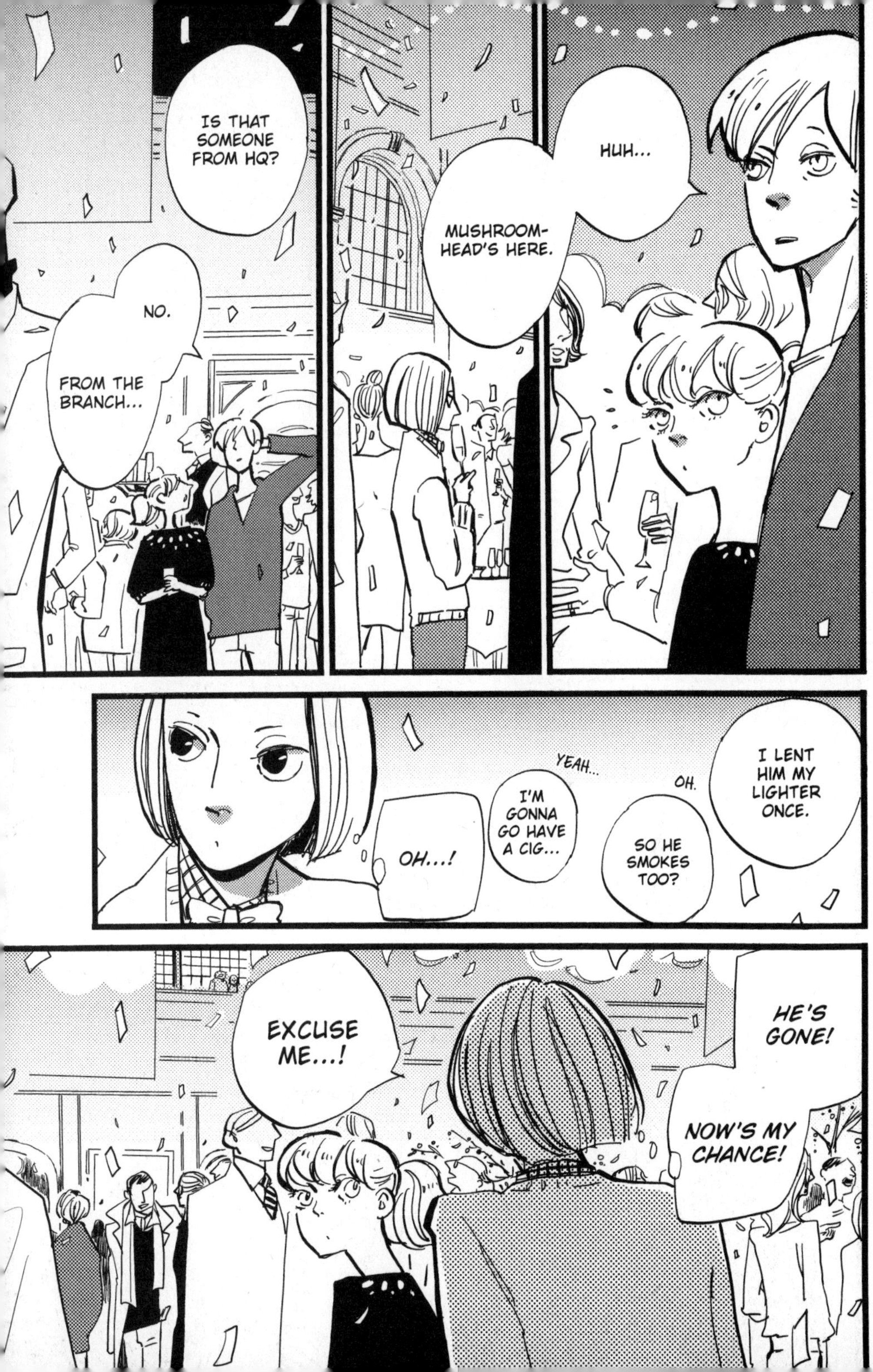
HUH...
MUSHROOM-HEAD'S HERE.
IS THAT SOMEONE FROM HQ?
NO.
FROM THE BRANCH...
I LENT HIM MY LIGHTER ONCE.
OH.
SO HE SMOKES TOO?
YEAH...
I'M GONNA GO HAVE A CIG...
OH...!
HE'S GONE!
NOW'S MY CHANCE!
EXCUSE ME...!

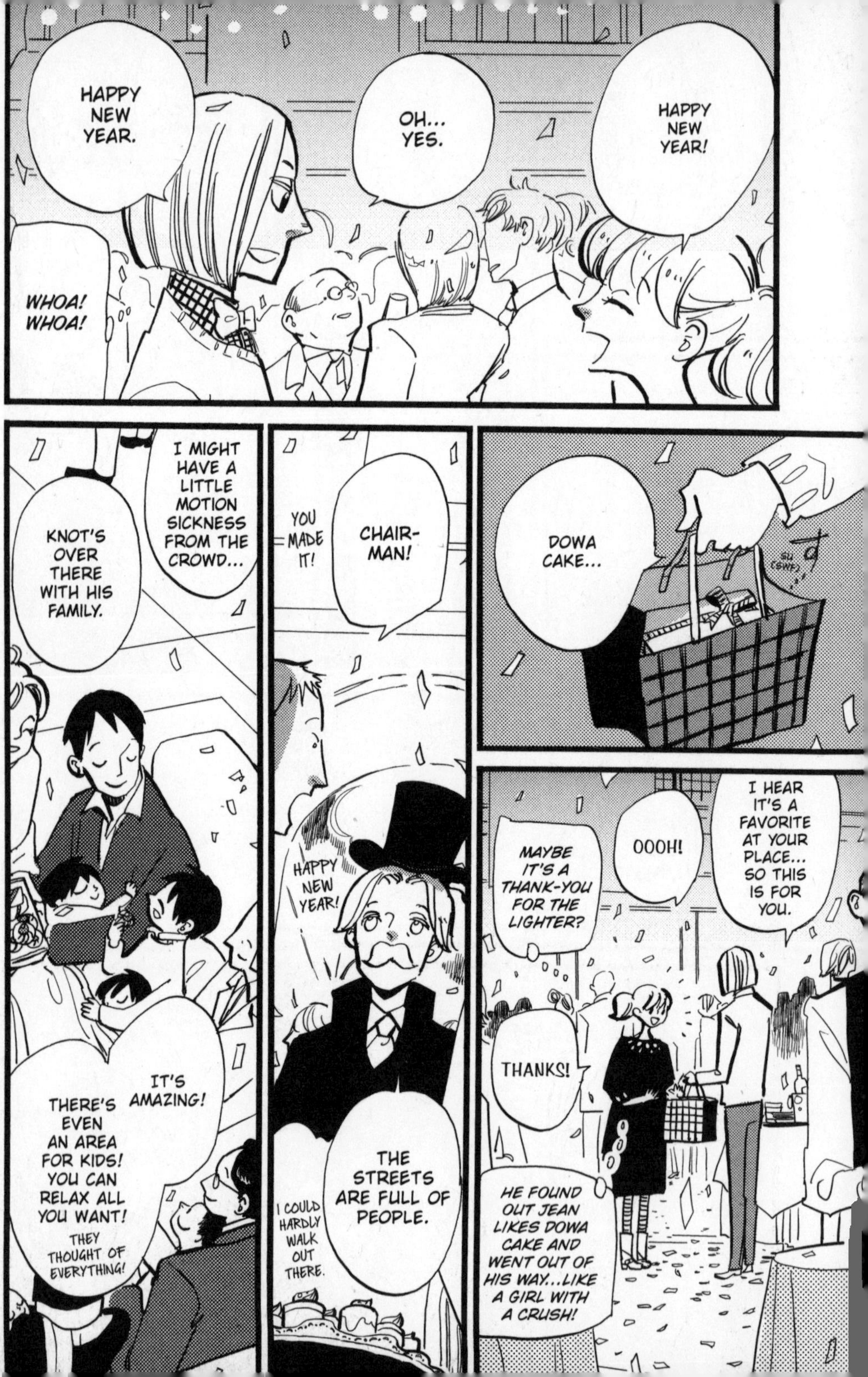
HAPPY NEW YEAR!
OH... YES.
HAPPY NEW YEAR.
WHOA! WHOA!
DOWA CAKE...
SU (SWF)
I HEAR IT'S A FAVORITE AT YOUR PLACE... SO THIS IS FOR YOU.
OOOH!
MAYBE IT'S A THANK-YOU FOR THE LIGHTER?
THANKS!
HE FOUND OUT JEAN LIKES DOWA CAKE AND WENT OUT OF HIS WAY...LIKE A GIRL WITH A CRUSH!
CHAIR-MAN!
YOU MADE IT!
HAPPY NEW YEAR!
THE STREETS ARE FULL OF PEOPLE.
I COULD HARDLY WALK OUT THERE.
I MIGHT HAVE A LITTLE MOTION SICKNESS FROM THE CROWD...
KNOT'S OVER THERE WITH HIS FAMILY.
IT'S AMAZING!
THERE'S EVEN AN AREA FOR KIDS! YOU CAN RELAX ALL YOU WANT!
THEY THOUGHT OF EVERYTHING!

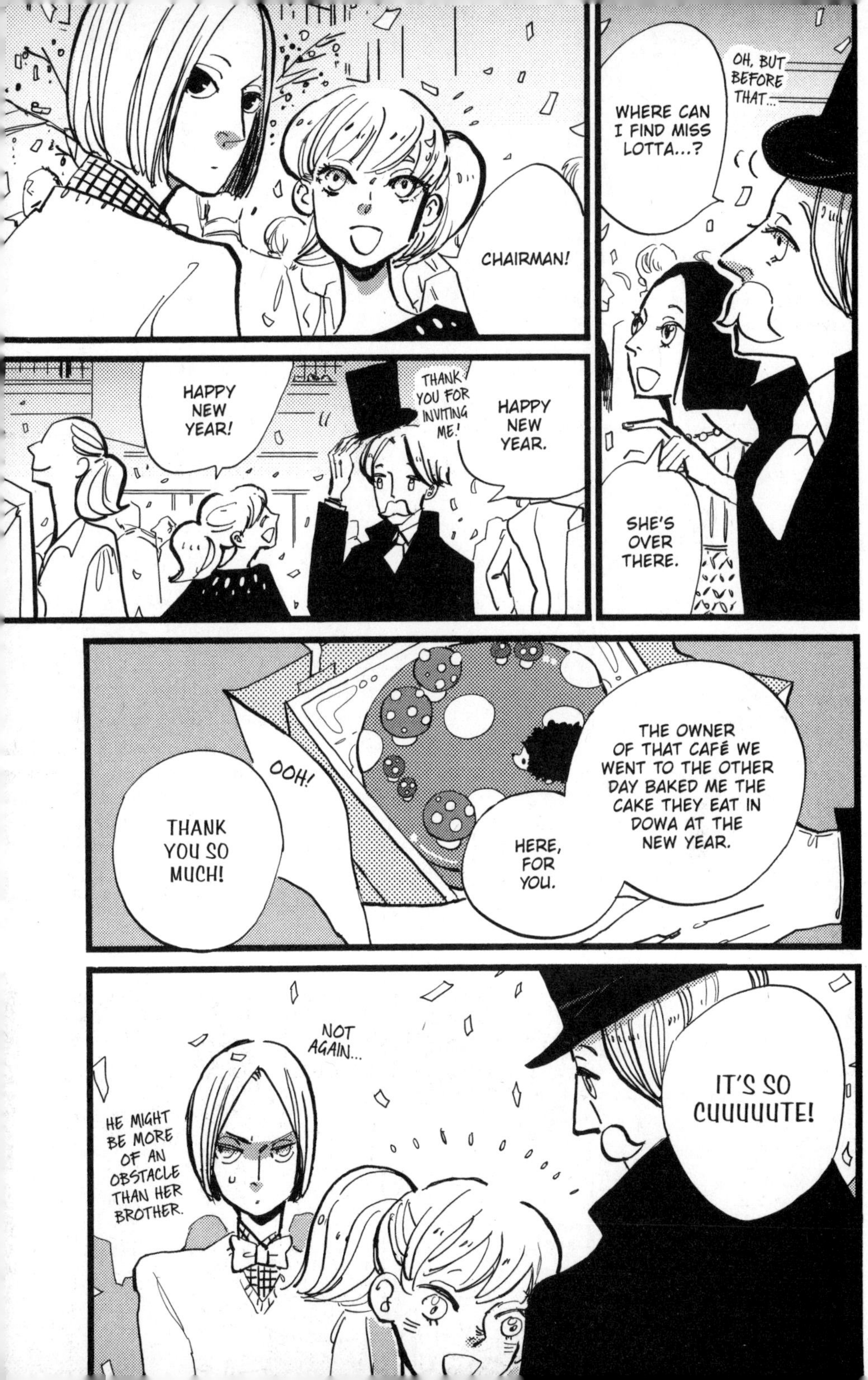
OH, BUT BEFORE THAT...
WHERE CAN I FIND MISS LOTTA...?
SHE'S OVER THERE.
CHAIRMAN!
HAPPY NEW YEAR.
THANK YOU FOR INVITING ME!
HAPPY NEW YEAR!
THE OWNER OF THAT CAFÉ WE WENT TO THE OTHER DAY BAKED ME THE CAKE THEY EAT IN DOWA AT THE NEW YEAR.
HERE, FOR YOU.
OOH!
THANK YOU SO MUCH!
IT'S SO CUUUUUTE!
NOT AGAIN...
HE MIGHT BE MORE OF AN OBSTACLE THAN HER BROTHER.

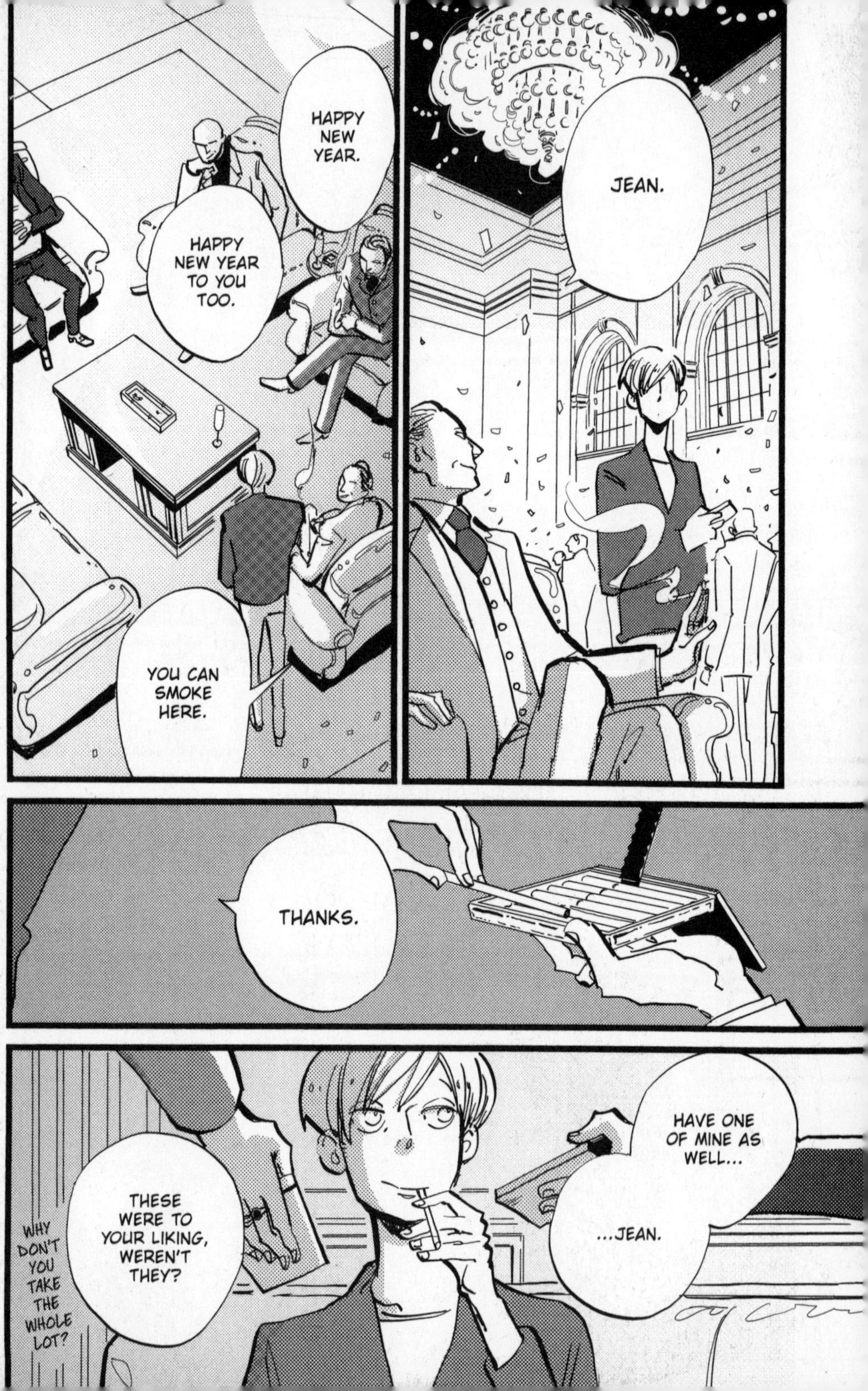
JEAN.
HAPPY NEW YEAR.
HAPPY NEW YEAR TO YOU TOO.
YOU CAN SMOKE HERE.
THANKS.
HAVE ONE OF MINE AS WELL...
...JEAN.
THESE WERE TO YOUR LIKING, WEREN'T THEY?
WHY DON'T YOU TAKE THE WHOLE LOT?

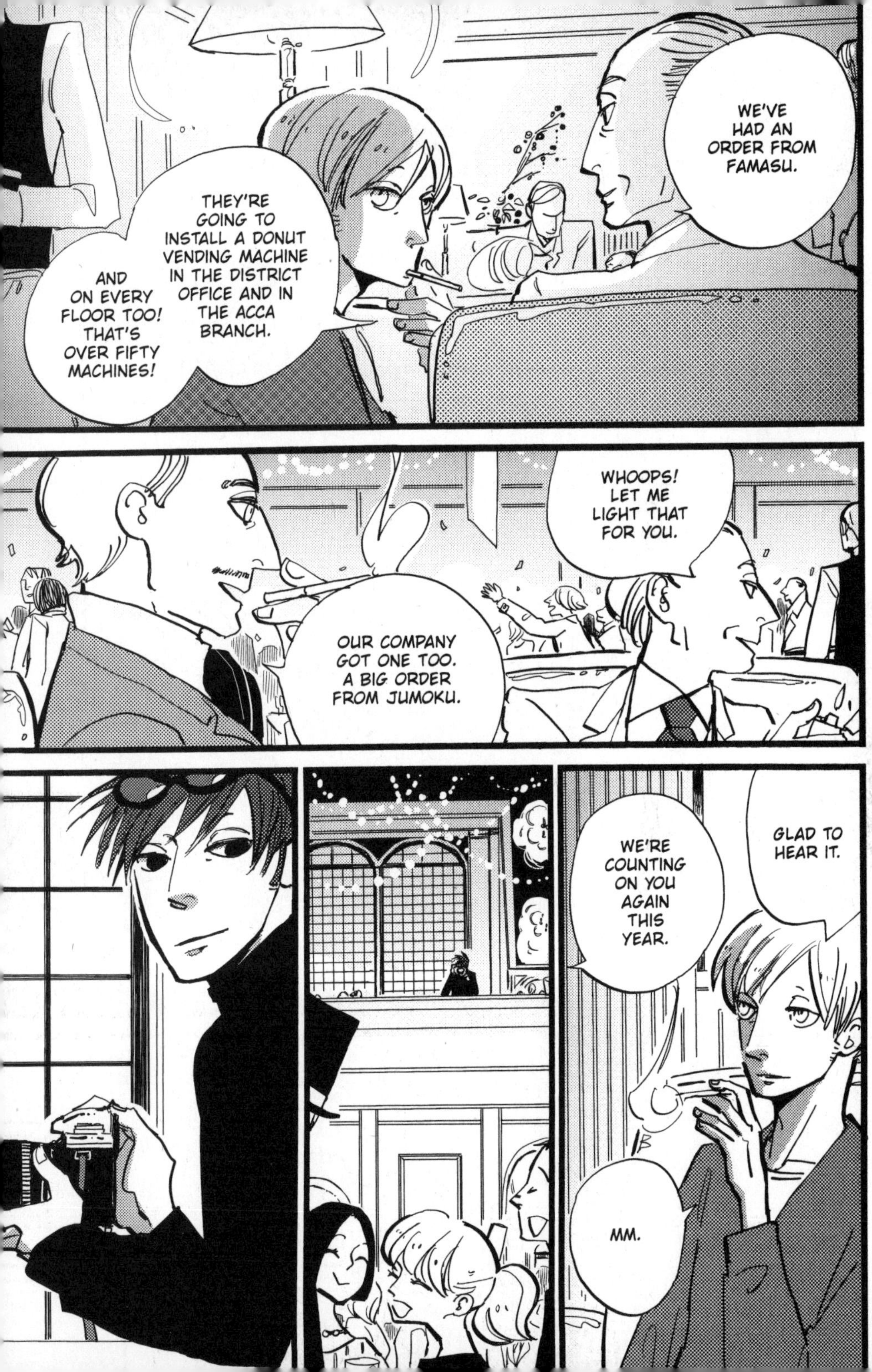
WE'VE HAD AN ORDER FROM FAMASU.
THEY'RE GOING TO INSTALL A DONUT VENDING MACHINE IN THE DISTRICT OFFICE AND IN THE ACCA BRANCH.
AND ON EVERY FLOOR TOO! THAT'S OVER FIFTY MACHINES!
WHOOPS! LET ME LIGHT THAT FOR YOU.
OUR COMPANY GOT ONE TOO. A BIG ORDER FROM JUMOKU.
GLAD TO HEAR IT.
WE'RE COUNTING ON YOU AGAIN THIS YEAR.
MM.

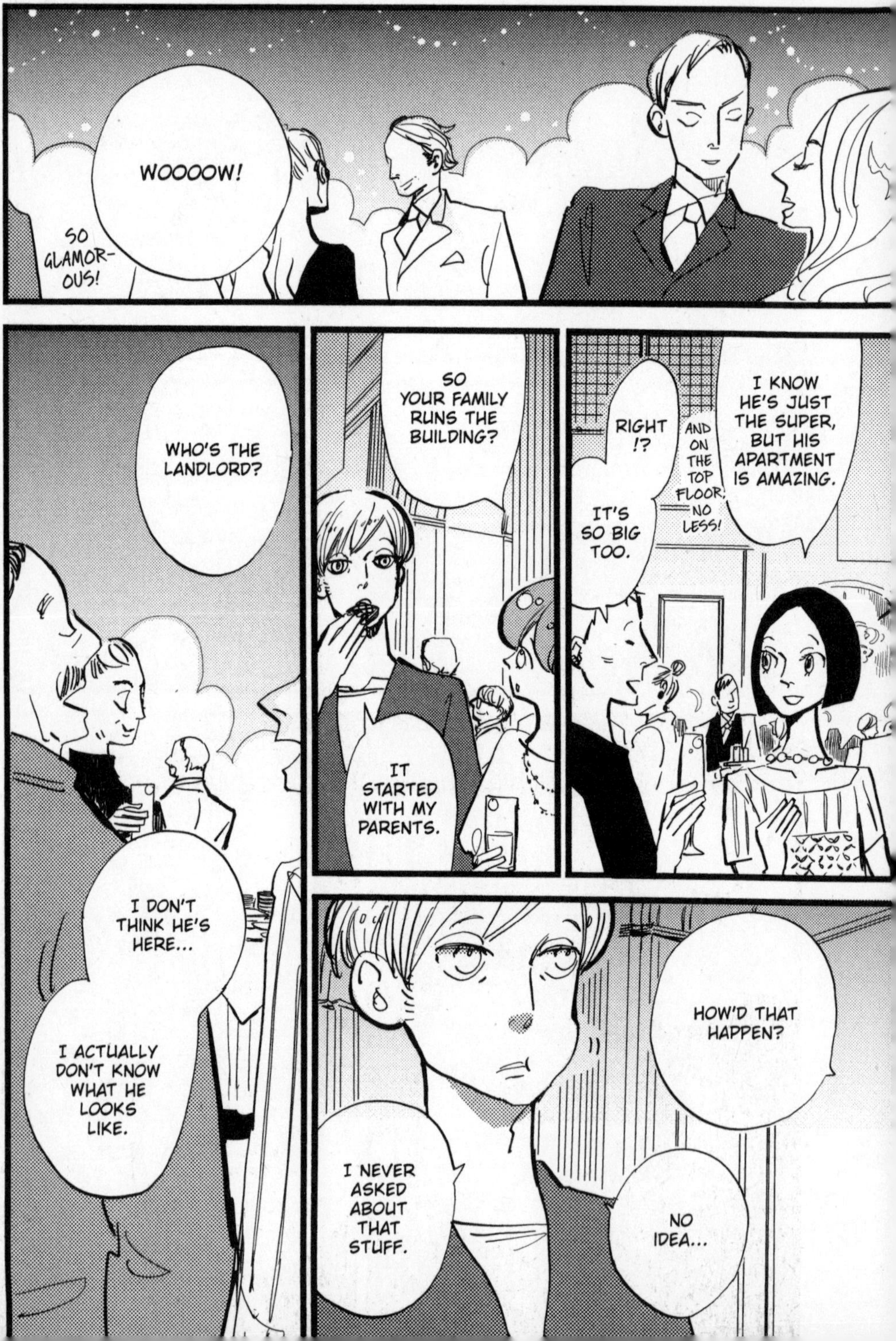
WOOOOW!
SO GLAMOR-OUS!
I KNOW HE'S JUST THE SUPER, BUT HIS APARTMENT IS AMAZING.
AND ON THE TOP FLOOR, NO LESS!
RIGHT !?
IT'S SO BIG TOO.
SO YOUR FAMILY RUNS THE BUILDING?
IT STARTED WITH MY PARENTS.
HOW'D THAT HAPPEN?
NO IDEA...
I NEVER ASKED ABOUT THAT STUFF.
WHO'S THE LANDLORD?
I DON'T THINK HE'S HERE...
I ACTUALLY DON'T KNOW WHAT HE LOOKS LIKE.

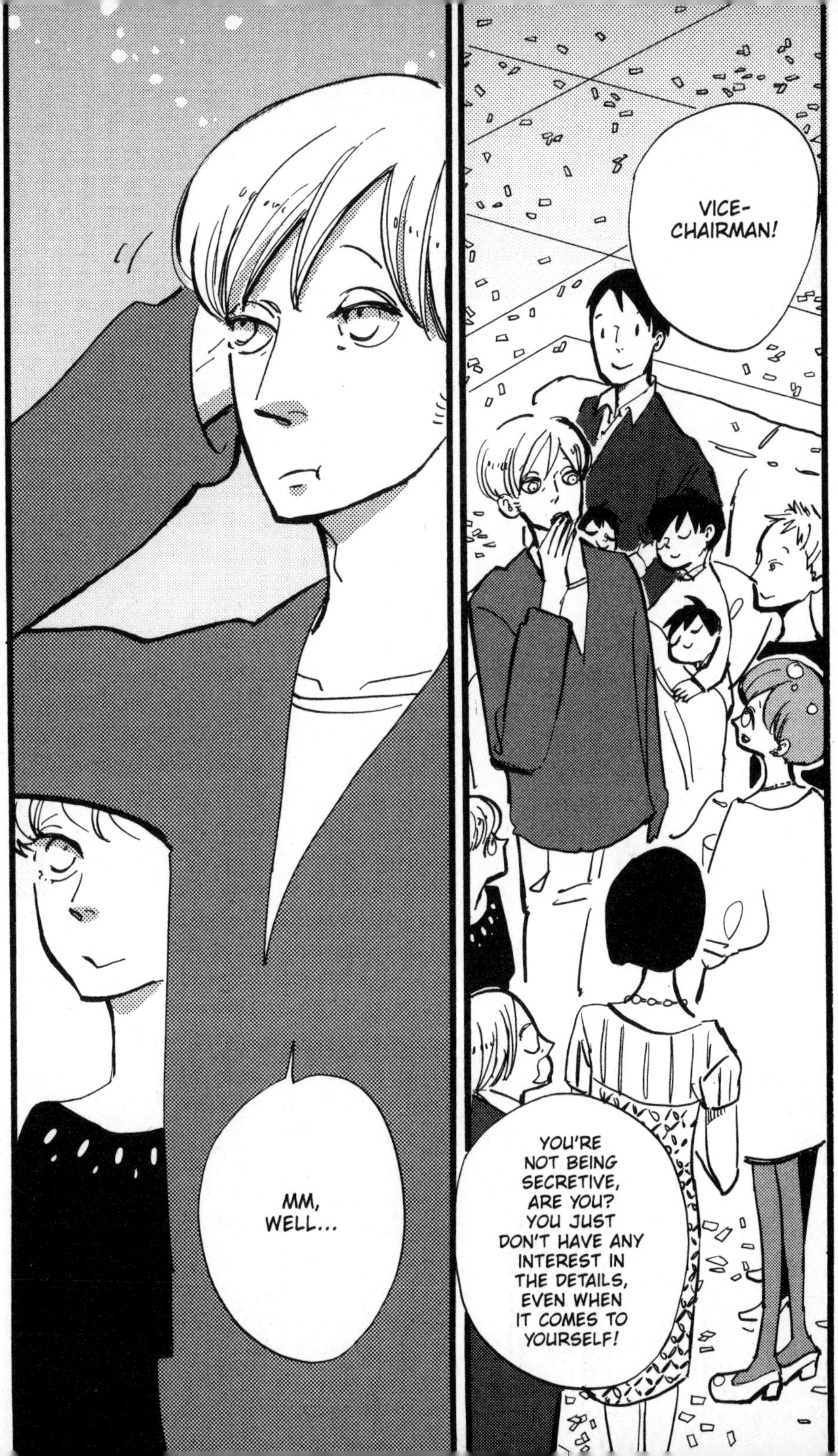
VICE-CHAIRMAN!
YOU'RE NOT BEING SECRETIVE, ARE YOU? YOU JUST DON'T HAVE ANY INTEREST IN THE DETAILS, EVEN WHEN IT COMES TO YOURSELF!
MM, WELL...

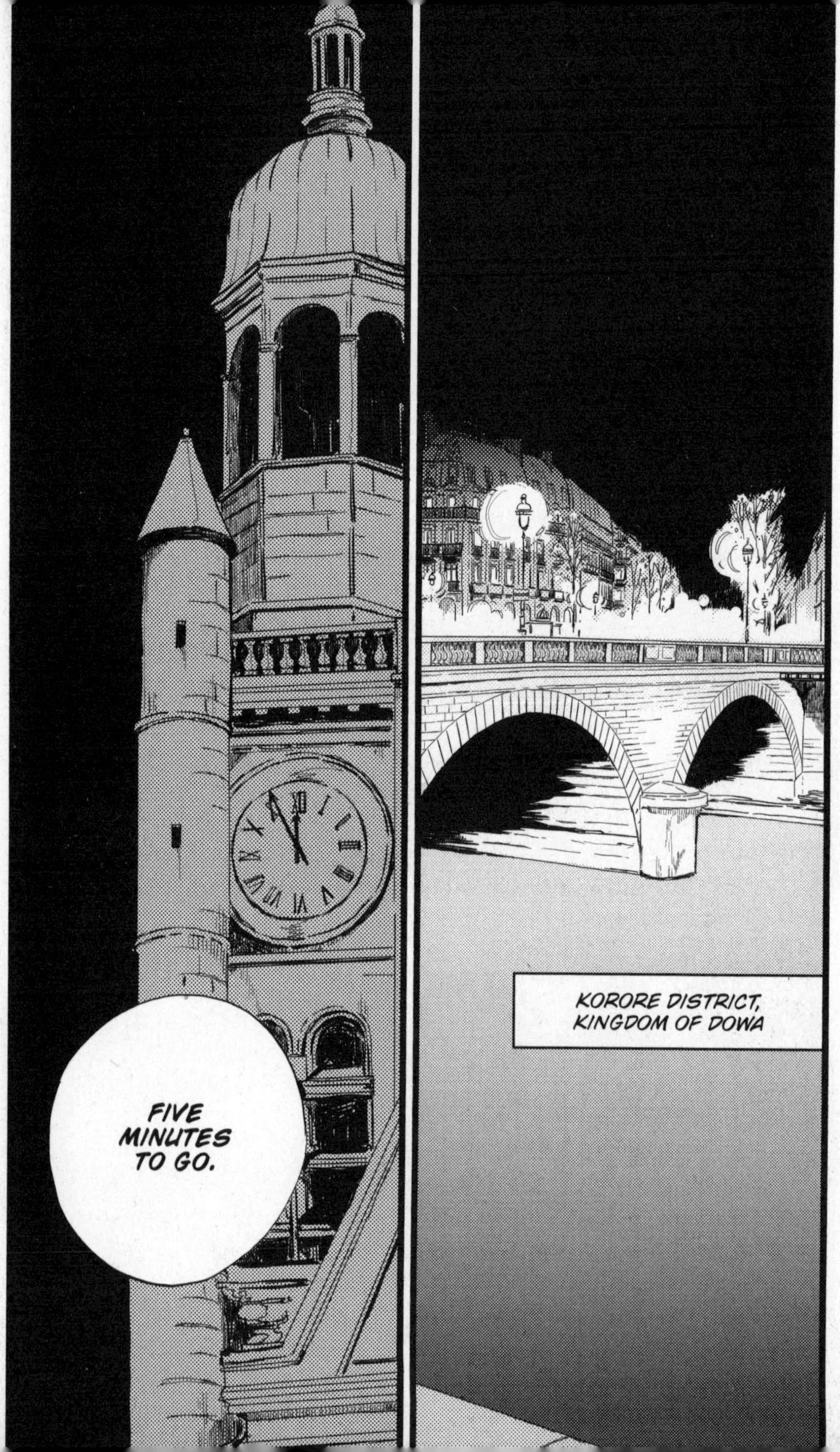
KORORE DISTRICT, KINGDOM OF DOWA
FIVE MINUTES TO GO.

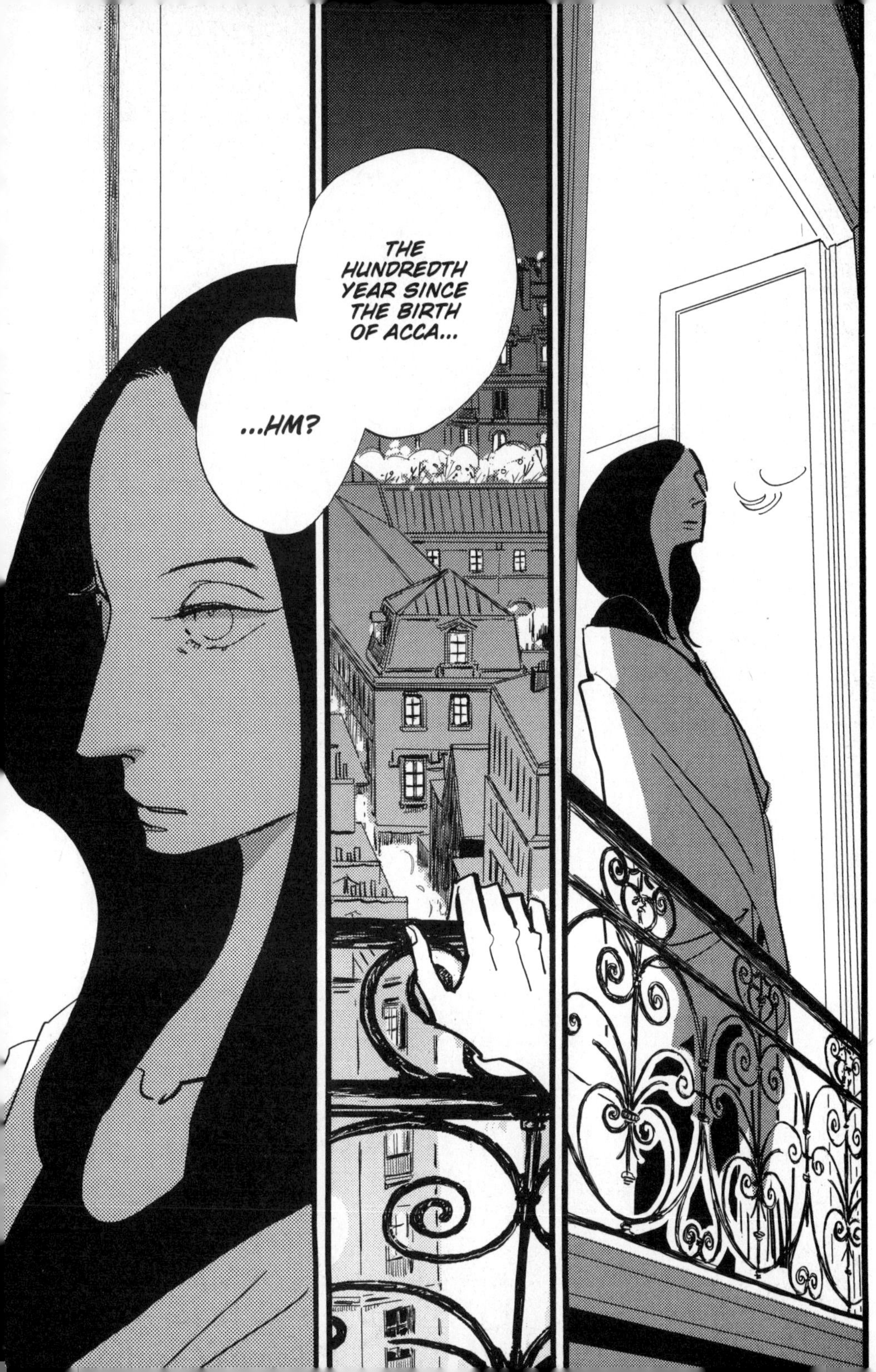
THE HUNDREDTH YEAR SINCE THE BIRTH OF ACCA...
...HM?

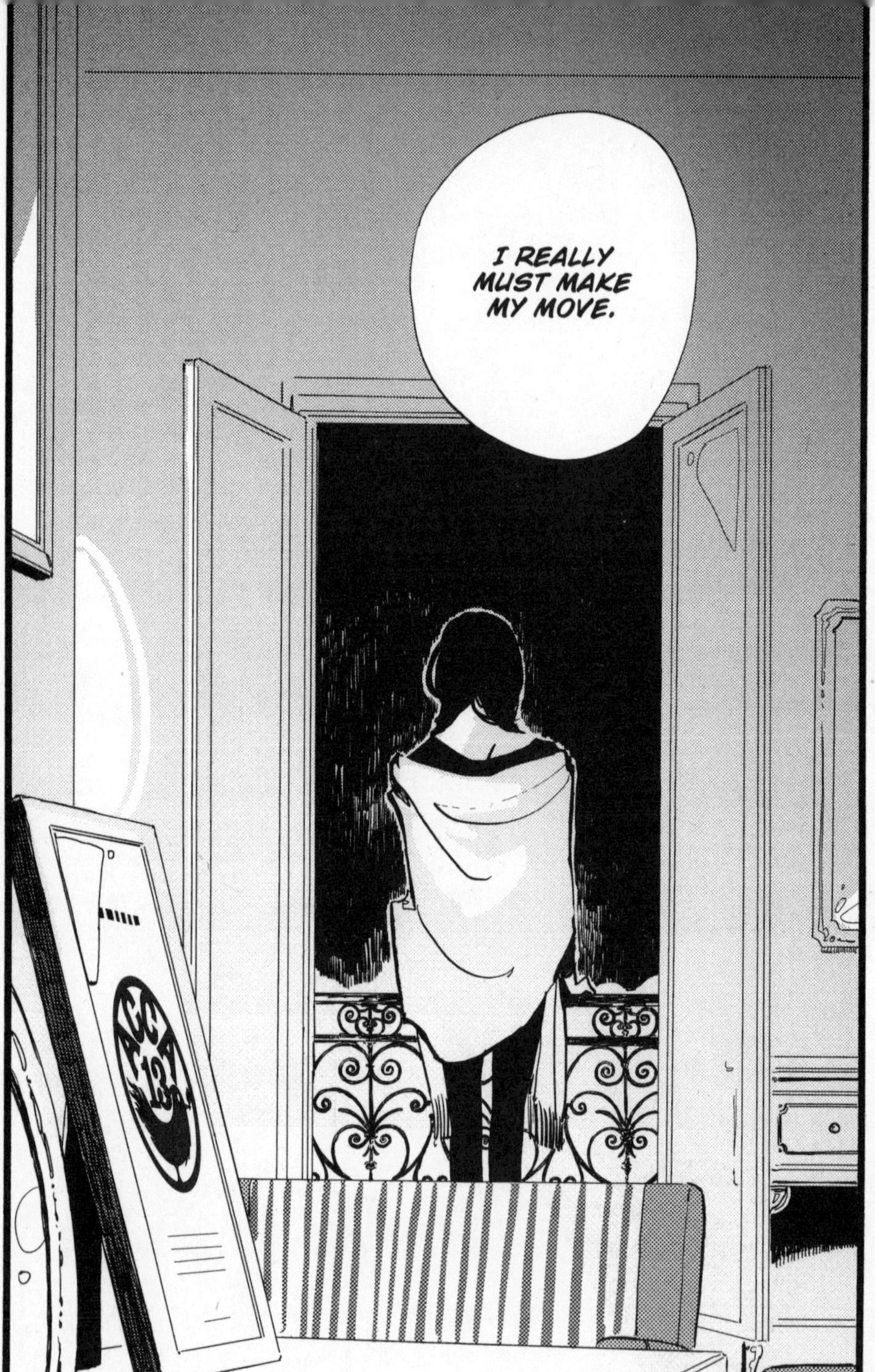
I REALLY MUST MAKE MY MOVE.

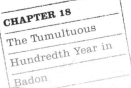

CHAPTER 18

The Tumultuous Hundredth Year in Badon

ACCA 13 TERRITORY INSPECTION DEPT
PASS

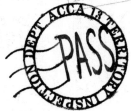

CHAPTER 19

The Reason for the Warm Welcome in Hare

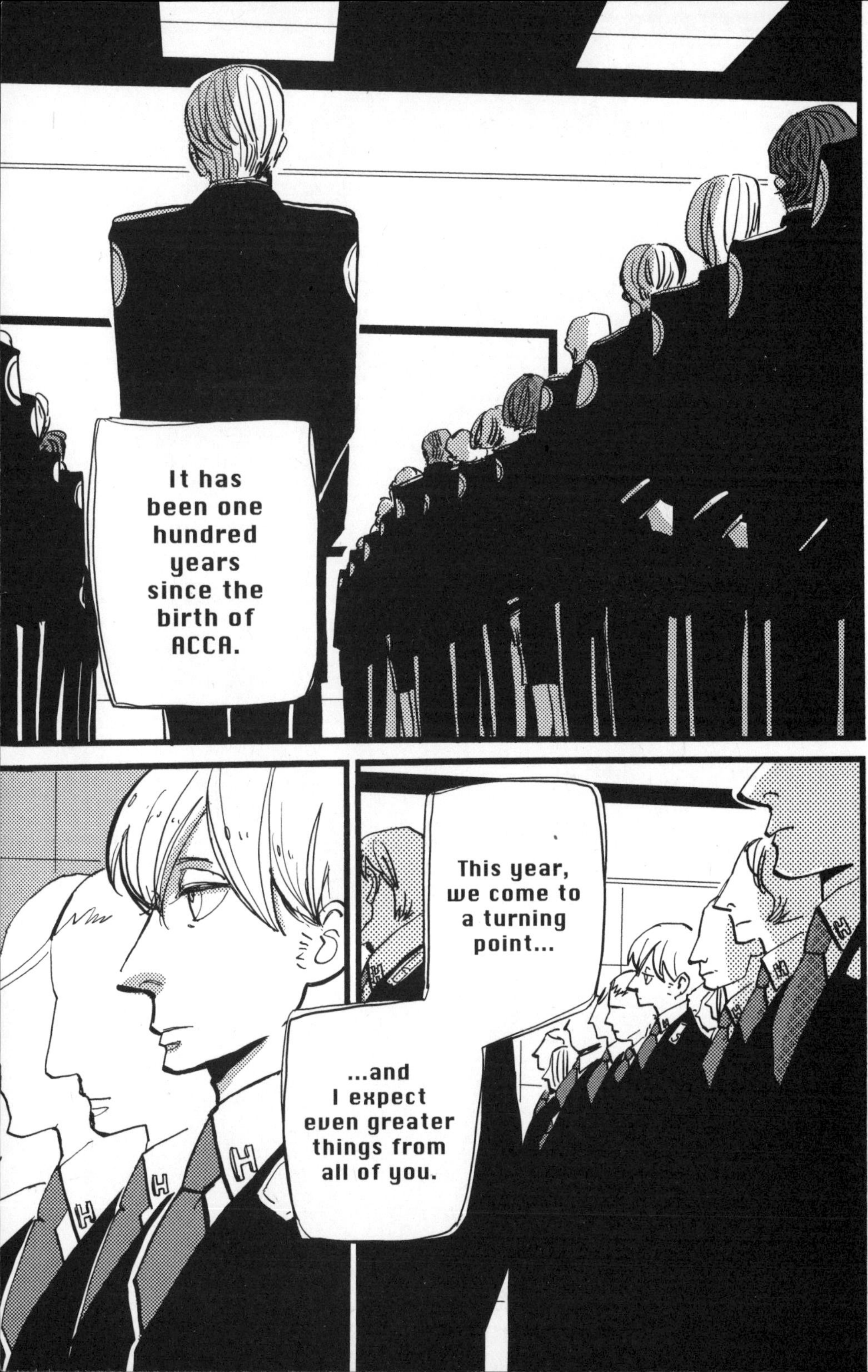
It has been one hundred years since the birth of ACCA.
This year, we come to a turning point...
...and I expect even greater things from all of you.

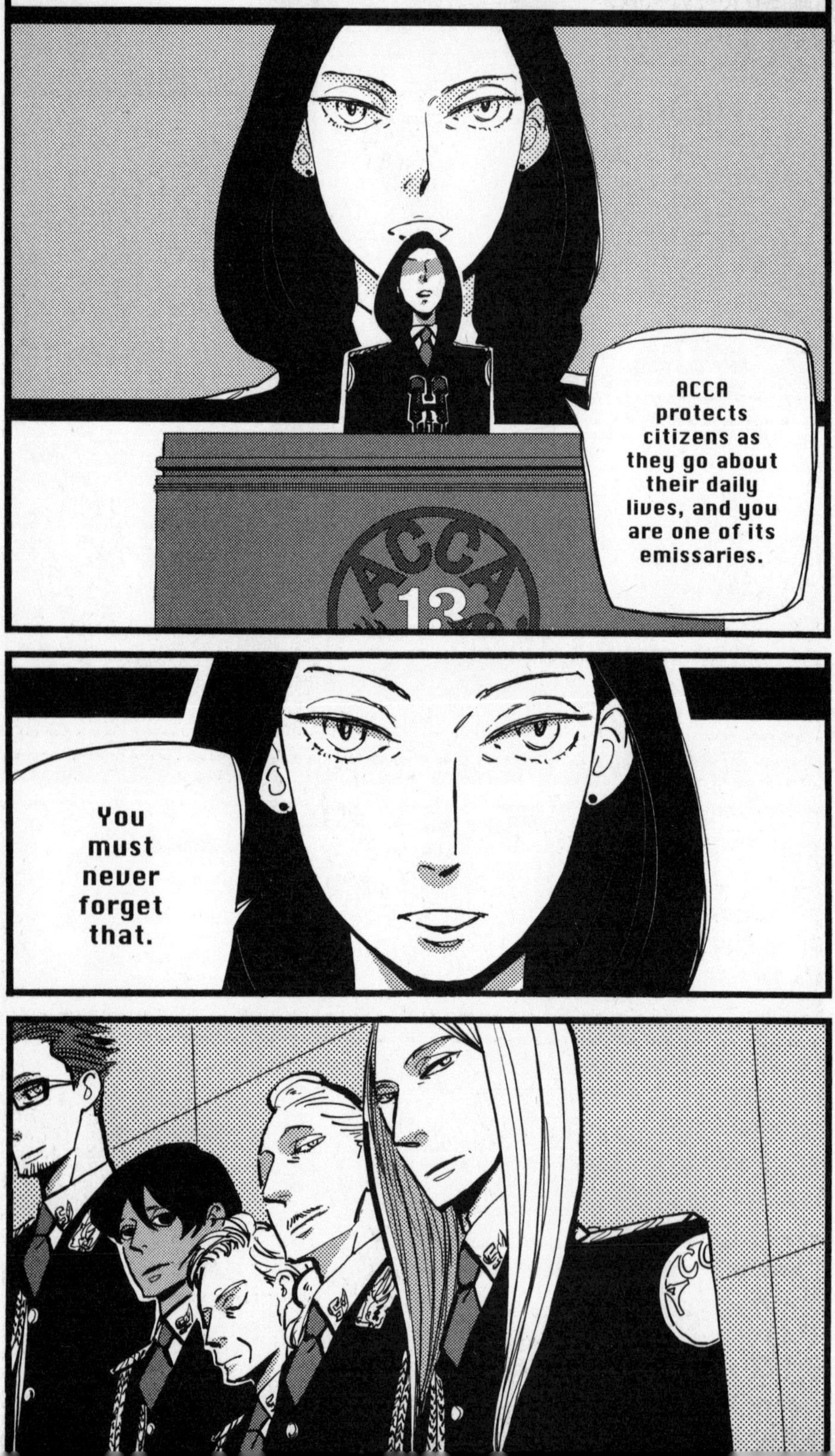
ACCA protects citizens as they go about their daily lives, and you are one of its emissaries.
You must never forget that.

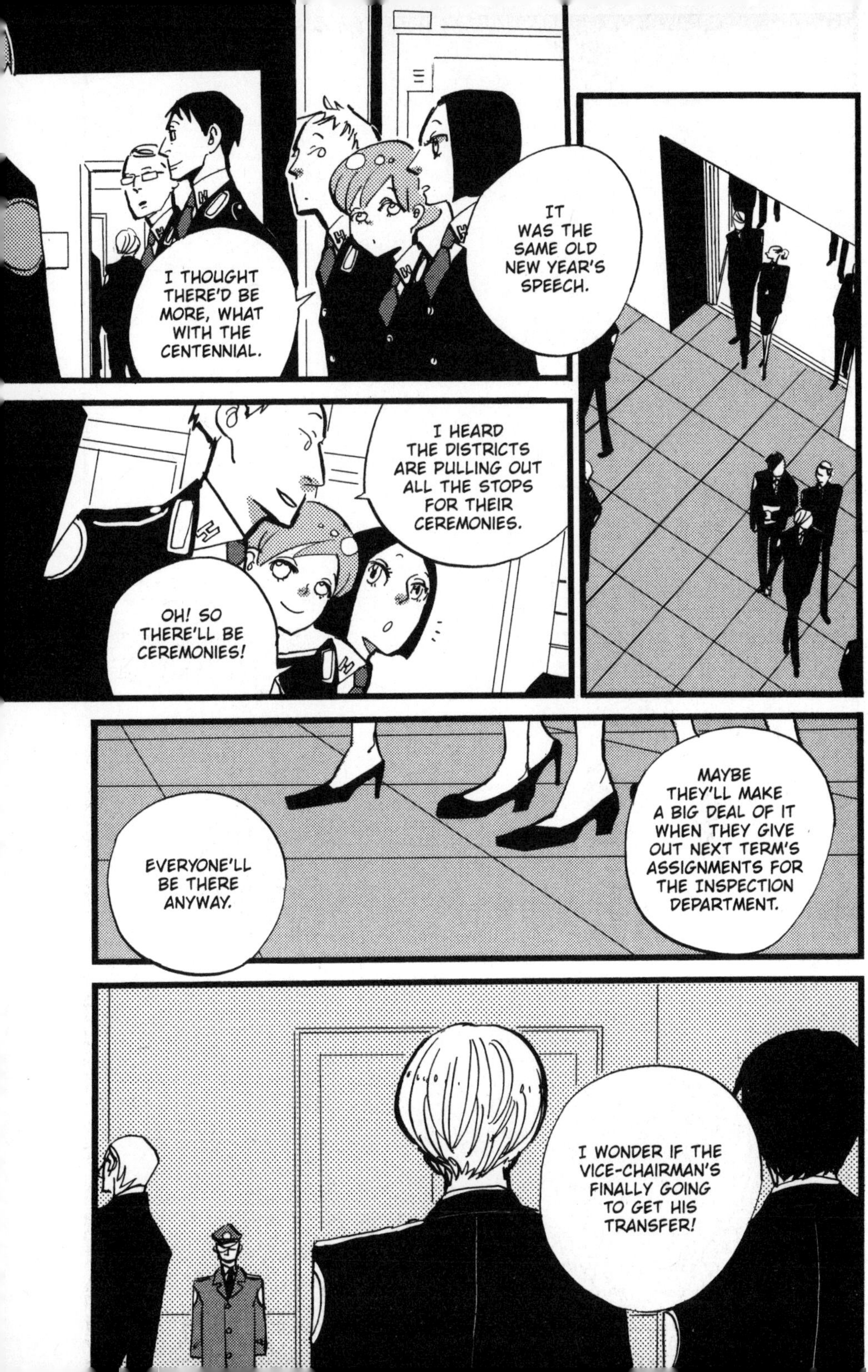
IT WAS THE SAME OLD NEW YEAR'S SPEECH.
I THOUGHT THERE'D BE MORE, WHAT WITH THE CENTENNIAL.
I HEARD THE DISTRICTS ARE PULLING OUT ALL THE STOPS FOR THEIR CEREMONIES.
OH! SO THERE'LL BE CEREMONIES!
MAYBE THEY'LL MAKE A BIG DEAL OF IT WHEN THEY GIVE OUT NEXT TERM'S ASSIGNMENTS FOR THE INSPECTION DEPARTMENT.
EVERYONE'LL BE THERE ANYWAY.
I WONDER IF THE VICE-CHAIRMAN'S FINALLY GOING TO GET HIS TRANSFER!

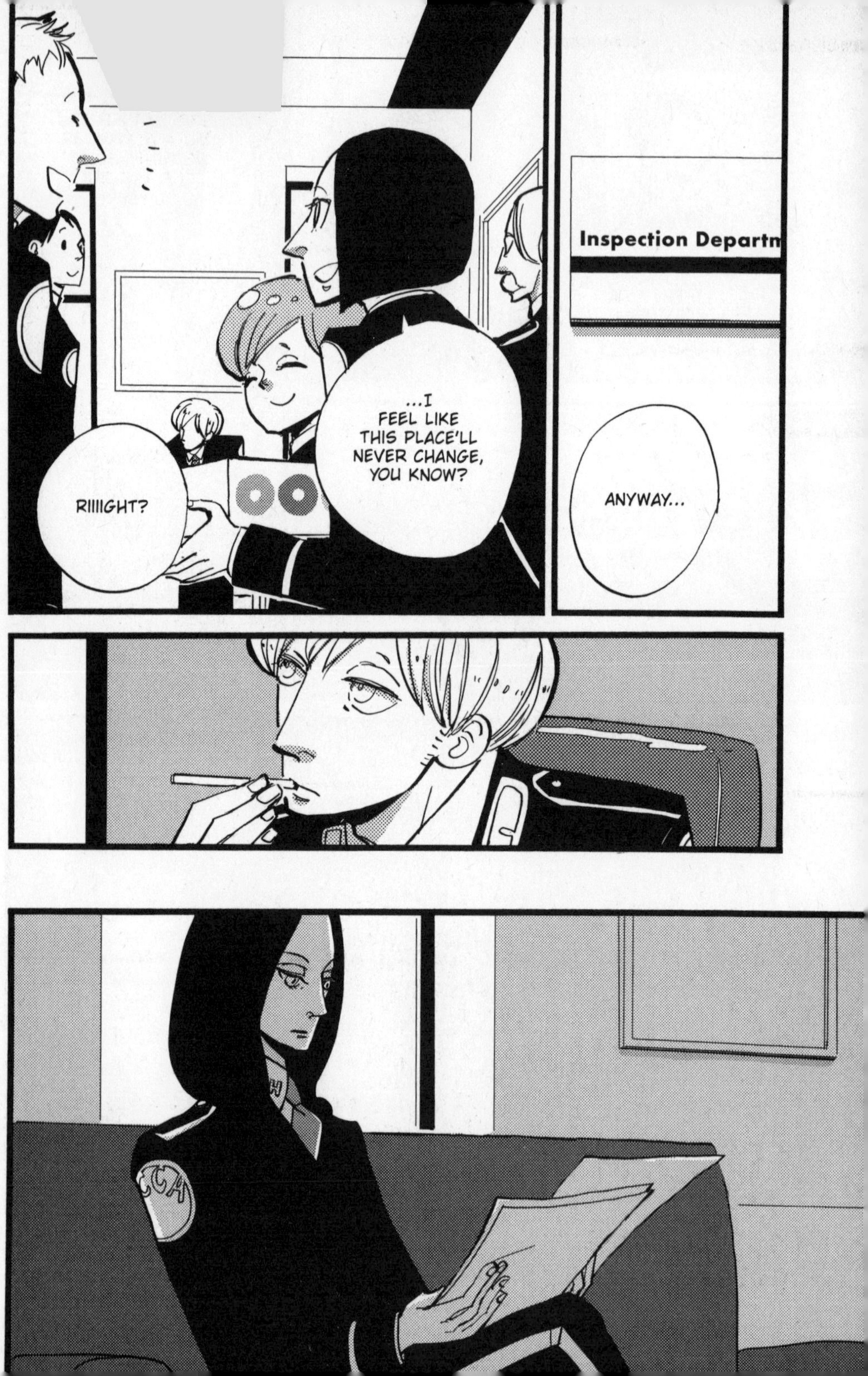
Inspection Departm
ANYWAY...
...I FEEL LIKE THIS PLACE'LL NEVER CHANGE, YOU KNOW?
RIIIIGHT?

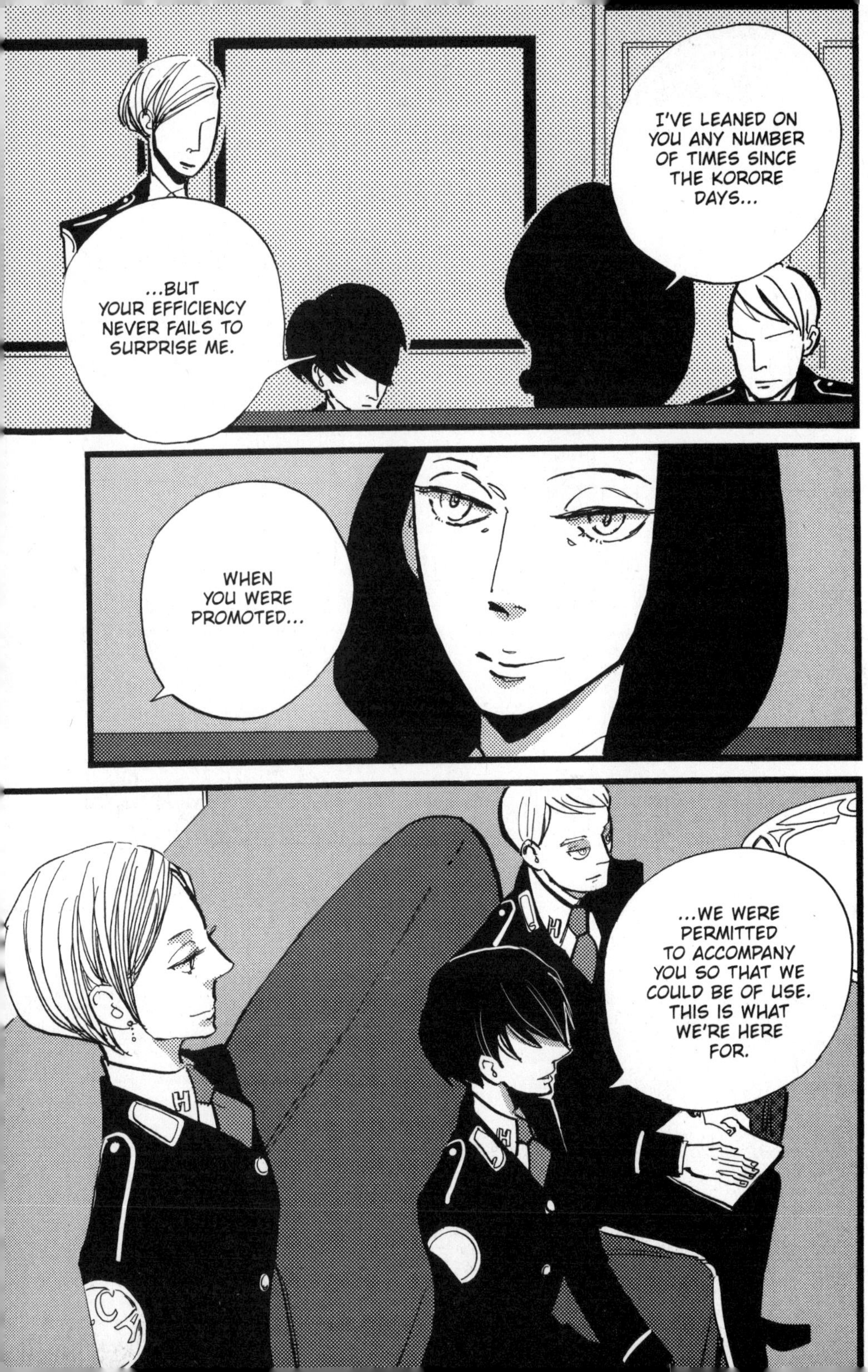

I'VE LEANED ON YOU ANY NUMBER OF TIMES SINCE THE KORORE DAYS...
...BUT YOUR EFFICIENCY NEVER FAILS TO SURPRISE ME.
WHEN YOU WERE PROMOTED...
...WE WERE PERMITTED TO ACCOMPANY YOU SO THAT WE COULD BE OF USE. THIS IS WHAT WE'RE HERE FOR.

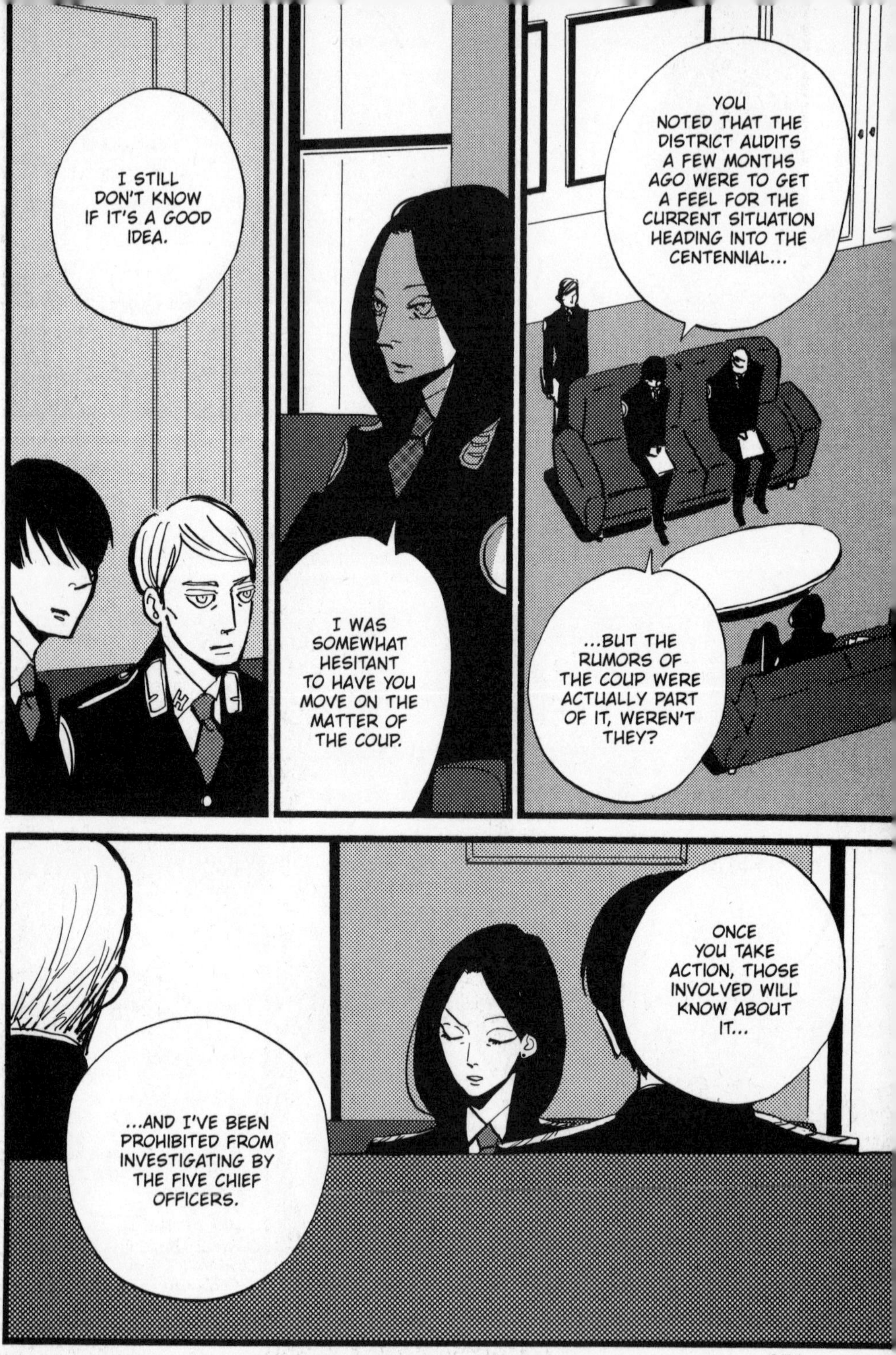
YOU NOTED THAT THE DISTRICT AUDITS A FEW MONTHS AGO WERE TO GET A FEEL FOR THE CURRENT SITUATION HEADING INTO THE CENTENNIAL...
...BUT THE RUMORS OF THE COUP WERE ACTUALLY PART OF IT, WEREN'T THEY?
I WAS SOMEWHAT HESITANT TO HAVE YOU MOVE ON THE MATTER OF THE COUP.
I STILL DON'T KNOW IF IT'S A GOOD IDEA.
ONCE YOU TAKE ACTION, THOSE INVOLVED WILL KNOW ABOUT IT...
...AND I'VE BEEN PROHIBITED FROM INVESTIGATING BY THE FIVE CHIEF OFFICERS.

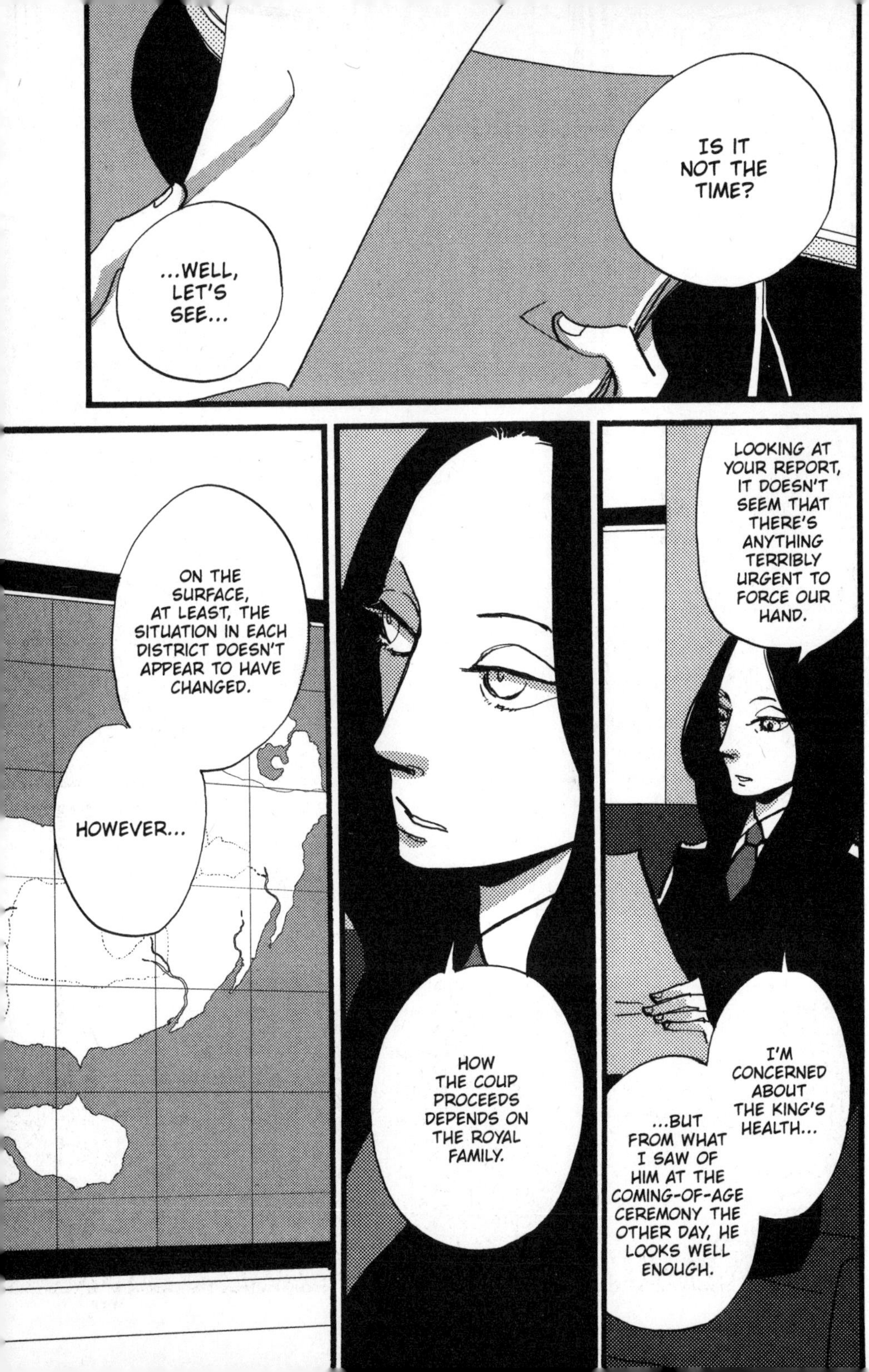
IS IT NOT THE TIME?
...WELL, LET'S SEE...
LOOKING AT YOUR REPORT, IT DOESN'T SEEM THAT THERE'S ANYTHING TERRIBLY URGENT TO FORCE OUR HAND.
I'M CONCERNED ABOUT THE KING'S HEALTH...
...BUT FROM WHAT I SAW OF HIM AT THE COMING-OF-AGE CEREMONY THE OTHER DAY, HE LOOKS WELL ENOUGH.
HOW THE COUP PROCEEDS DEPENDS ON THE ROYAL FAMILY.
ON THE SURFACE, AT LEAST, THE SITUATION IN EACH DISTRICT DOESN'T APPEAR TO HAVE CHANGED.
HOWEVER...

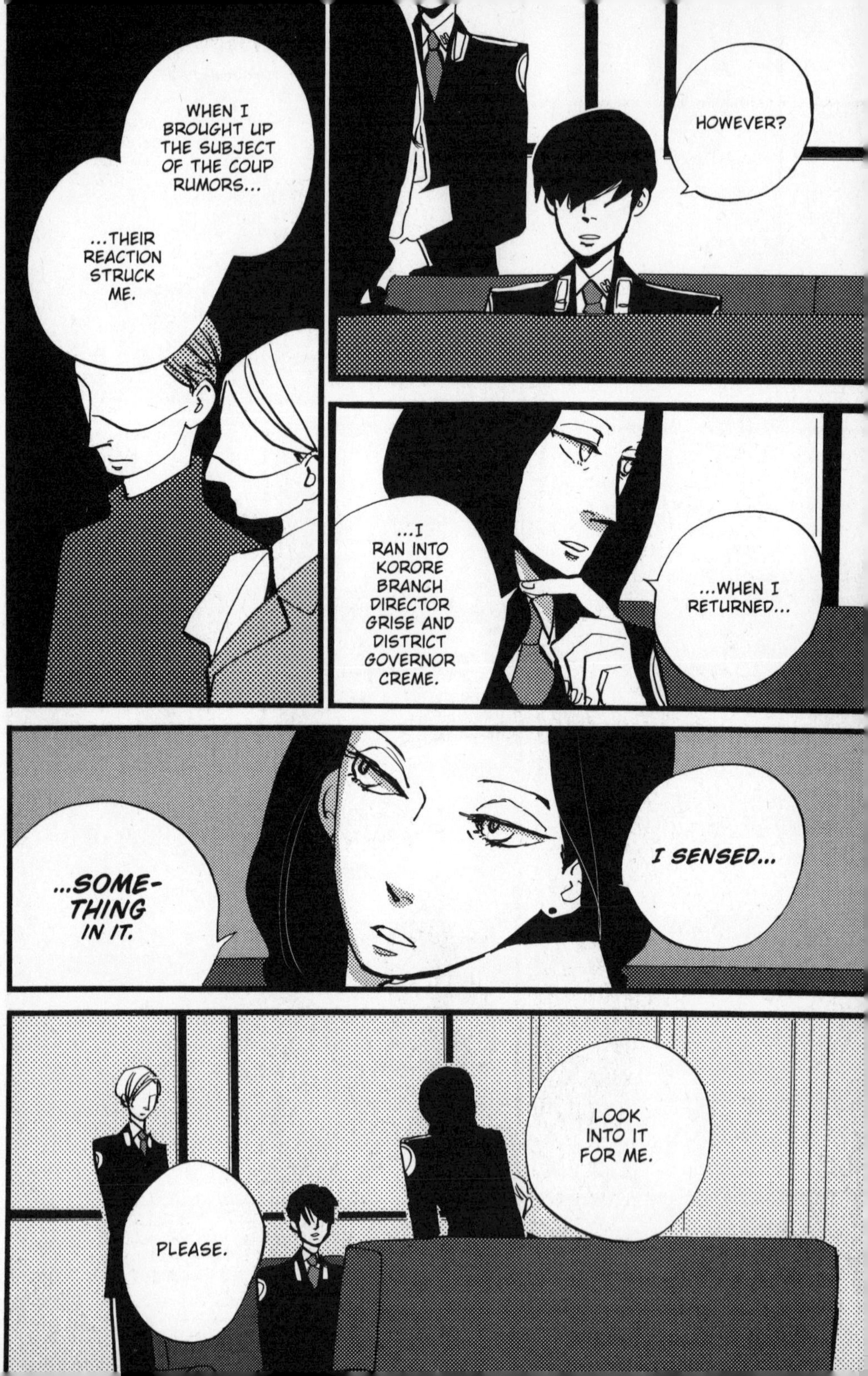
HOWEVER?
...WHEN I RETURNED...
...I RAN INTO KORORE BRANCH DIRECTOR GRISE AND DISTRICT GOVERNOR CREME.
WHEN I BROUGHT UP THE SUBJECT OF THE COUP RUMORS...
...THEIR REACTION STRUCK ME.
I SENSED...
...SOME-THING IN IT.
LOOK INTO IT FOR ME.
PLEASE.

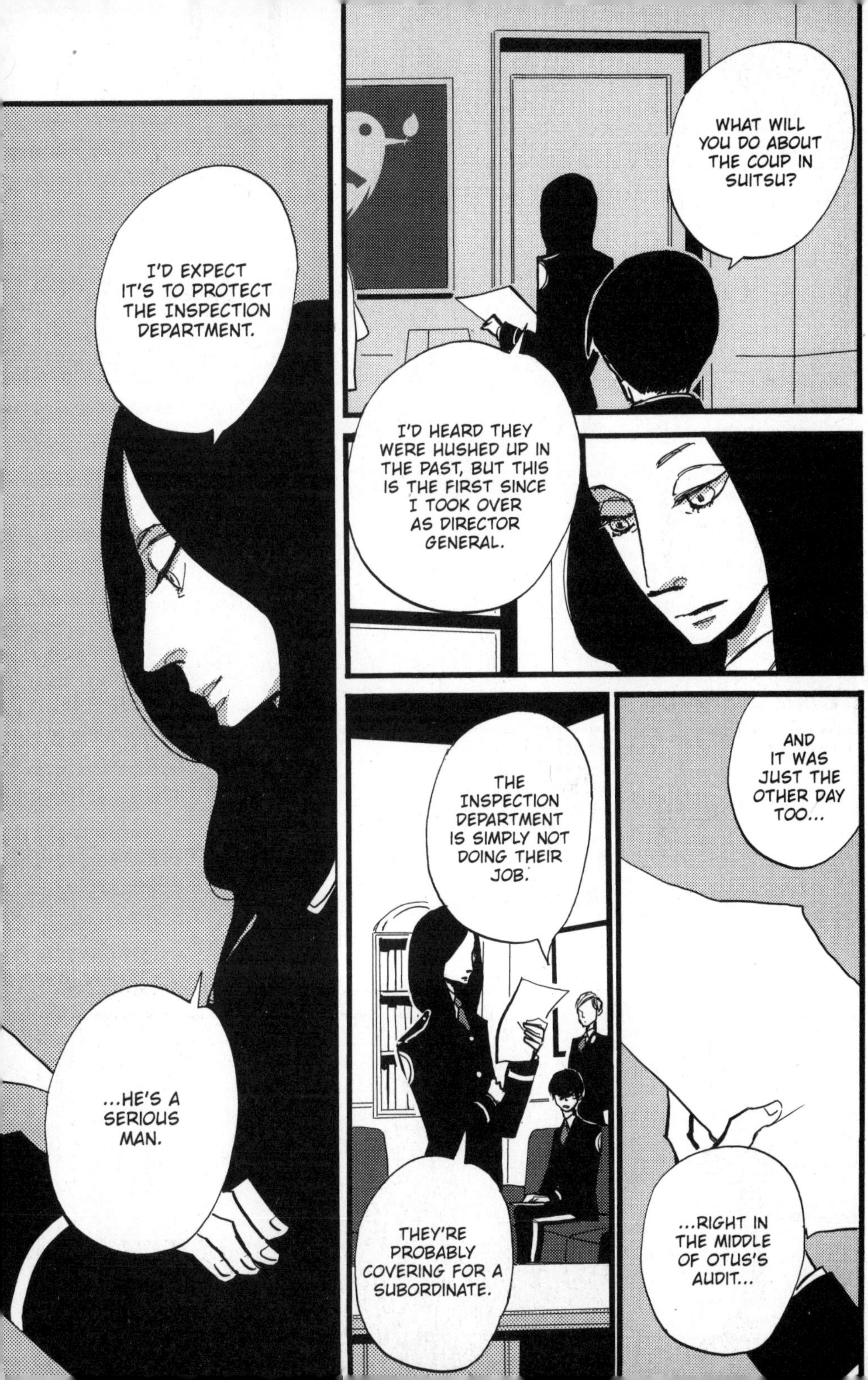
WHAT WILL YOU DO ABOUT THE COUP IN SUITSU?
I'D HEARD THEY WERE HUSHED UP IN THE PAST, BUT THIS IS THE FIRST SINCE I TOOK OVER AS DIRECTOR GENERAL.
AND IT WAS JUST THE OTHER DAY TOO...
...RIGHT IN THE MIDDLE OF OTUS'S AUDIT...
THE INSPECTION DEPARTMENT IS SIMPLY NOT DOING THEIR JOB.
THEY'RE PROBABLY COVERING FOR A SUBORDINATE.
I'D EXPECT IT'S TO PROTECT THE INSPECTION DEPARTMENT.
...HE'S A SERIOUS MAN.

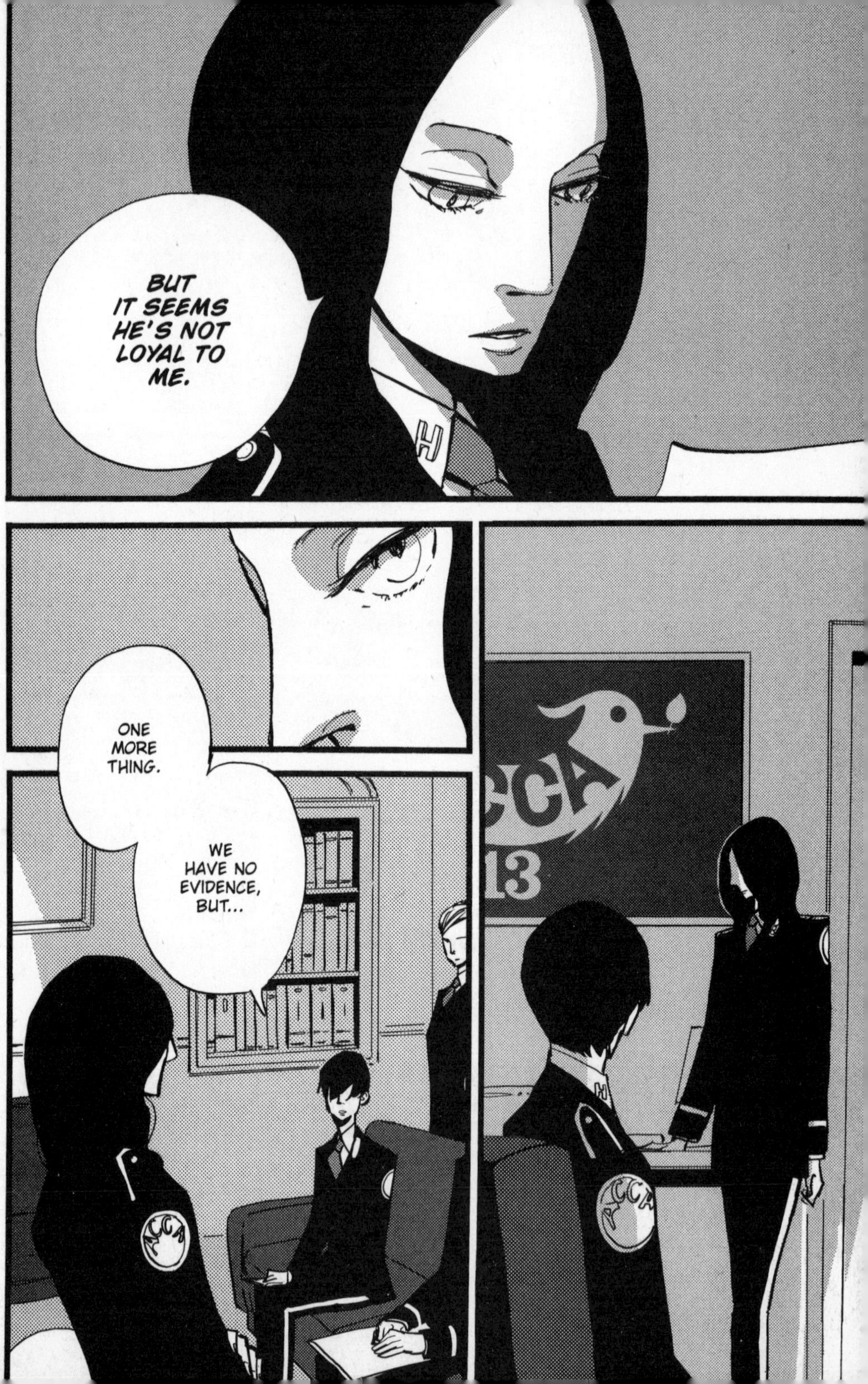
BUT IT SEEMS HE'S NOT LOYAL TO ME.
ONE MORE THING.
WE HAVE NO EVIDENCE, BUT...

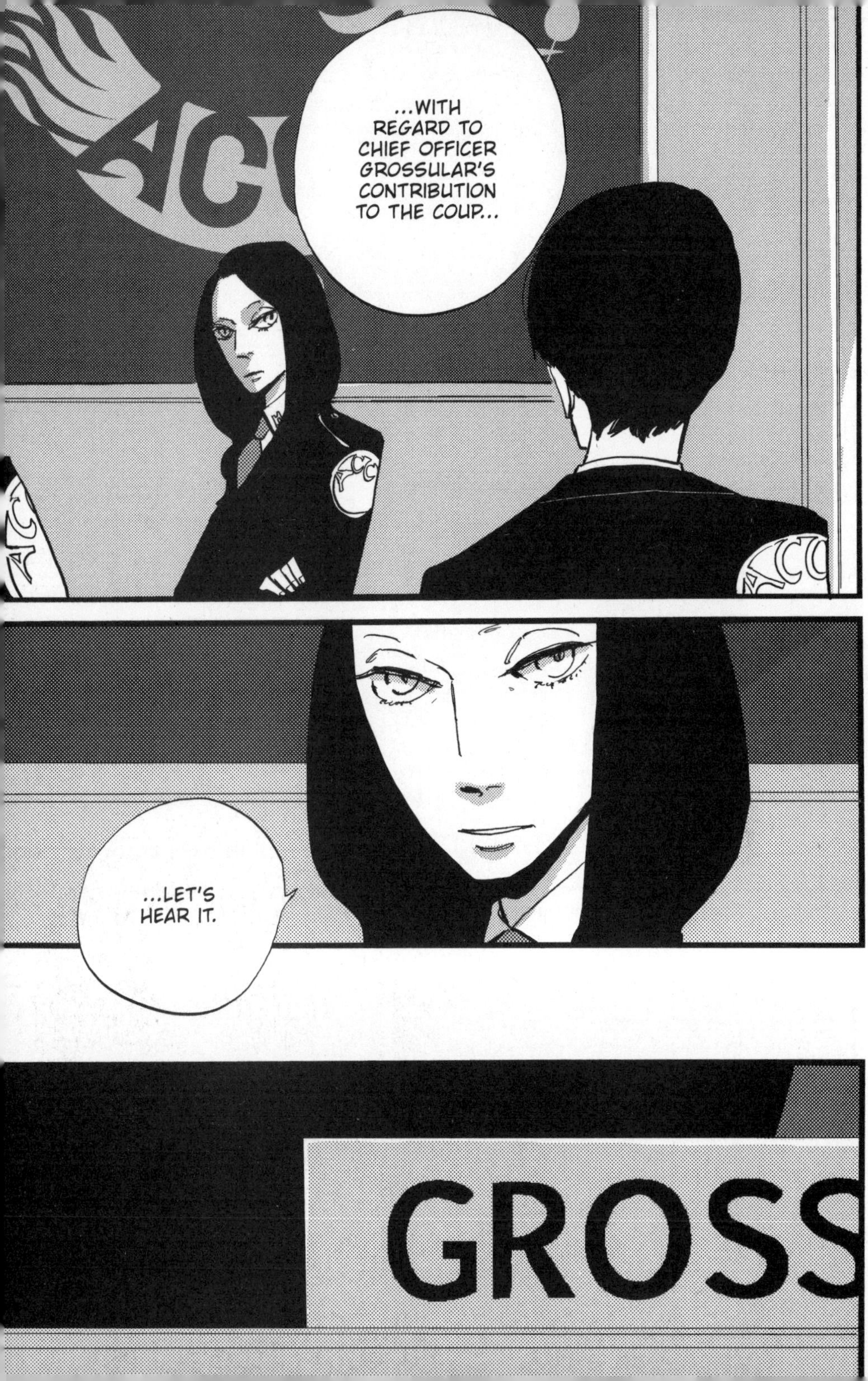
...WITH REGARD TO CHIEF OFFICER GROSSULAR'S CONTRIBUTION TO THE COUP...
...LET'S HEAR IT.
GROSS

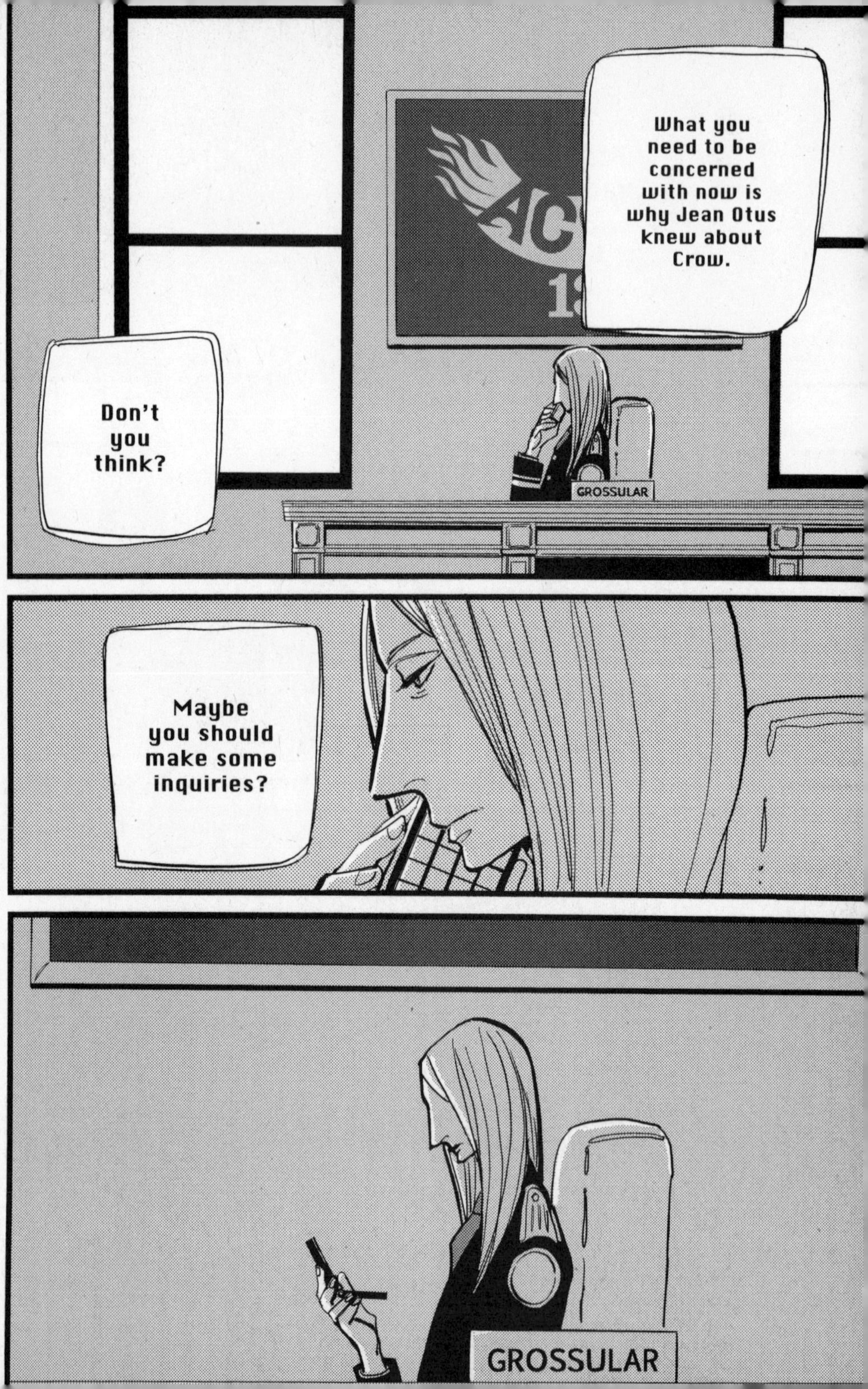
What you need to be concerned with now is why Jean Otus knew about Crow.
Don't you think?
GROSSULAR
Maybe you should make some inquiries?
GROSSULAR

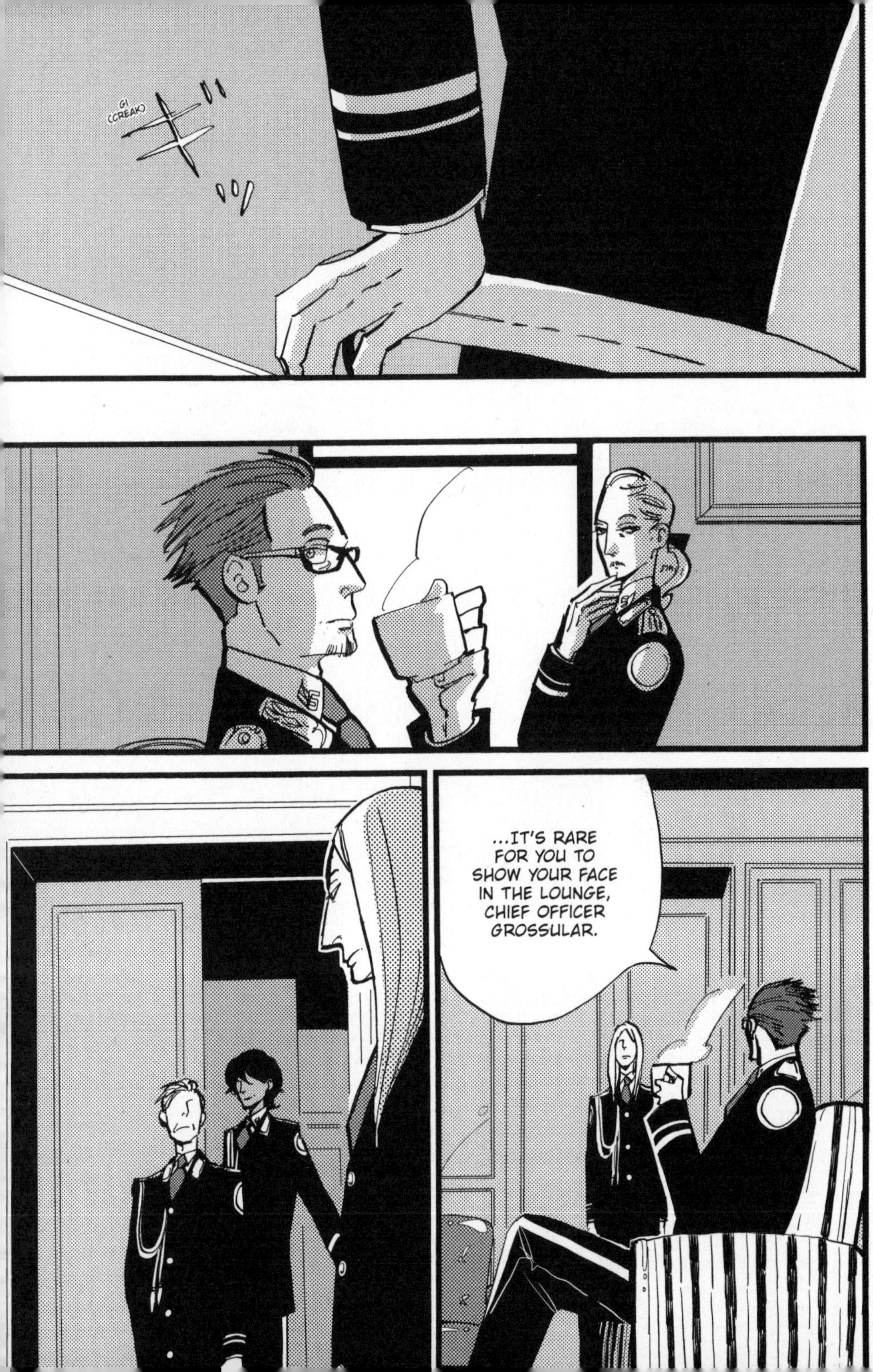
GI
(CREAK)
...IT'S RARE FOR YOU TO SHOW YOUR FACE IN THE LOUNGE, CHIEF OFFICER GROSSULAR.

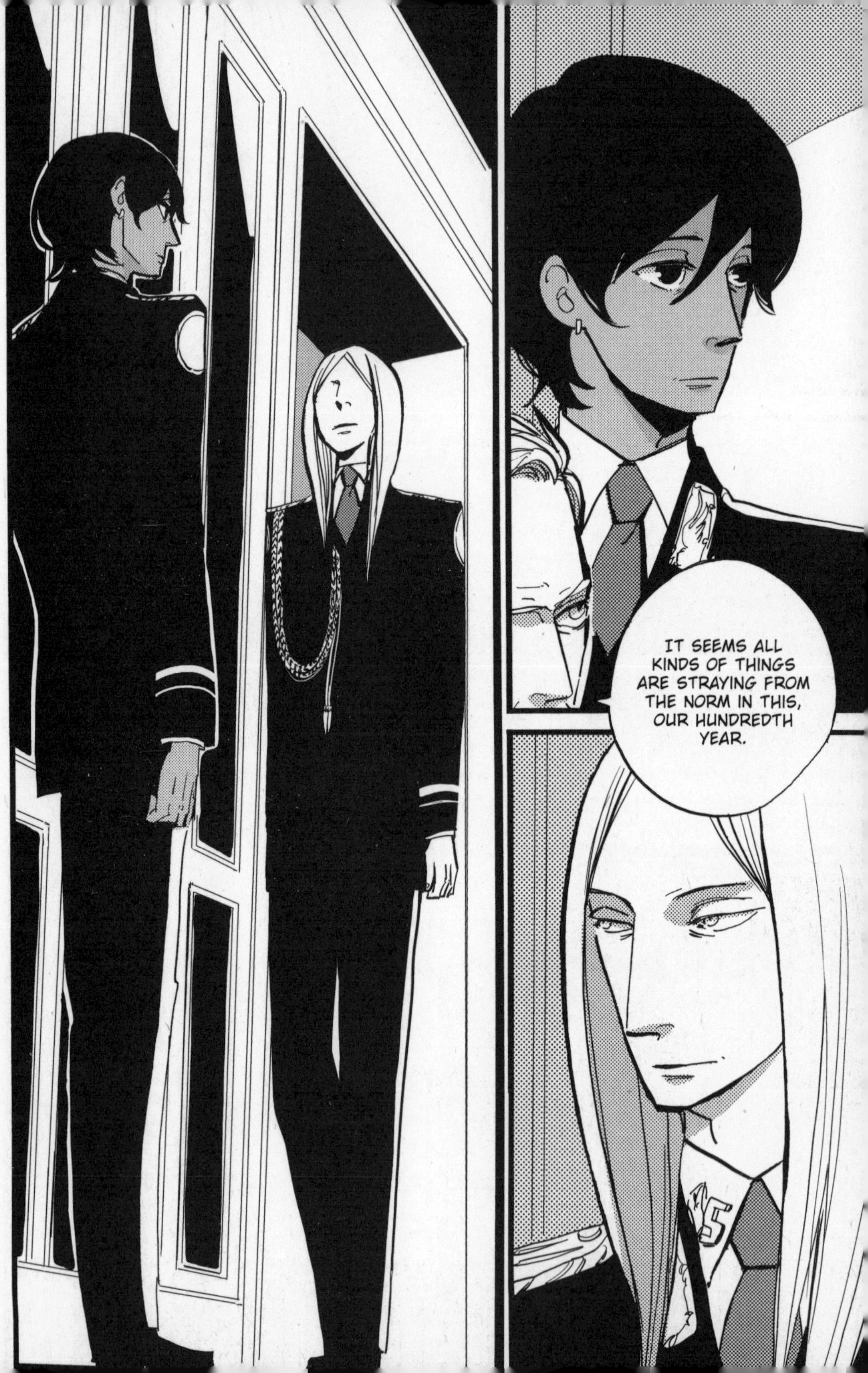
IT SEEMS ALL KINDS OF THINGS ARE STRAYING FROM THE NORM IN THIS, OUR HUNDREDTH YEAR.

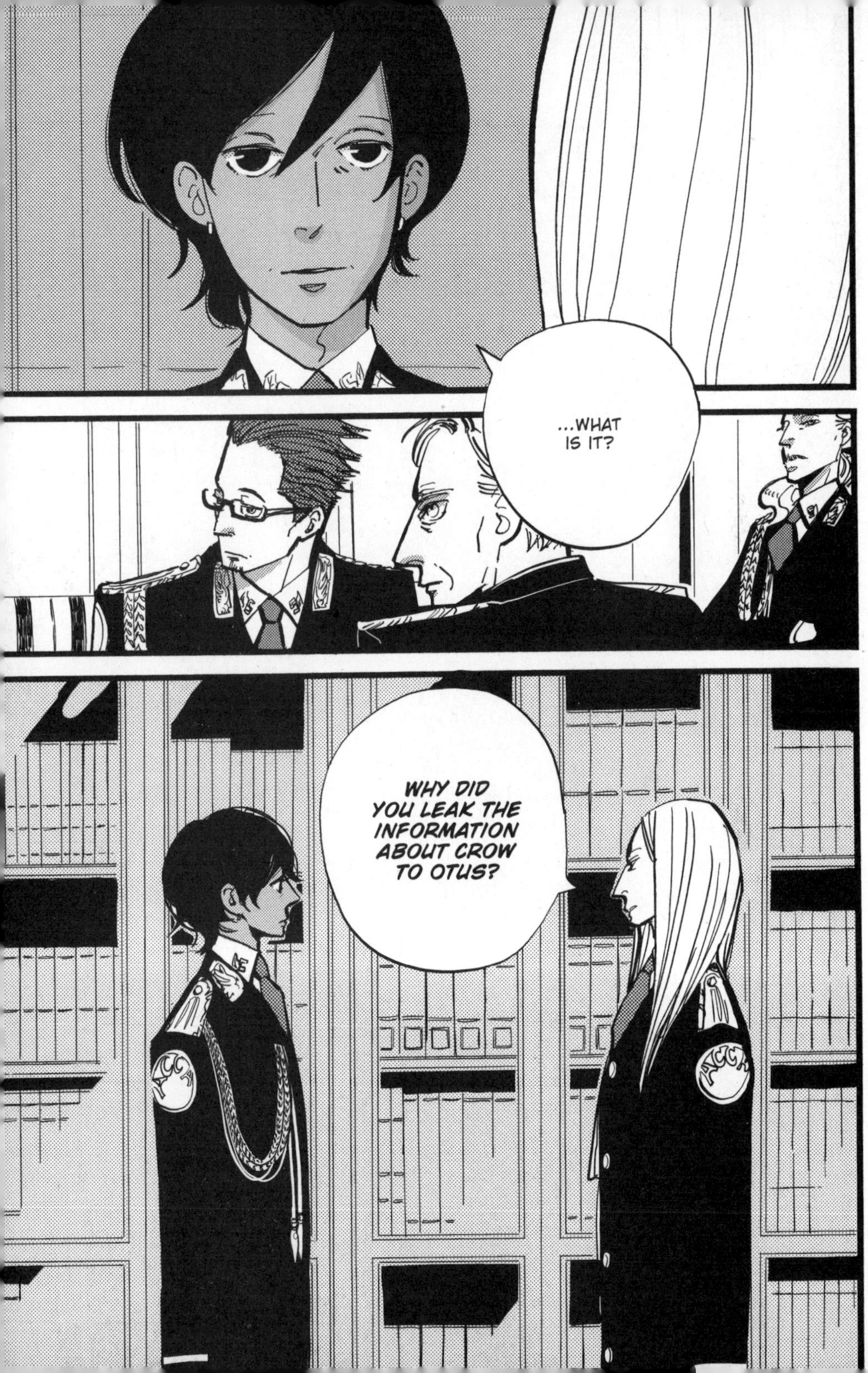
...WHAT IS IT?
WHY DID YOU LEAK THE INFORMATION ABOUT CROW TO OTUS?

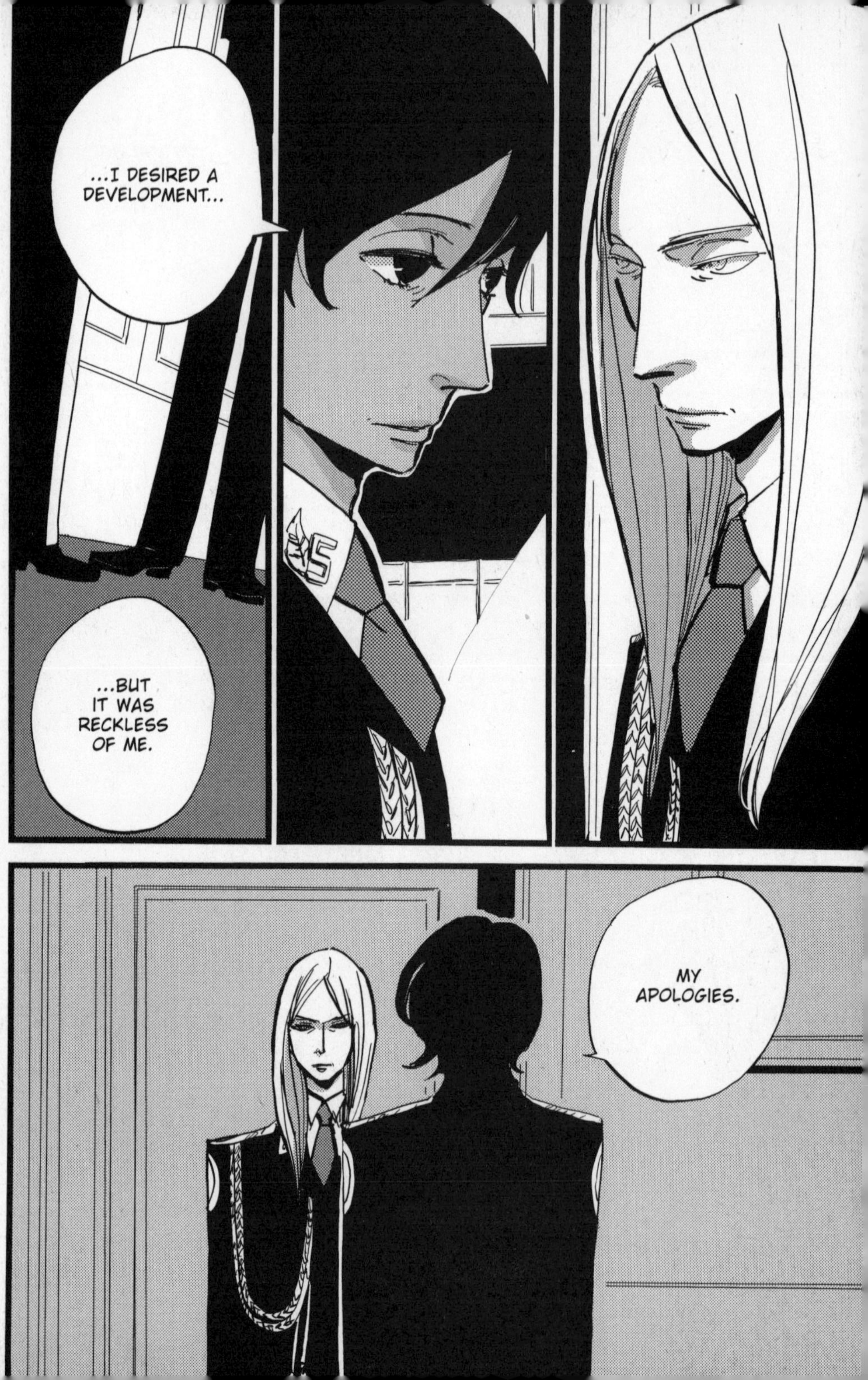
...I DESIRED A DEVELOPMENT...
...BUT IT WAS RECKLESS OF ME.
MY APOLOGIES.

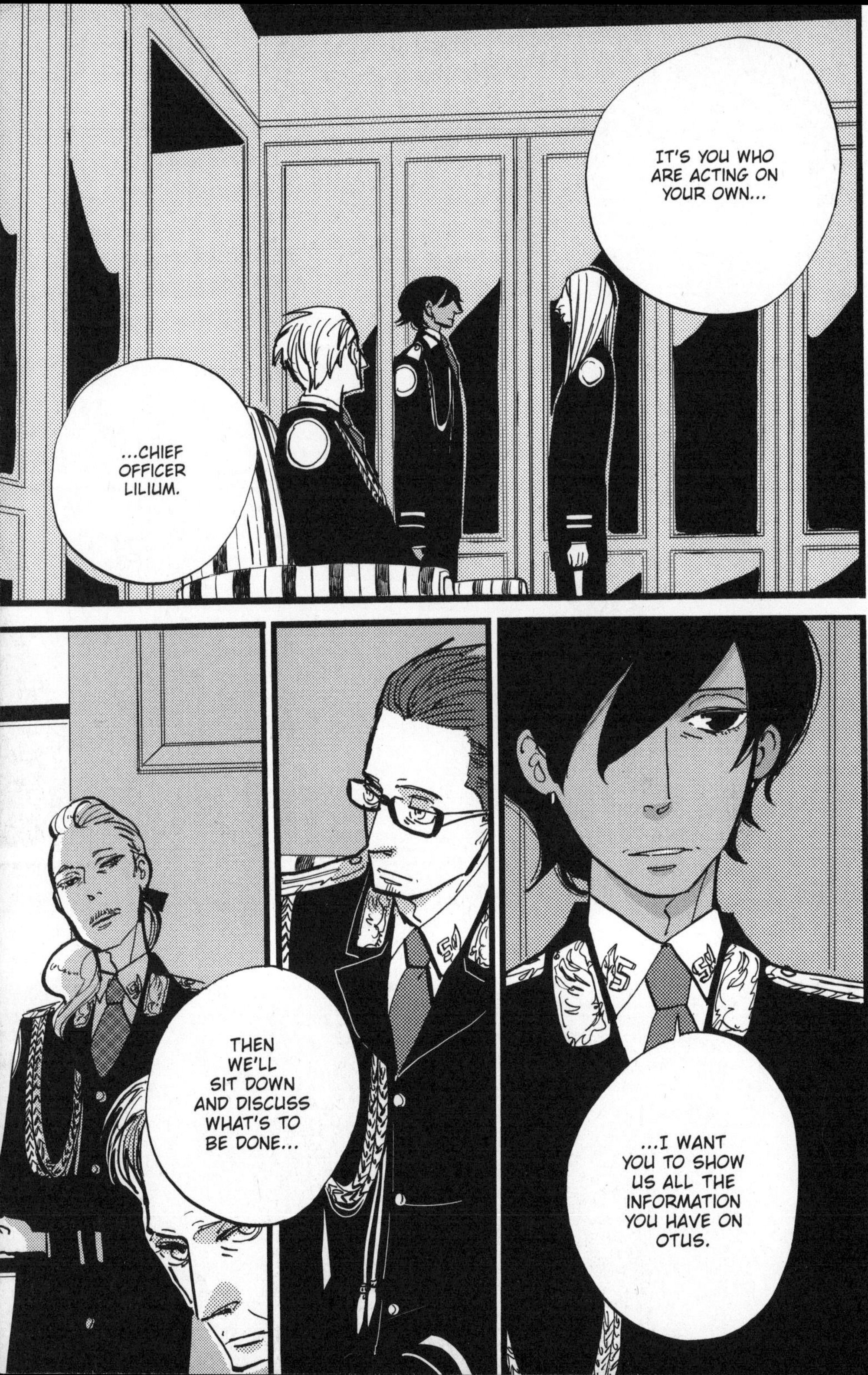
IT'S YOU WHO ARE ACTING ON YOUR OWN...
...CHIEF OFFICER LILIUM.
...I WANT YOU TO SHOW US ALL THE INFORMATION YOU HAVE ON OTUS.
THEN WE'LL SIT DOWN AND DISCUSS WHAT'S TO BE DONE...

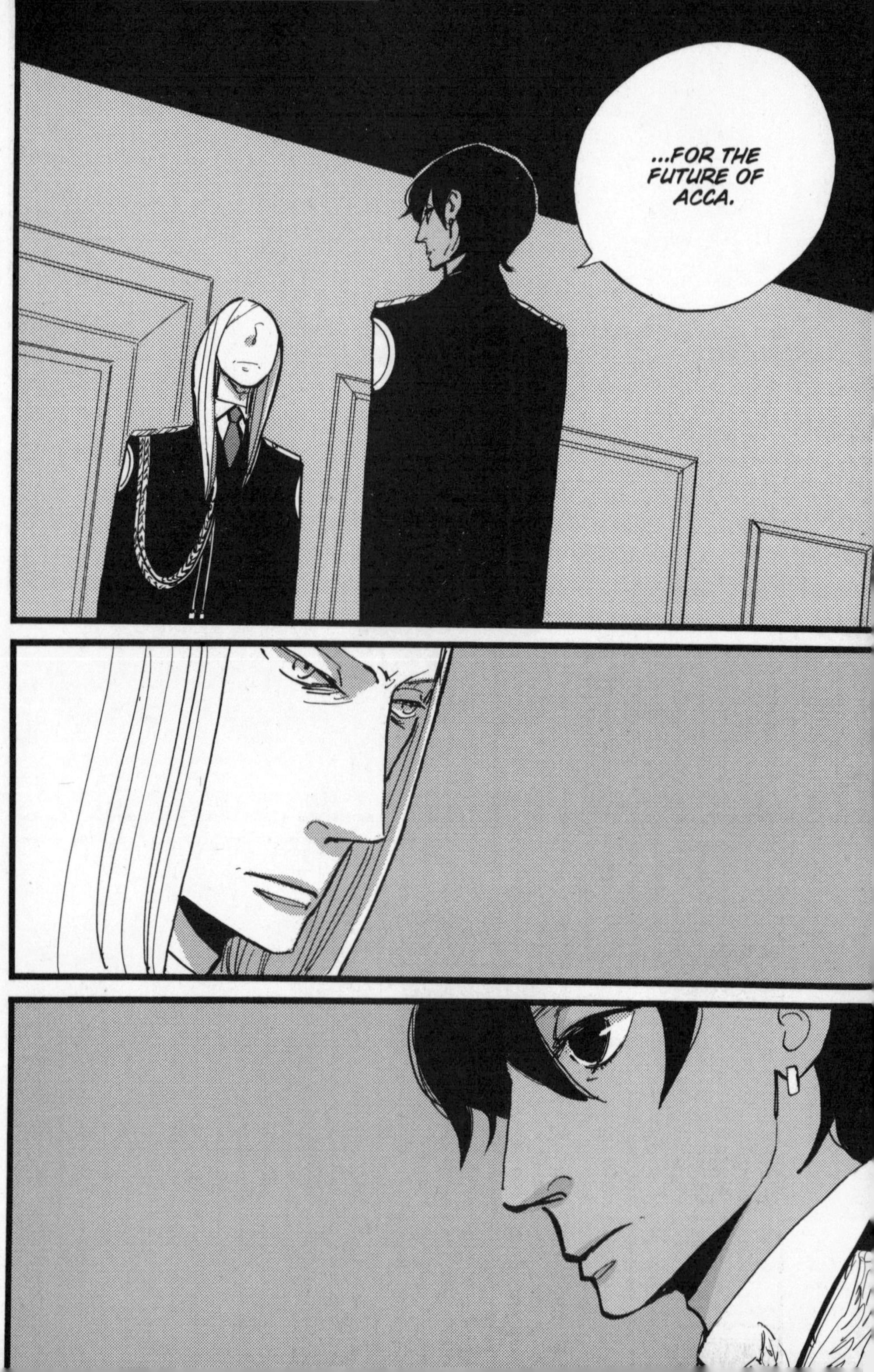
...FOR THE FUTURE OF ACCA.

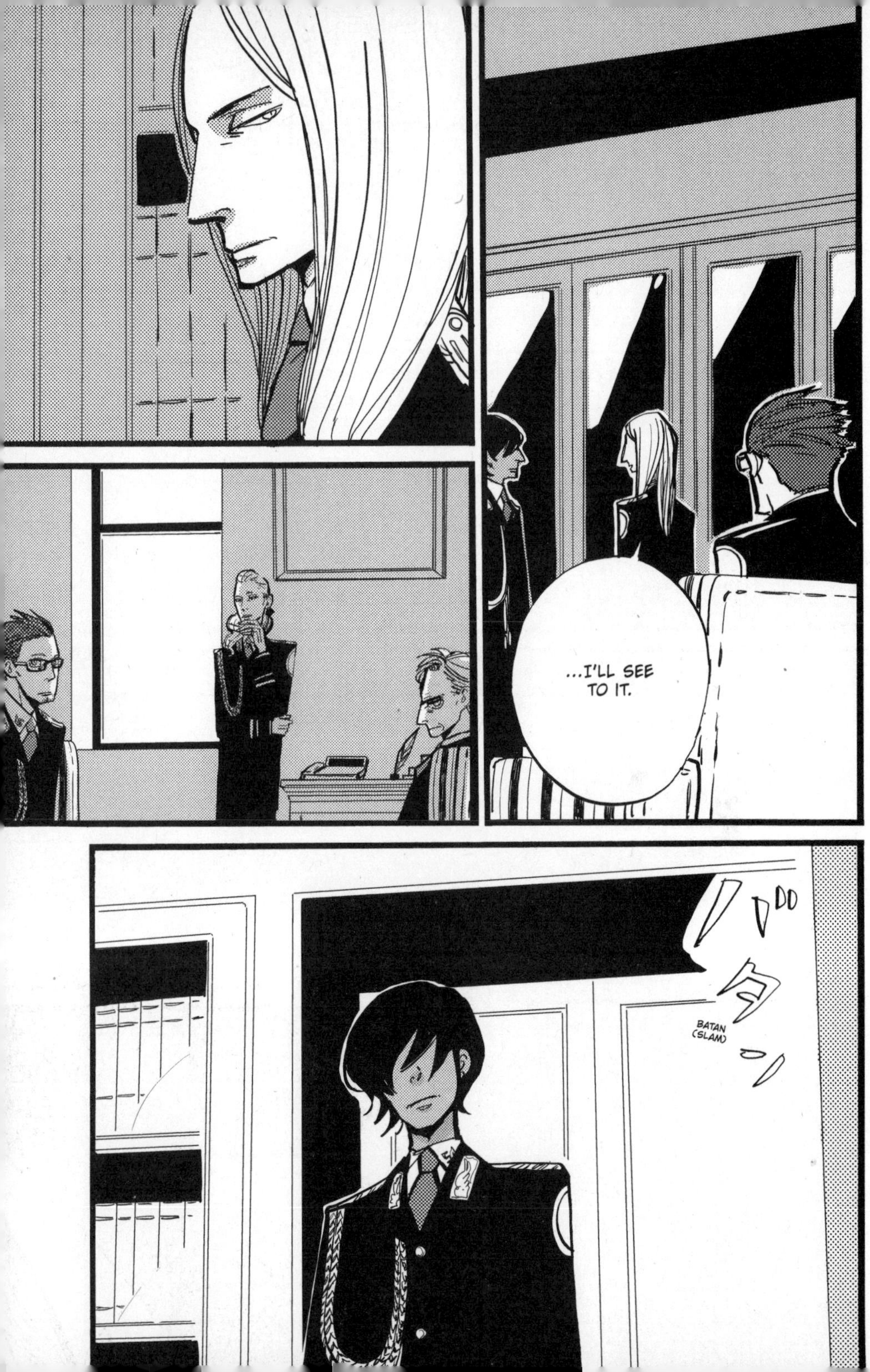
...I'LL SEE TO IT.
BATAN (SLAM)

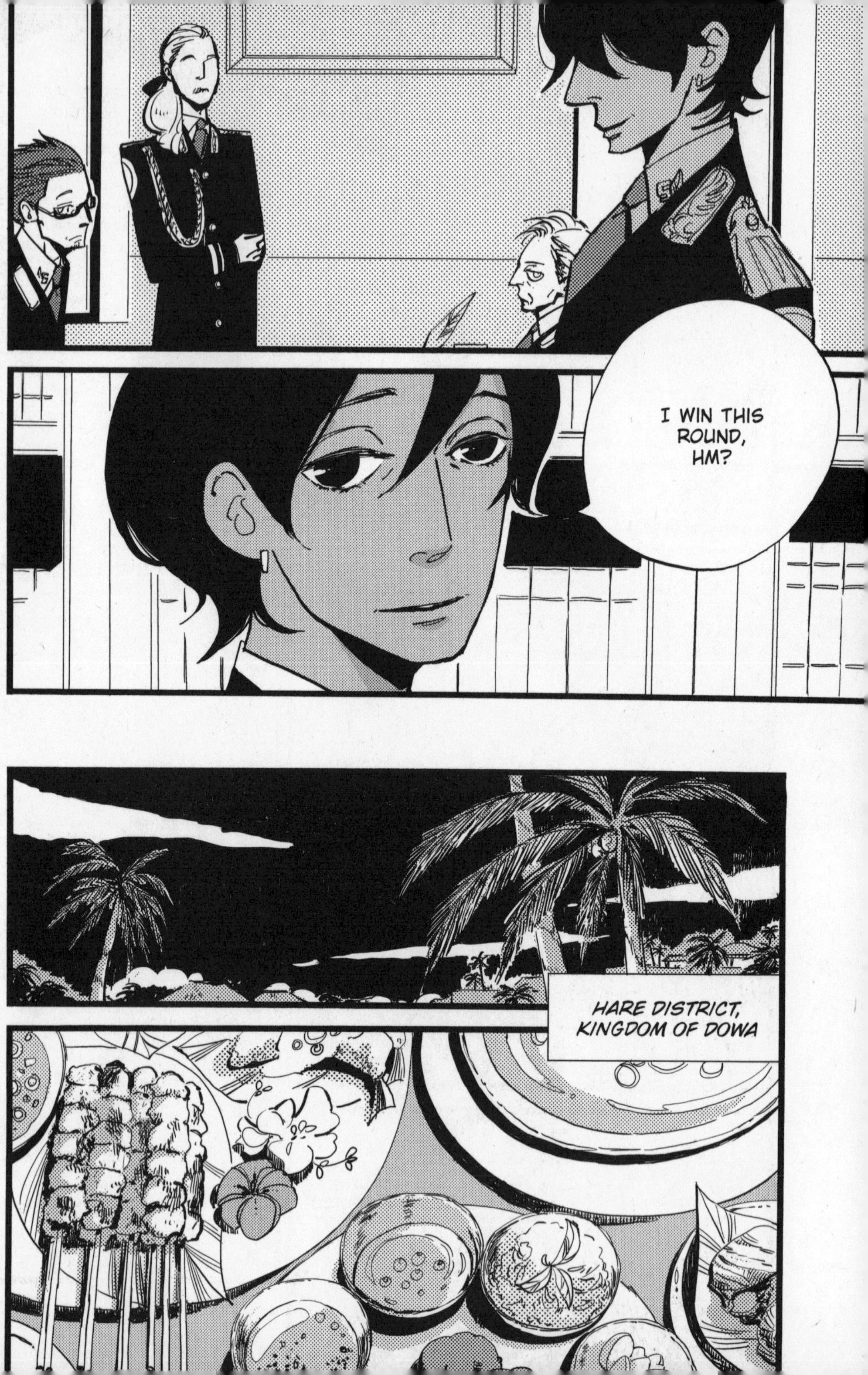
I WIN THIS ROUND, HM?
HARE DISTRICT, KINGDOM OF DOWA

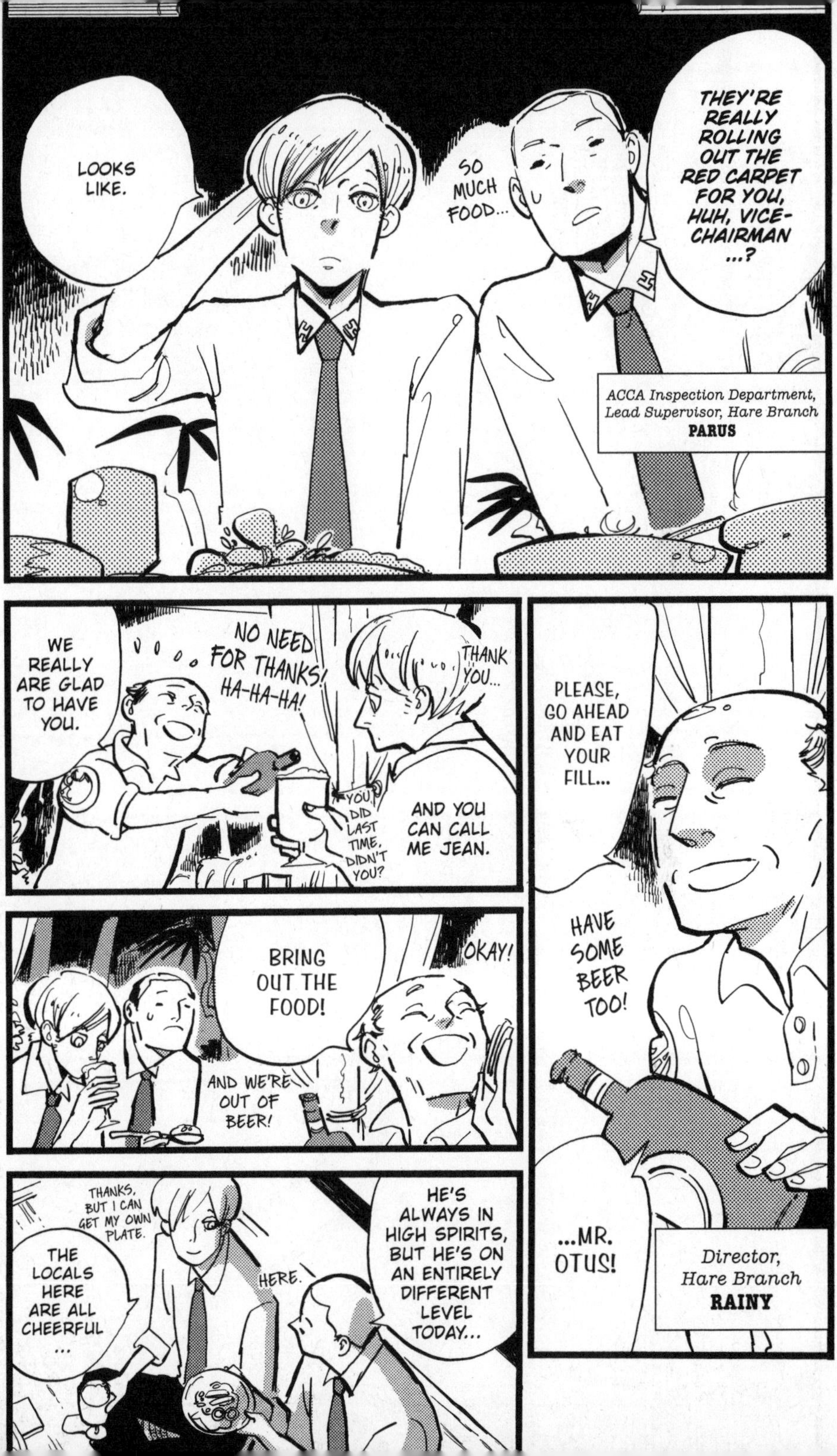
THEY'RE REALLY ROLLING OUT THE RED CARPET FOR YOU, HUH, VICE-CHAIRMAN...?
SO MUCH FOOD...
LOOKS LIKE.
ACCA Inspection Department, Lead Supervisor, Hare Branch PARUS
PLEASE, GO AHEAD AND EAT YOUR FILL...
HAVE SOME BEER TOO!
...MR. OTUS!
Director, Hare Branch RAINY
THANK YOU...
NO NEED FOR THANKS! HA-HA-HA!
WE REALLY ARE GLAD TO HAVE YOU.
AND YOU CAN CALL ME JEAN.
YOU DID LAST TIME, DIDN'T YOU?
OKAY!
BRING OUT THE FOOD!
AND WE'RE OUT OF BEER!
HE'S ALWAYS IN HIGH SPIRITS, BUT HE'S ON AN ENTIRELY DIFFERENT LEVEL TODAY...
HERE.
THANKS, BUT I CAN GET MY OWN PLATE.
THE LOCALS HERE ARE ALL CHEERFUL...

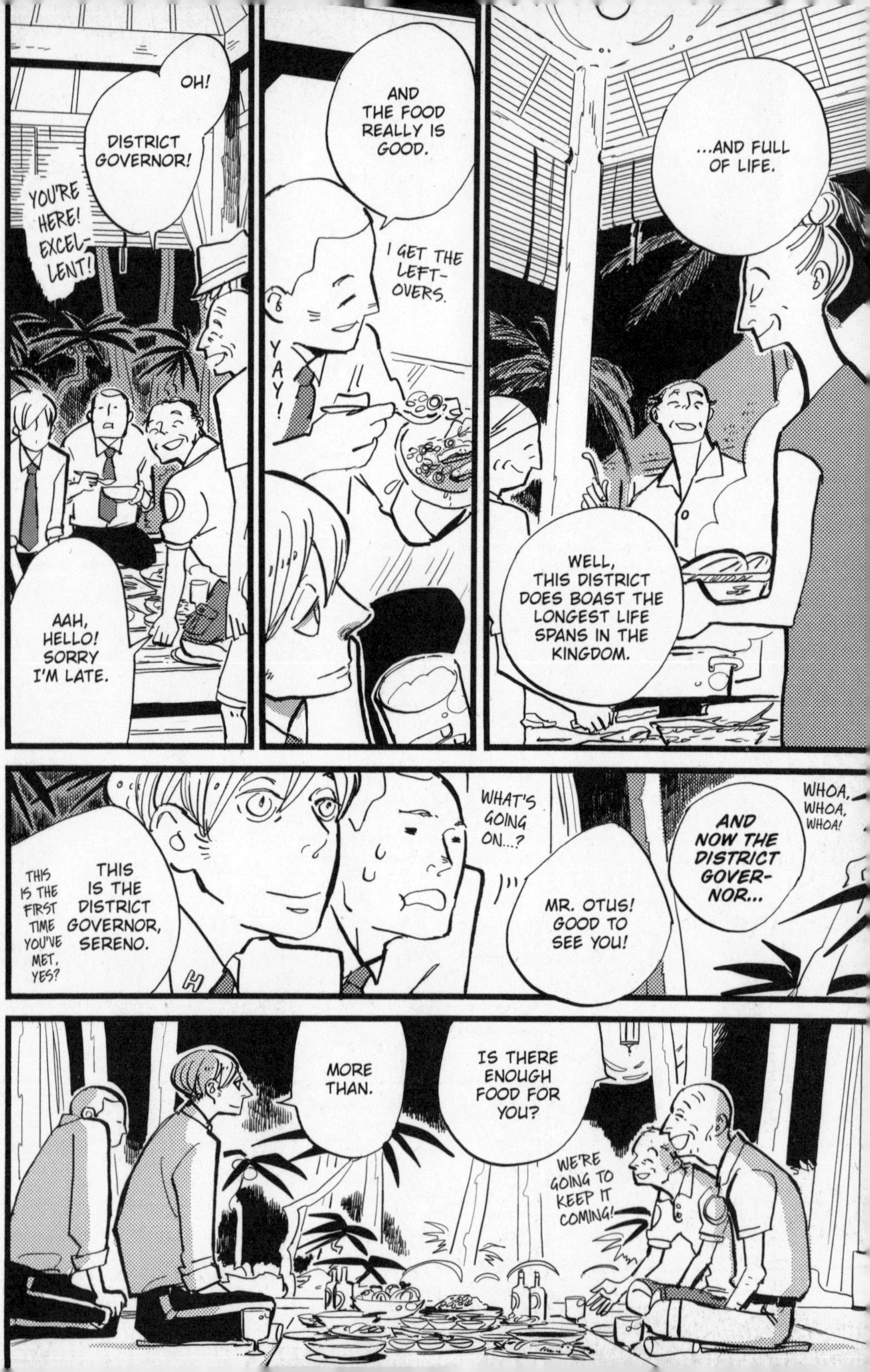
...AND FULL OF LIFE.
WELL, THIS DISTRICT DOES BOAST THE LONGEST LIFE SPANS IN THE KINGDOM.
AND THE FOOD REALLY IS GOOD.
I GET THE LEFTOVERS.
YAY!
OH!
DISTRICT GOVERNOR!
YOU'RE HERE! EXCELLENT!
AAH, HELLO! SORRY I'M LATE.
WHOA, WHOA, WHOA!
AND NOW THE DISTRICT GOVERNOR...
WHAT'S GOING ON...?
MR. OTUS! GOOD TO SEE YOU!
THIS IS THE DISTRICT GOVERNOR, SERENO.
THIS IS THE FIRST TIME YOU'VE MET, YES?
IS THERE ENOUGH FOOD FOR YOU?
WE'RE GOING TO KEEP IT COMING!
MORE THAN.

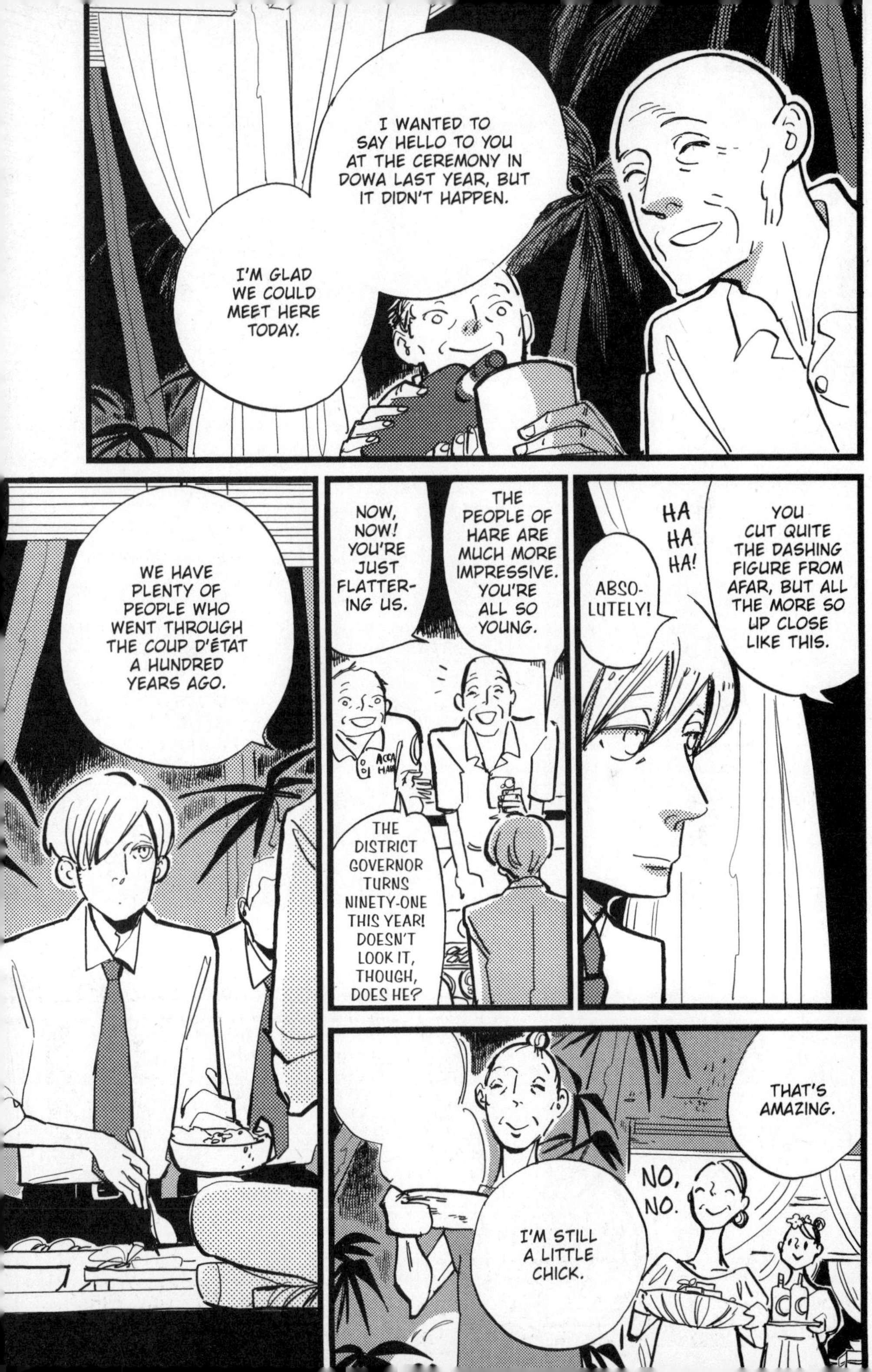
I WANTED TO SAY HELLO TO YOU AT THE CEREMONY IN DOWA LAST YEAR, BUT IT DIDN'T HAPPEN.
I'M GLAD WE COULD MEET HERE TODAY.
YOU CUT QUITE THE DASHING FIGURE FROM AFAR, BUT ALL THE MORE SO UP CLOSE LIKE THIS.
HA HA HA!
ABSO-LUTELY!
THE PEOPLE OF HARE ARE MUCH MORE IMPRESSIVE. YOU'RE ALL SO YOUNG.
NOW, NOW! YOU'RE JUST FLATTER-ING US.
THE DISTRICT GOVERNOR TURNS NINETY-ONE THIS YEAR! DOESN'T LOOK IT, THOUGH, DOES HE?
THAT'S AMAZING.
NO, NO.
I'M STILL A LITTLE CHICK.
WE HAVE PLENTY OF PEOPLE WHO WENT THROUGH THE COUP D'ÉTAT A HUNDRED YEARS AGO.

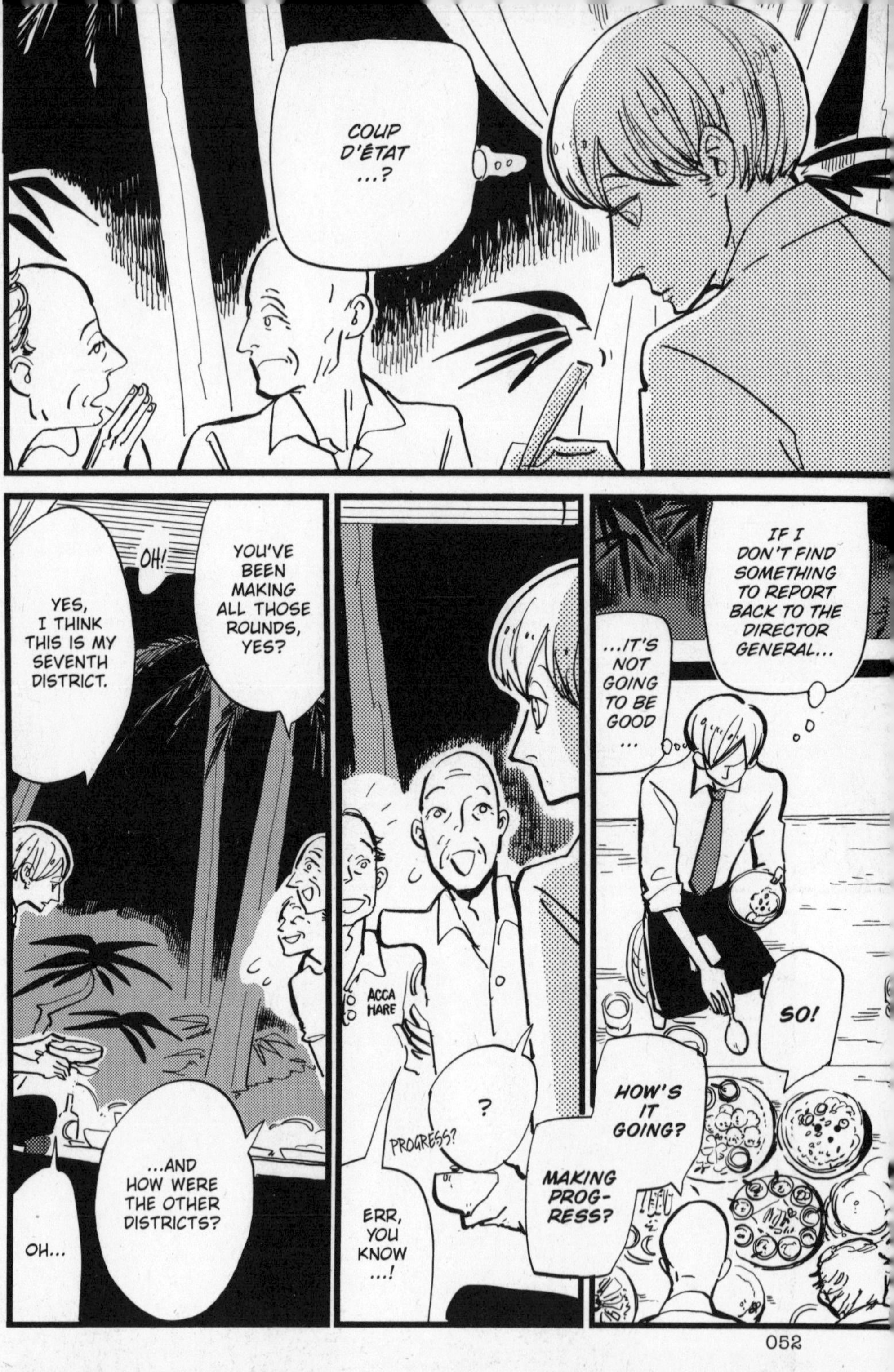
COUP D'ÉTAT ...?
IF I DON'T FIND SOMETHING TO REPORT BACK TO THE DIRECTOR GENERAL...
...IT'S NOT GOING TO BE GOOD ...
SO!
HOW'S IT GOING?
MAKING PROG-RESS?
?
PROGRESS?
ACCA HARE
ERR, YOU KNOW ...!
YOU'VE BEEN MAKING ALL THOSE ROUNDS, YES?
OH!
YES, I THINK THIS IS MY SEVENTH DISTRICT.
...AND HOW WERE THE OTHER DISTRICTS?
OH...

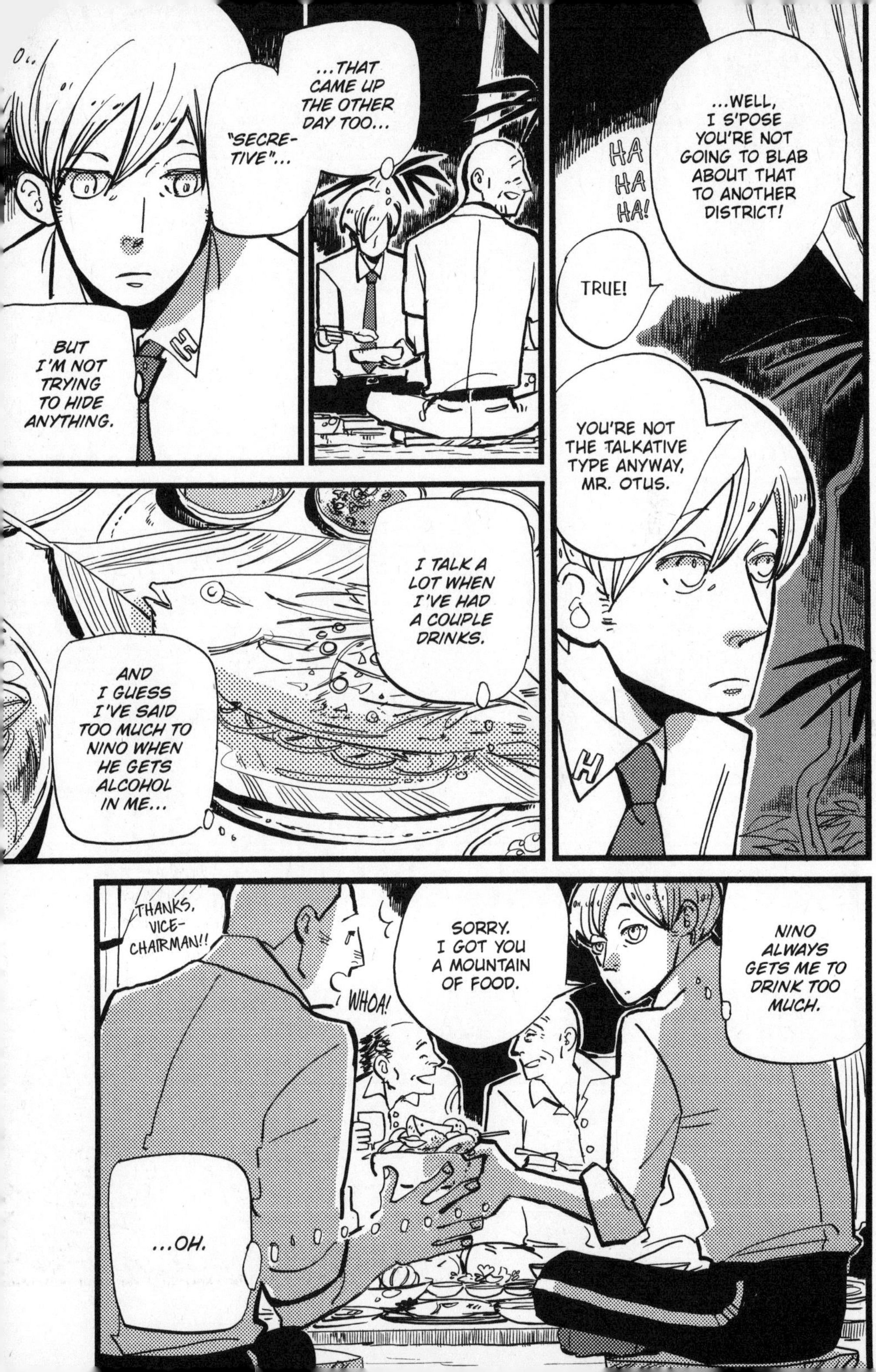

...WELL, I S'POSE YOU'RE NOT GOING TO BLAB ABOUT THAT TO ANOTHER DISTRICT!
HA HA HA!
TRUE!
YOU'RE NOT THE TALKATIVE TYPE ANYWAY, MR. OTUS.
"SECRE-TIVE"...
...THAT CAME UP THE OTHER DAY TOO...
O..
BUT I'M NOT TRYING TO HIDE ANYTHING.
I TALK A LOT WHEN I'VE HAD A COUPLE DRINKS.
AND I GUESS I'VE SAID TOO MUCH TO NINO WHEN HE GETS ALCOHOL IN ME...
NINO ALWAYS GETS ME TO DRINK TOO MUCH.
SORRY. I GOT YOU A MOUNTAIN OF FOOD.
WHOA!
THANKS, VICE-CHAIRMAN!!
...OH.

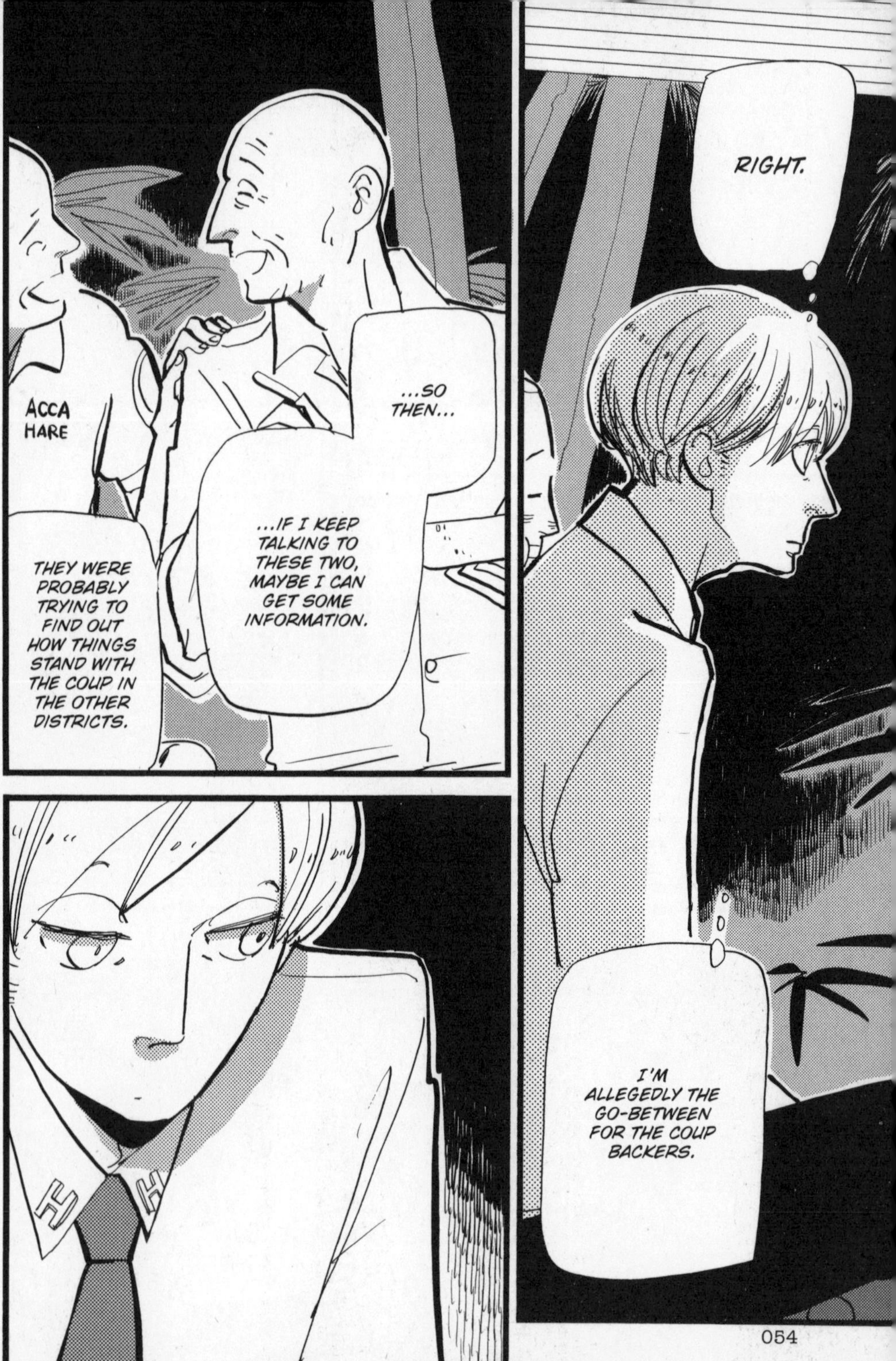
RIGHT.
I'M ALLEGEDLY THE GO-BETWEEN FOR THE COUP BACKERS.
...SO THEN...
...IF I KEEP TALKING TO THESE TWO, MAYBE I CAN GET SOME INFORMATION.
ACCA HARE
THEY WERE PROBABLY TRYING TO FIND OUT HOW THINGS STAND WITH THE COUP IN THE OTHER DISTRICTS.

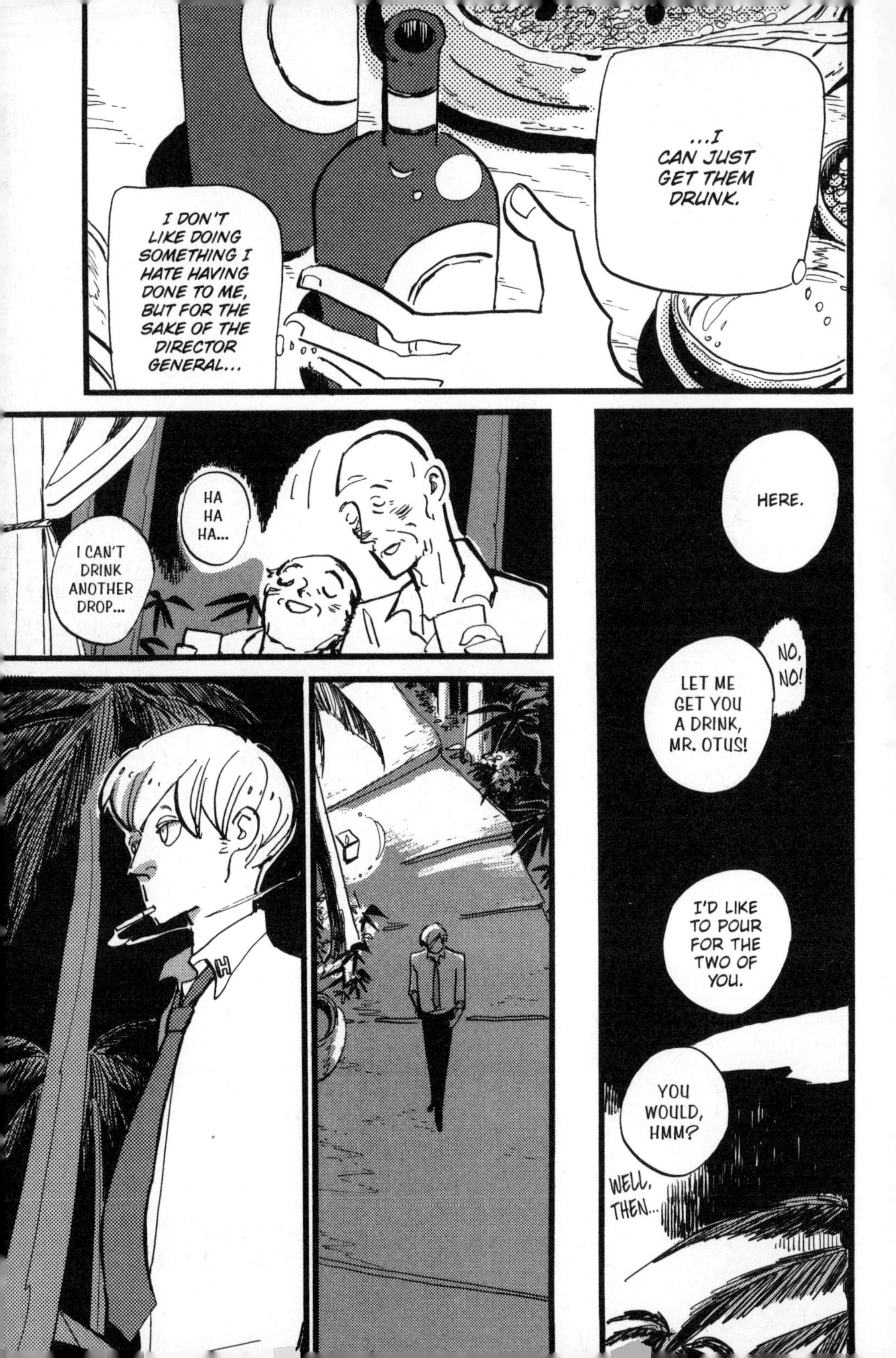
I DON'T LIKE DOING SOMETHING I HATE HAVING DONE TO ME, BUT FOR THE SAKE OF THE DIRECTOR GENERAL...
...I CAN JUST GET THEM DRUNK.
HERE.
NO, NO!
LET ME GET YOU A DRINK, MR. OTUS!
I'D LIKE TO POUR FOR THE TWO OF YOU.
YOU WOULD, HMM?
WELL, THEN...
HA HA HA...
I CAN'T DRINK ANOTHER DROP...

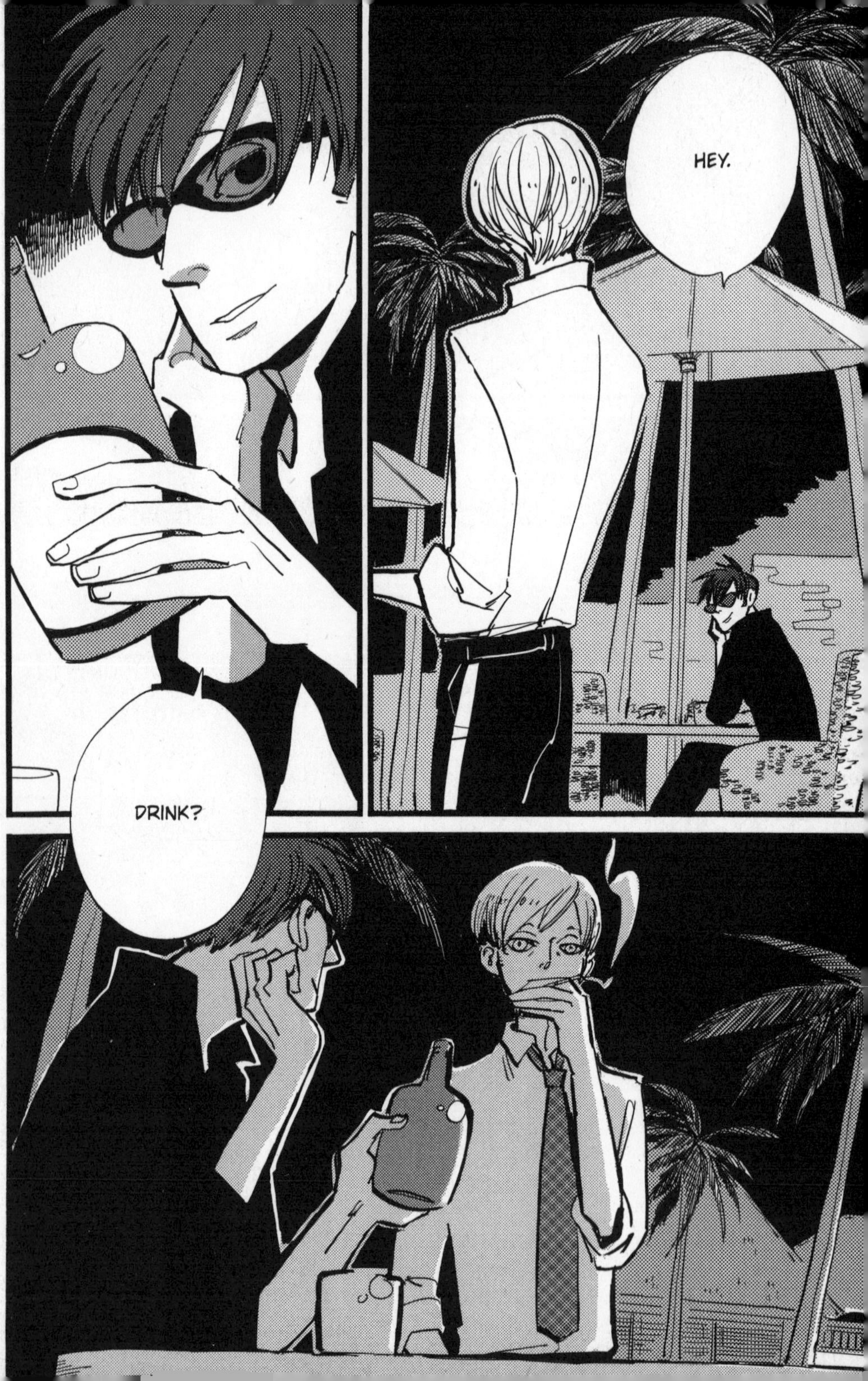
HEY.
DRINK?

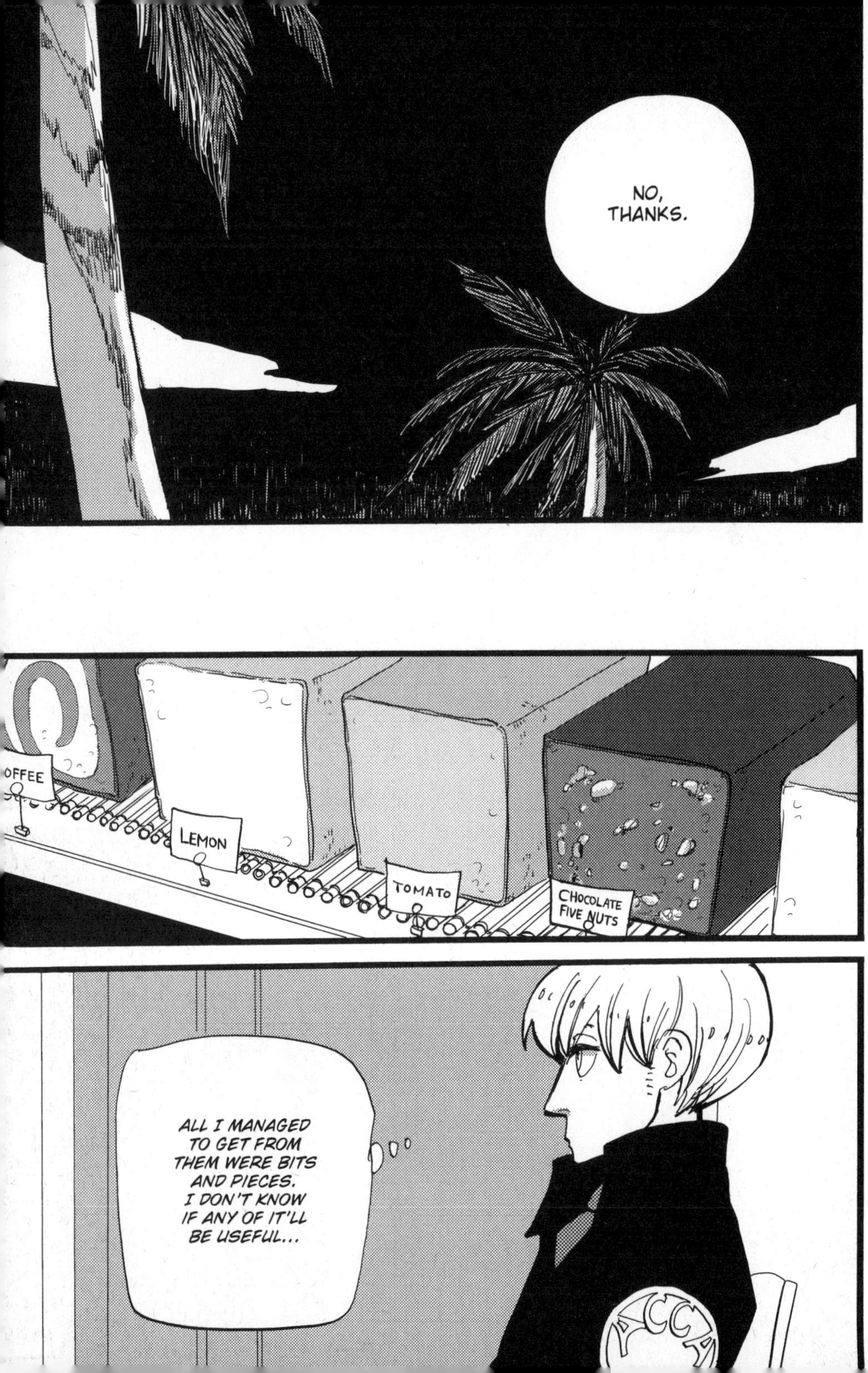
NO, THANKS.
CHOCOLATE FIVE NUTS
TOMATO
LEMON
OFFEE
ALL I MANAGED TO GET FROM THEM WERE BITS AND PIECES. I DON'T KNOW IF ANY OF IT'LL BE USEFUL...

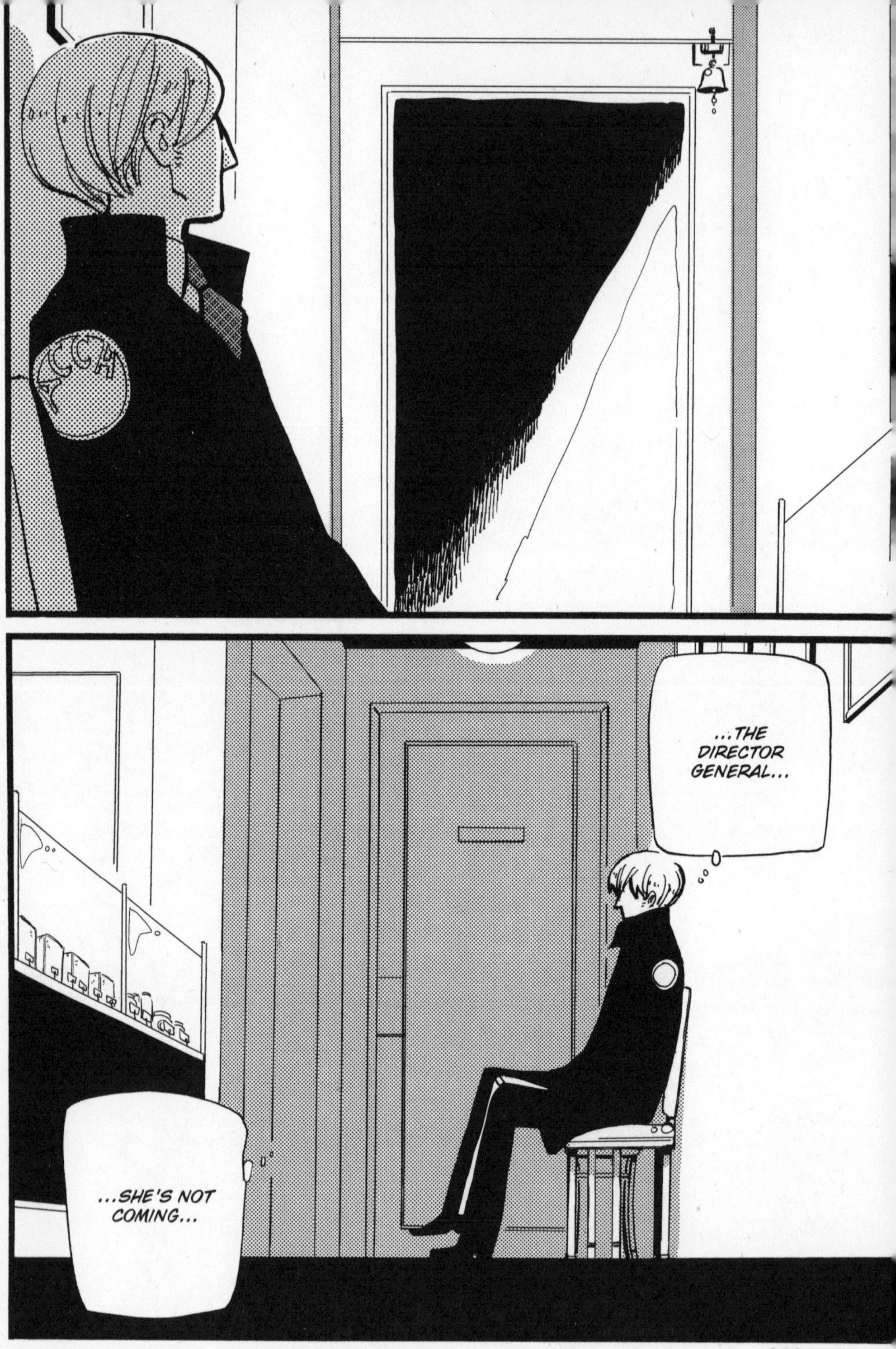
...THE DIRECTOR GENERAL...
...SHE'S NOT COMING...

ACCA Branch Uniforms | 7

Hare District

The climate in Hare is mild, and many of its people are quite long-lived. The citizens tend to have a sunny, cheerful disposition. Even at ACCA, the elderly vigorously carry out their duties in short sleeves and shorts.

ACCA
HARE

CHAPTER 19

The Reason for the Warm Welcome in Hare

DEPT ACCA 13 TERRITORY INSPECTION

PASS

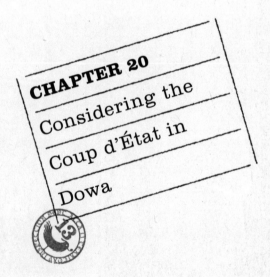

CHAPTER 20

Considering the
Coup d'État in
Dowa

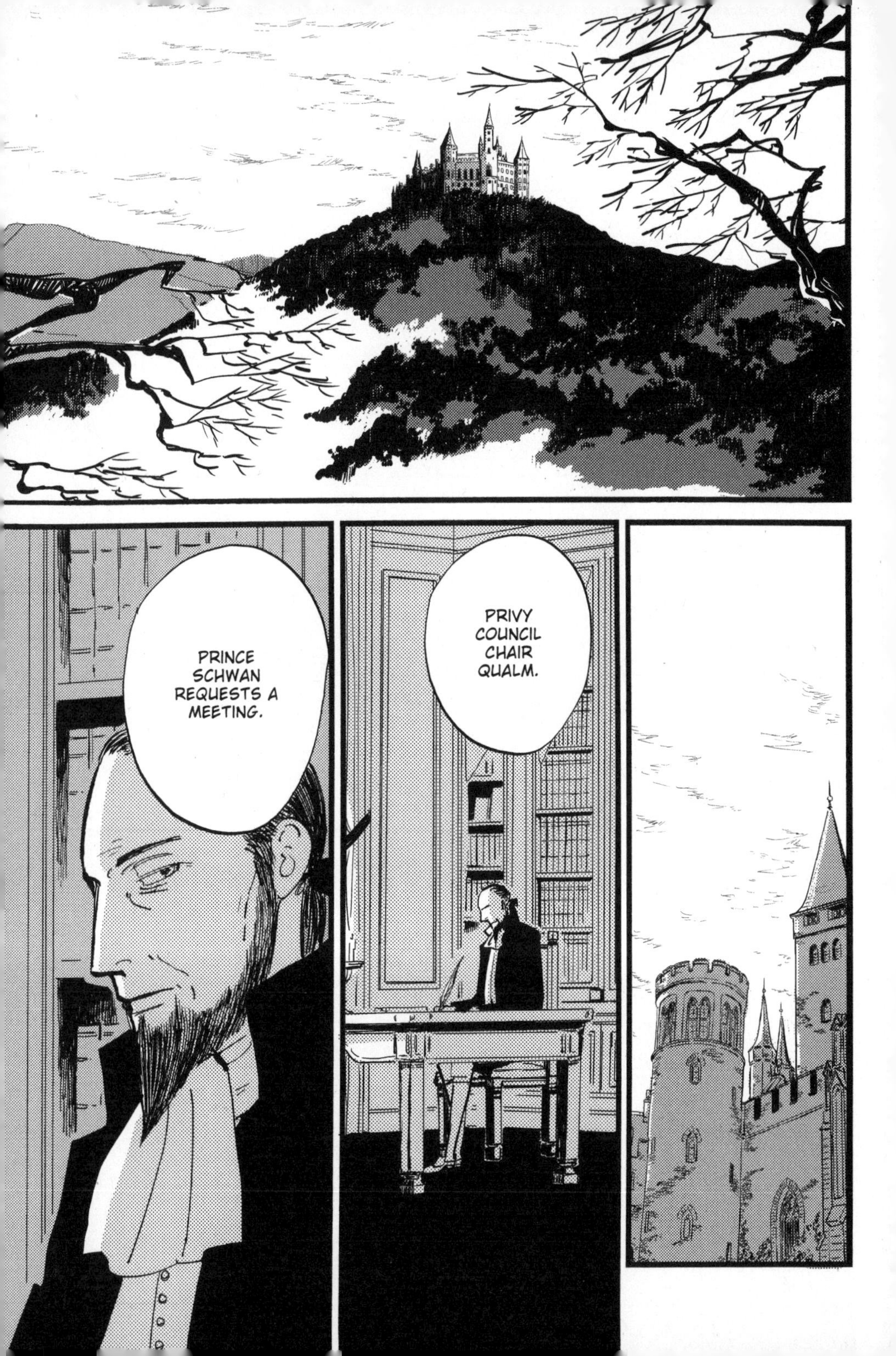
PRIVY COUNCIL CHAIR QUALM.
PRINCE SCHWAN REQUESTS A MEETING.

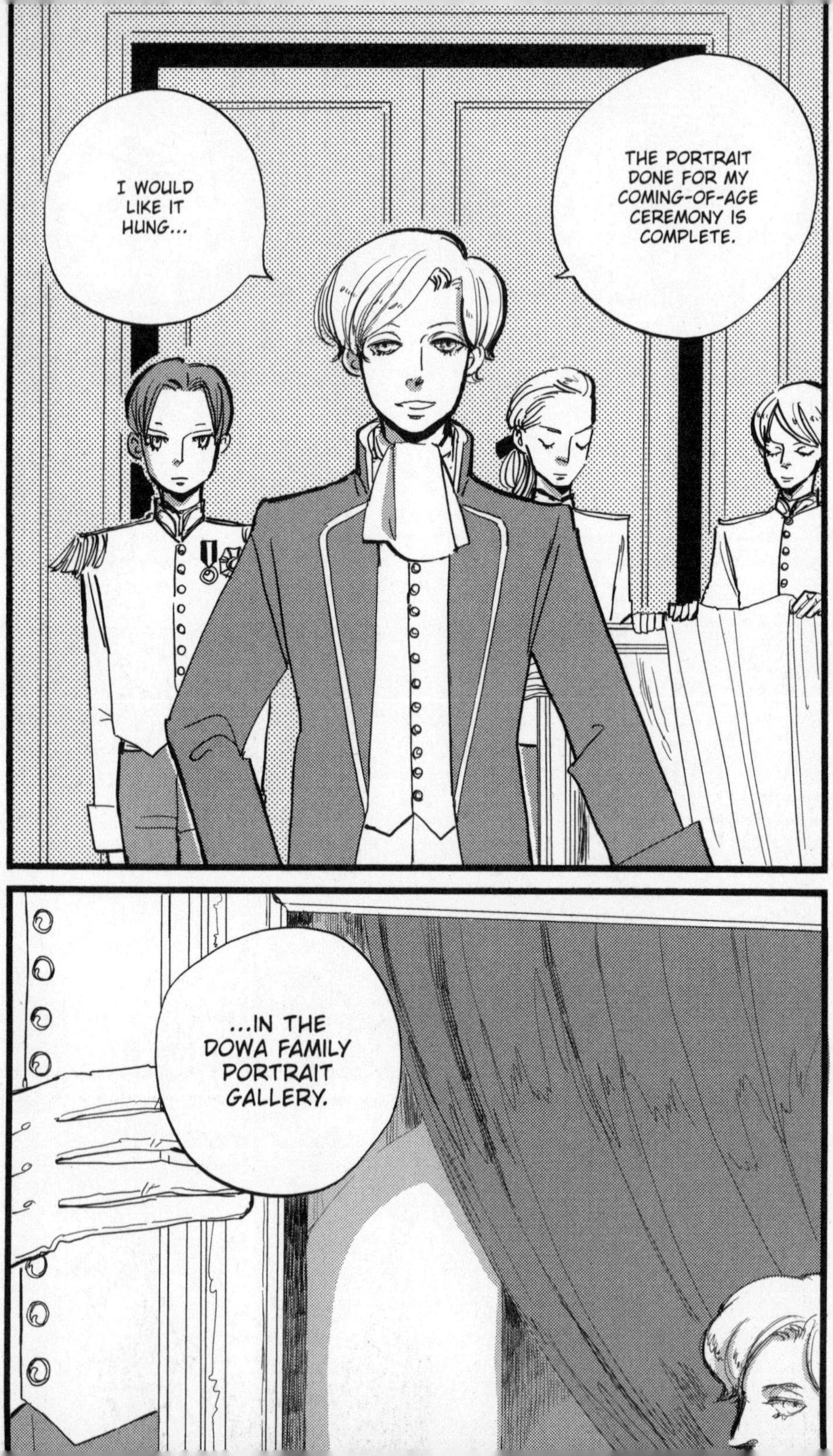
THE PORTRAIT DONE FOR MY COMING-OF-AGE CEREMONY IS COMPLETE.
I WOULD LIKE IT HUNG...
...IN THE DOWA FAMILY PORTRAIT GALLERY.

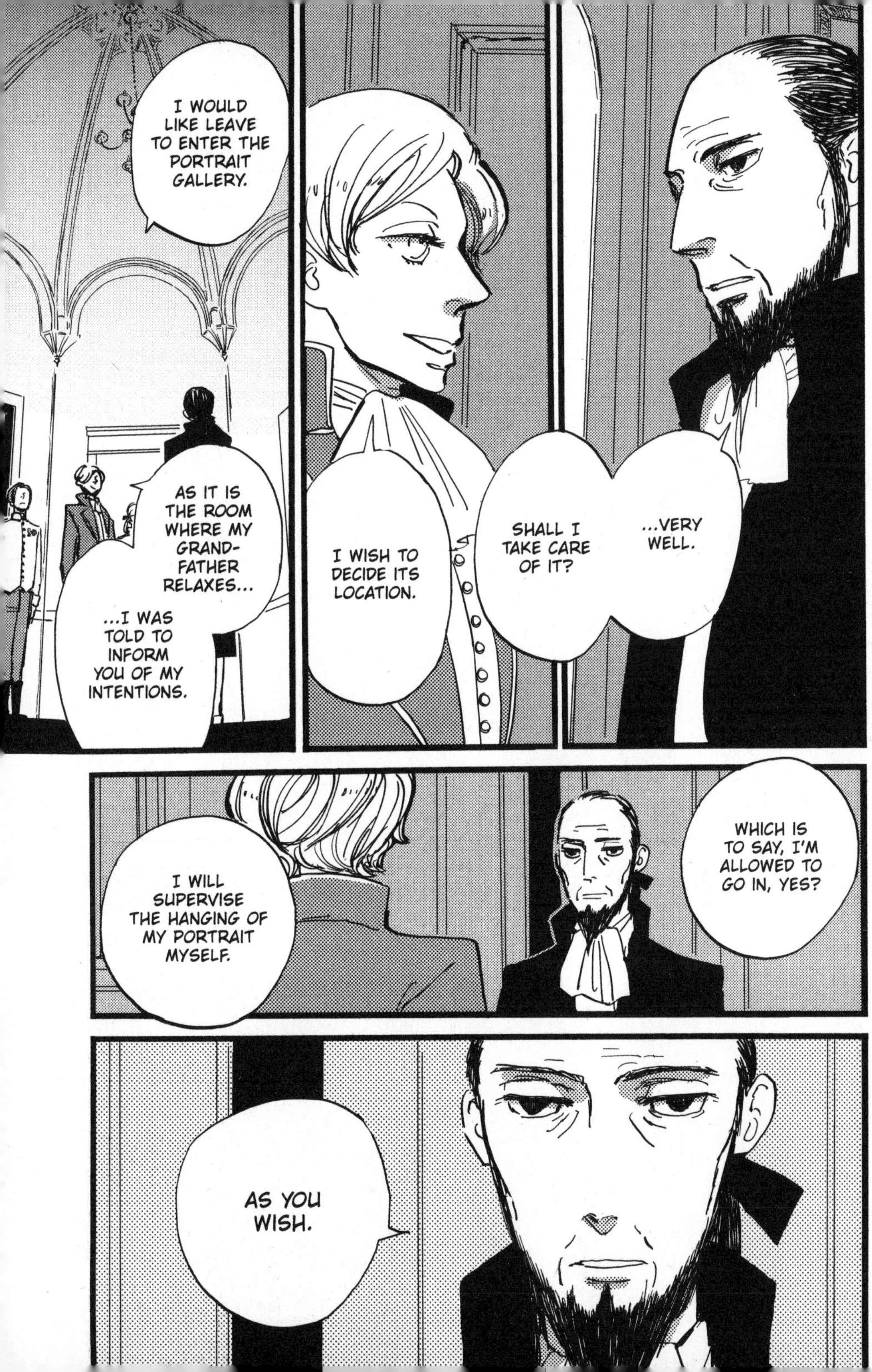
...VERY WELL.
SHALL I TAKE CARE OF IT?
I WISH TO DECIDE ITS LOCATION.
I WOULD LIKE LEAVE TO ENTER THE PORTRAIT GALLERY.
AS IT IS THE ROOM WHERE MY GRAND-FATHER RELAXES...
...I WAS TOLD TO INFORM YOU OF MY INTENTIONS.
WHICH IS TO SAY, I'M ALLOWED TO GO IN, YES?
I WILL SUPERVISE THE HANGING OF MY PORTRAIT MYSELF.
AS YOU WISH.

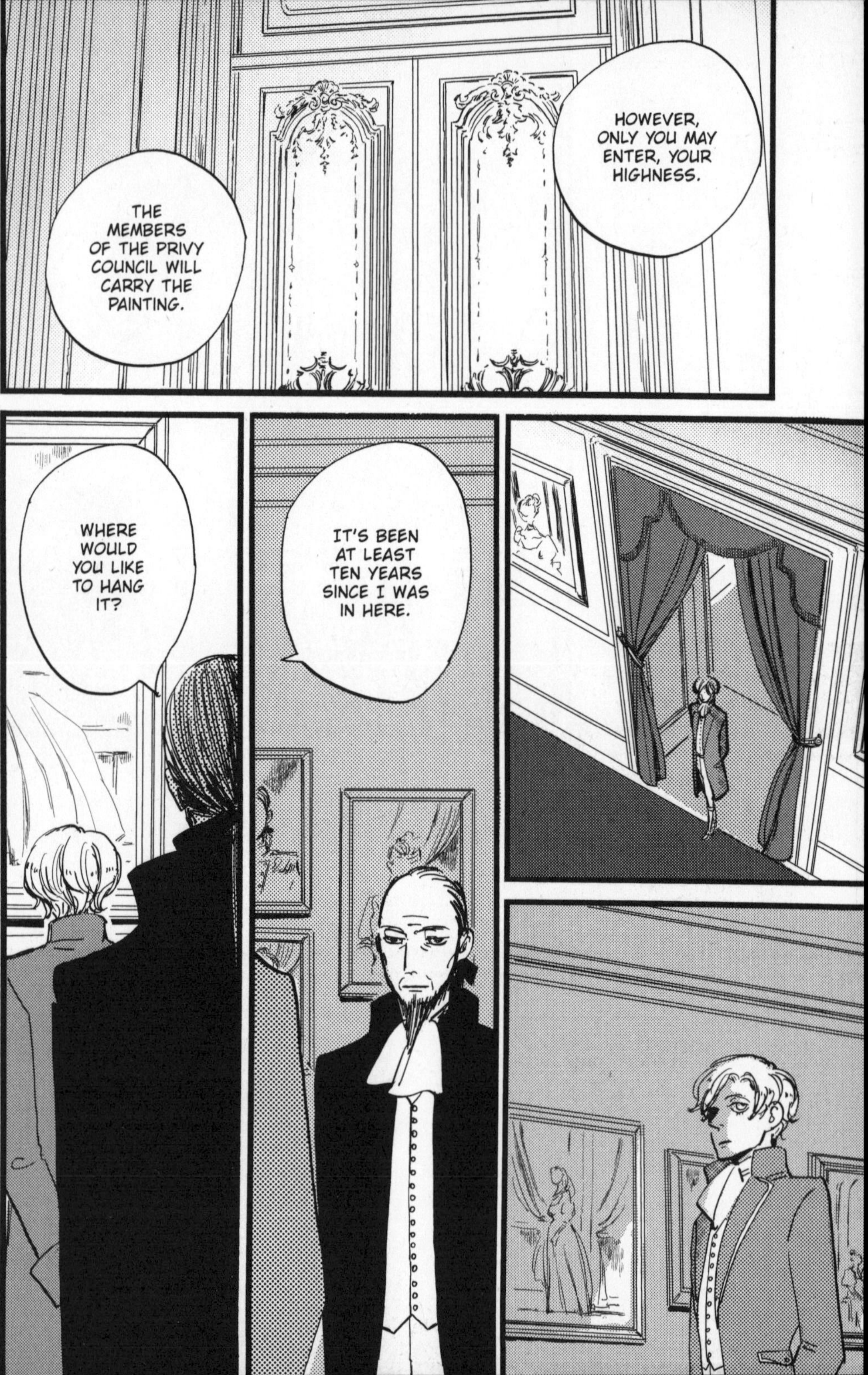
HOWEVER, ONLY YOU MAY ENTER, YOUR HIGHNESS.
THE MEMBERS OF THE PRIVY COUNCIL WILL CARRY THE PAINTING.
IT'S BEEN AT LEAST TEN YEARS SINCE I WAS IN HERE.
WHERE WOULD YOU LIKE TO HANG IT?

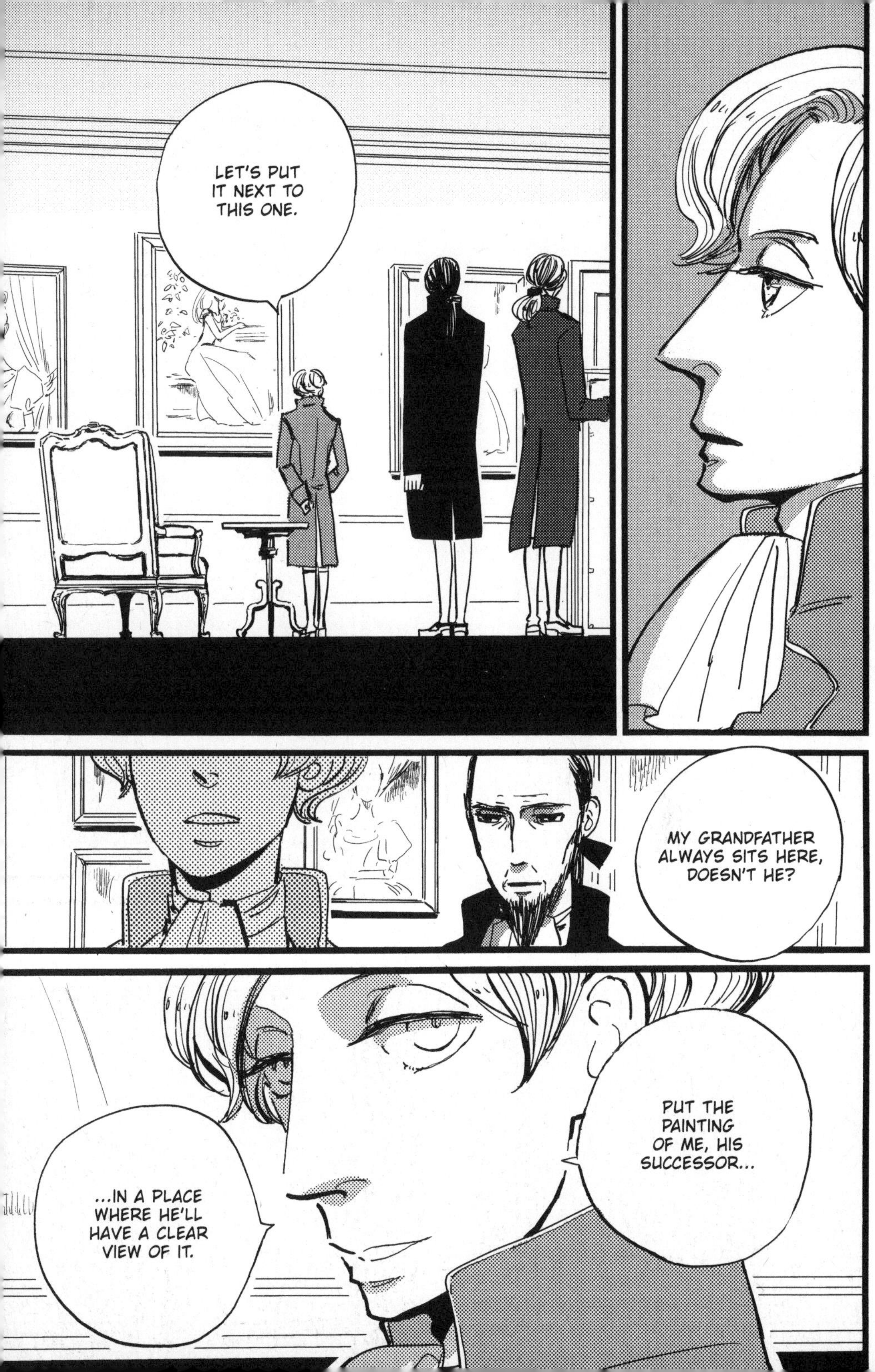
LET'S PUT IT NEXT TO THIS ONE.
MY GRANDFATHER ALWAYS SITS HERE, DOESN'T HE?
PUT THE PAINTING OF ME, HIS SUCCESSOR...
...IN A PLACE WHERE HE'LL HAVE A CLEAR VIEW OF IT.

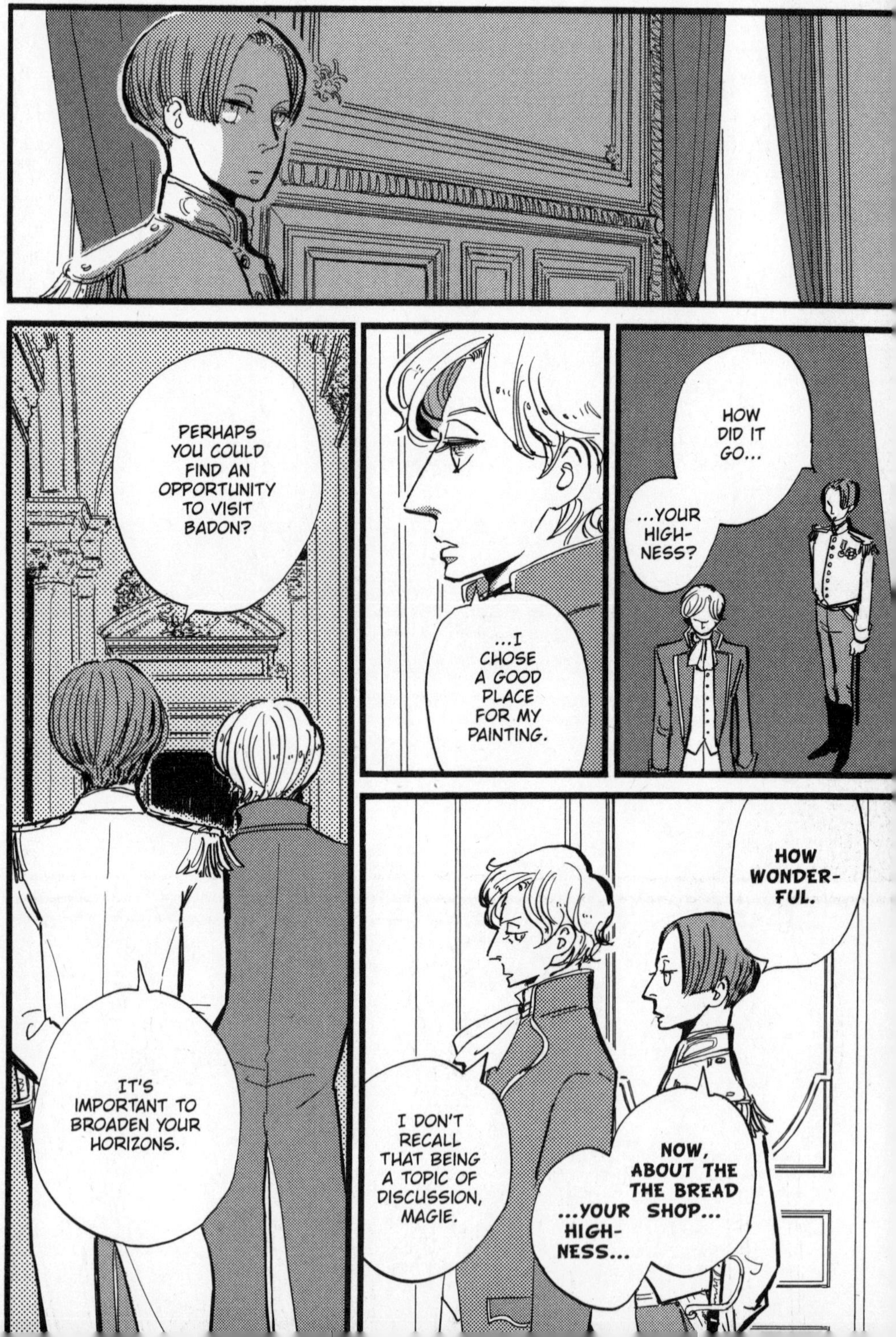
HOW DID IT GO...
...YOUR HIGHNESS?
...I CHOSE A GOOD PLACE FOR MY PAINTING.
HOW WONDERFUL.
NOW, ABOUT THE THE BREAD SHOP...
...YOUR HIGHNESS...
I DON'T RECALL THAT BEING A TOPIC OF DISCUSSION, MAGIE.
PERHAPS YOU COULD FIND AN OPPORTUNITY TO VISIT BADON?
IT'S IMPORTANT TO BROADEN YOUR HORIZONS.

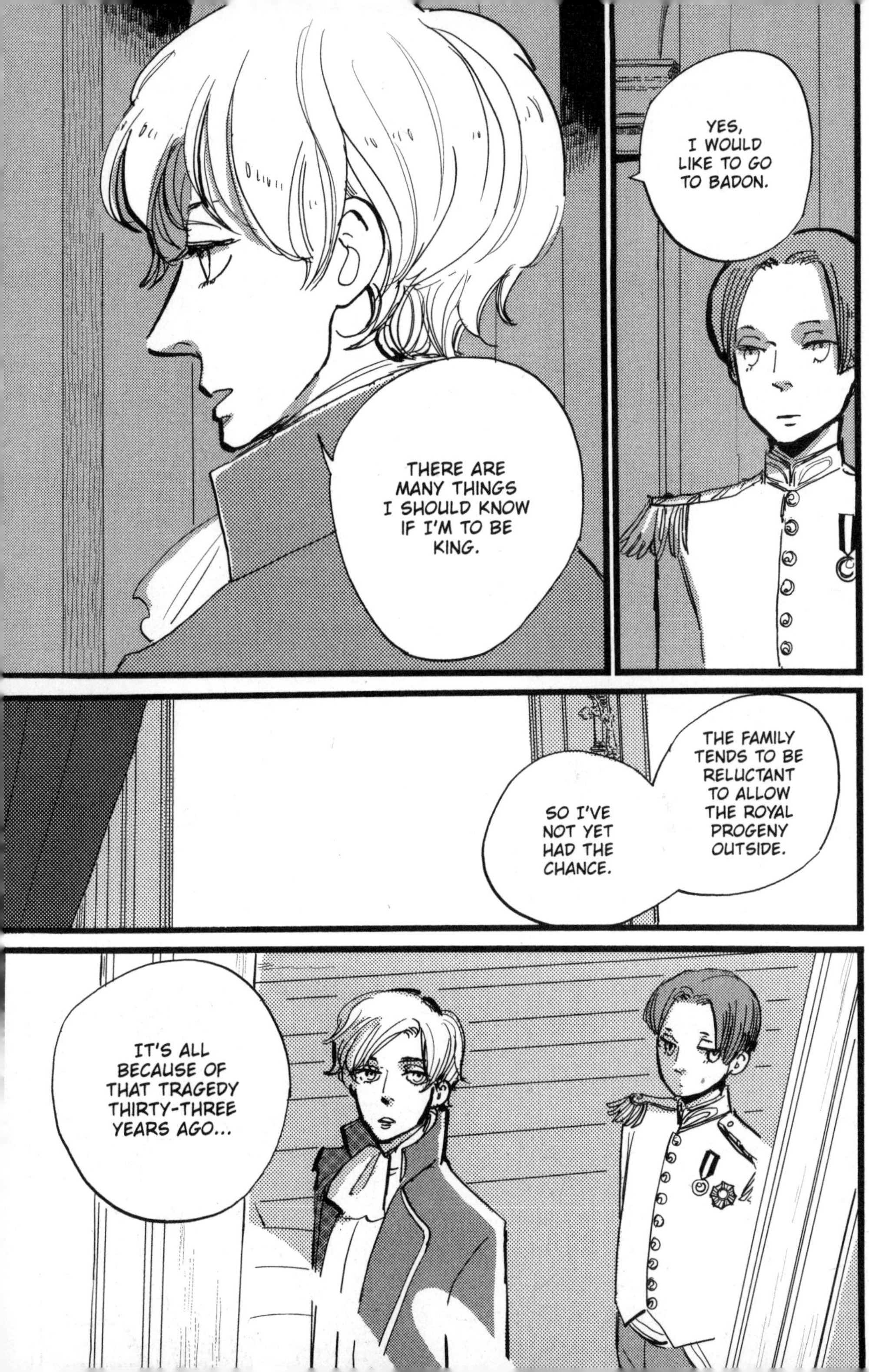
YES, I WOULD LIKE TO GO TO BADON.
THERE ARE MANY THINGS I SHOULD KNOW IF I'M TO BE KING.
THE FAMILY TENDS TO BE RELUCTANT TO ALLOW THE ROYAL PROGENY OUTSIDE.
SO I'VE NOT YET HAD THE CHANCE.
IT'S ALL BECAUSE OF THAT TRAGEDY THIRTY-THREE YEARS AGO...

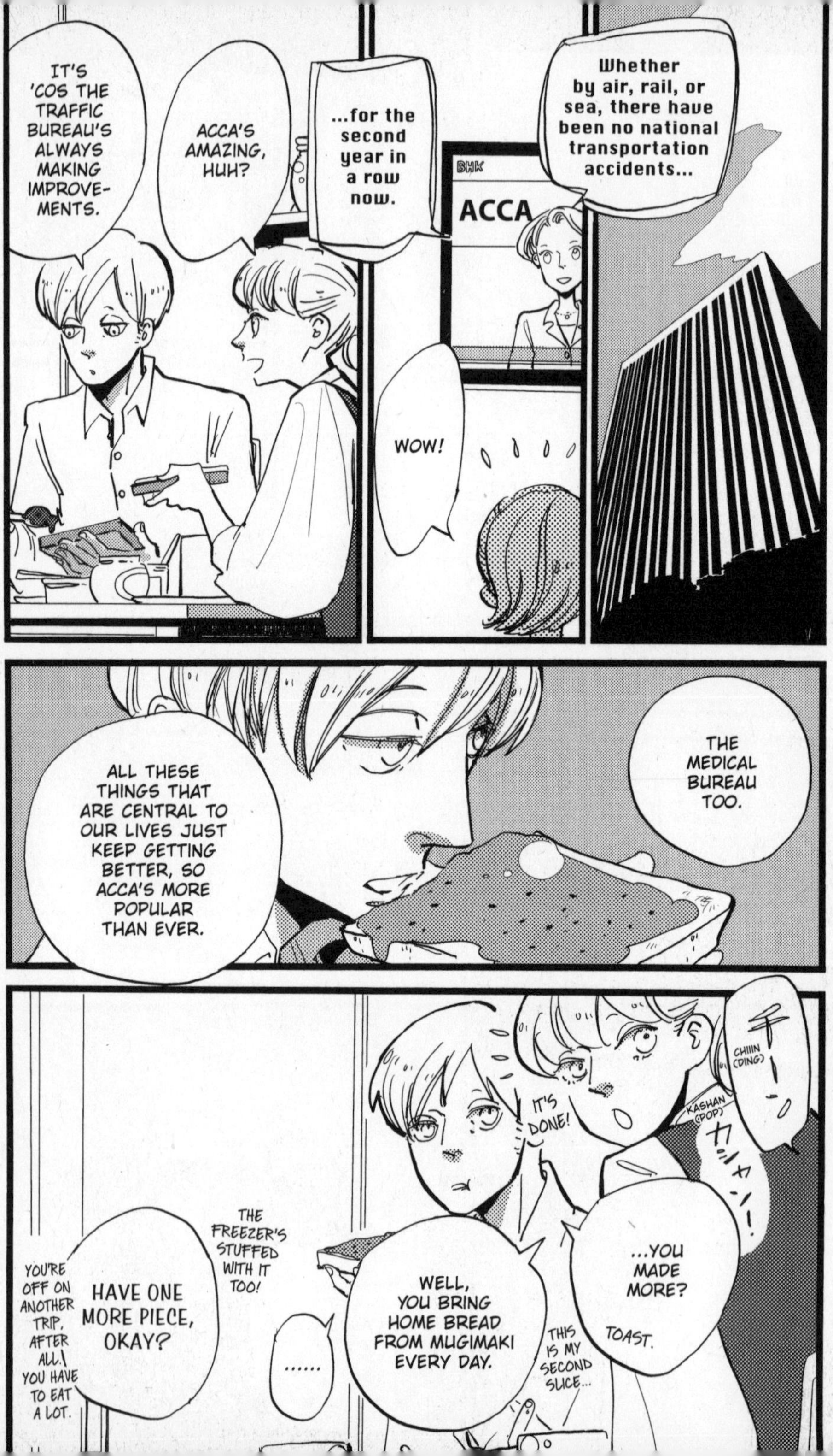
Whether by air, rail, or sea, there have been no national transportation accidents...
...for the second year in a row now.
BHK
ACCA
WOW!
ACCA'S AMAZING, HUH?
IT'S 'COS THE TRAFFIC BUREAU'S ALWAYS MAKING IMPROVEMENTS.
THE MEDICAL BUREAU TOO.
ALL THESE THINGS THAT ARE CENTRAL TO OUR LIVES JUST KEEP GETTING BETTER, SO ACCA'S MORE POPULAR THAN EVER.
CHIIIN (DING)
KASHAN (POP)
IT'S DONE!
...YOU MADE MORE?
TOAST.
THIS IS MY SECOND SLICE...
WELL, YOU BRING HOME BREAD FROM MUGIMAKI EVERY DAY.
......
THE FREEZER'S STUFFED WITH IT TOO!
HAVE ONE MORE PIECE, OKAY?
YOU'RE OFF ON ANOTHER TRIP, AFTER ALL. YOU HAVE TO EAT A LOT.

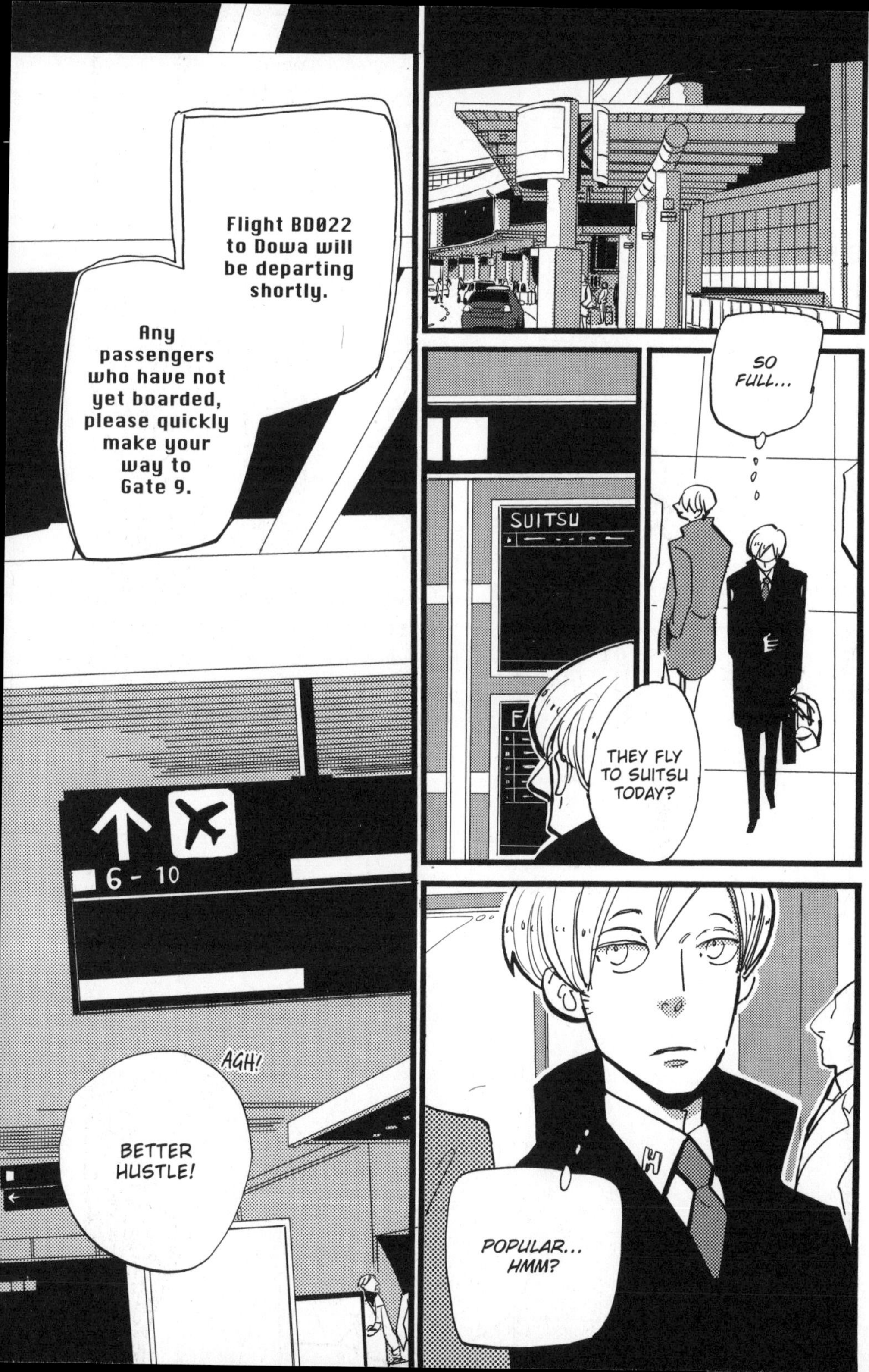
SO FULL...
SUITSU
THEY FLY TO SUITSU TODAY?
POPULAR... HMM?
Flight BD022 to Dowa will be departing shortly.
Any passengers who have not yet boarded, please quickly make your way to Gate 9.
6 - 10
AGH!
BETTER HUSTLE!

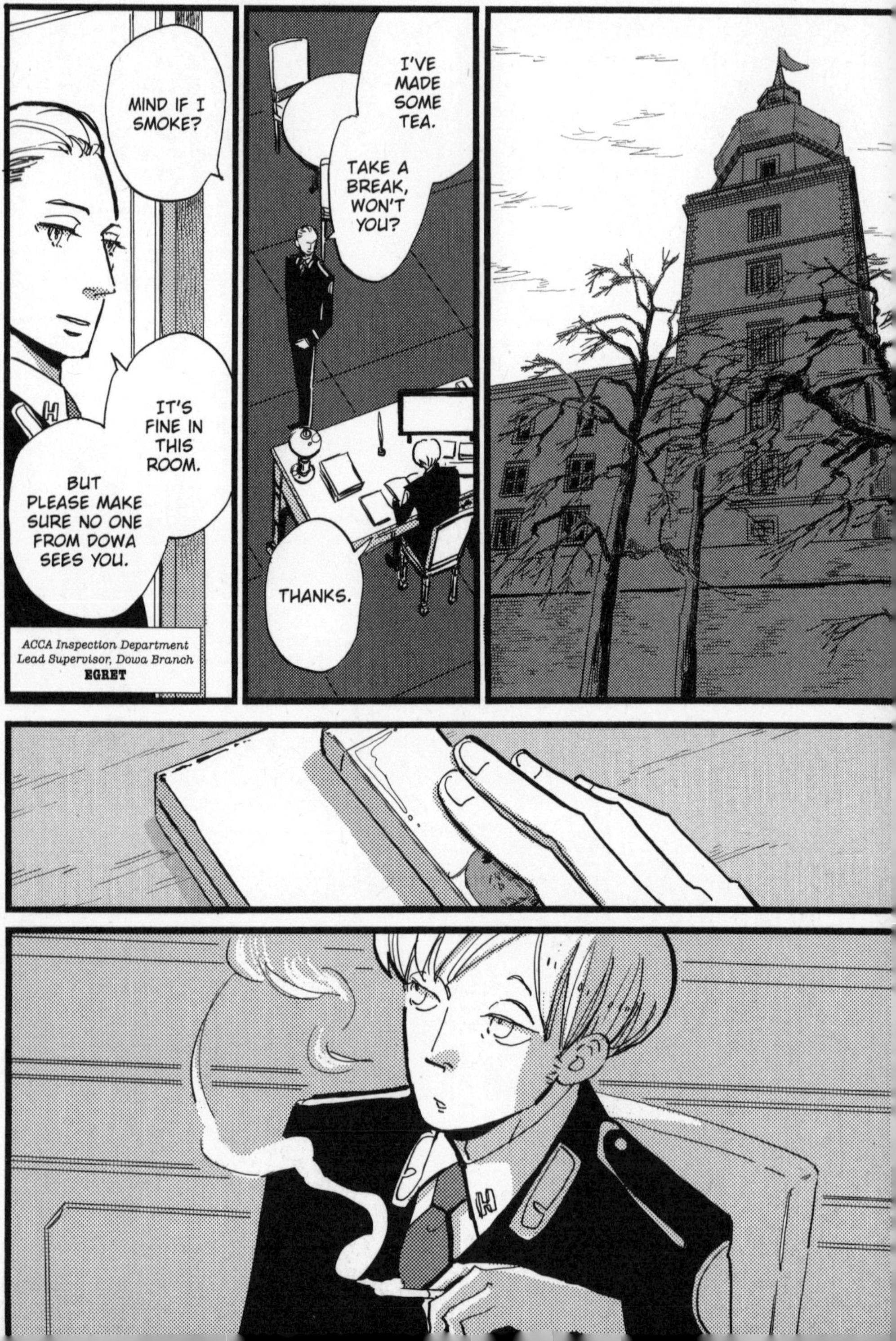
I'VE MADE SOME TEA.
TAKE A BREAK, WON'T YOU?
THANKS.
MIND IF I SMOKE?
IT'S FINE IN THIS ROOM.
BUT PLEASE MAKE SURE NO ONE FROM DOWA SEES YOU.
ACCA Inspection Department
Lead Supervisor, Dowa Branch
EGRET

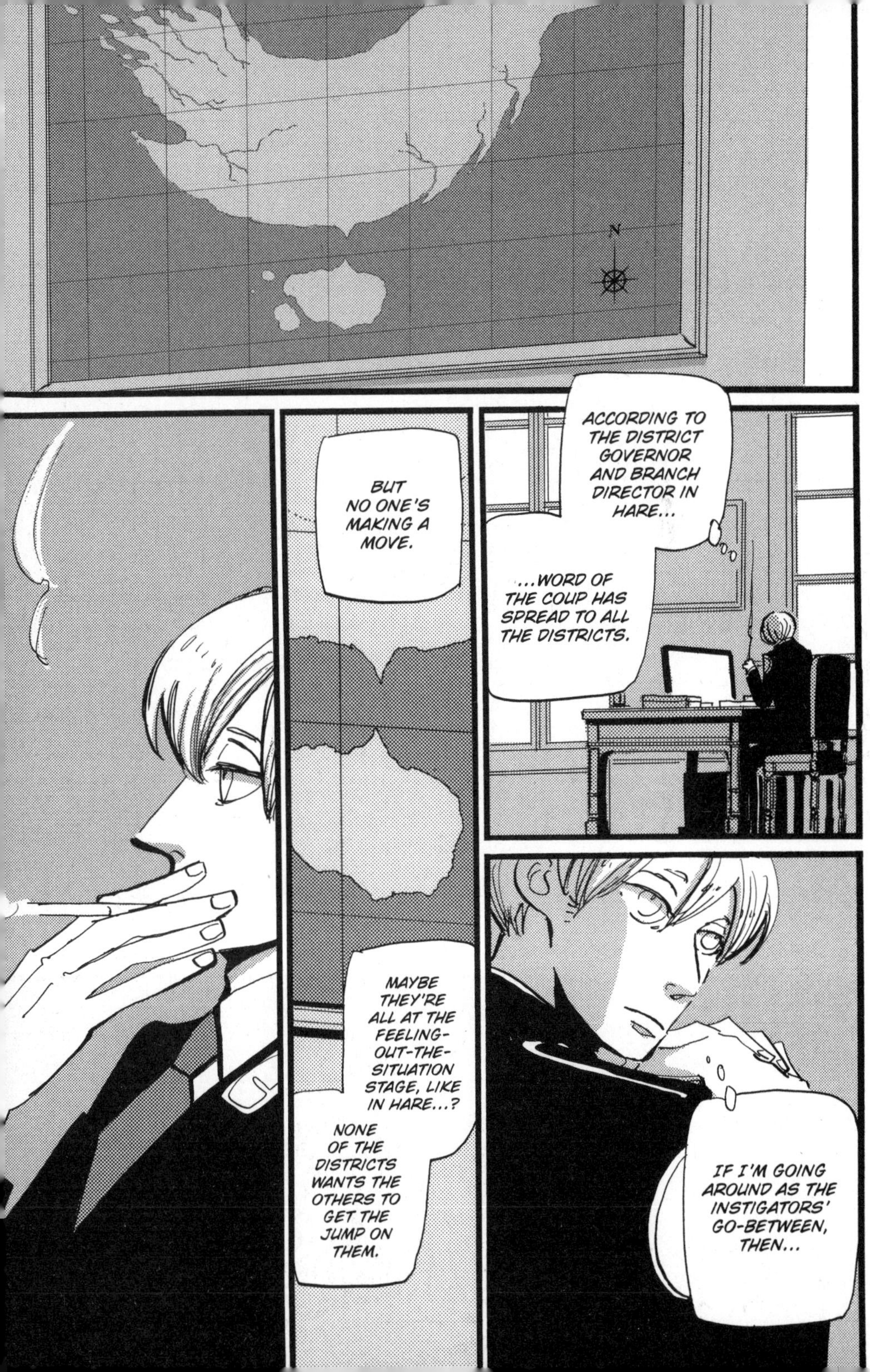

ACCORDING TO THE DISTRICT GOVERNOR AND BRANCH DIRECTOR IN HARE...
...WORD OF THE COUP HAS SPREAD TO ALL THE DISTRICTS.
IF I'M GOING AROUND AS THE INSTIGATORS' GO-BETWEEN, THEN...
BUT NO ONE'S MAKING A MOVE.
MAYBE THEY'RE ALL AT THE FEELING-OUT-THE-SITUATION STAGE, LIKE IN HARE...?
NONE OF THE DISTRICTS WANTS THE OTHERS TO GET THE JUMP ON THEM.

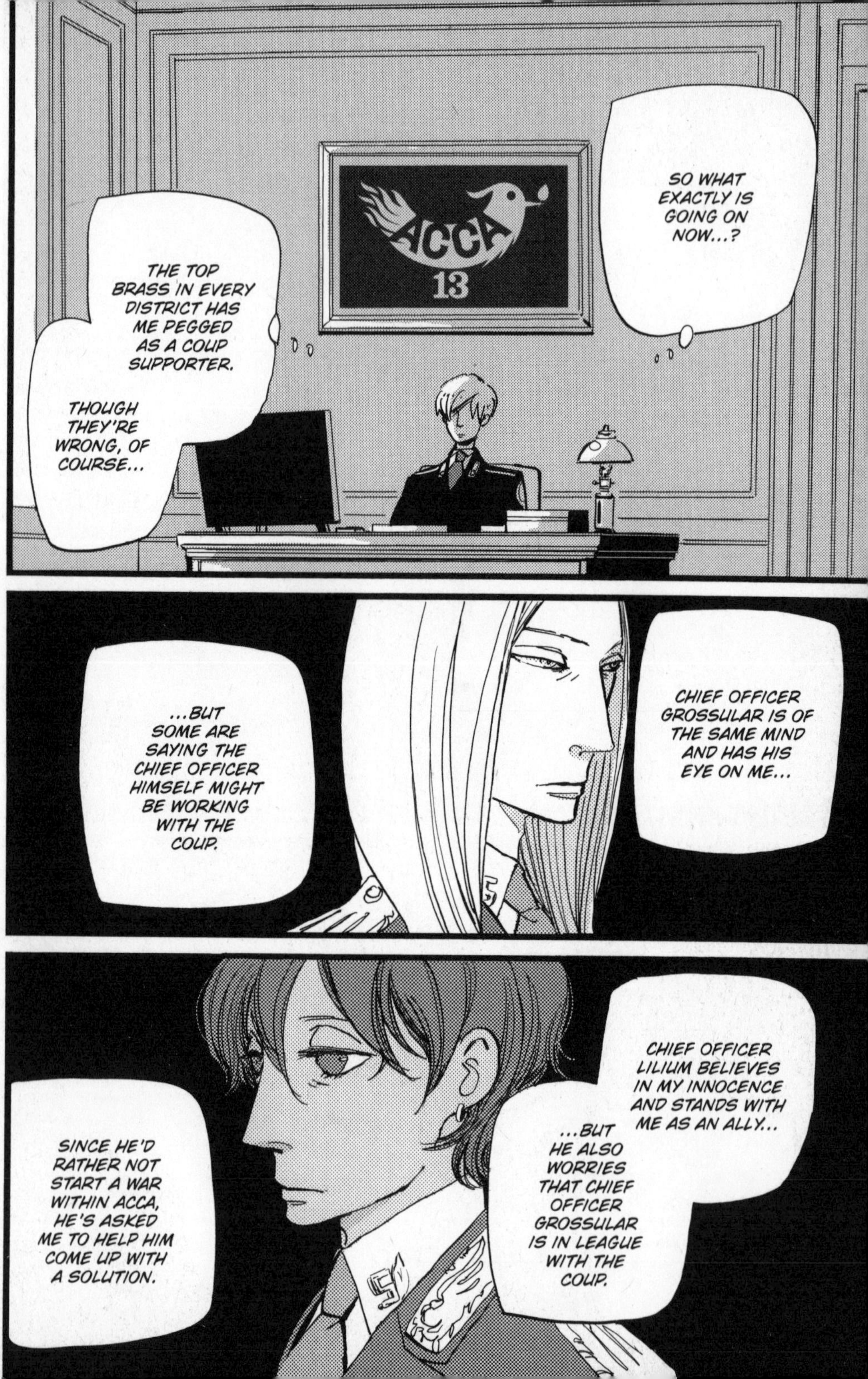
SO WHAT EXACTLY IS GOING ON NOW...?
THE TOP BRASS IN EVERY DISTRICT HAS ME PEGGED AS A COUP SUPPORTER.
THOUGH THEY'RE WRONG, OF COURSE...
CHIEF OFFICER GROSSULAR IS OF THE SAME MIND AND HAS HIS EYE ON ME...
...BUT SOME ARE SAYING THE CHIEF OFFICER HIMSELF MIGHT BE WORKING WITH THE COUP.
CHIEF OFFICER LILIUM BELIEVES IN MY INNOCENCE AND STANDS WITH ME AS AN ALLY...
...BUT HE ALSO WORRIES THAT CHIEF OFFICER GROSSULAR IS IN LEAGUE WITH THE COUP.
SINCE HE'D RATHER NOT START A WAR WITHIN ACCA, HE'S ASKED ME TO HELP HIM COME UP WITH A SOLUTION.

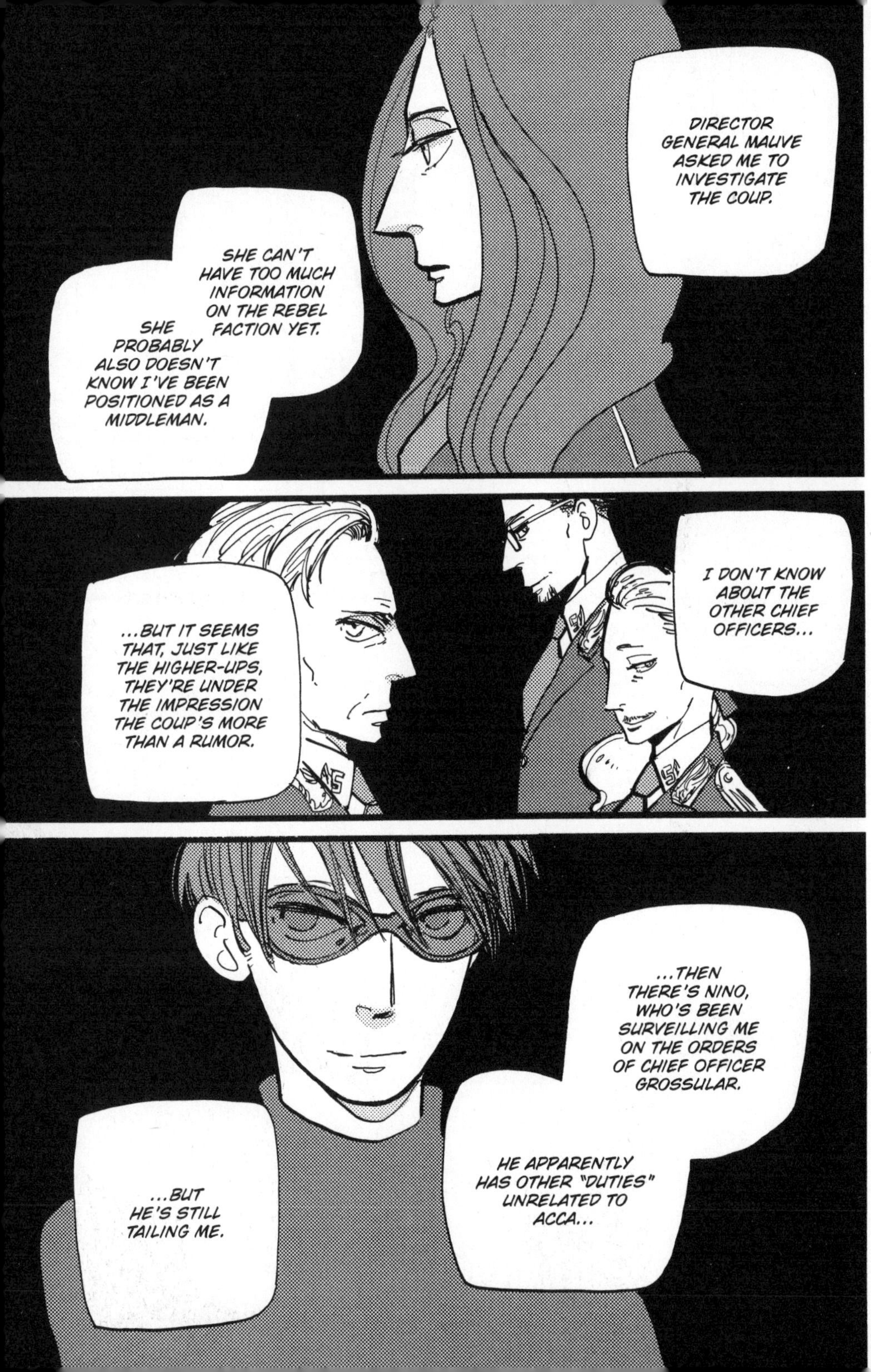
DIRECTOR GENERAL MAUVE ASKED ME TO INVESTIGATE THE COUP.
SHE CAN'T HAVE TOO MUCH INFORMATION ON THE REBEL FACTION YET.
SHE PROBABLY ALSO DOESN'T KNOW I'VE BEEN POSITIONED AS A MIDDLEMAN.
I DON'T KNOW ABOUT THE OTHER CHIEF OFFICERS...
...BUT IT SEEMS THAT, JUST LIKE THE HIGHER-UPS, THEY'RE UNDER THE IMPRESSION THE COUP'S MORE THAN A RUMOR.
...THEN THERE'S NINO, WHO'S BEEN SURVEILLING ME ON THE ORDERS OF CHIEF OFFICER GROSSULAR.
HE APPARENTLY HAS OTHER "DUTIES" UNRELATED TO ACCA...
...BUT HE'S STILL TAILING ME.

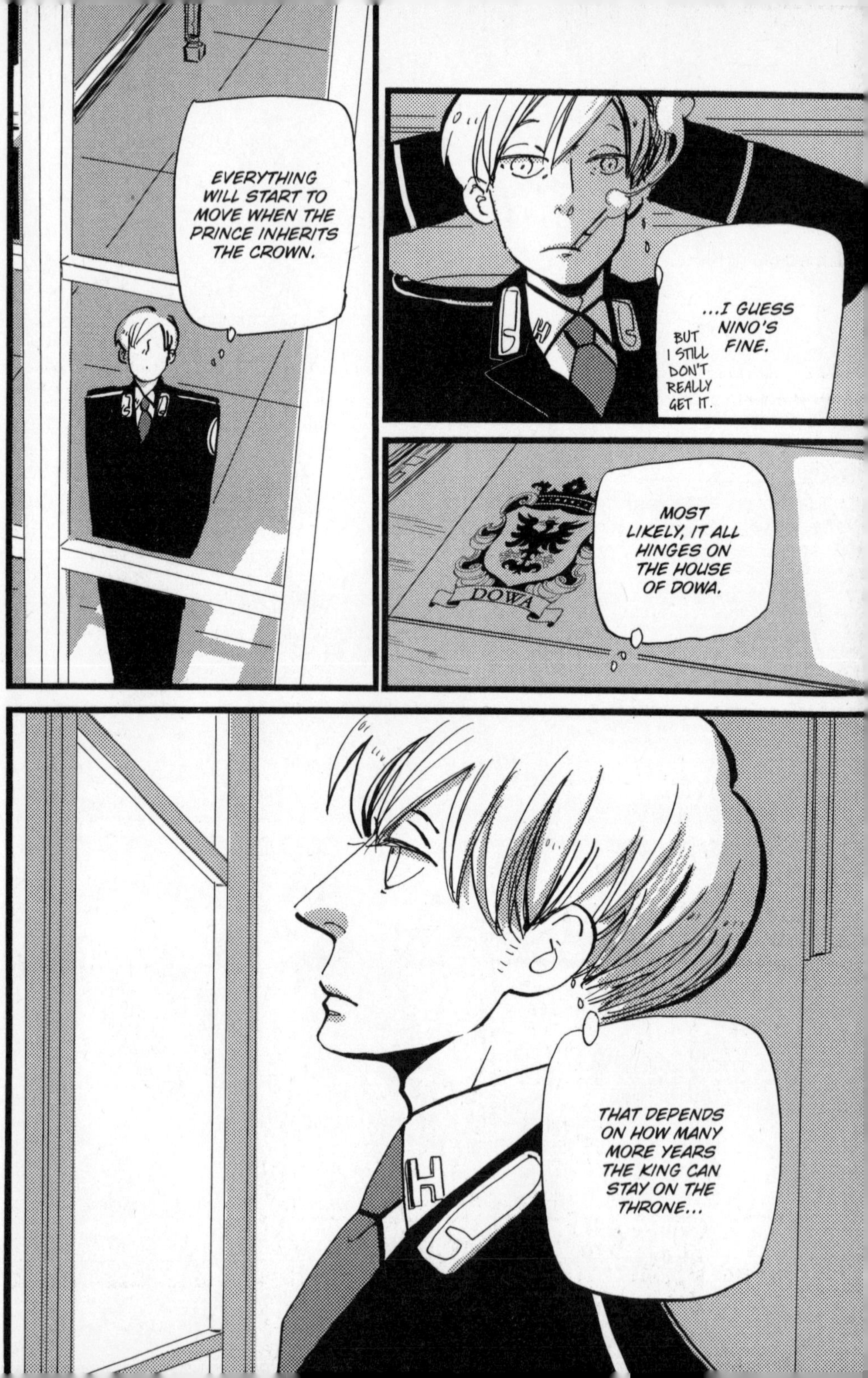
...I GUESS NINO'S FINE.
BUT I STILL DON'T REALLY GET IT.
MOST LIKELY, IT ALL HINGES ON THE HOUSE OF DOWA.
DOWA
EVERYTHING WILL START TO MOVE WHEN THE PRINCE INHERITS THE CROWN.
THAT DEPENDS ON HOW MANY MORE YEARS THE KING CAN STAY ON THE THRONE...

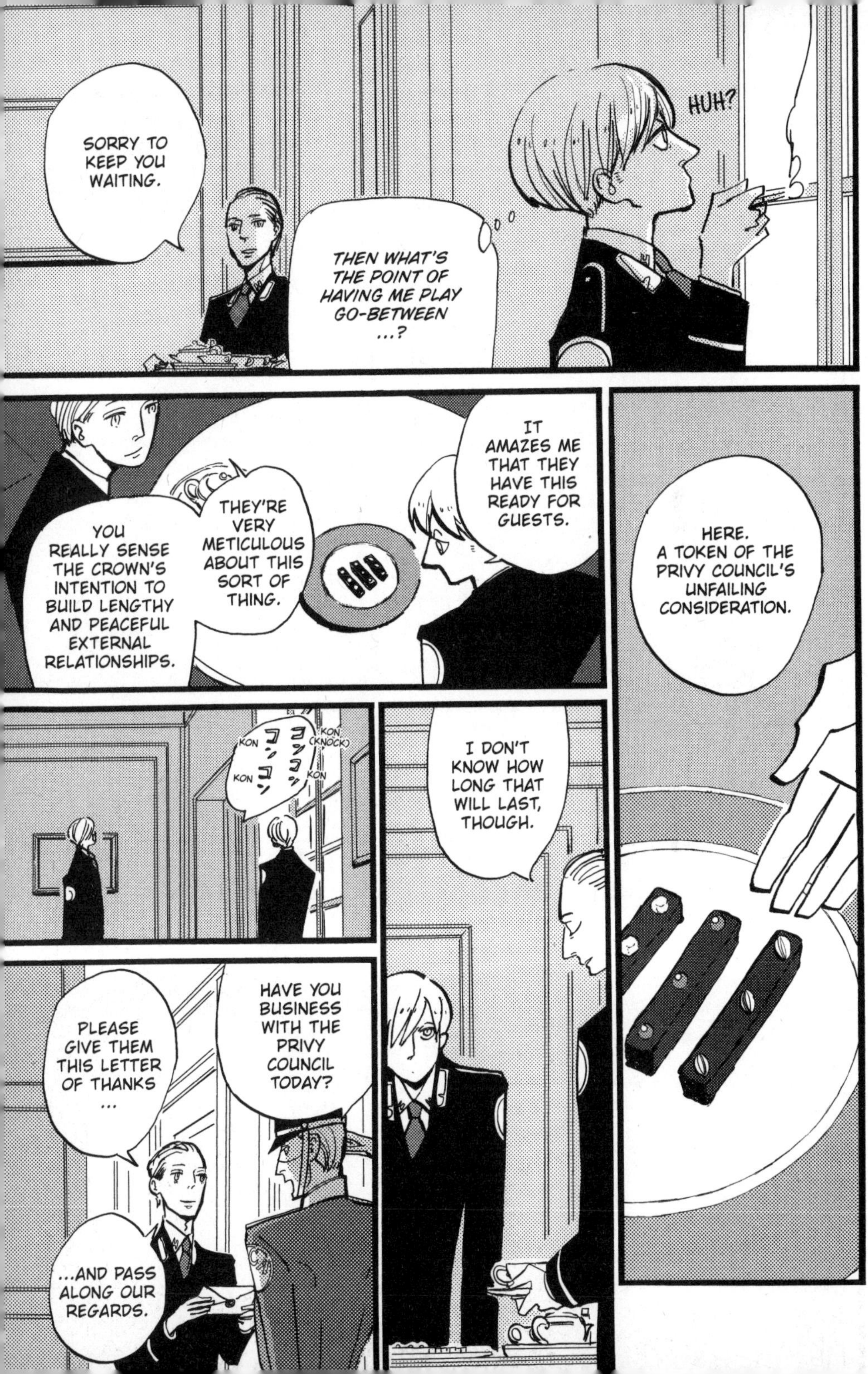
HUH?
THEN WHAT'S THE POINT OF HAVING ME PLAY GO-BETWEEN ...?
SORRY TO KEEP YOU WAITING.
HERE. A TOKEN OF THE PRIVY COUNCIL'S UNFAILING CONSIDERATION.
IT AMAZES ME THAT THEY HAVE THIS READY FOR GUESTS.
THEY'RE VERY METICULOUS ABOUT THIS SORT OF THING.
YOU REALLY SENSE THE CROWN'S INTENTION TO BUILD LENGTHY AND PEACEFUL EXTERNAL RELATIONSHIPS.
I DON'T KNOW HOW LONG THAT WILL LAST, THOUGH.
KON (KNOCK) KON
KON KON
HAVE YOU BUSINESS WITH THE PRIVY COUNCIL TODAY?
PLEASE GIVE THEM THIS LETTER OF THANKS ...
...AND PASS ALONG OUR REGARDS.

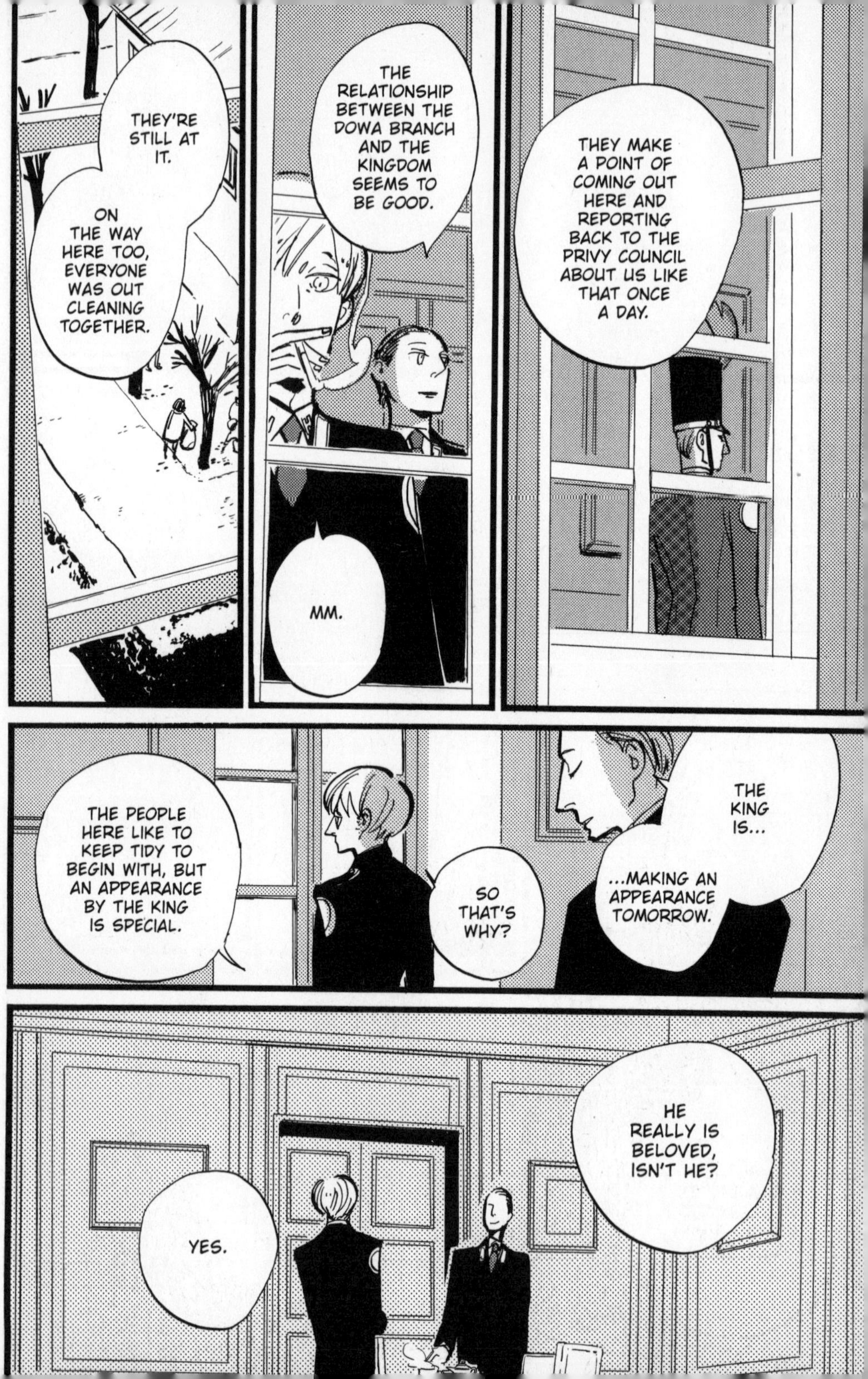
THEY MAKE A POINT OF COMING OUT HERE AND REPORTING BACK TO THE PRIVY COUNCIL ABOUT US LIKE THAT ONCE A DAY.
THE RELATIONSHIP BETWEEN THE DOWA BRANCH AND THE KINGDOM SEEMS TO BE GOOD.
MM.
THEY'RE STILL AT IT.
ON THE WAY HERE TOO, EVERYONE WAS OUT CLEANING TOGETHER.
THE KING IS...
...MAKING AN APPEARANCE TOMORROW.
SO THAT'S WHY?
THE PEOPLE HERE LIKE TO KEEP TIDY TO BEGIN WITH, BUT AN APPEARANCE BY THE KING IS SPECIAL.
HE REALLY IS BELOVED, ISN'T HE?
YES.

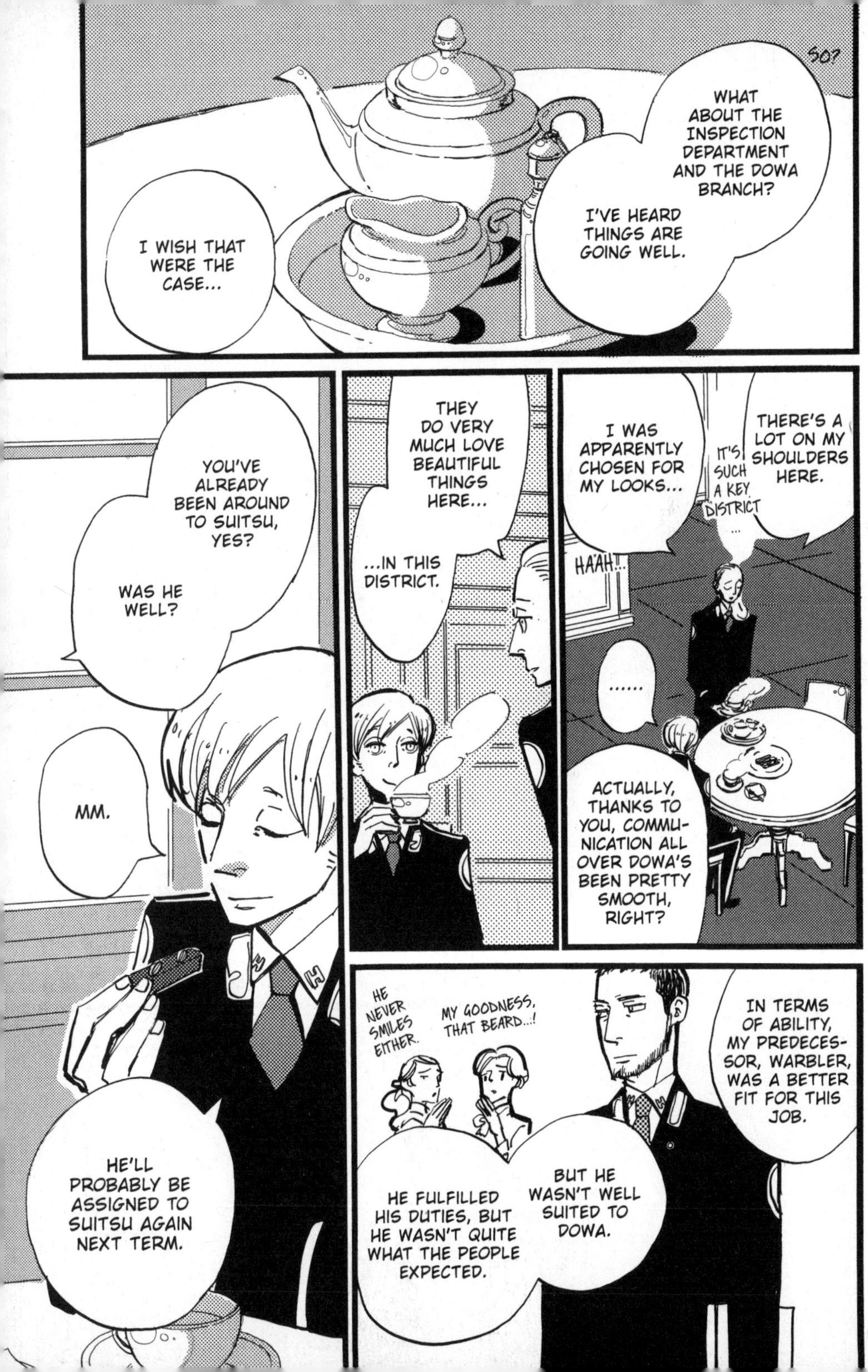
WHAT ABOUT THE INSPECTION DEPARTMENT AND THE DOWA BRANCH?
I'VE HEARD THINGS ARE GOING WELL.
I WISH THAT WERE THE CASE...
THERE'S A LOT ON MY SHOULDERS HERE.
IT'S SUCH A KEY DISTRICT...
I WAS APPARENTLY CHOSEN FOR MY LOOKS...
HAAH...
......
ACTUALLY, THANKS TO YOU, COMMUNICATION ALL OVER DOWA'S BEEN PRETTY SMOOTH, RIGHT?
THEY DO VERY MUCH LOVE BEAUTIFUL THINGS HERE...
...IN THIS DISTRICT.
IN TERMS OF ABILITY, MY PREDECESSOR, WARBLER, WAS A BETTER FIT FOR THIS JOB.
MY GOODNESS, THAT BEARD...!
HE NEVER SMILES EITHER.
BUT HE WASN'T WELL SUITED TO DOWA.
HE FULFILLED HIS DUTIES, BUT HE WASN'T QUITE WHAT THE PEOPLE EXPECTED.
YOU'VE ALREADY BEEN AROUND TO SUITSU, YES?
WAS HE WELL?
MM.
HE'LL PROBABLY BE ASSIGNED TO SUITSU AGAIN NEXT TERM.

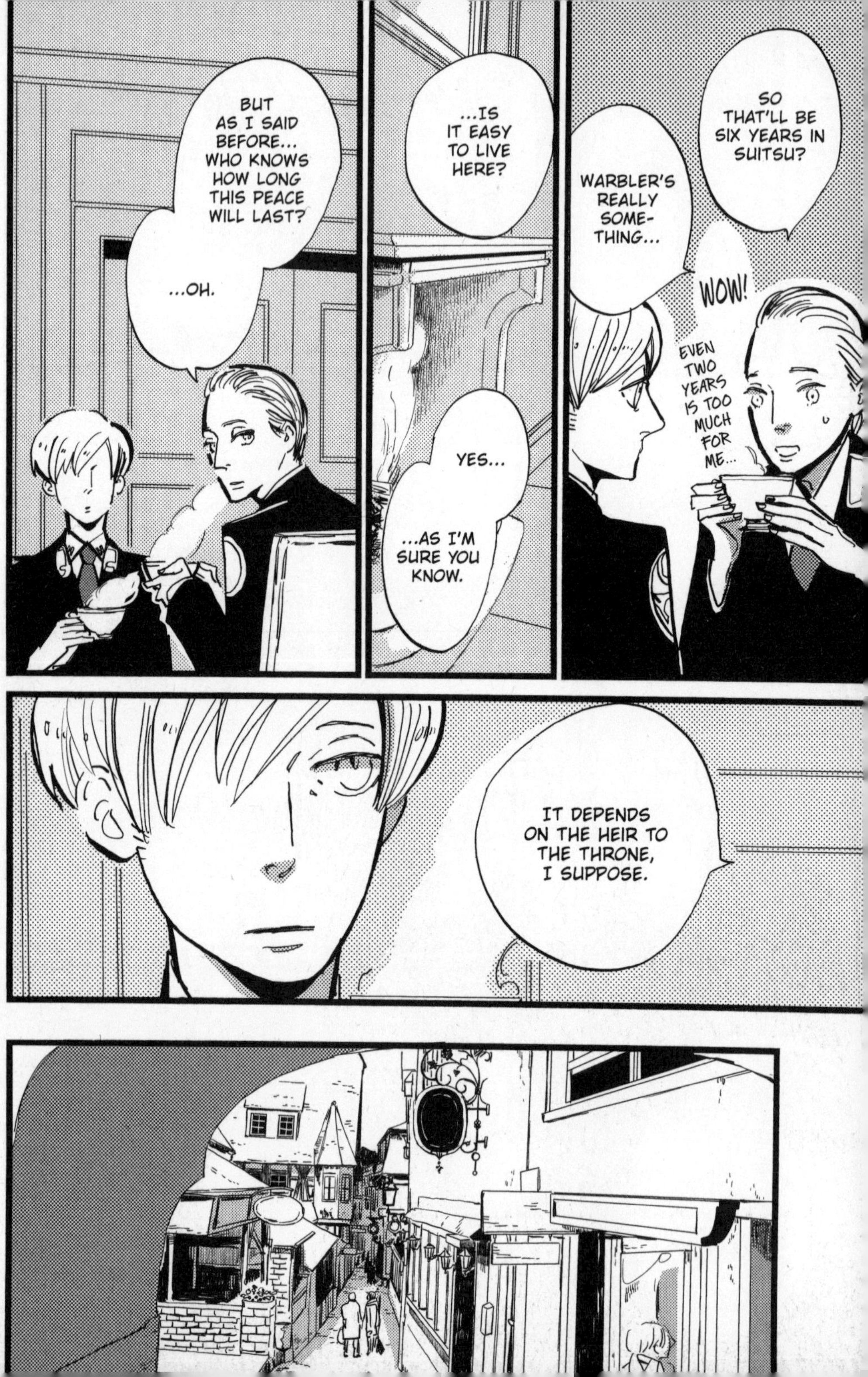
SO THAT'LL BE SIX YEARS IN SUITSU?
WARBLER'S REALLY SOME-THING...
WOW!
EVEN TWO YEARS IS TOO MUCH FOR ME...
...IS IT EASY TO LIVE HERE?
YES...
...AS I'M SURE YOU KNOW.
BUT AS I SAID BEFORE... WHO KNOWS HOW LONG THIS PEACE WILL LAST?
...OH.
IT DEPENDS ON THE HEIR TO THE THRONE, I SUPPOSE.

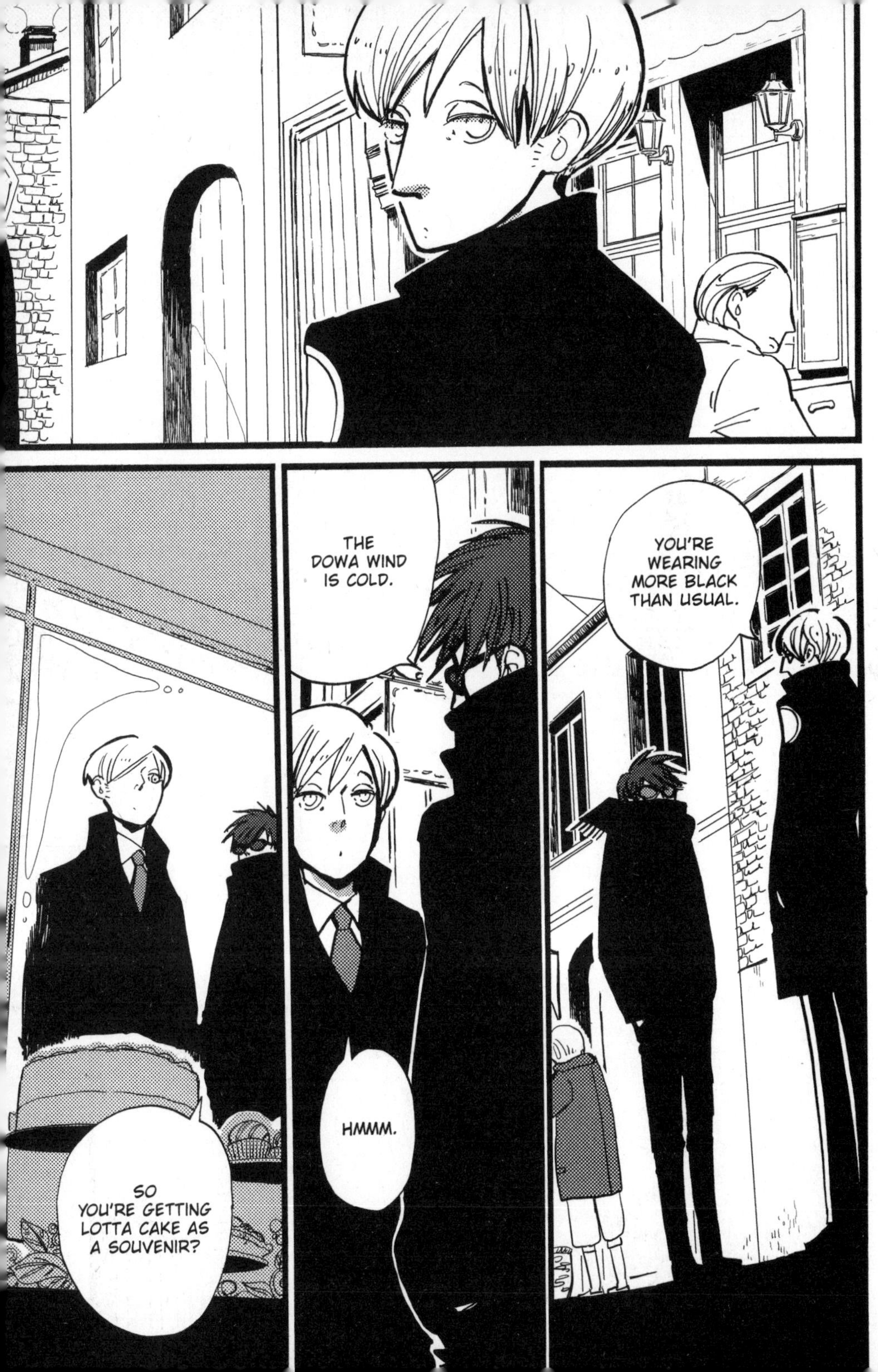
YOU'RE WEARING MORE BLACK THAN USUAL.
THE DOWA WIND IS COLD.
HMMM.
SO YOU'RE GETTING LOTTA CAKE AS A SOUVENIR?

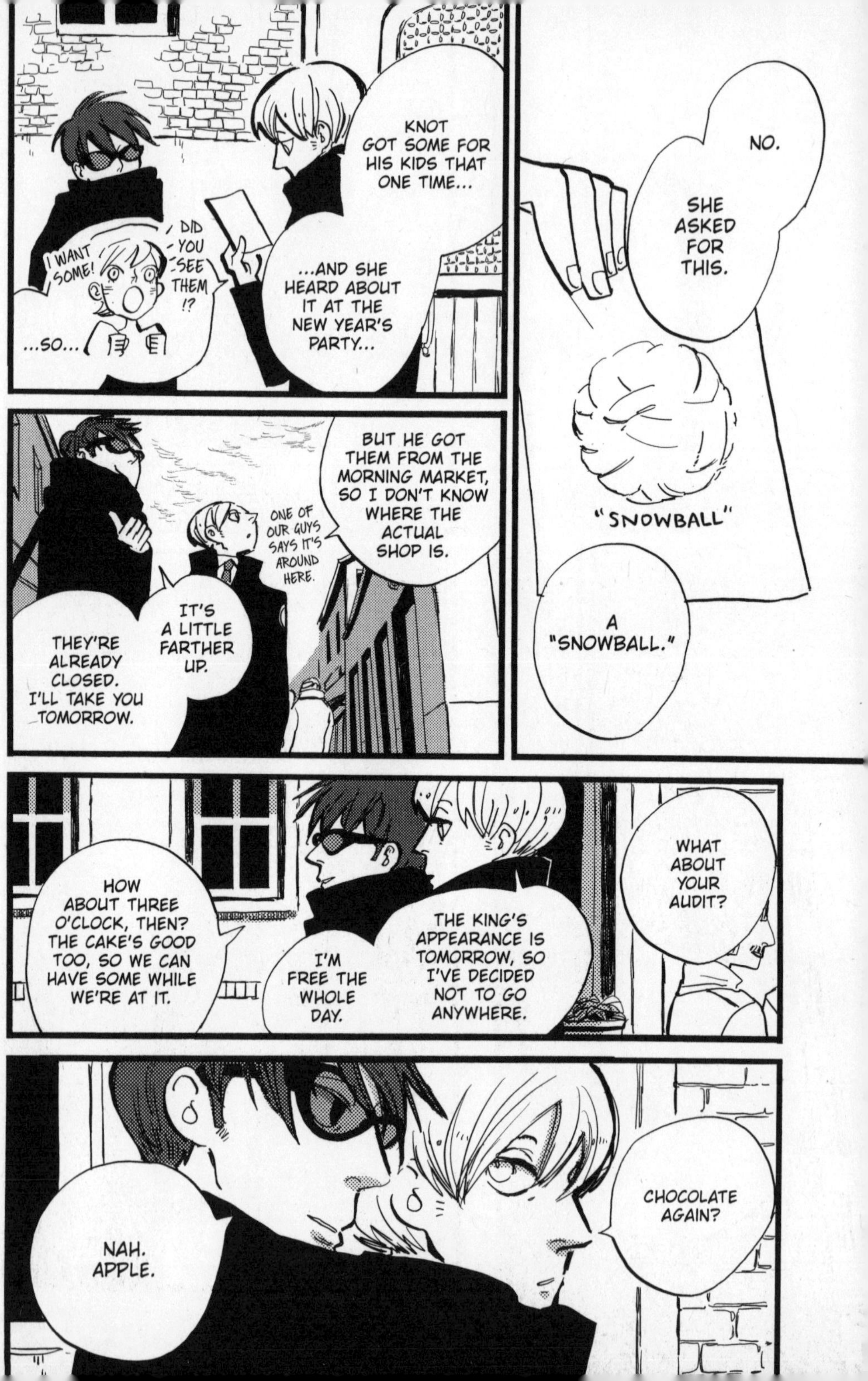
NO.
SHE ASKED FOR THIS.
"SNOWBALL"
A "SNOWBALL."
KNOT GOT SOME FOR HIS KIDS THAT ONE TIME...
...AND SHE HEARD ABOUT IT AT THE NEW YEAR'S PARTY...
DID YOU SEE THEM!?
I WANT SOME!
...SO...
BUT HE GOT THEM FROM THE MORNING MARKET, SO I DON'T KNOW WHERE THE ACTUAL SHOP IS.
ONE OF OUR GUYS SAYS IT'S AROUND HERE.
IT'S A LITTLE FARTHER UP.
THEY'RE ALREADY CLOSED. I'LL TAKE YOU TOMORROW.
WHAT ABOUT YOUR AUDIT?
THE KING'S APPEARANCE IS TOMORROW, SO I'VE DECIDED NOT TO GO ANYWHERE.
I'M FREE THE WHOLE DAY.
HOW ABOUT THREE O'CLOCK, THEN? THE CAKE'S GOOD TOO, SO WE CAN HAVE SOME WHILE WE'RE AT IT.
CHOCOLATE AGAIN?
NAH. APPLE.

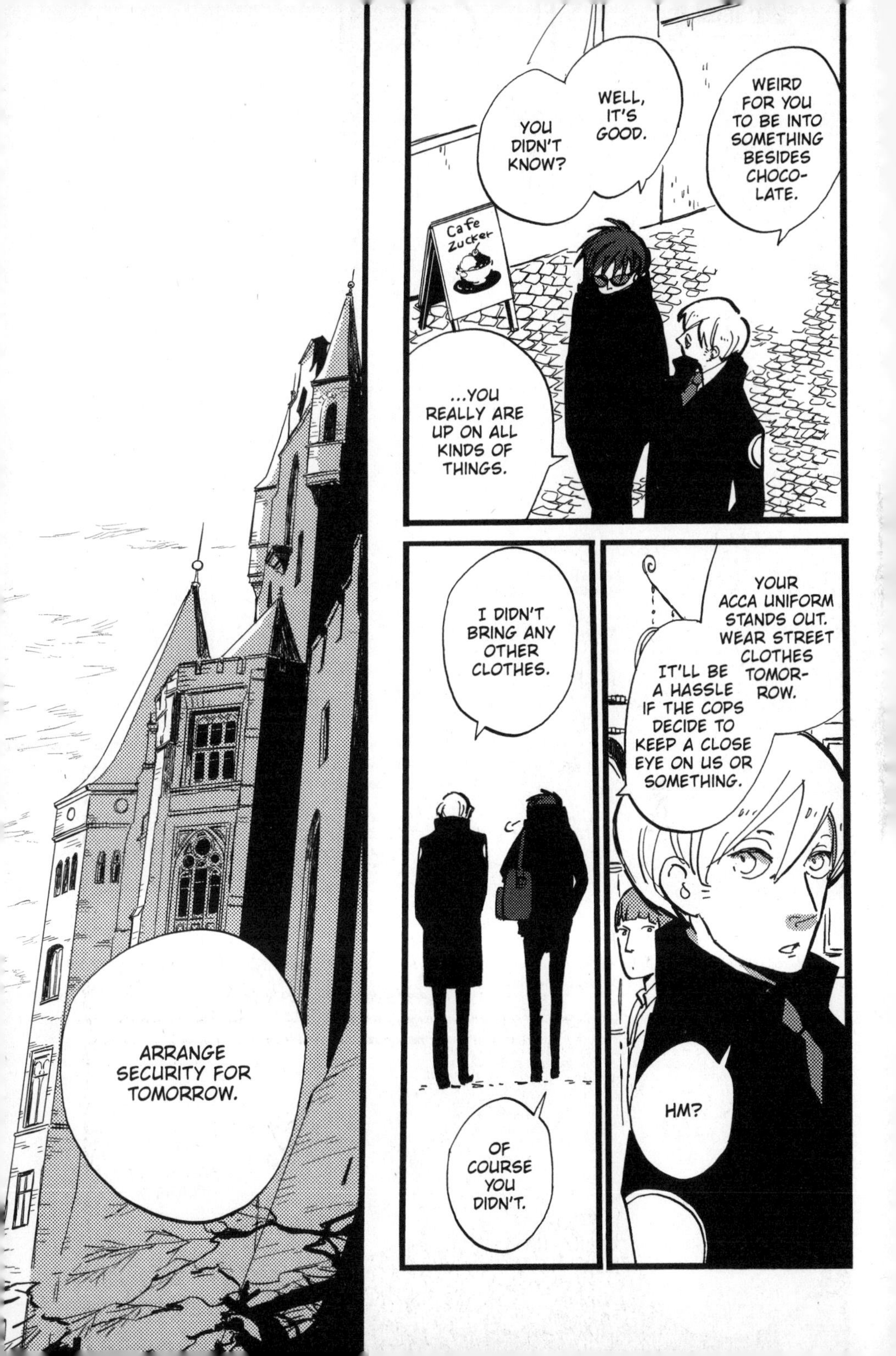
WEIRD FOR YOU TO BE INTO SOMETHING BESIDES CHOCO-LATE.
WELL, IT'S GOOD.
YOU DIDN'T KNOW?
Cafe Zucker
...YOU REALLY ARE UP ON ALL KINDS OF THINGS.
YOUR ACCA UNIFORM STANDS OUT. WEAR STREET CLOTHES TOMOR-ROW.
IT'LL BE A HASSLE IF THE COPS DECIDE TO KEEP A CLOSE EYE ON US OR SOMETHING.
HM?
I DIDN'T BRING ANY OTHER CLOTHES.
OF COURSE YOU DIDN'T.
ARRANGE SECURITY FOR TOMORROW.

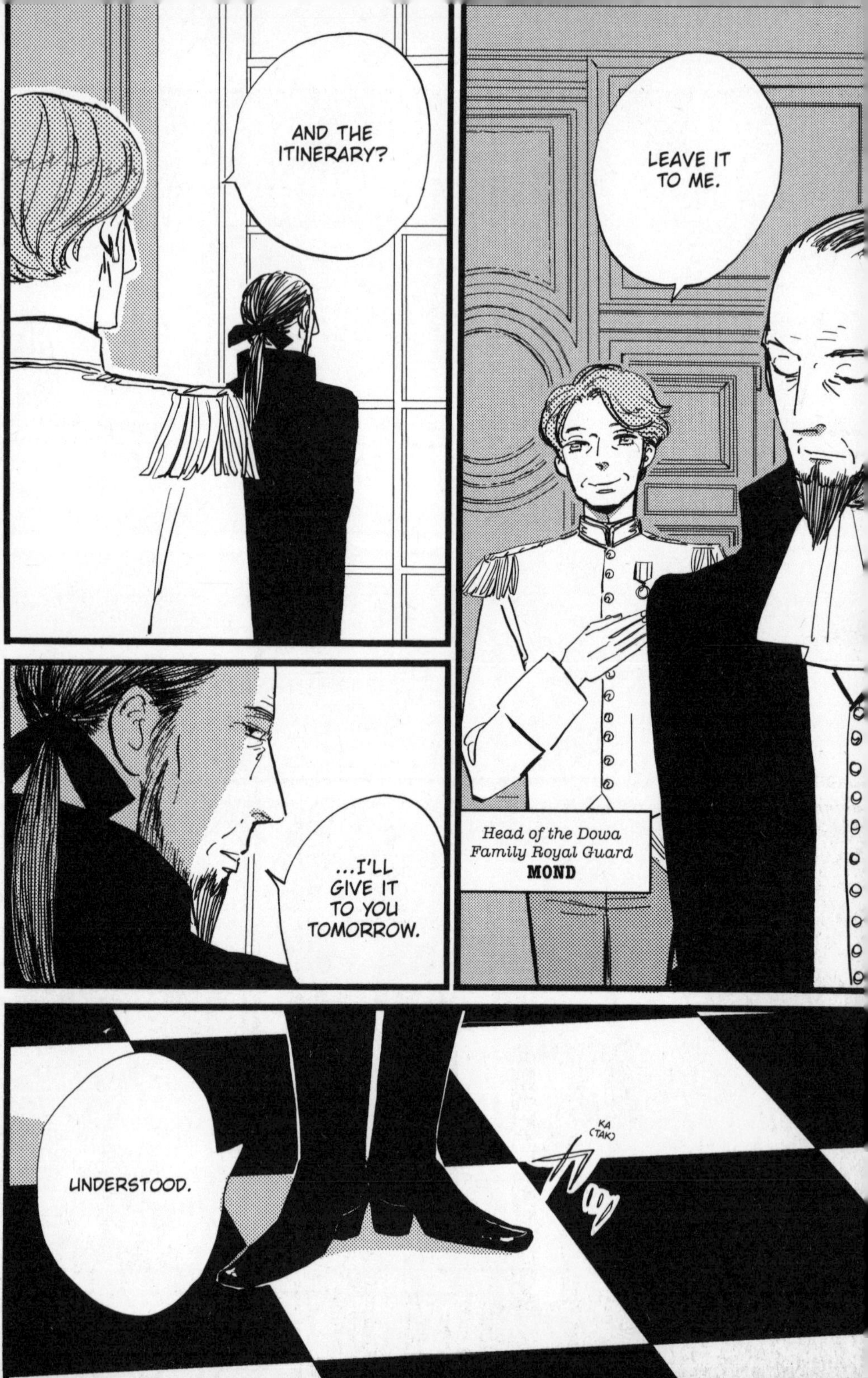
LEAVE IT TO ME.
Head of the Dowa Family Royal Guard MOND
AND THE ITINERARY?
...I'LL GIVE IT TO YOU TOMORROW.
KA (TAK)
UNDERSTOOD.

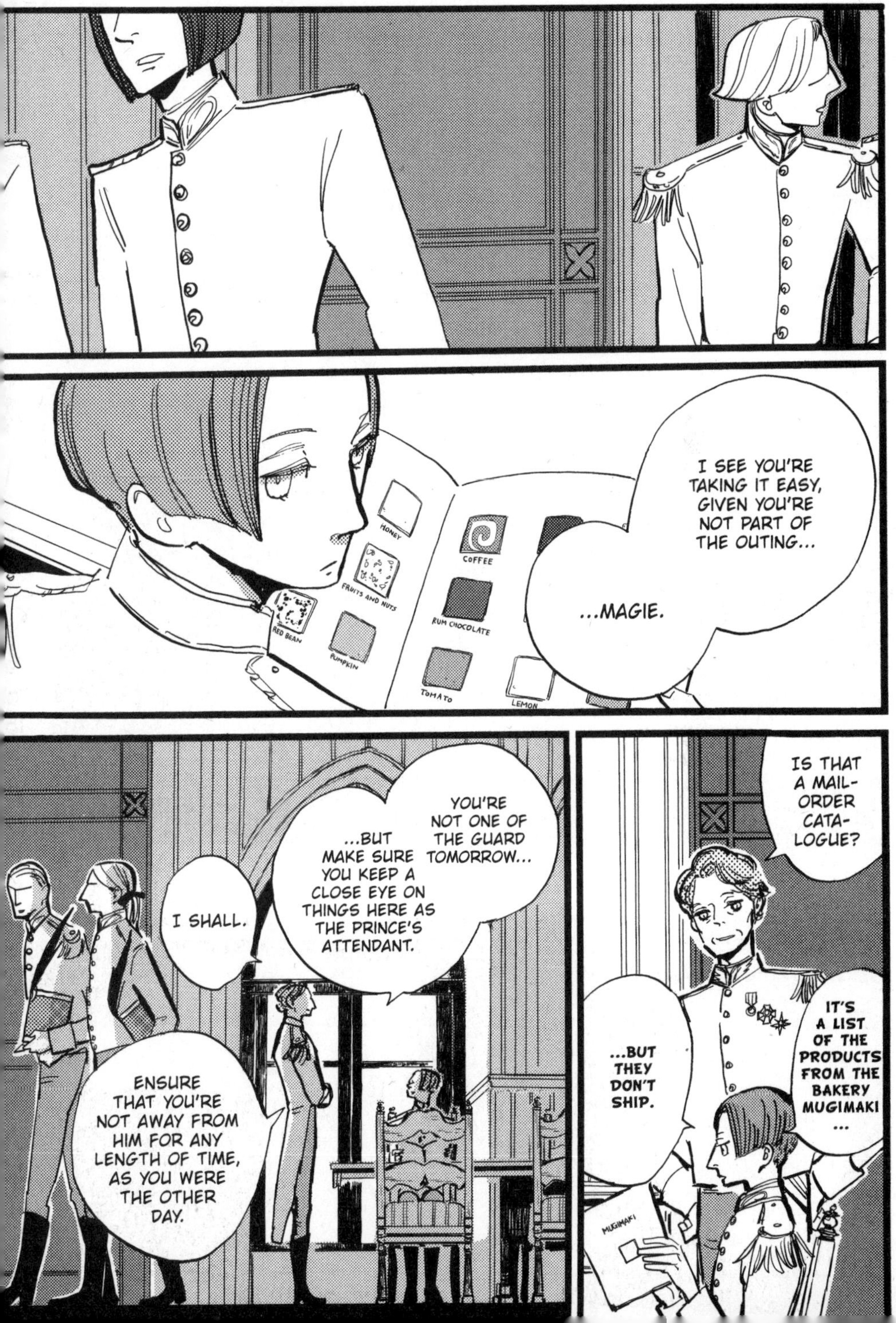
I SEE YOU'RE TAKING IT EASY, GIVEN YOU'RE NOT PART OF THE OUTING...
...MAGIE.
HONEY
COFFEE
FRUITS AND NUTS
RUM CHOCOLATE
RED BEAN
PUMPKIN
TOMATO
LEMON
IS THAT A MAIL-ORDER CATALOGUE?
IT'S A LIST OF THE PRODUCTS FROM THE BAKERY MUGIMAKI ...
...BUT THEY DON'T SHIP.
MUGIMAKI
YOU'RE NOT ONE OF THE GUARD TOMORROW...
...BUT MAKE SURE YOU KEEP A CLOSE EYE ON THINGS HERE AS THE PRINCE'S ATTENDANT.
I SHALL.
ENSURE THAT YOU'RE NOT AWAY FROM HIM FOR ANY LENGTH OF TIME, AS YOU WERE THE OTHER DAY.

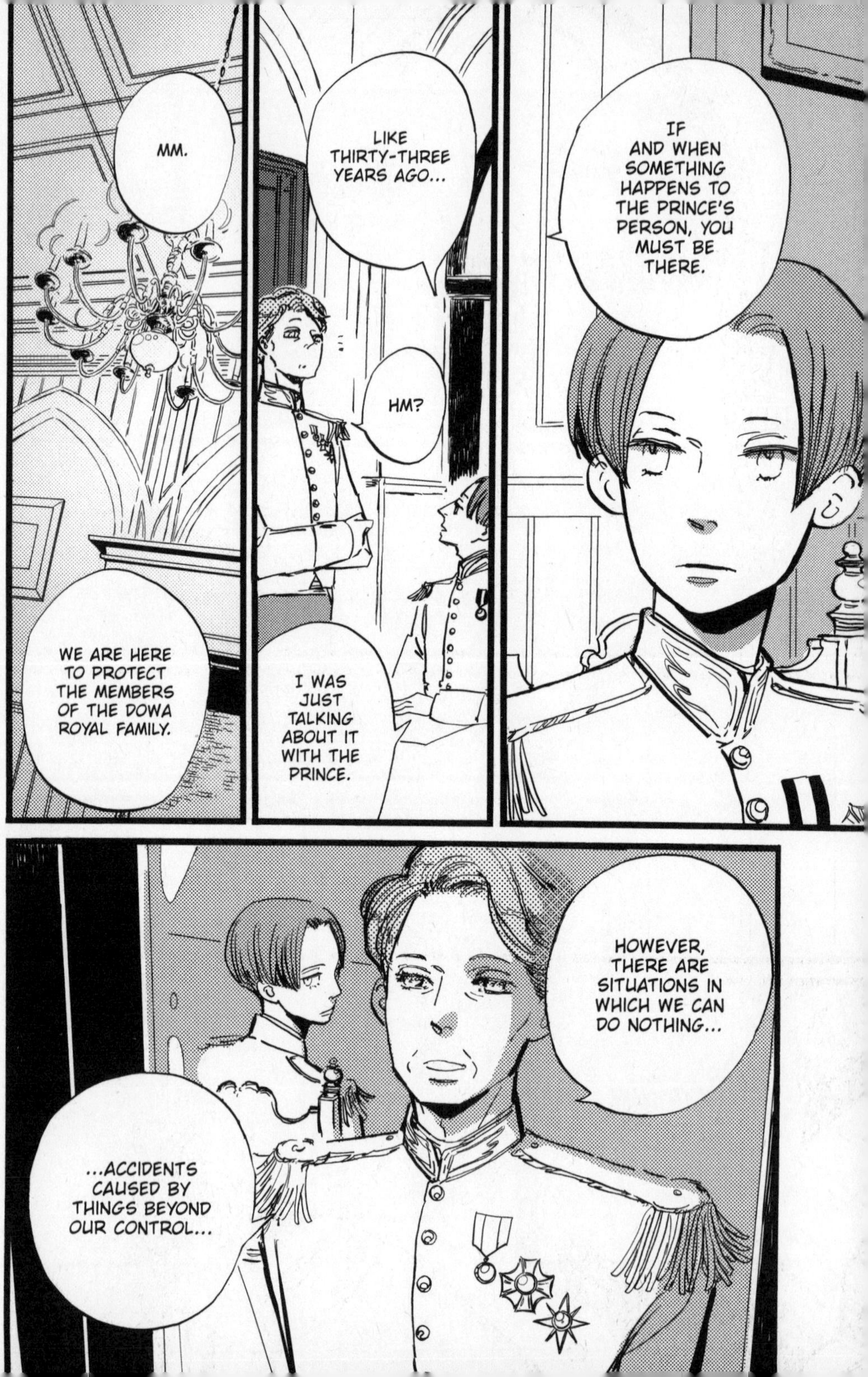
IF AND WHEN SOMETHING HAPPENS TO THE PRINCE'S PERSON, YOU MUST BE THERE.
LIKE THIRTY-THREE YEARS AGO...
HM?
I WAS JUST TALKING ABOUT IT WITH THE PRINCE.
MM.
WE ARE HERE TO PROTECT THE MEMBERS OF THE DOWA ROYAL FAMILY.
HOWEVER, THERE ARE SITUATIONS IN WHICH WE CAN DO NOTHING...
...ACCIDENTS CAUSED BY THINGS BEYOND OUR CONTROL...

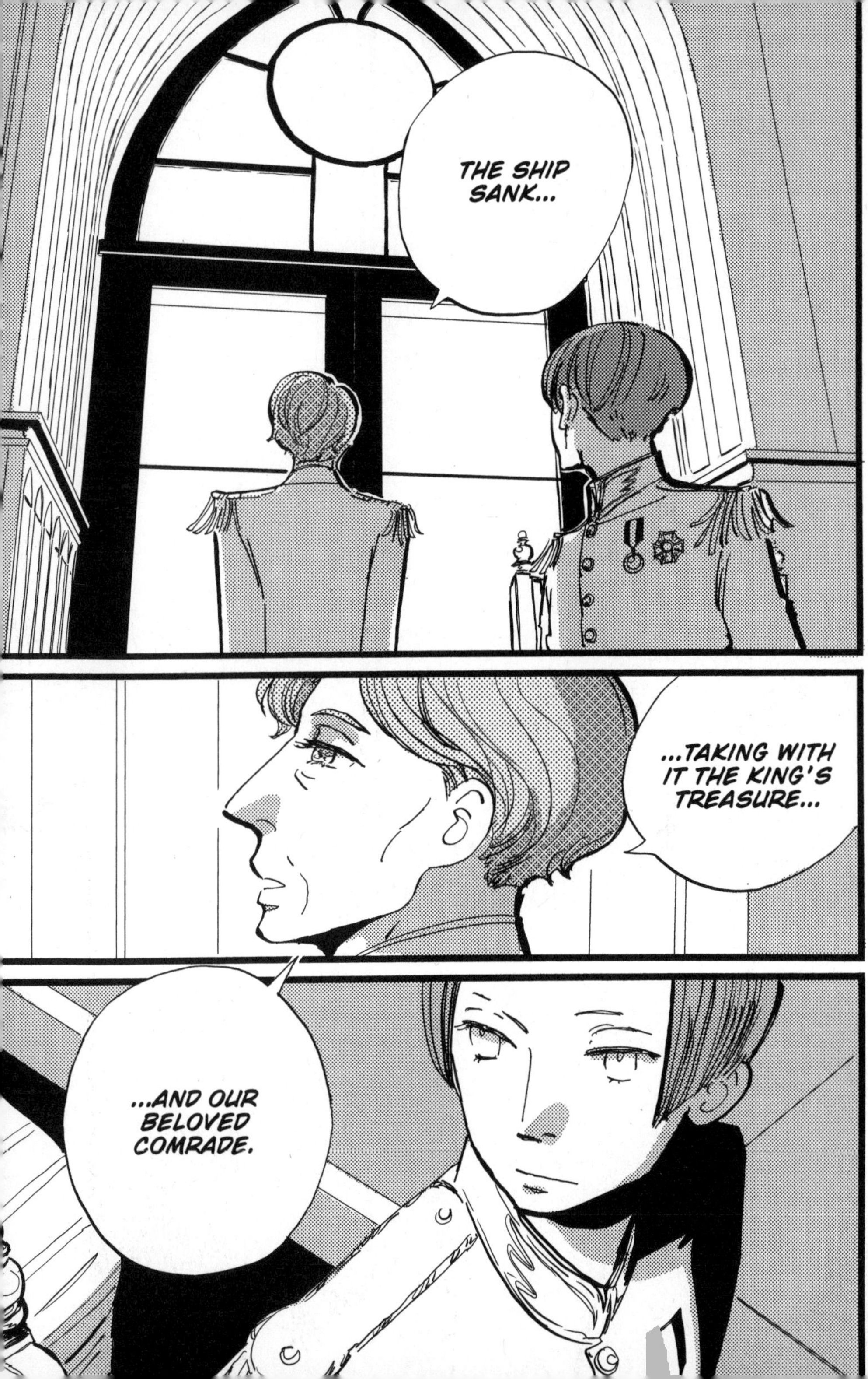
THE SHIP SANK...
...TAKING WITH IT THE KING'S TREASURE...
...AND OUR BELOVED COMRADE.

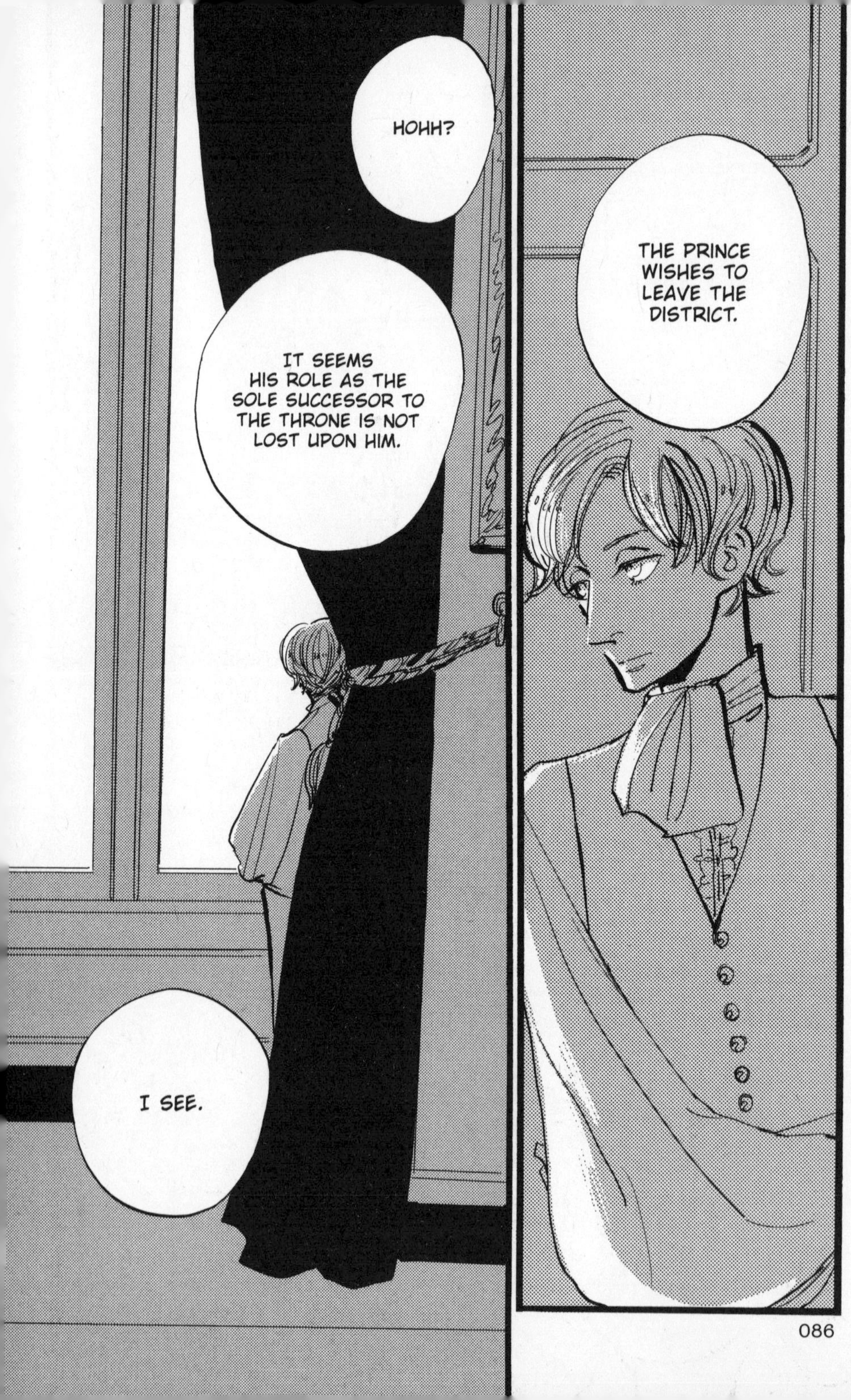
THE PRINCE WISHES TO LEAVE THE DISTRICT.
HOHH?
IT SEEMS HIS ROLE AS THE SOLE SUCCESSOR TO THE THRONE IS NOT LOST UPON HIM.
I SEE.

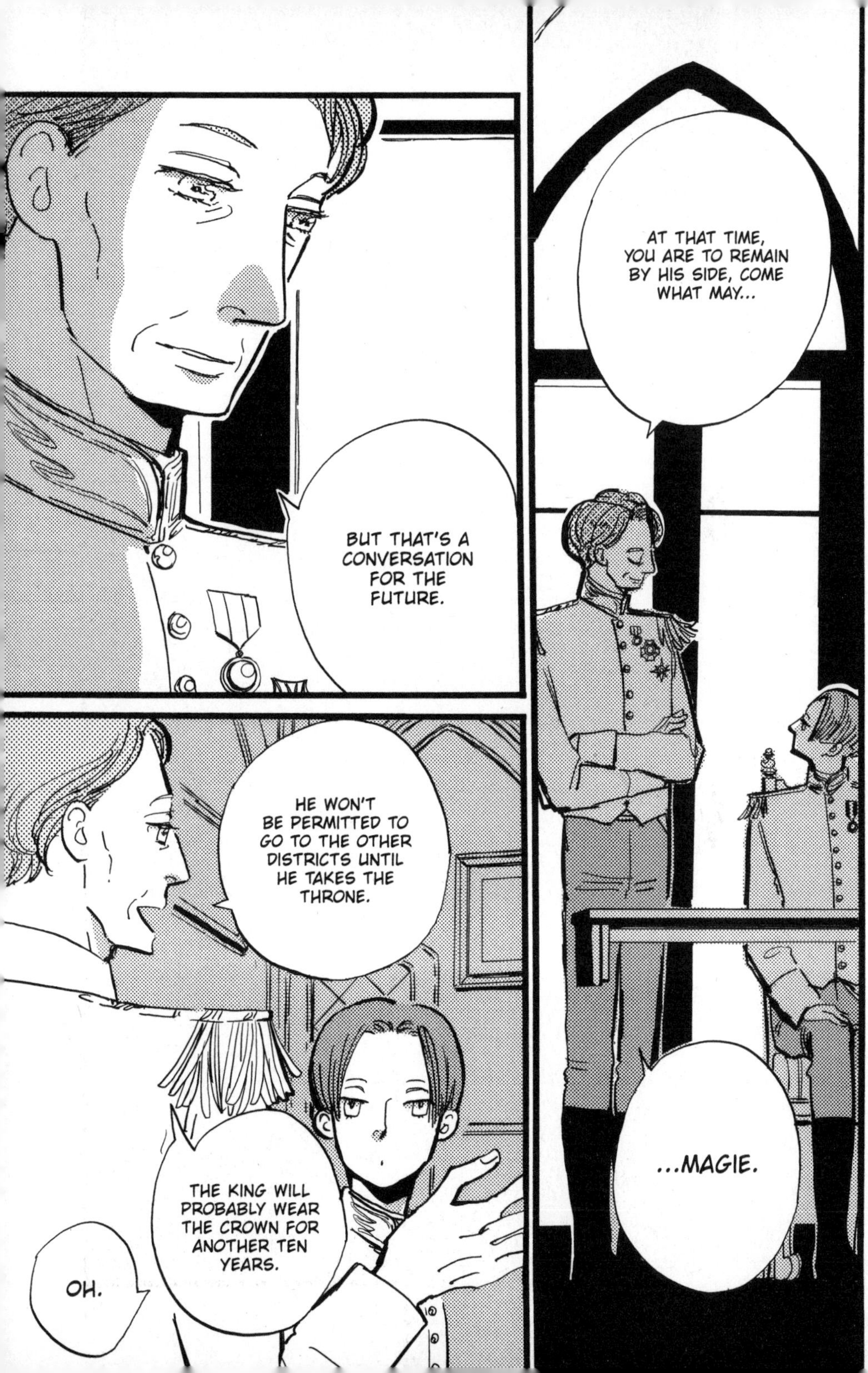
AT THAT TIME, YOU ARE TO REMAIN BY HIS SIDE, COME WHAT MAY...
...MAGIE.
BUT THAT'S A CONVERSATION FOR THE FUTURE.
HE WON'T BE PERMITTED TO GO TO THE OTHER DISTRICTS UNTIL HE TAKES THE THRONE.
THE KING WILL PROBABLY WEAR THE CROWN FOR ANOTHER TEN YEARS.
OH.

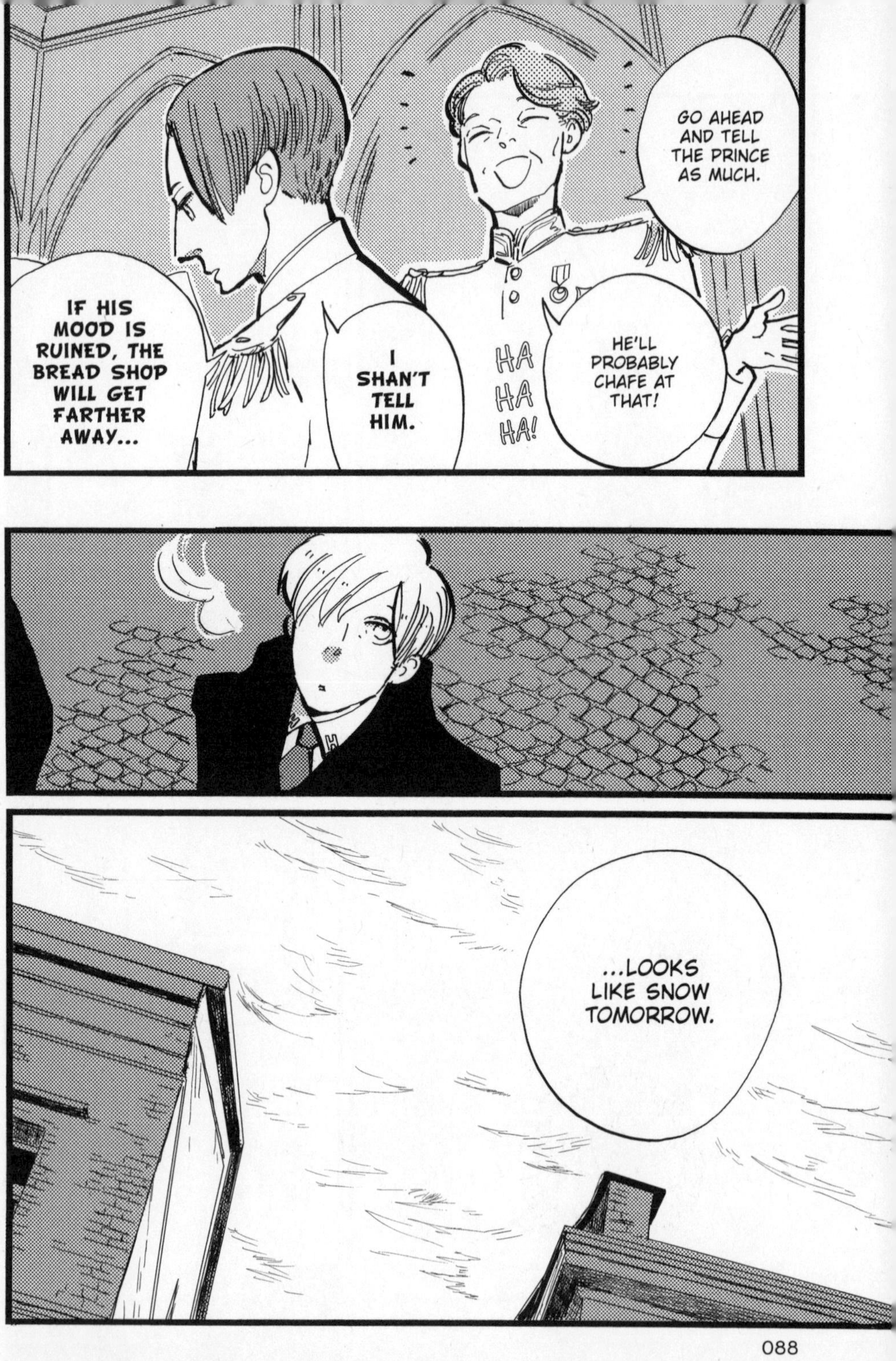
GO AHEAD AND TELL THE PRINCE AS MUCH.
HE'LL PROBABLY CHAFE AT THAT!
HA HA HA!
I SHAN'T TELL HIM.
IF HIS MOOD IS RUINED, THE BREAD SHOP WILL GET FARTHER AWAY...
...LOOKS LIKE SNOW TOMORROW.

CHAPTER 20

Considering the Coup d'État in Dowa

INSPECTION DEPT ACCA 13 TERRITORY
PASS

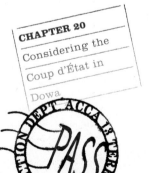

CHAPTER 21

Snack Time with a
Certain Someone
in Dowa

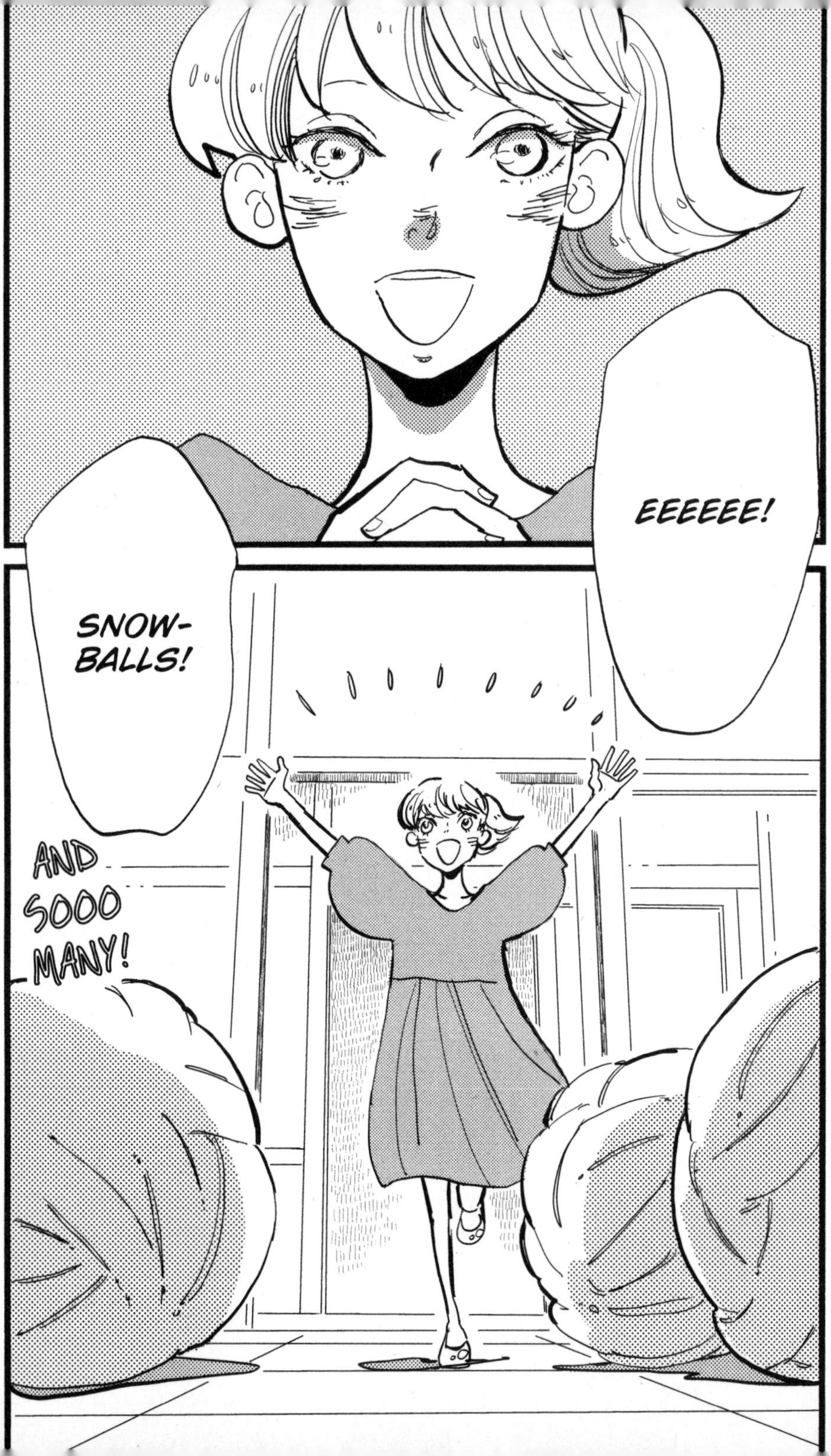
EEEEEE!
SNOW-BALLS!
AND SOOO MANY!

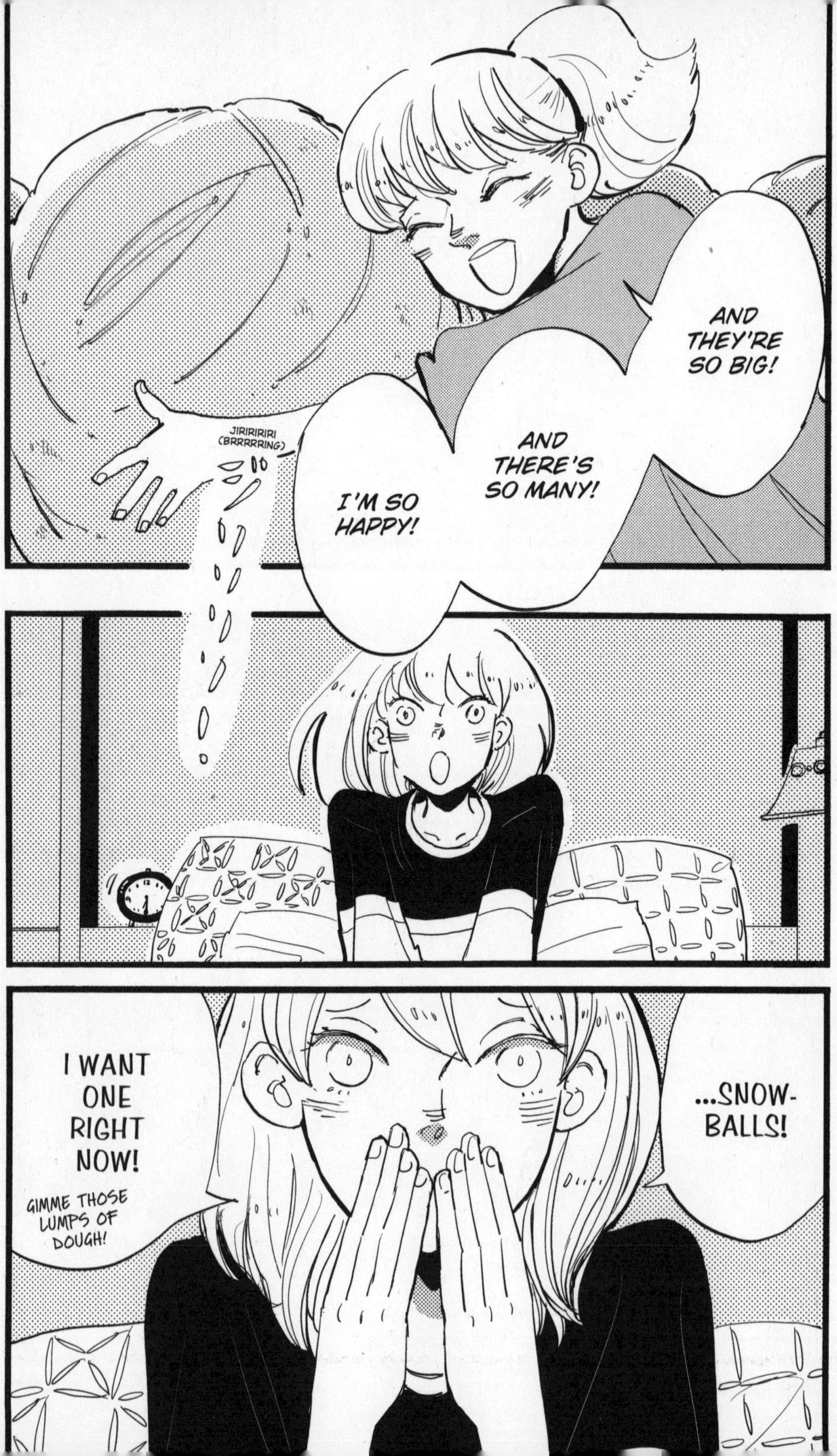
AND THEY'RE SO BIG!
AND THERE'S SO MANY!
I'M SO HAPPY!
JIRIRIRIRI (BRRRRRING)
...SNOW-BALLS!
I WANT ONE RIGHT NOW!
GIMME THOSE LUMPS OF DOUGH!

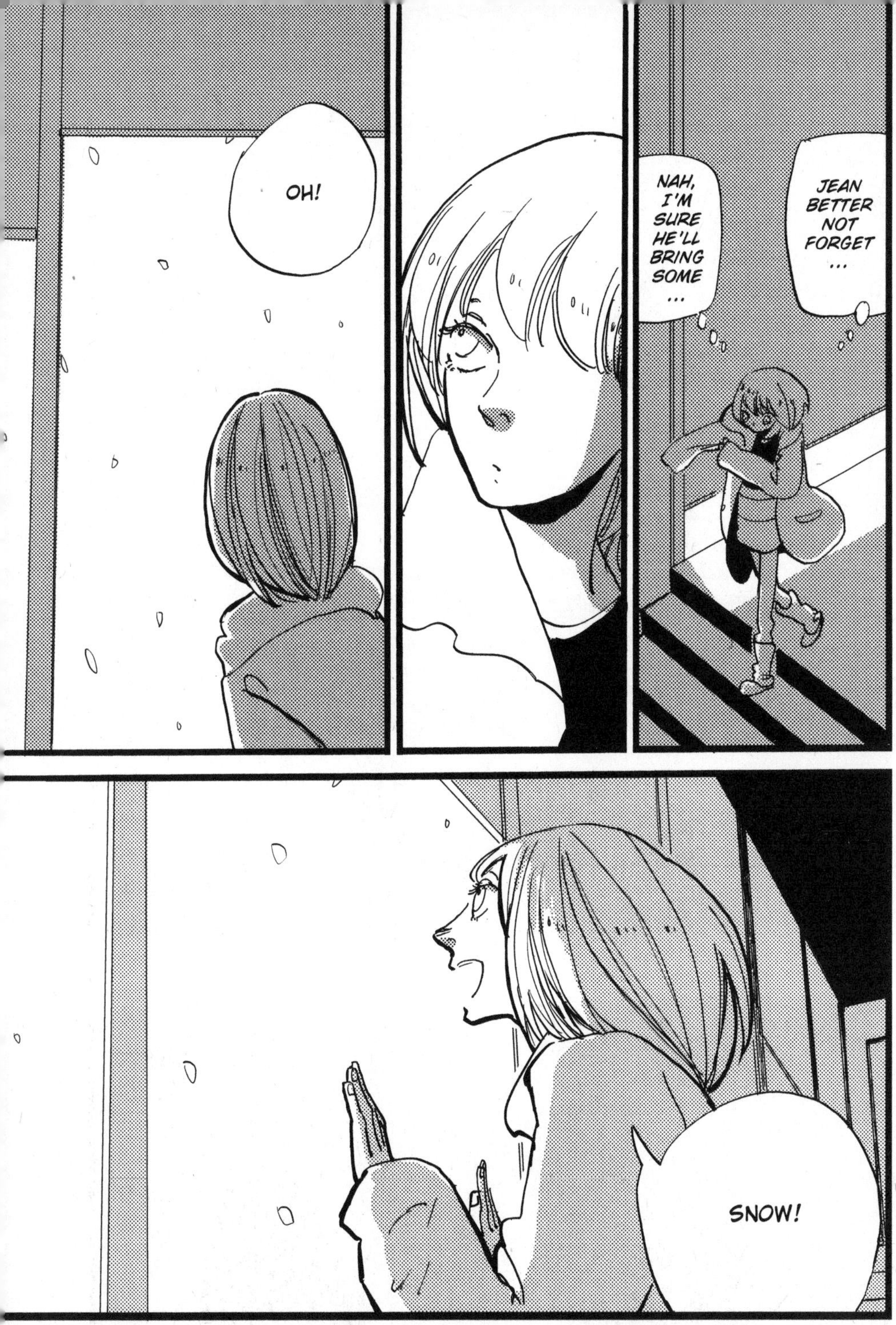
JEAN BETTER NOT FORGET ...
NAH, I'M SURE HE'LL BRING SOME ...
OH!
SNOW!

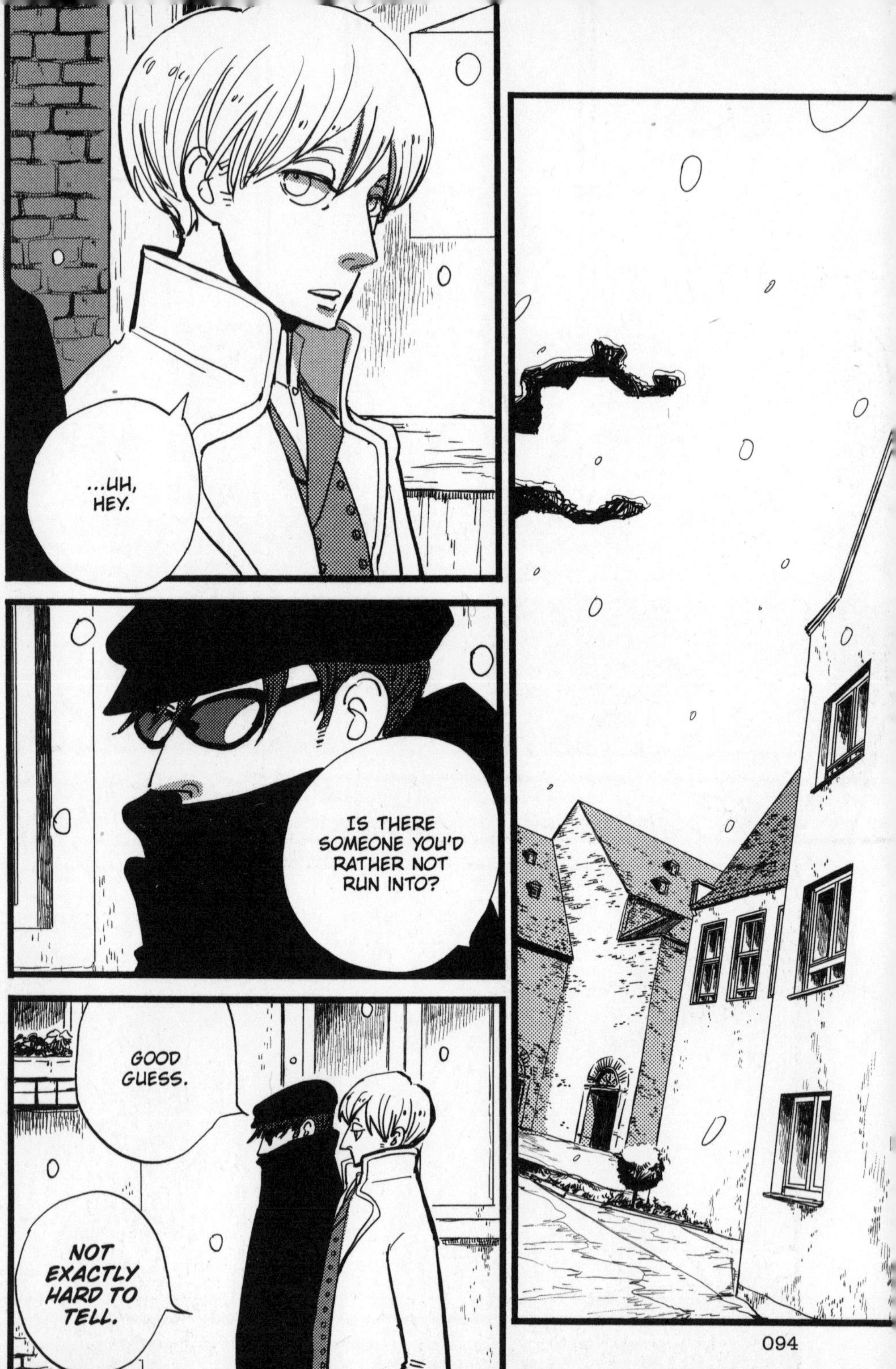
...UH, HEY.
IS THERE SOMEONE YOU'D RATHER NOT RUN INTO?
GOOD GUESS.
NOT EXACTLY HARD TO TELL.

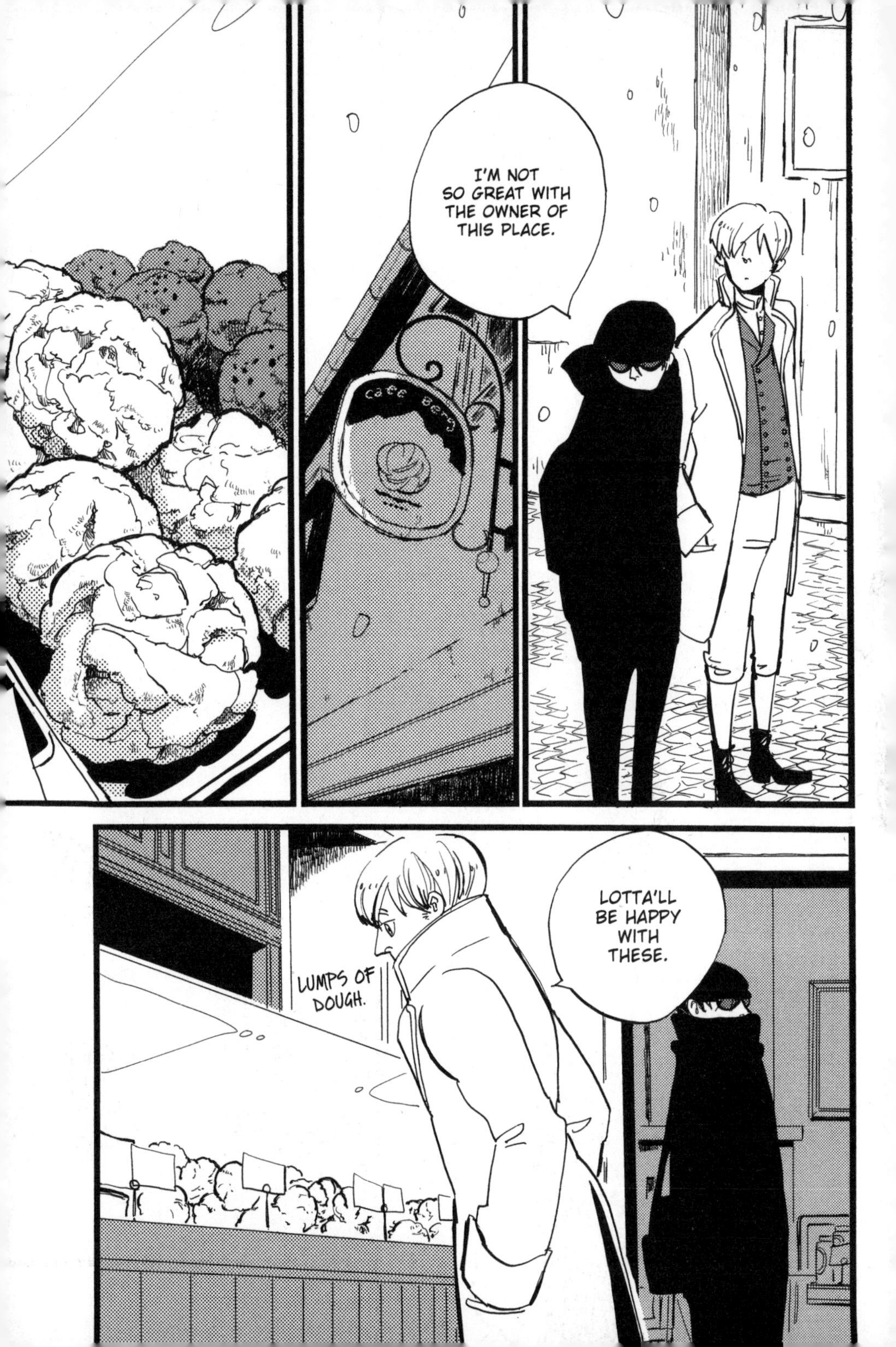

I'M NOT SO GREAT WITH THE OWNER OF THIS PLACE.
Cafe Berg
LOTTA'LL BE HAPPY WITH THESE.
LUMPS OF DOUGH.

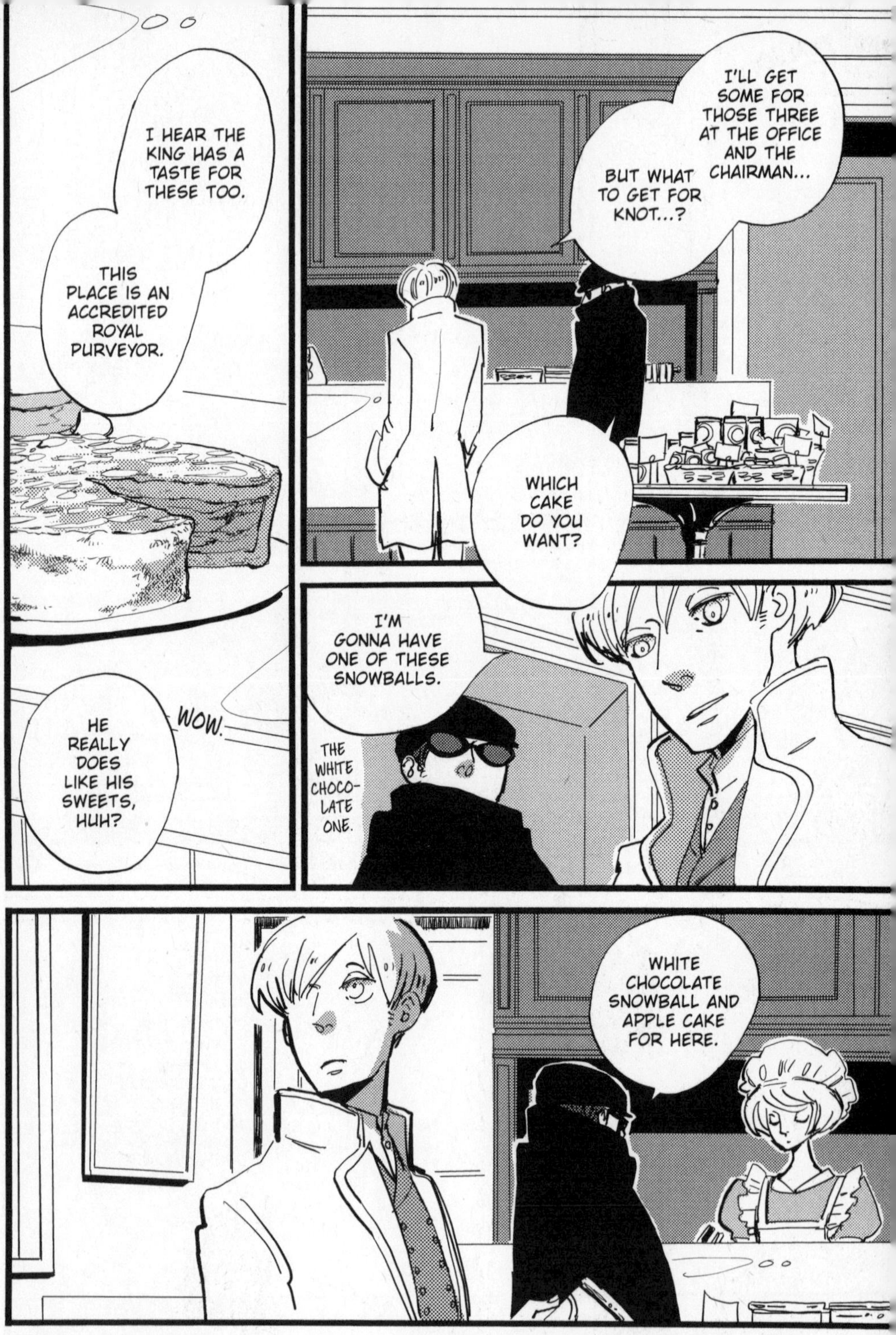
I'LL GET SOME FOR THOSE THREE AT THE OFFICE AND THE CHAIRMAN...
BUT WHAT TO GET FOR KNOT...?
WHICH CAKE DO YOU WANT?
I HEAR THE KING HAS A TASTE FOR THESE TOO.
THIS PLACE IS AN ACCREDITED ROYAL PURVEYOR.
I'M GONNA HAVE ONE OF THESE SNOWBALLS.
THE WHITE CHOCOLATE ONE.
WOW.
HE REALLY DOES LIKE HIS SWEETS, HUH?
WHITE CHOCOLATE SNOWBALL AND APPLE CAKE FOR HERE.

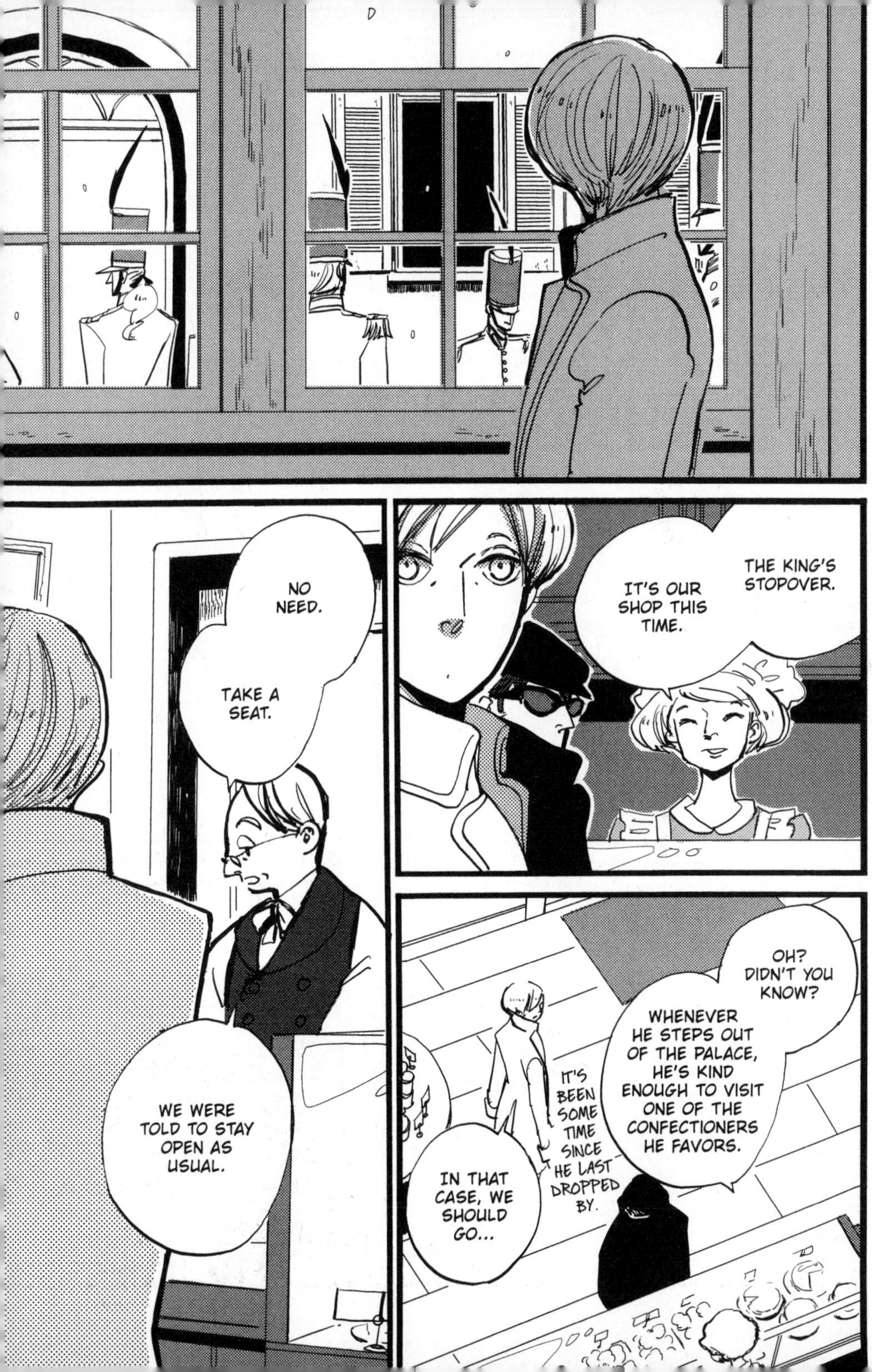
THE KING'S STOPOVER.
IT'S OUR SHOP THIS TIME.
OH? DIDN'T YOU KNOW?
WHENEVER HE STEPS OUT OF THE PALACE, HE'S KIND ENOUGH TO VISIT ONE OF THE CONFECTIONERS HE FAVORS.
IT'S BEEN SOME TIME SINCE HE LAST DROPPED BY.
IN THAT CASE, WE SHOULD GO...
NO NEED.
TAKE A SEAT.
WE WERE TOLD TO STAY OPEN AS USUAL.

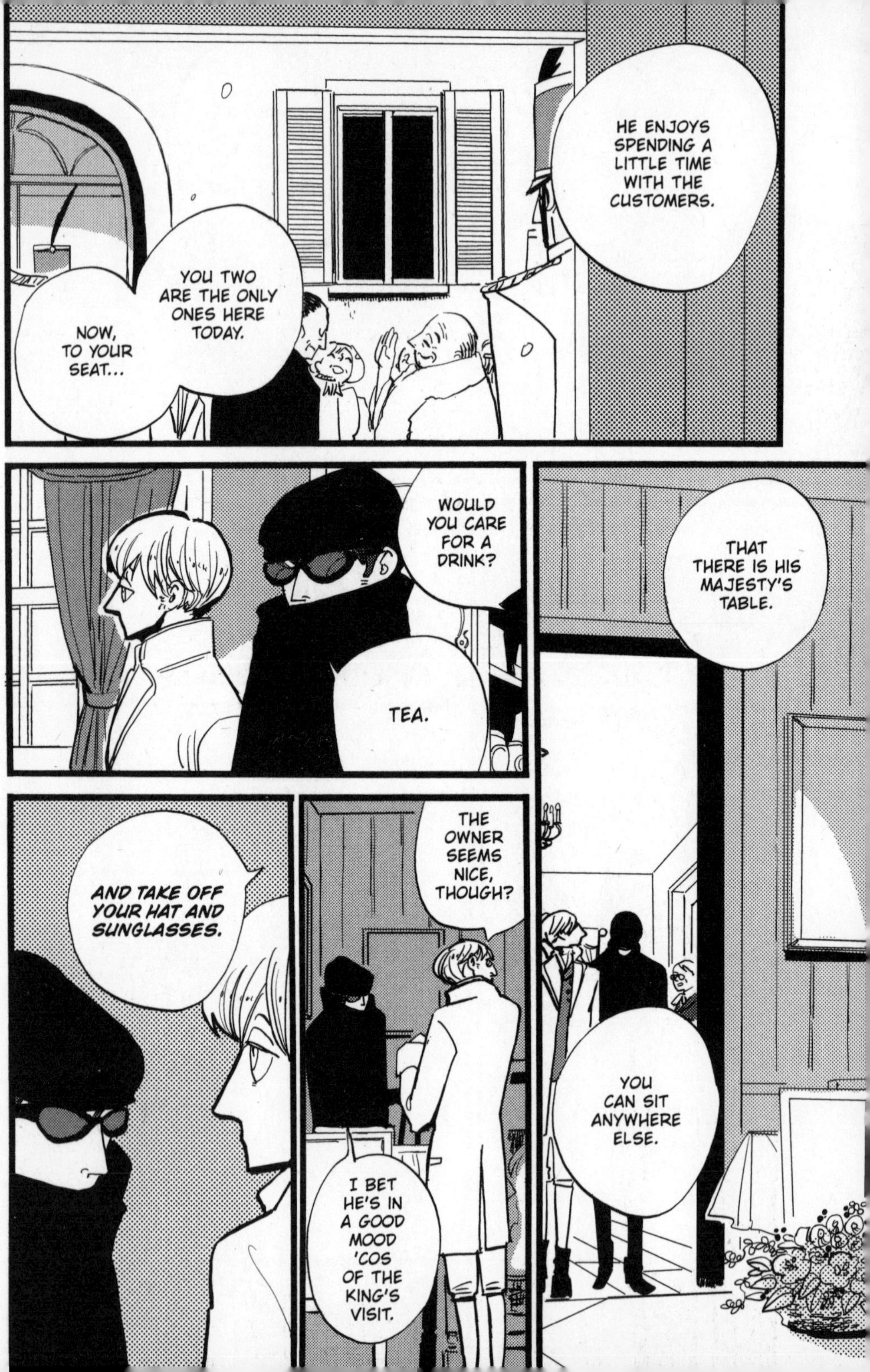
HE ENJOYS SPENDING A LITTLE TIME WITH THE CUSTOMERS.
YOU TWO ARE THE ONLY ONES HERE TODAY.
NOW, TO YOUR SEAT...
THAT THERE IS HIS MAJESTY'S TABLE.
YOU CAN SIT ANYWHERE ELSE.
WOULD YOU CARE FOR A DRINK?
TEA.
THE OWNER SEEMS NICE, THOUGH?
I BET HE'S IN A GOOD MOOD 'COS OF THE KING'S VISIT.
AND TAKE OFF YOUR HAT AND SUNGLASSES.

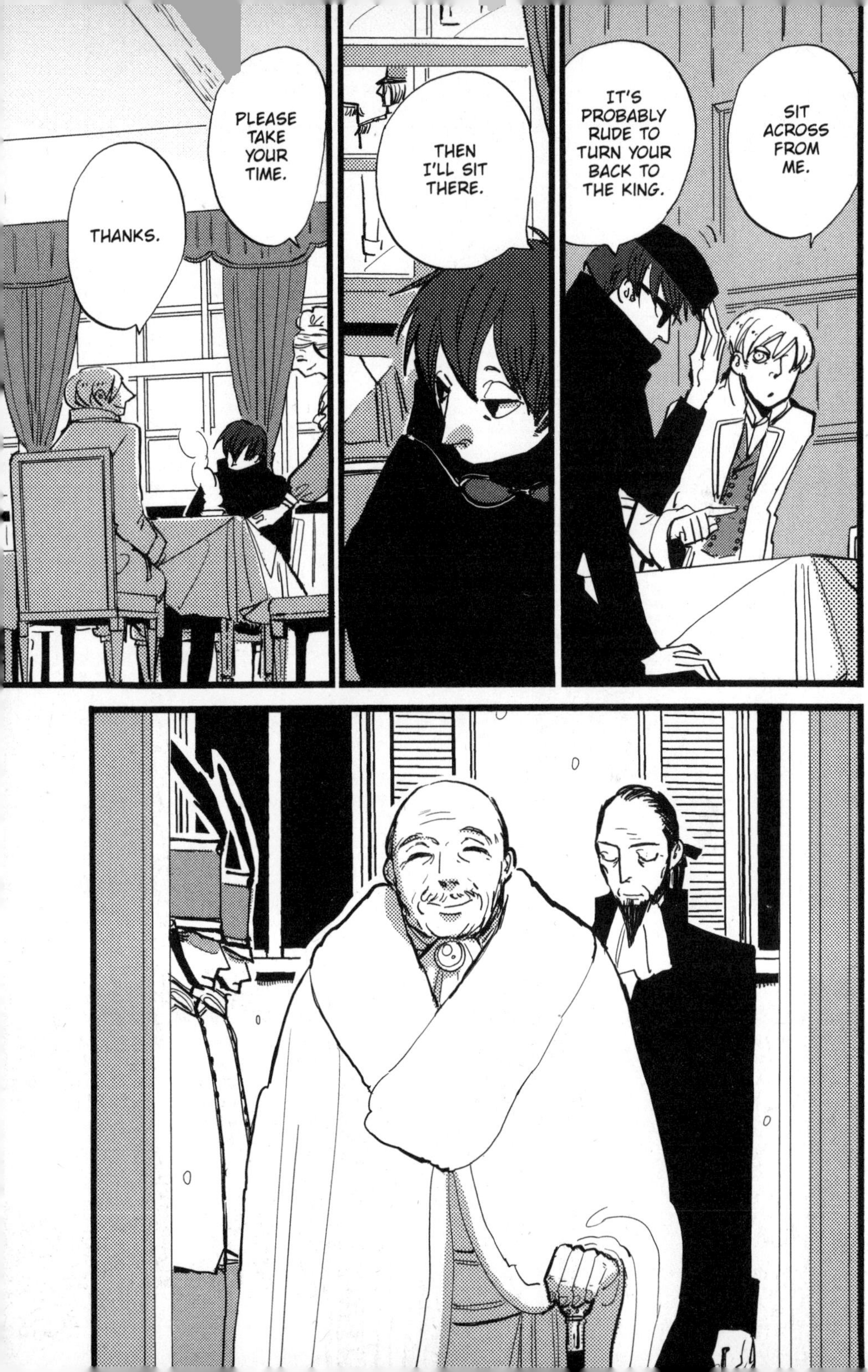
SIT ACROSS FROM ME.
IT'S PROBABLY RUDE TO TURN YOUR BACK TO THE KING.
THEN I'LL SIT THERE.
PLEASE TAKE YOUR TIME.
THANKS.

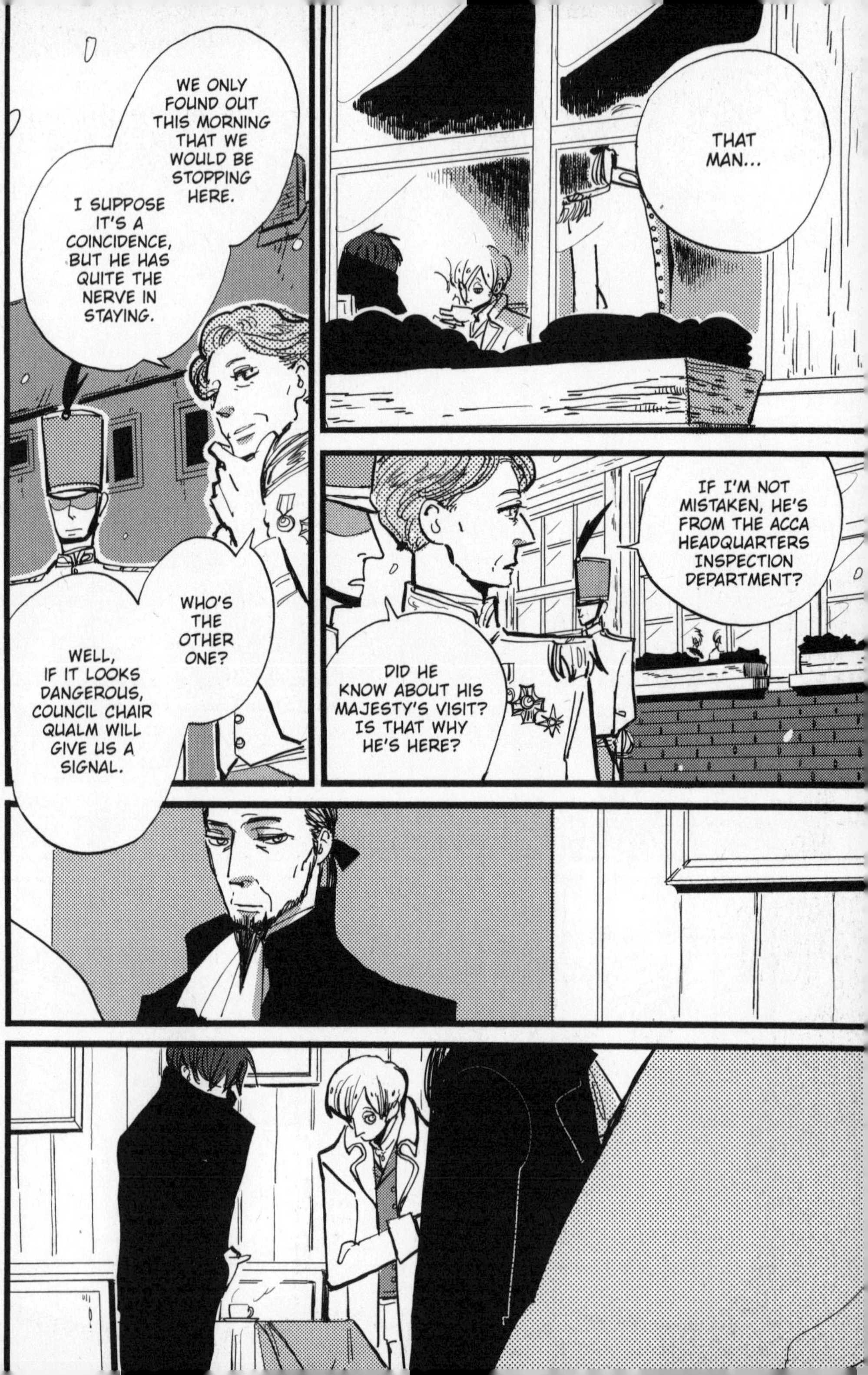
THAT MAN...
IF I'M NOT MISTAKEN, HE'S FROM THE ACCA HEADQUARTERS INSPECTION DEPARTMENT?
DID HE KNOW ABOUT HIS MAJESTY'S VISIT? IS THAT WHY HE'S HERE?
WE ONLY FOUND OUT THIS MORNING THAT WE WOULD BE STOPPING HERE.
I SUPPOSE IT'S A COINCIDENCE, BUT HE HAS QUITE THE NERVE IN STAYING.
WHO'S THE OTHER ONE?
WELL, IF IT LOOKS DANGEROUS, COUNCIL CHAIR QUALM WILL GIVE US A SIGNAL.

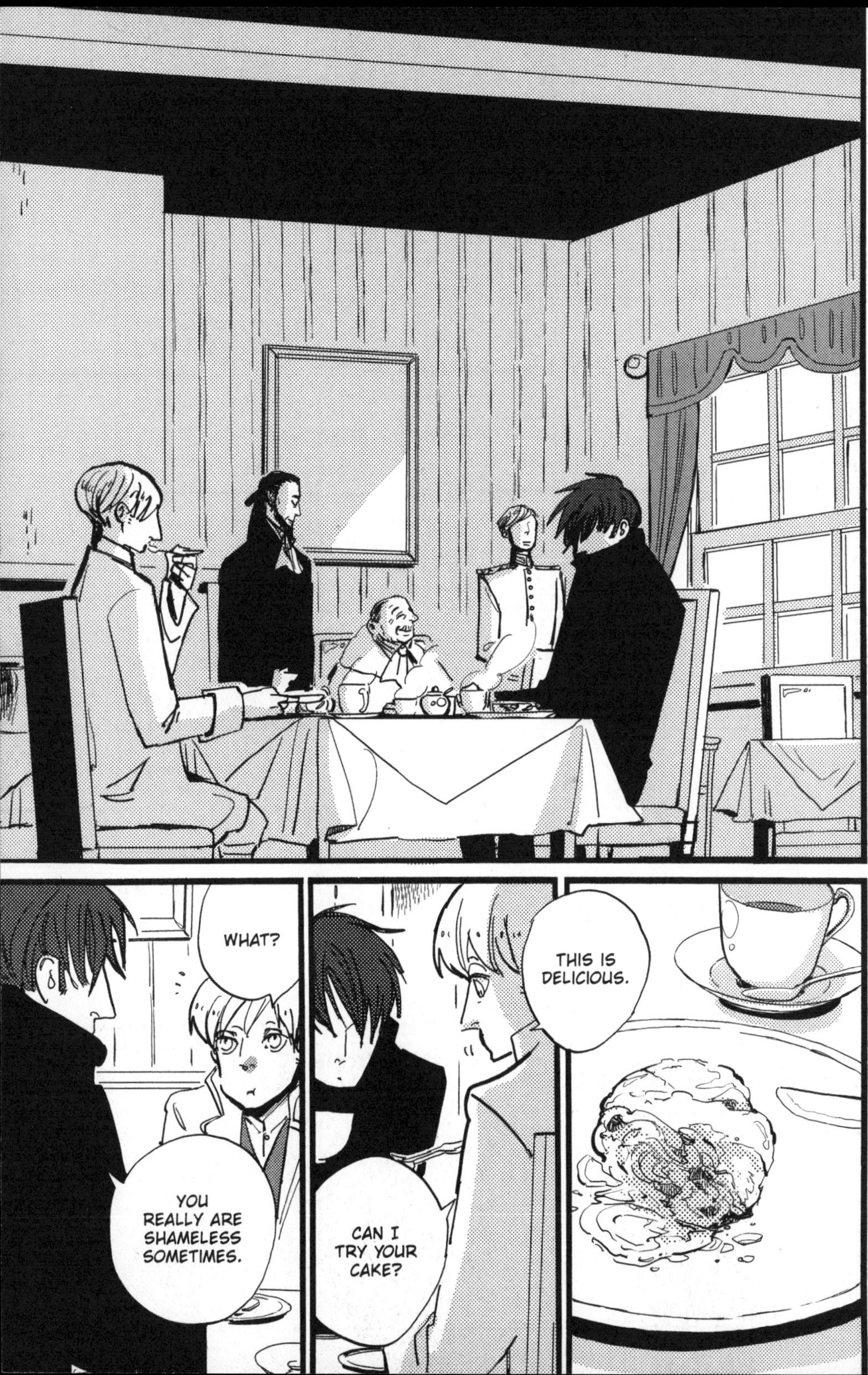
THIS IS DELICIOUS.
CAN I TRY YOUR CAKE?
WHAT?
YOU REALLY ARE SHAMELESS SOMETIMES.

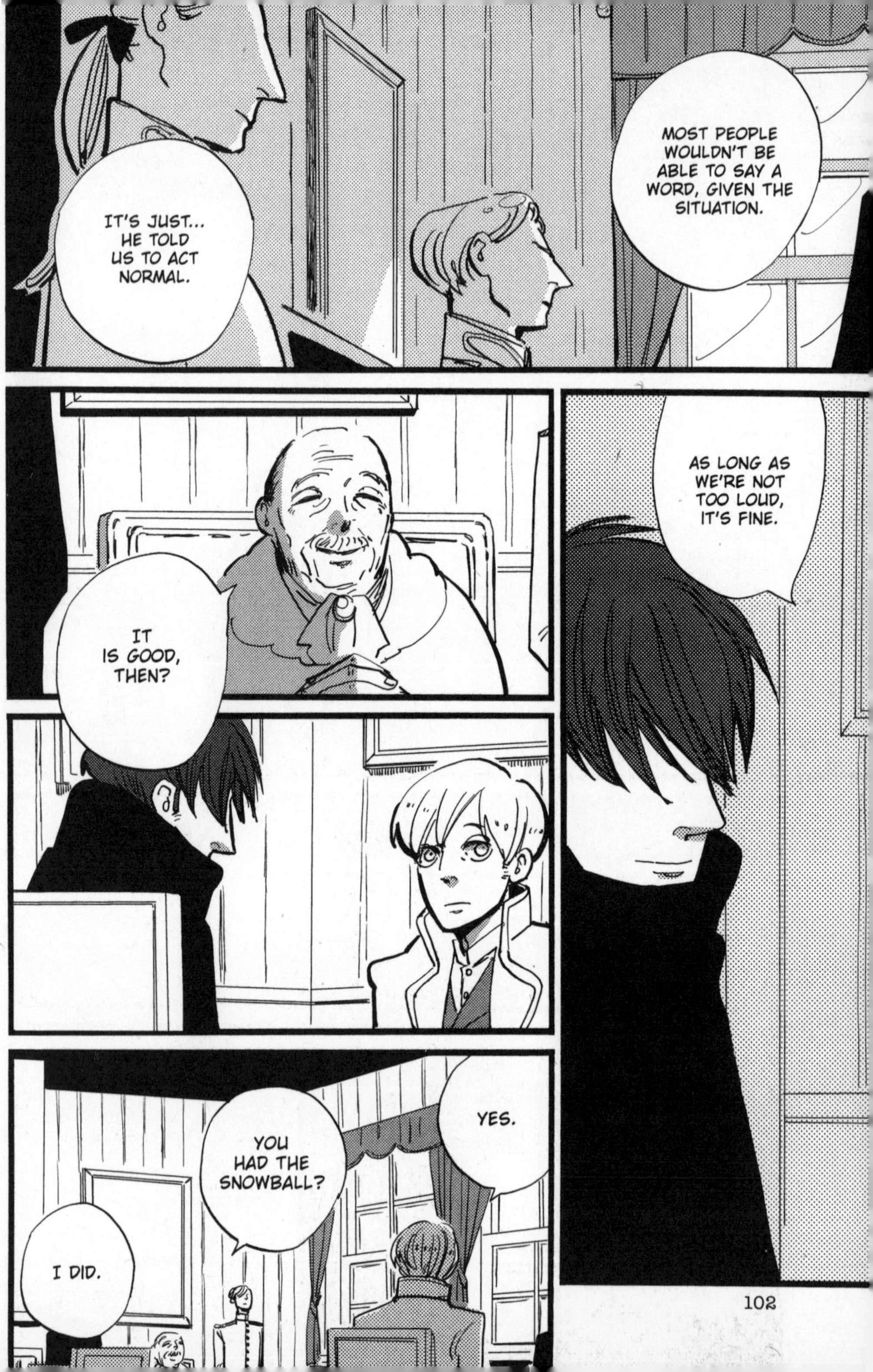
MOST PEOPLE WOULDN'T BE ABLE TO SAY A WORD, GIVEN THE SITUATION.
IT'S JUST... HE TOLD US TO ACT NORMAL.
AS LONG AS WE'RE NOT TOO LOUD, IT'S FINE.
IT IS GOOD, THEN?
YES.
YOU HAD THE SNOWBALL?
I DID.

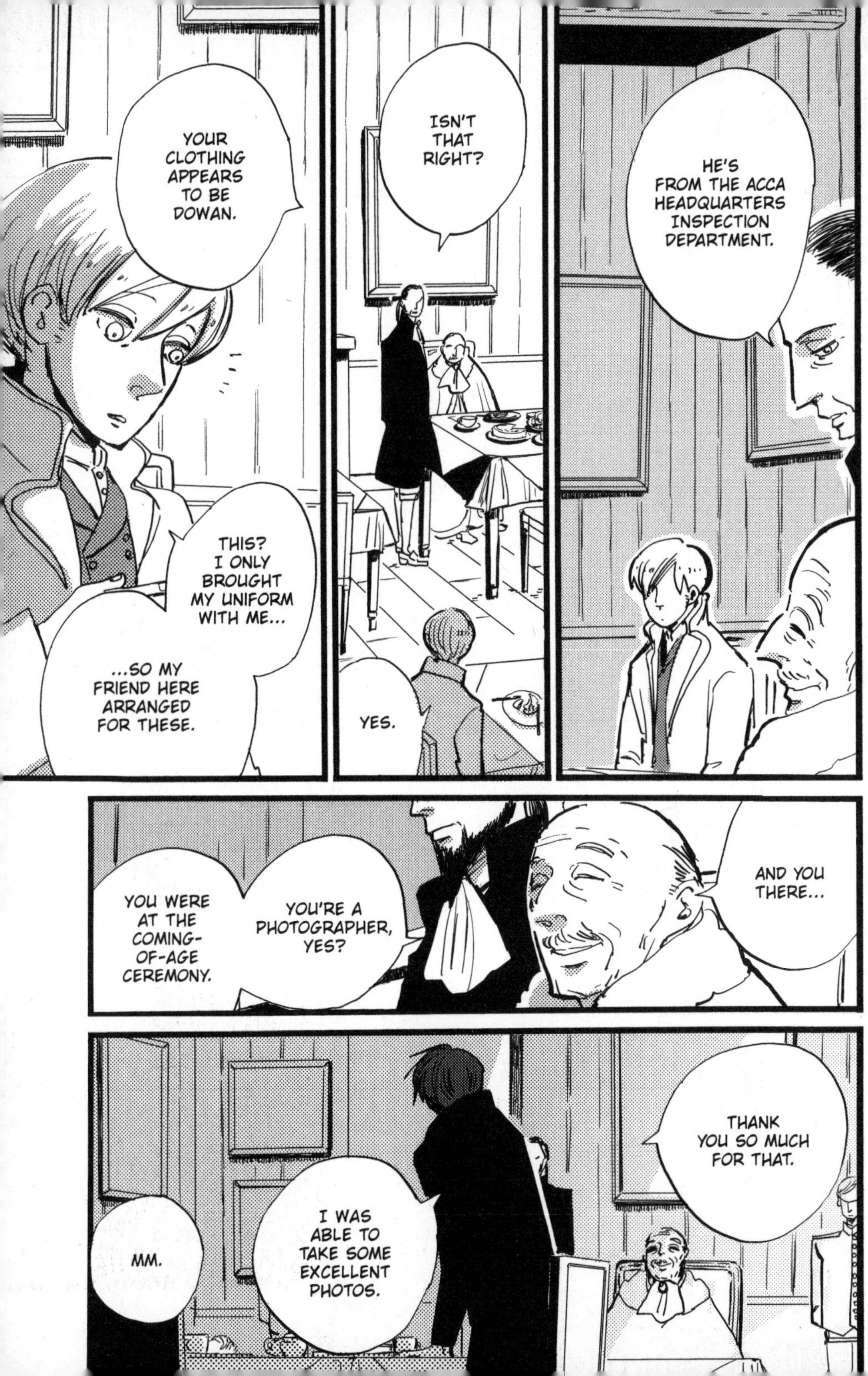
HE'S FROM THE ACCA HEADQUARTERS INSPECTION DEPARTMENT.
ISN'T THAT RIGHT?
YES.
YOUR CLOTHING APPEARS TO BE DOWAN.
THIS? I ONLY BROUGHT MY UNIFORM WITH ME...
...SO MY FRIEND HERE ARRANGED FOR THESE.
AND YOU THERE...
YOU'RE A PHOTOGRAPHER, YES?
YOU WERE AT THE COMING-OF-AGE CEREMONY.
THANK YOU SO MUCH FOR THAT.
I WAS ABLE TO TAKE SOME EXCELLENT PHOTOS.
MM.

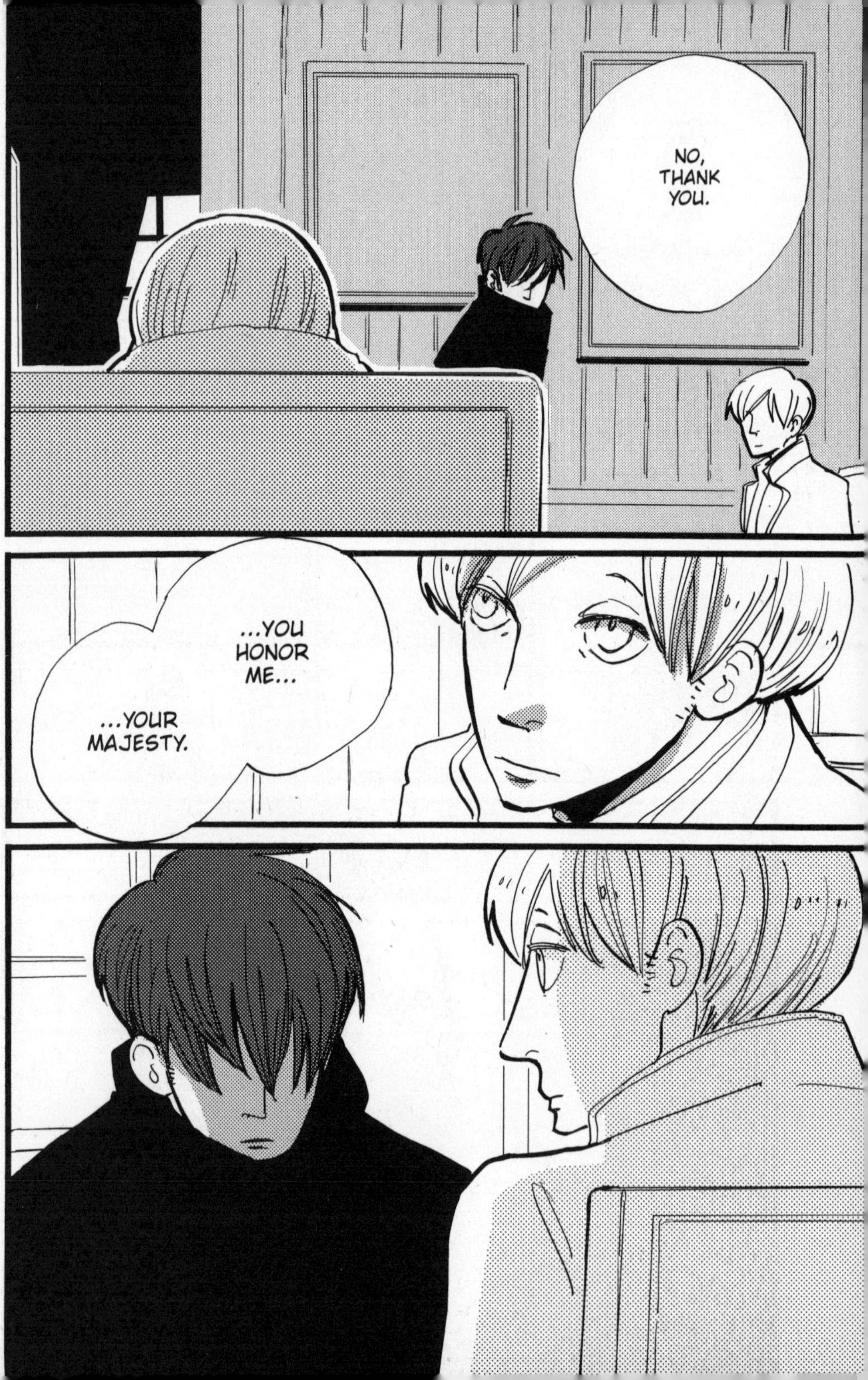
NO, THANK YOU.
...YOU HONOR ME...
...YOUR MAJESTY.

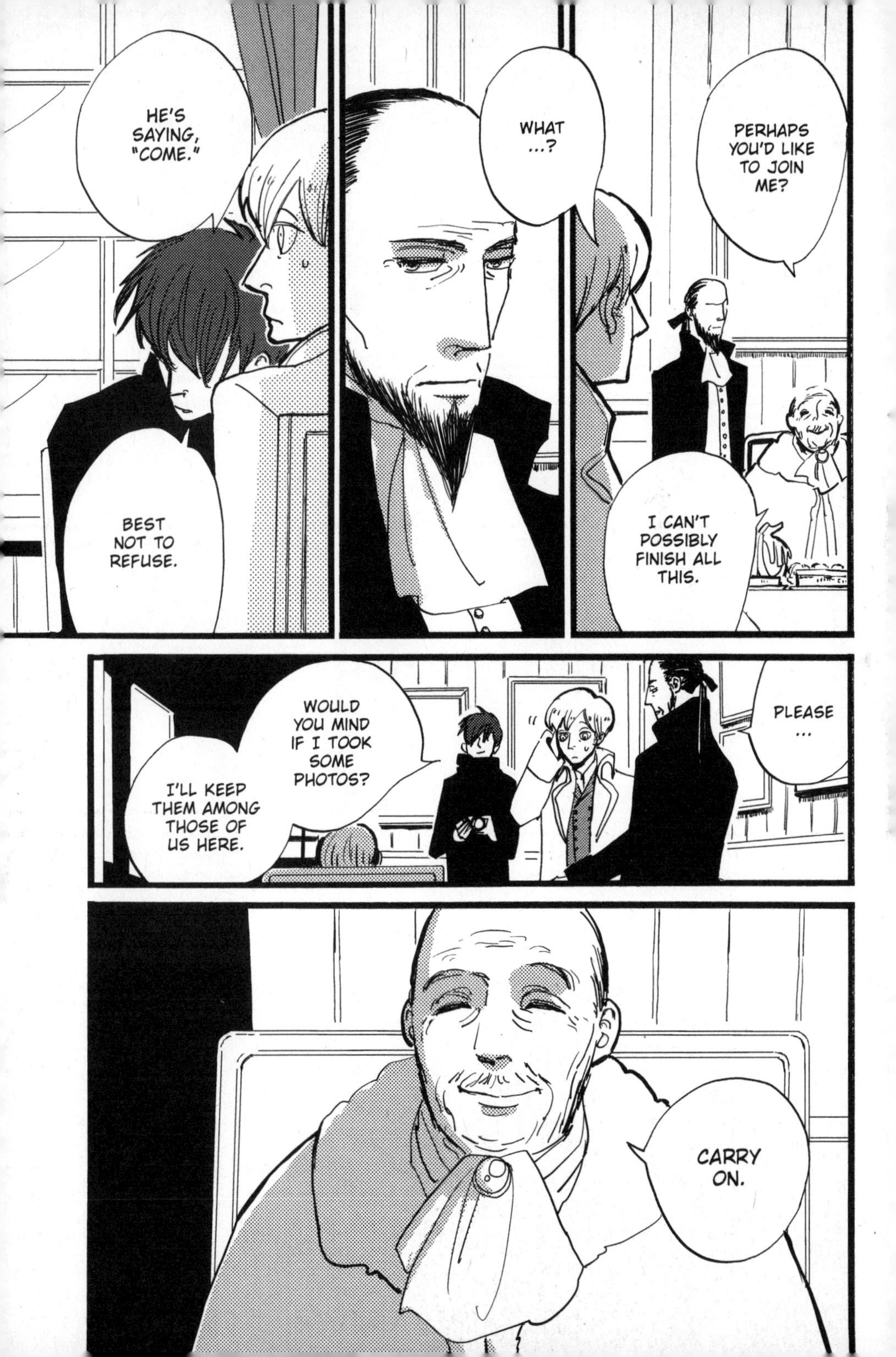
PERHAPS YOU'D LIKE TO JOIN ME?
I CAN'T POSSIBLY FINISH ALL THIS.
WHAT ...?
HE'S SAYING, "COME."
BEST NOT TO REFUSE.
PLEASE ...
WOULD YOU MIND IF I TOOK SOME PHOTOS?
I'LL KEEP THEM AMONG THOSE OF US HERE.
CARRY ON.

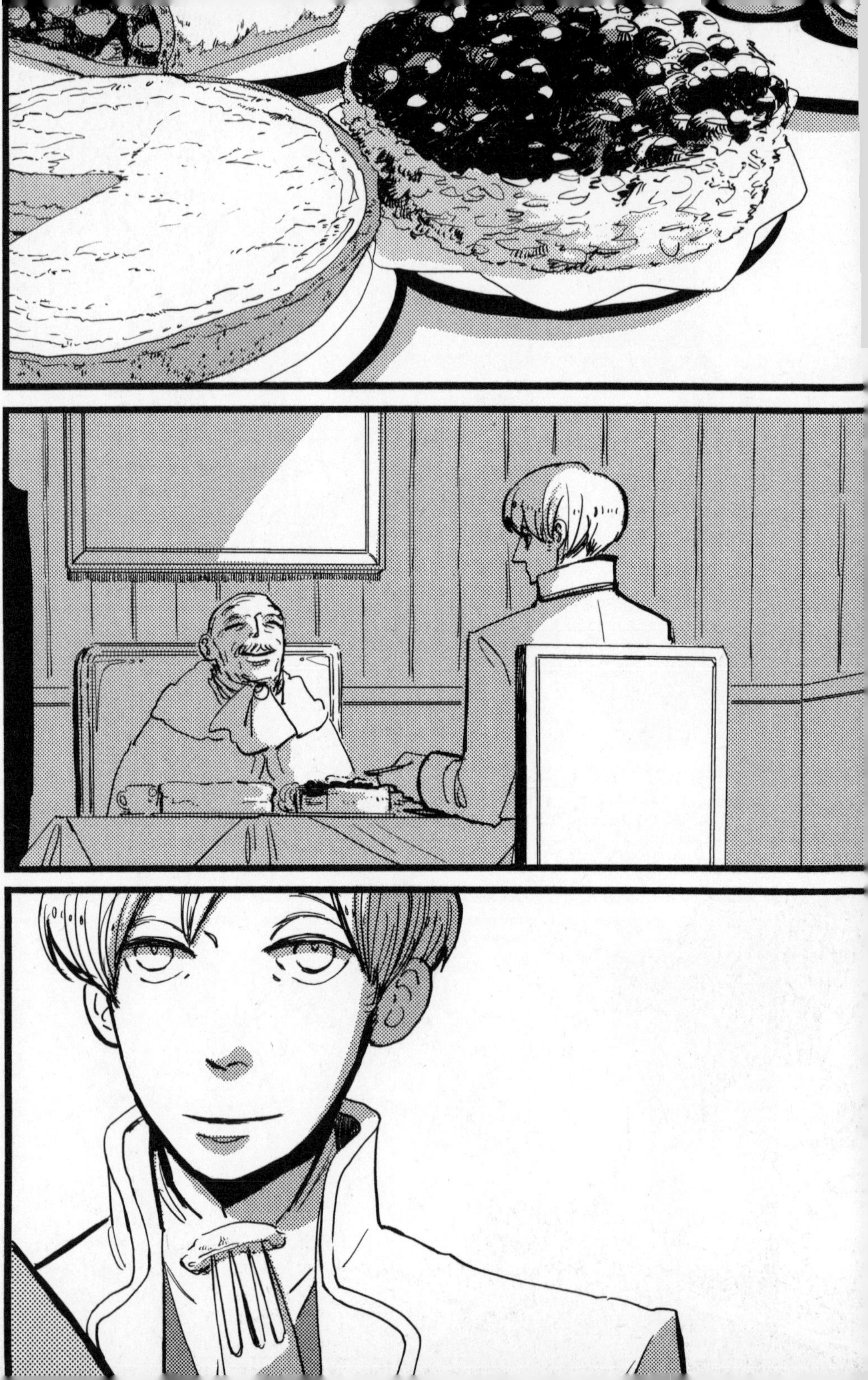

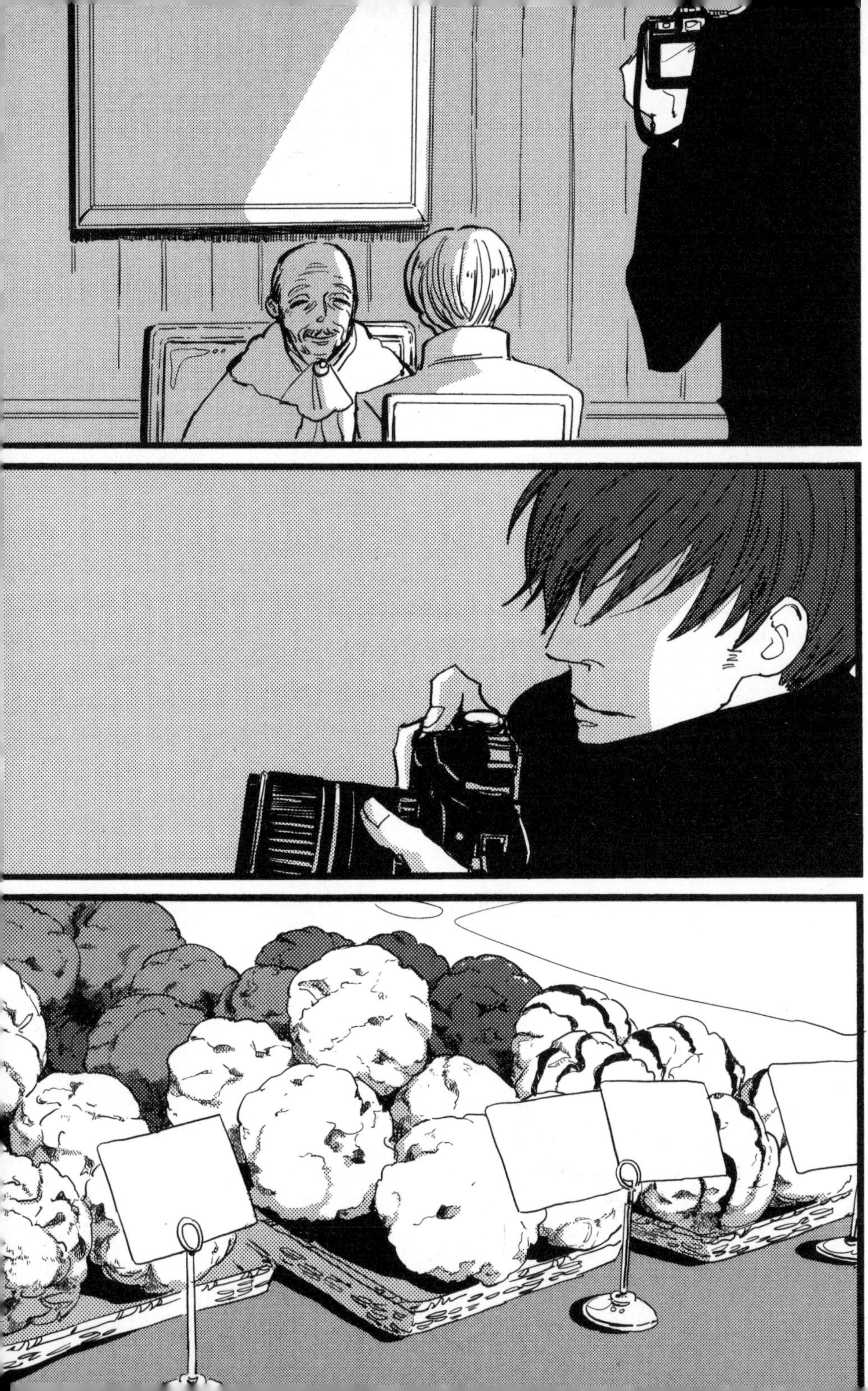

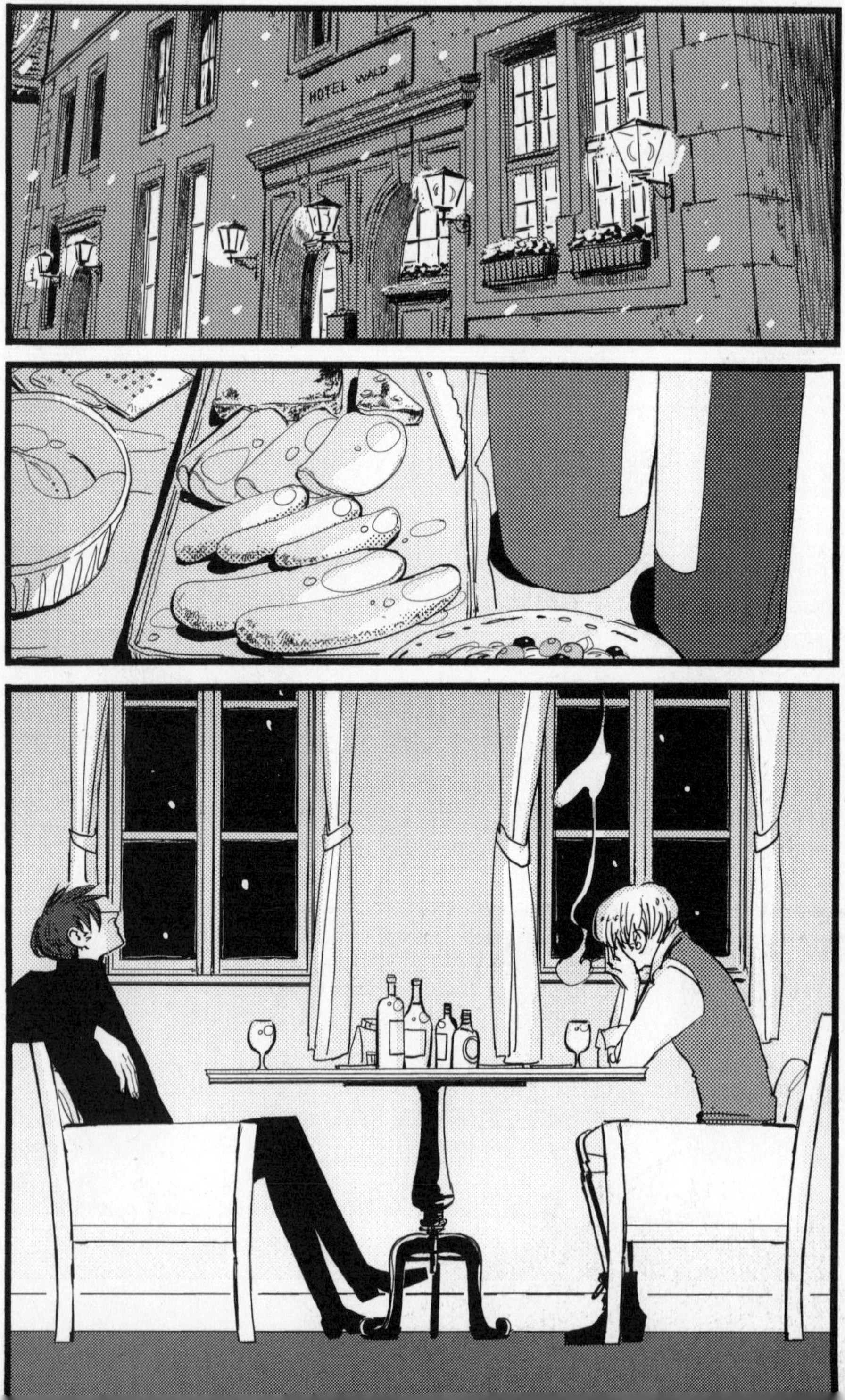
HOTEL WALD

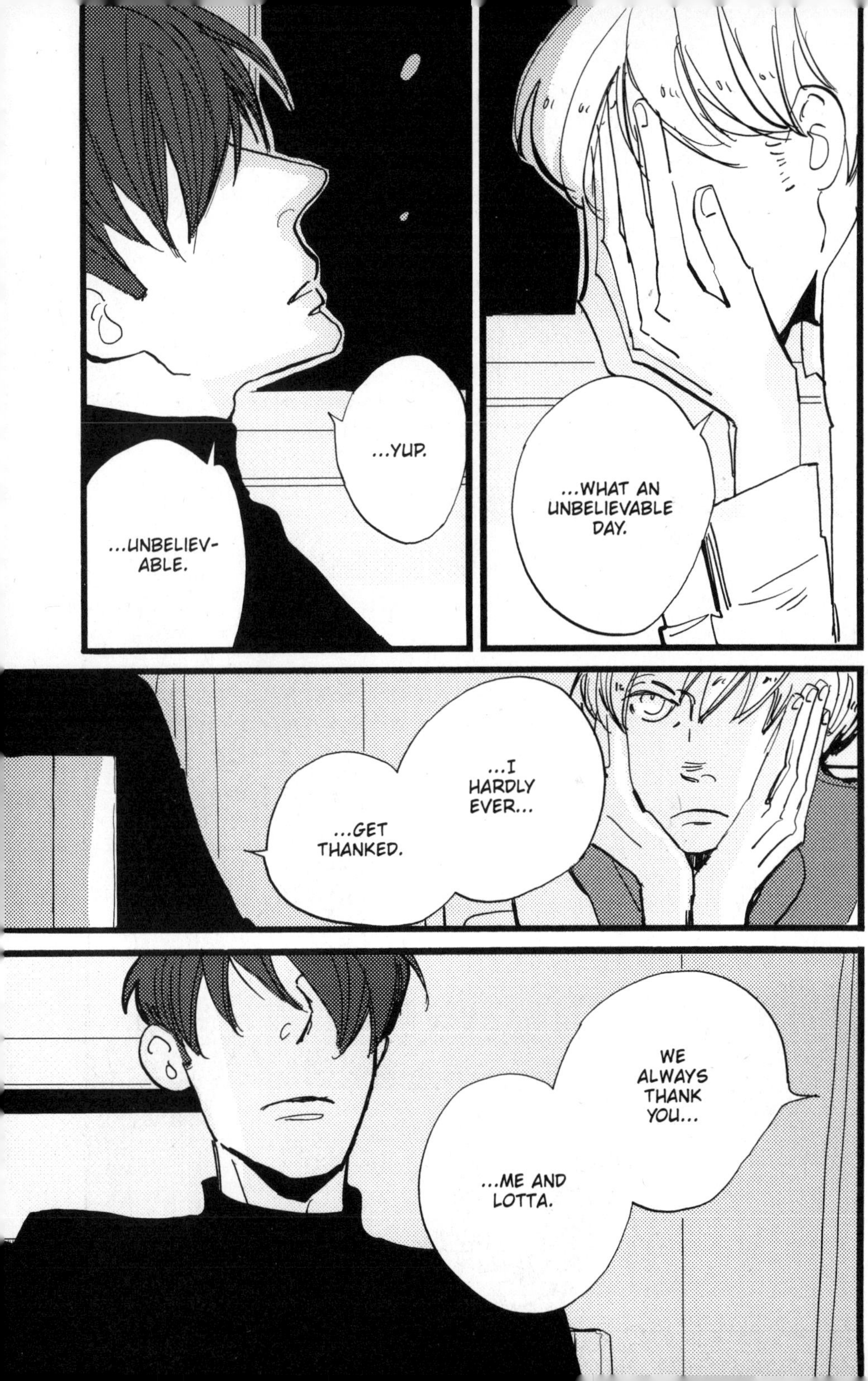
...WHAT AN UNBELIEVABLE DAY.
...YUP.
...UNBELIEV-ABLE.
...I HARDLY EVER...
...GET THANKED.
WE ALWAYS THANK YOU...
...ME AND LOTTA.

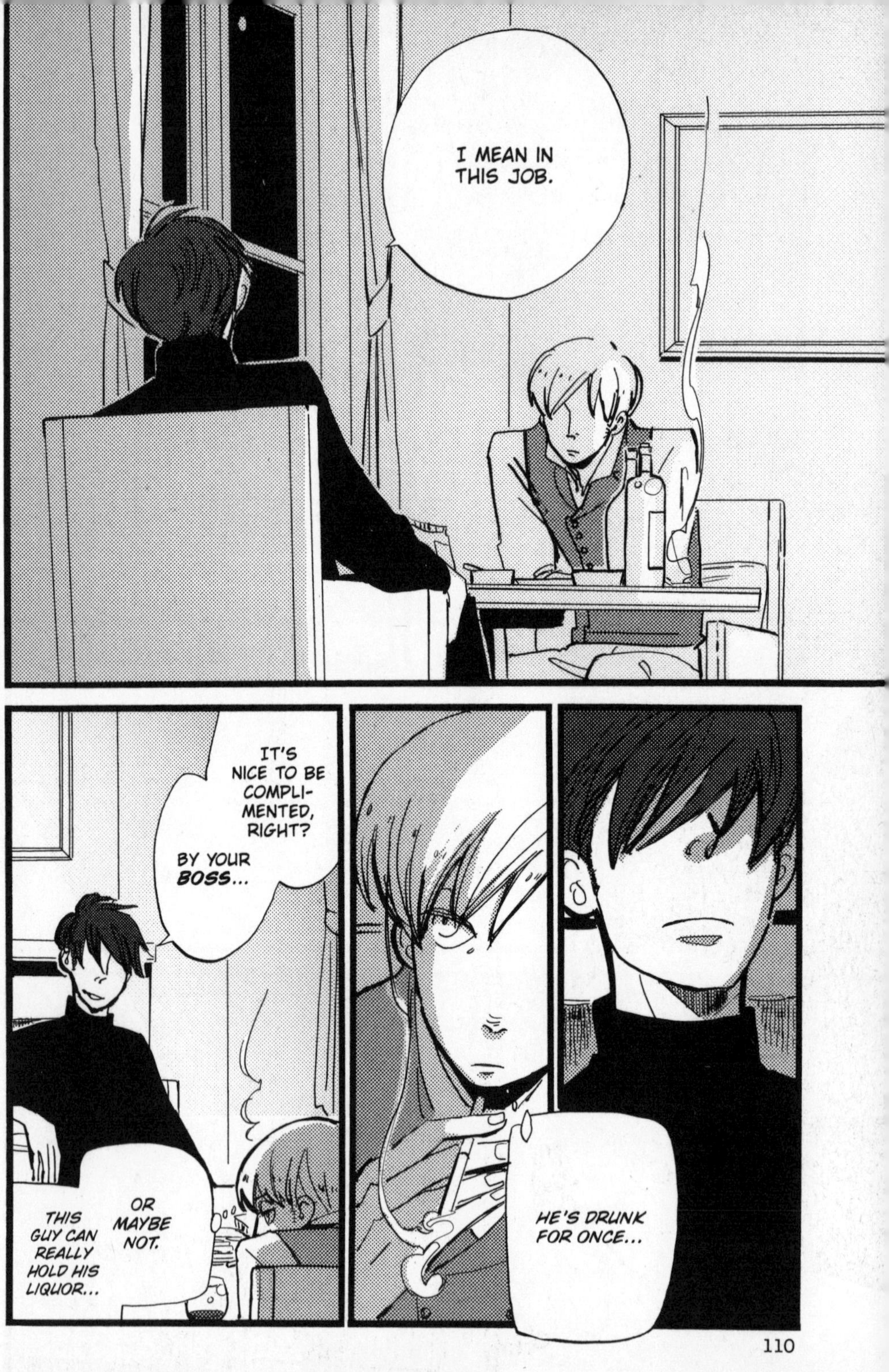
I MEAN IN THIS JOB.
HE'S DRUNK FOR ONCE...
IT'S NICE TO BE COMPLIMENTED, RIGHT?
BY YOUR *BOSS*...
OR MAYBE NOT.
THIS GUY CAN REALLY HOLD HIS LIQUOR...

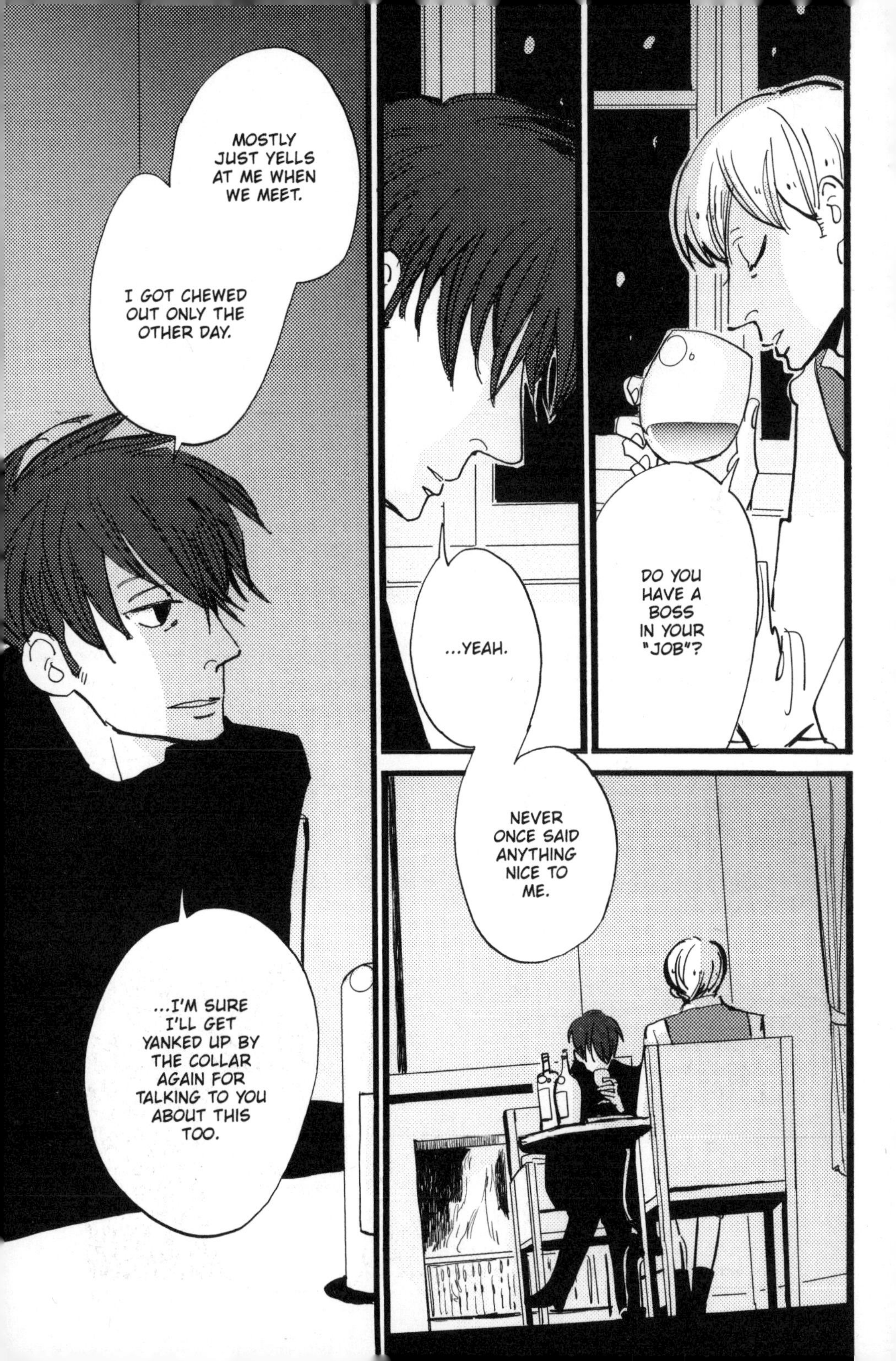
DO YOU HAVE A BOSS IN YOUR "JOB"?
...YEAH.
NEVER ONCE SAID ANYTHING NICE TO ME.
MOSTLY JUST YELLS AT ME WHEN WE MEET.
I GOT CHEWED OUT ONLY THE OTHER DAY.
...I'M SURE I'LL GET YANKED UP BY THE COLLAR AGAIN FOR TALKING TO YOU ABOUT THIS TOO.

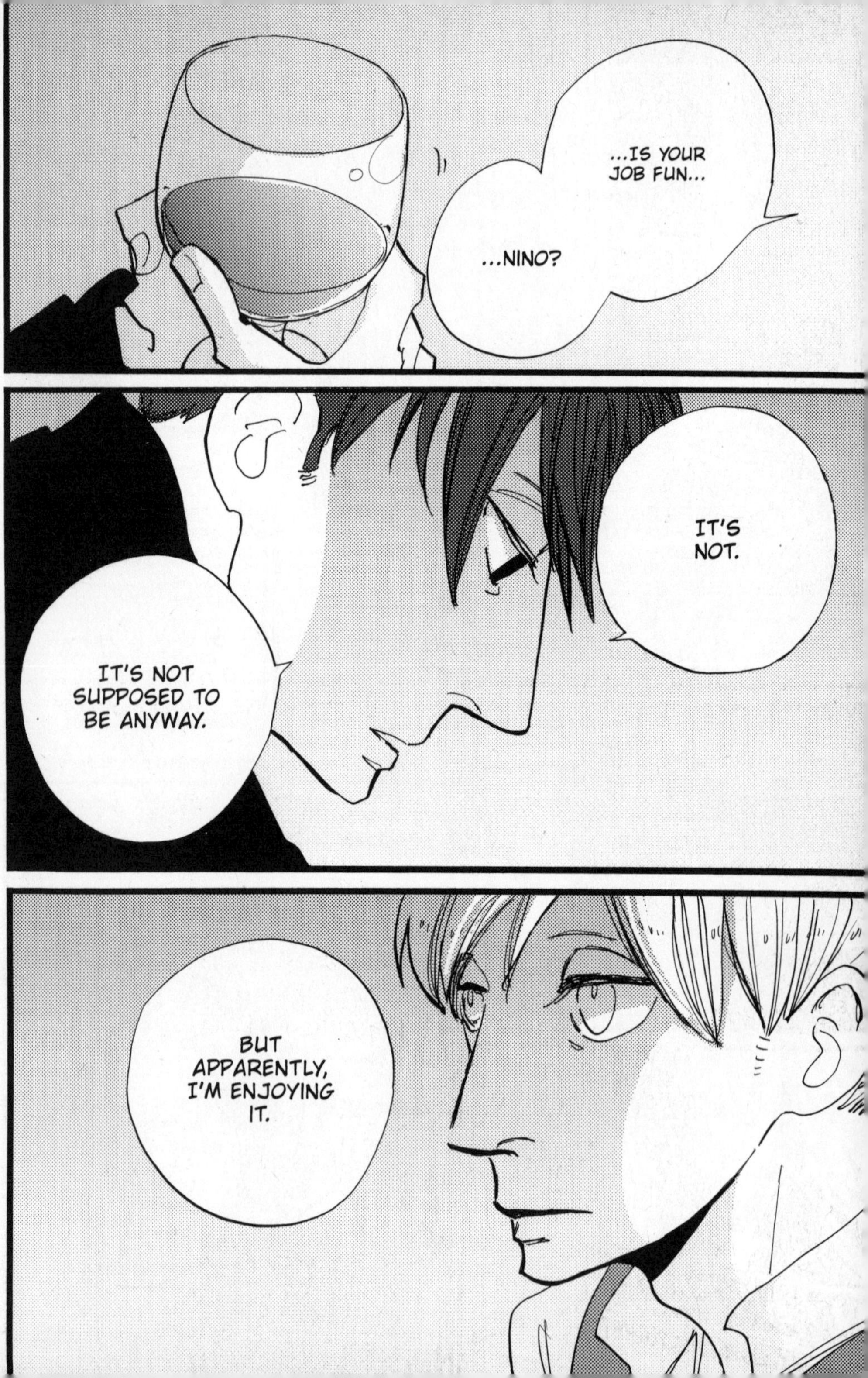
...IS YOUR JOB FUN...
...NINO?
IT'S NOT.
IT'S NOT SUPPOSED TO BE ANYWAY.
BUT APPARENTLY, I'M ENJOYING IT.

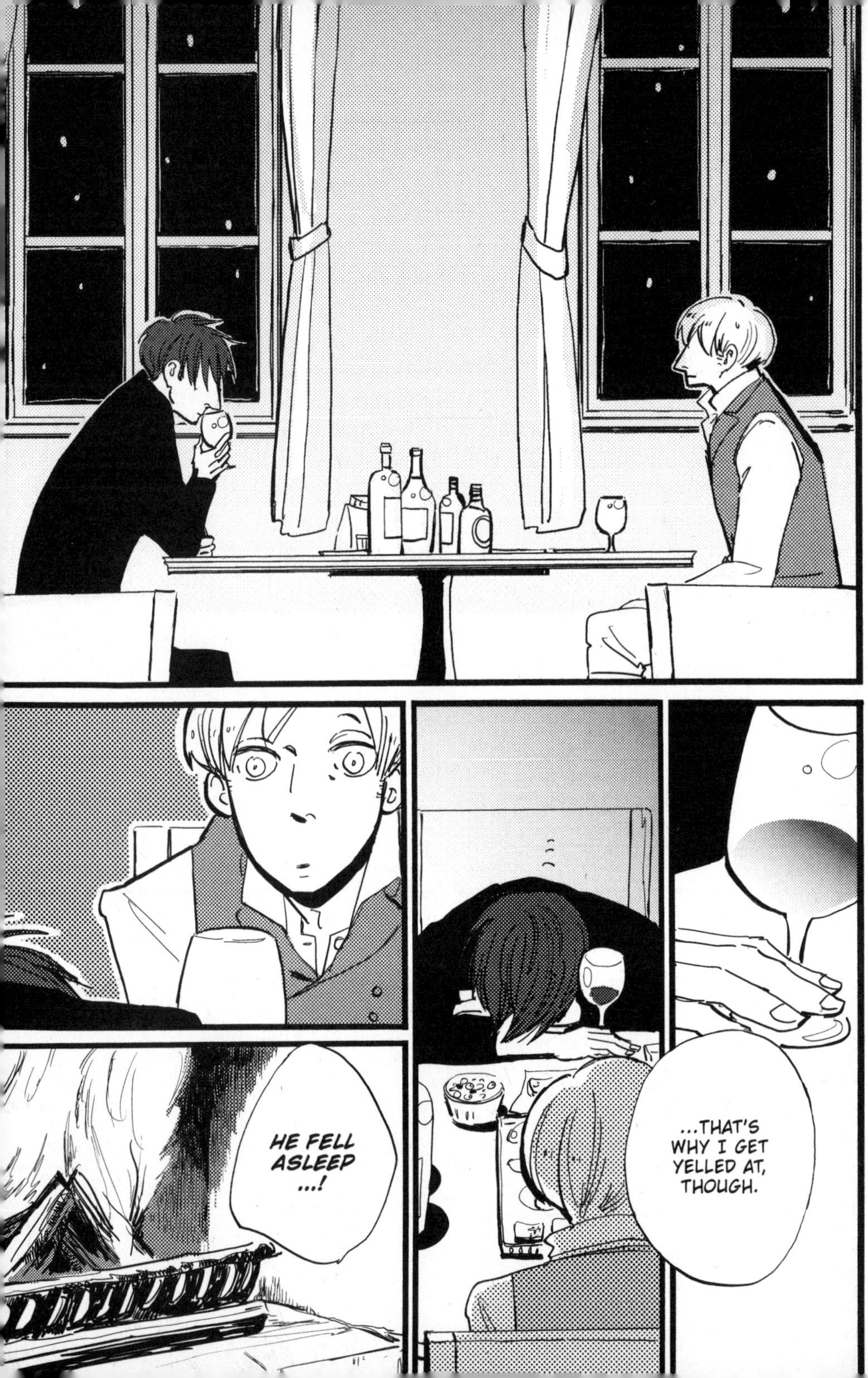
HE FELL ASLEEP ...!
...THAT'S WHY I GET YELLED AT, THOUGH.

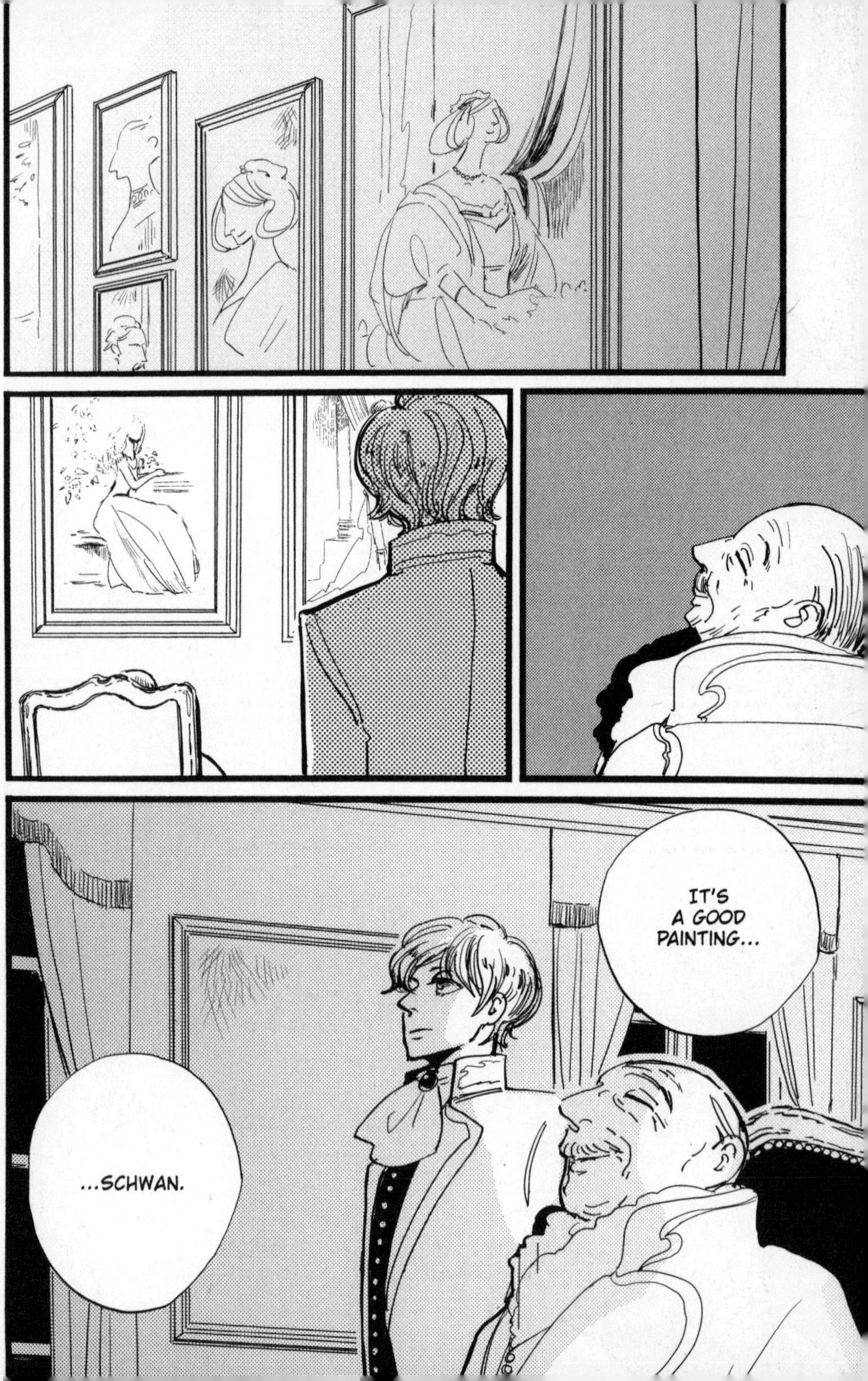
IT'S A GOOD PAINTING...
...SCHWAN.

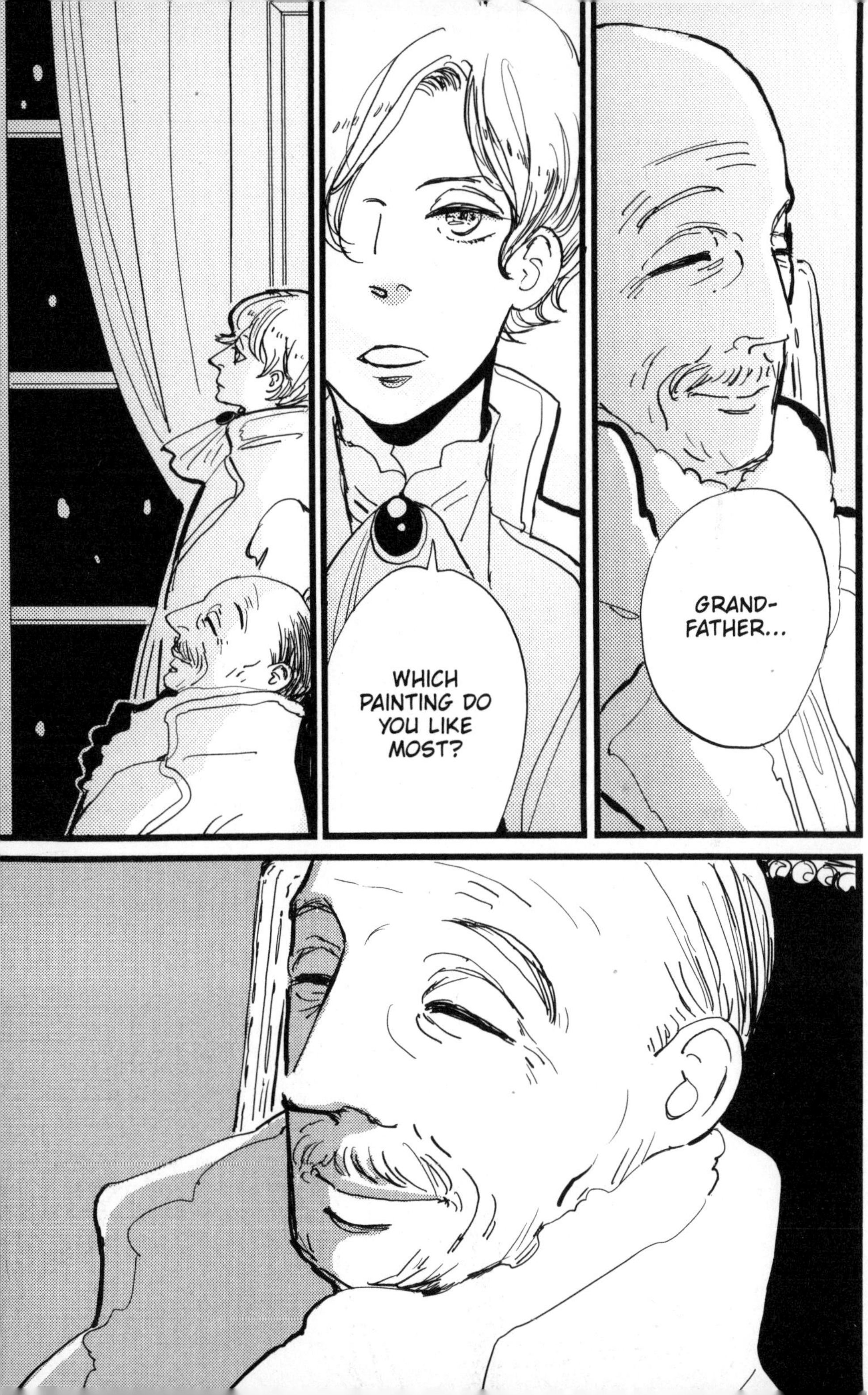
GRAND-FATHER...
WHICH PAINTING DO YOU LIKE MOST?

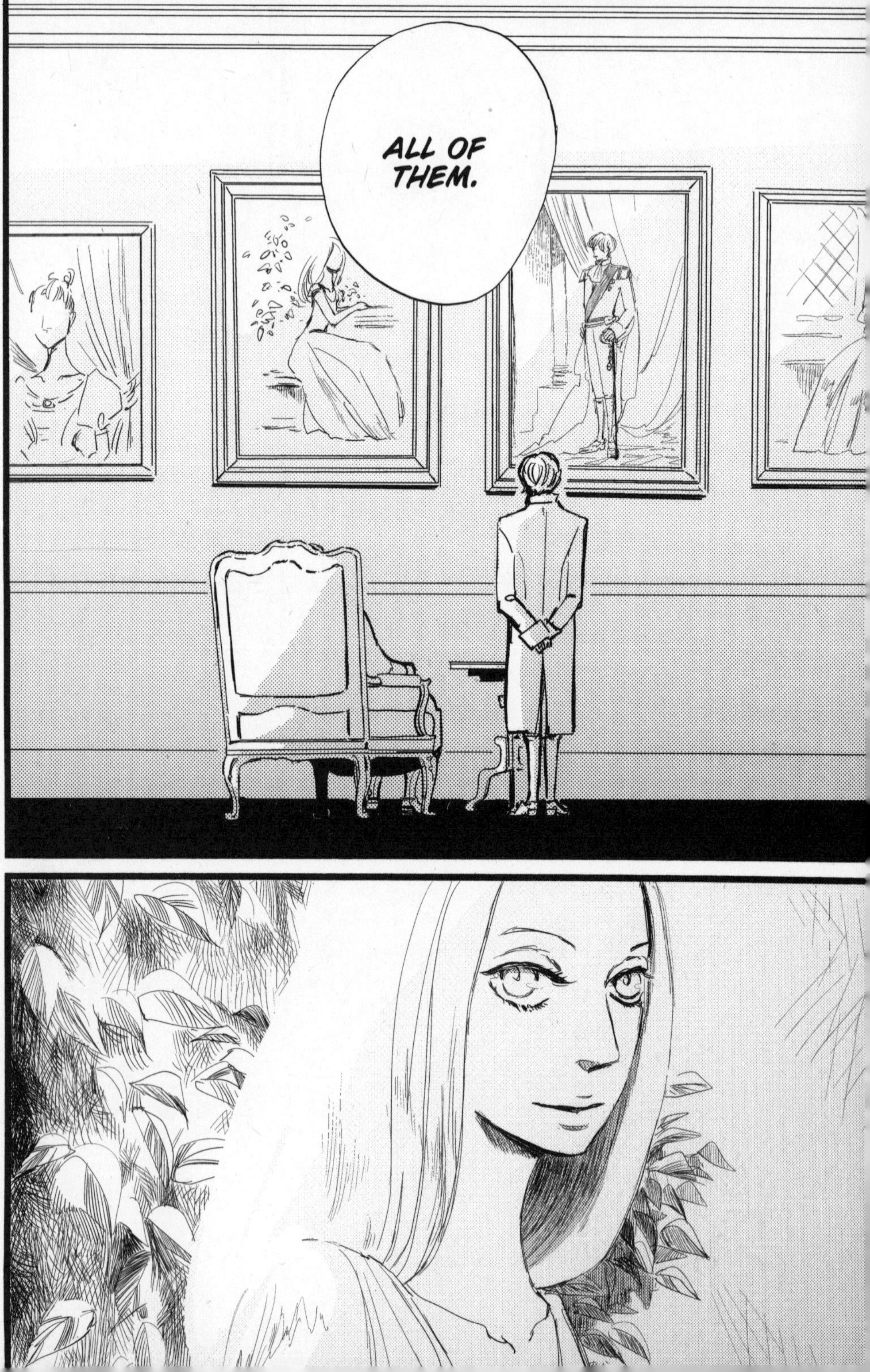
ALL OF THEM.

CHAPTER 21

Snack Time with a Certain Someone in Dowa

DEPT. ACCA 13 TERRITORY INSPECTION

PASS

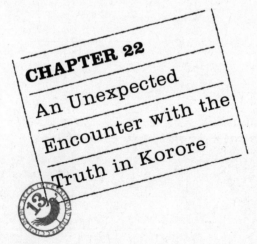

CHAPTER 22

An Unexpected

Encounter with the

Truth in Korore

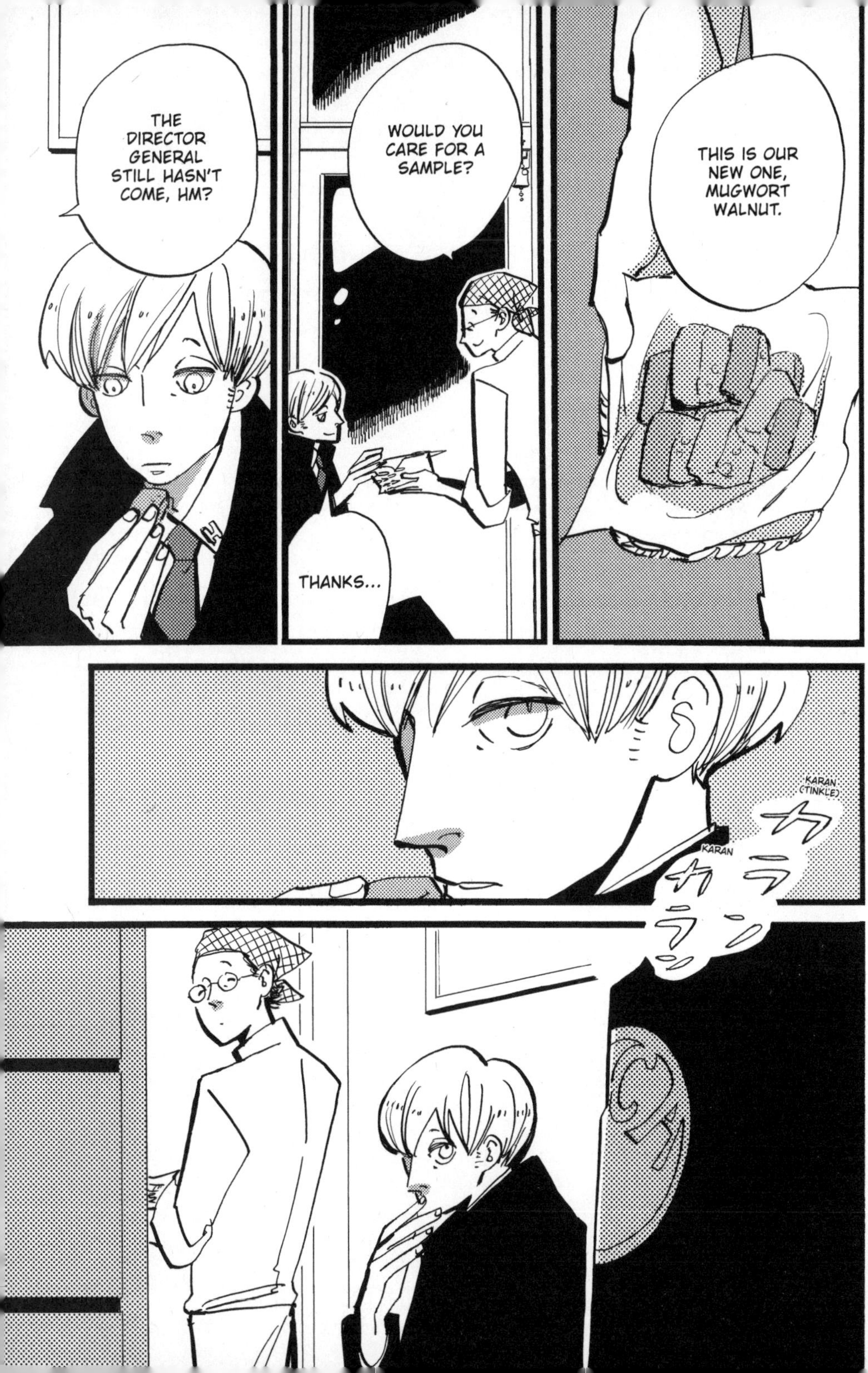
THIS IS OUR NEW ONE, MUGWORT WALNUT.
WOULD YOU CARE FOR A SAMPLE?
THANKS...
THE DIRECTOR GENERAL STILL HASN'T COME, HM?
KARAN (TINKLE)
カラン
KARAN
カラン

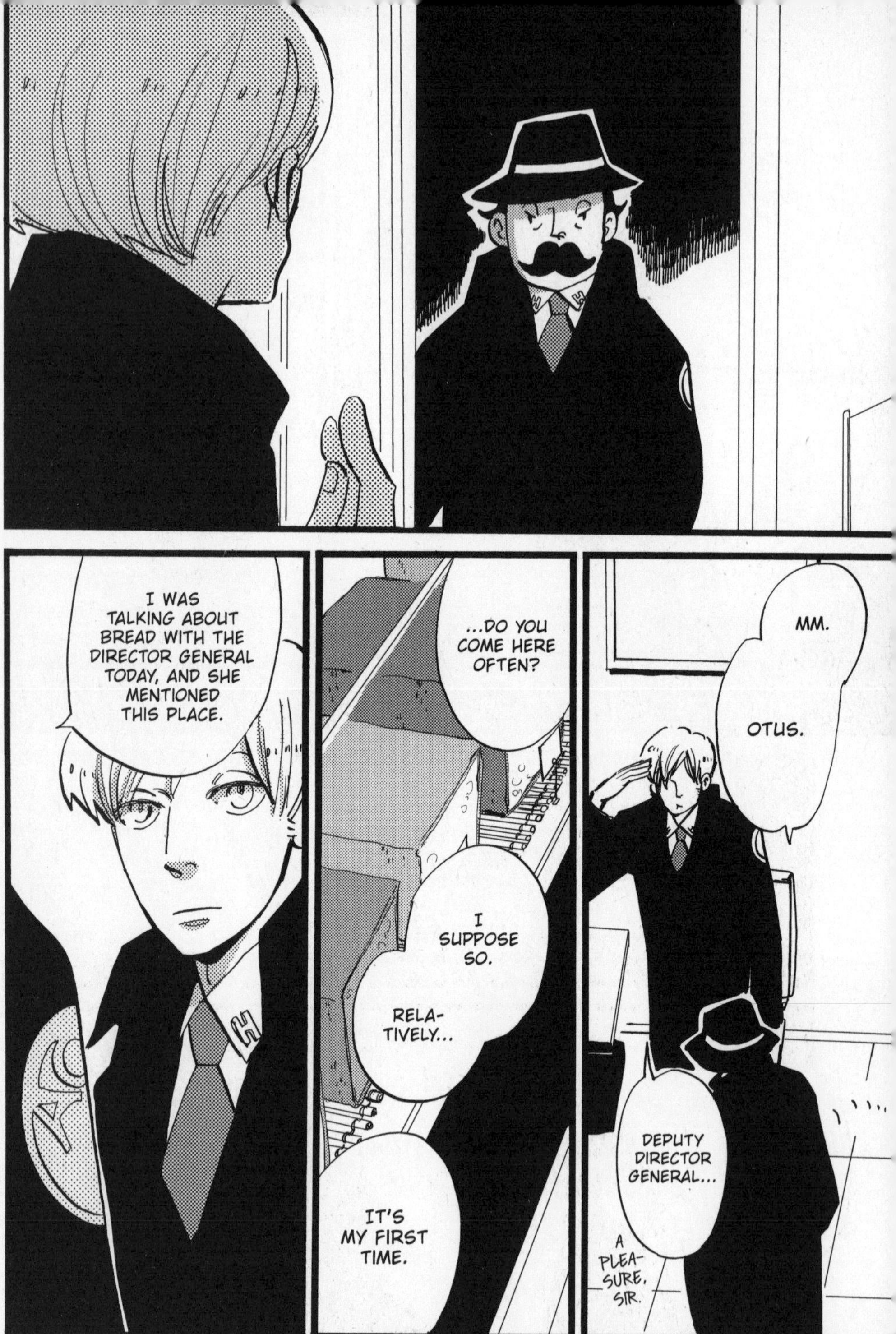
MM.
OTUS.
DEPUTY DIRECTOR GENERAL...
A PLEASURE, SIR.
...DO YOU COME HERE OFTEN?
I SUPPOSE SO.
RELATIVELY...
IT'S MY FIRST TIME.
I WAS TALKING ABOUT BREAD WITH THE DIRECTOR GENERAL TODAY, AND SHE MENTIONED THIS PLACE.

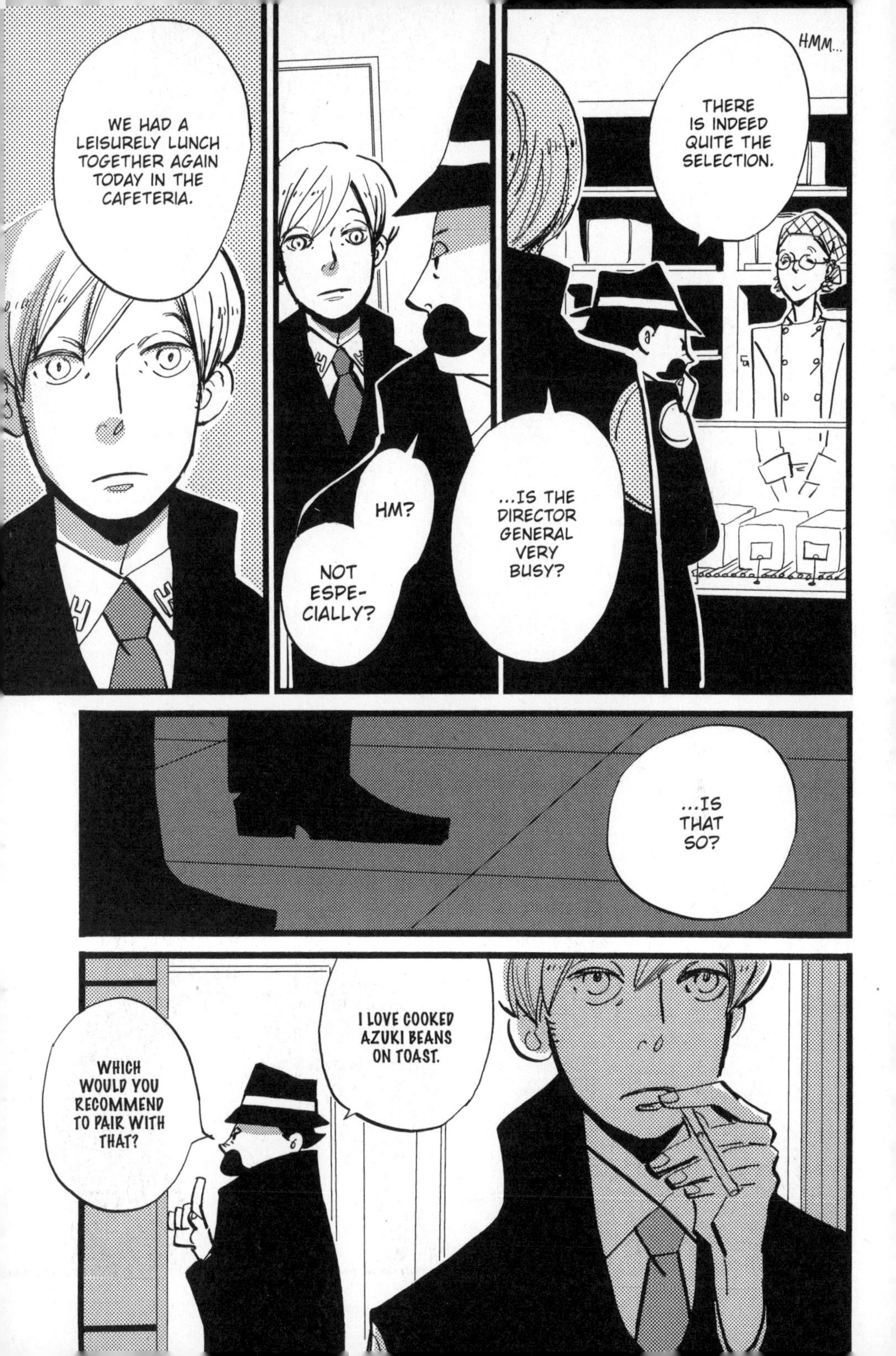
HMM...
THERE IS INDEED QUITE THE SELECTION.
...IS THE DIRECTOR GENERAL VERY BUSY?
HM?
NOT ESPE-CIALLY?
WE HAD A LEISURELY LUNCH TOGETHER AGAIN TODAY IN THE CAFETERIA.
...IS THAT SO?
I LOVE COOKED AZUKI BEANS ON TOAST.
WHICH WOULD YOU RECOMMEND TO PAIR WITH THAT?

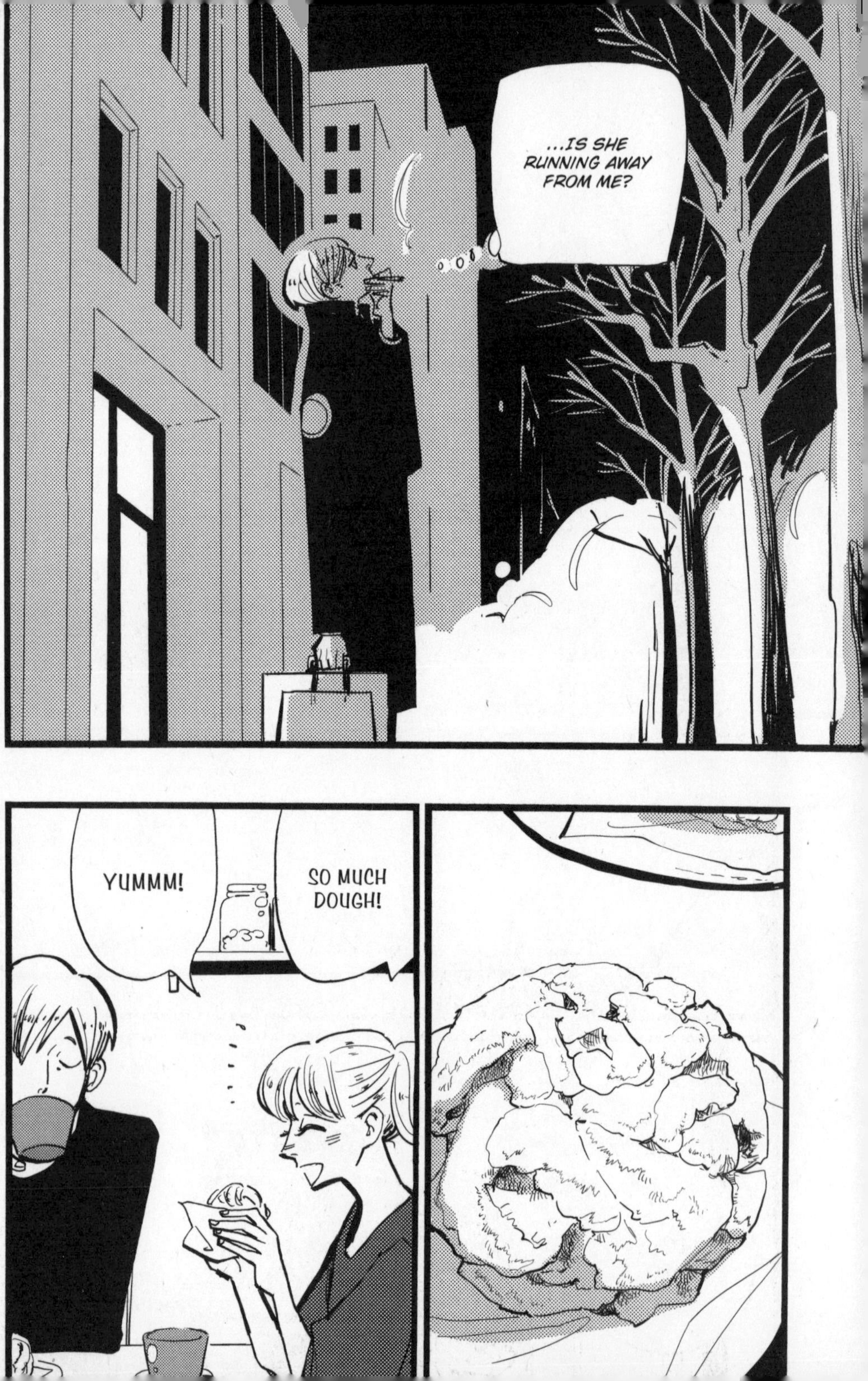
...IS SHE RUNNING AWAY FROM ME?
SO MUCH DOUGH!
YUMMM!

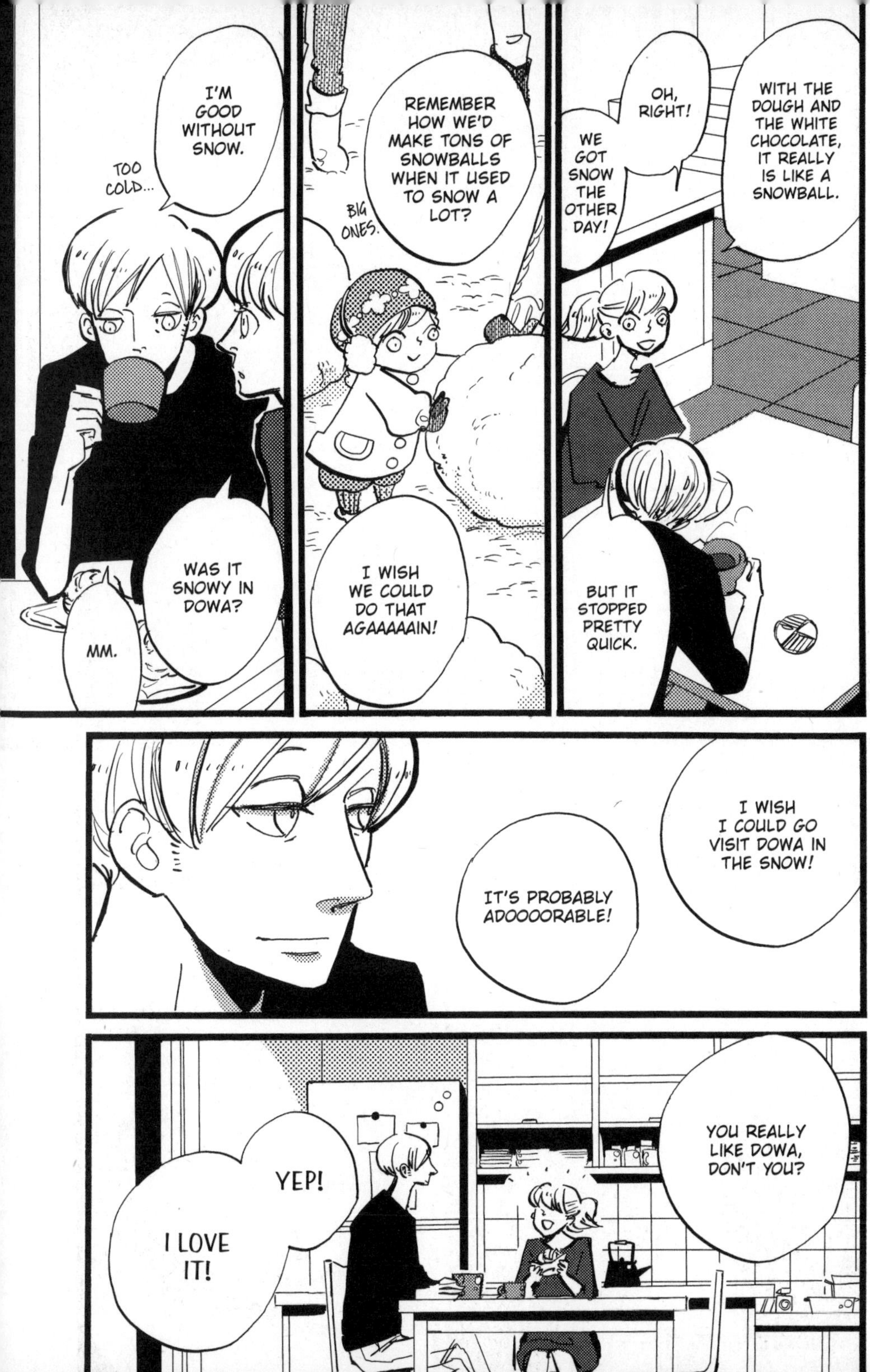
WITH THE DOUGH AND THE WHITE CHOCOLATE, IT REALLY IS LIKE A SNOWBALL.
OH, RIGHT!
WE GOT SNOW THE OTHER DAY!
BUT IT STOPPED PRETTY QUICK.
REMEMBER HOW WE'D MAKE TONS OF SNOWBALLS WHEN IT USED TO SNOW A LOT?
BIG ONES.
I WISH WE COULD DO THAT AGAAAAAIN!
I'M GOOD WITHOUT SNOW.
TOO COLD...
WAS IT SNOWY IN DOWA?
MM.
I WISH I COULD GO VISIT DOWA IN THE SNOW!
IT'S PROBABLY ADOOOORABLE!
YOU REALLY LIKE DOWA, DON'T YOU?
YEP!
I LOVE IT!

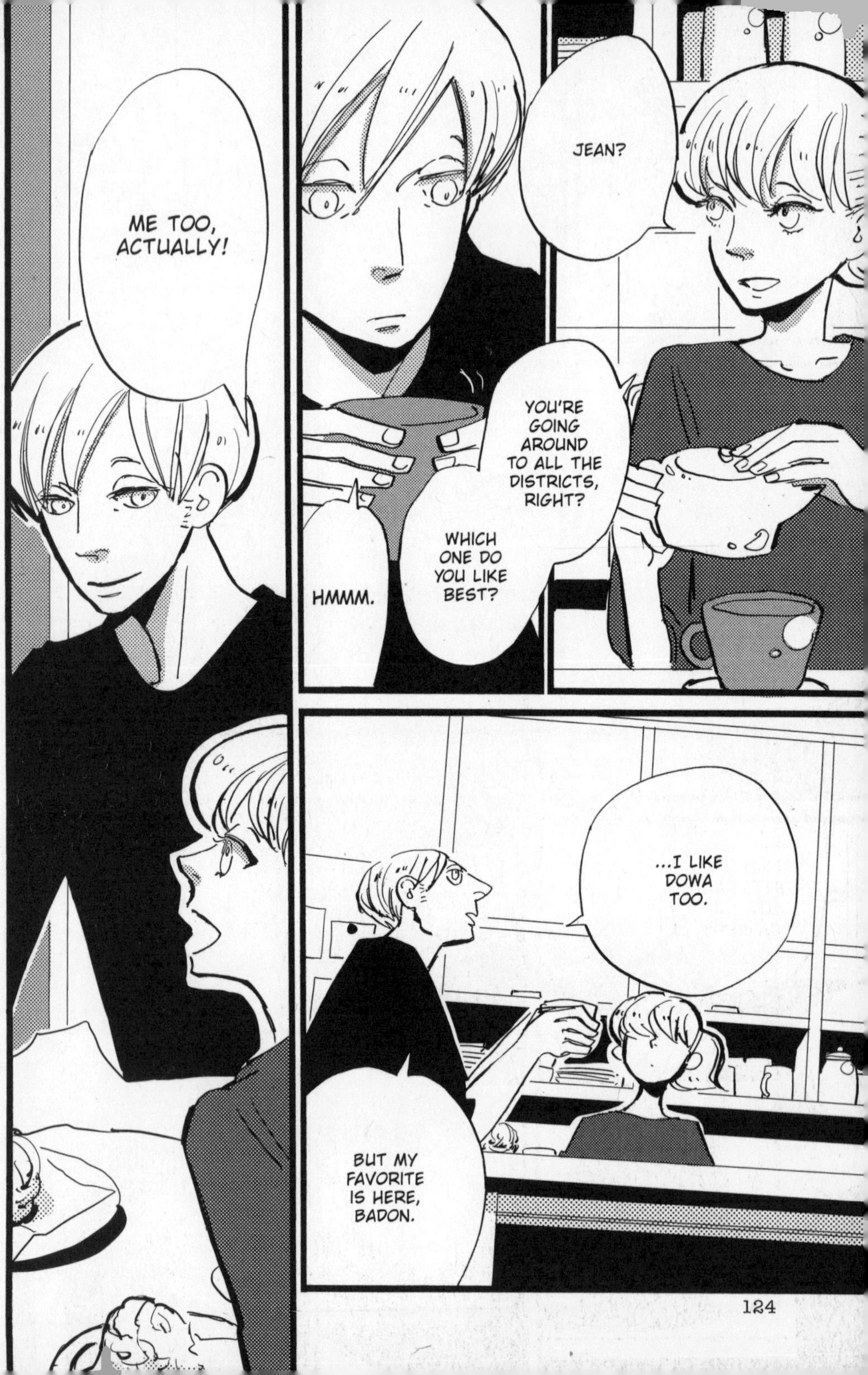
JEAN?
YOU'RE GOING AROUND TO ALL THE DISTRICTS, RIGHT?
WHICH ONE DO YOU LIKE BEST?
HMMM.
...I LIKE DOWA TOO.
BUT MY FAVORITE IS HERE, BADON.
ME TOO, ACTUALLY!

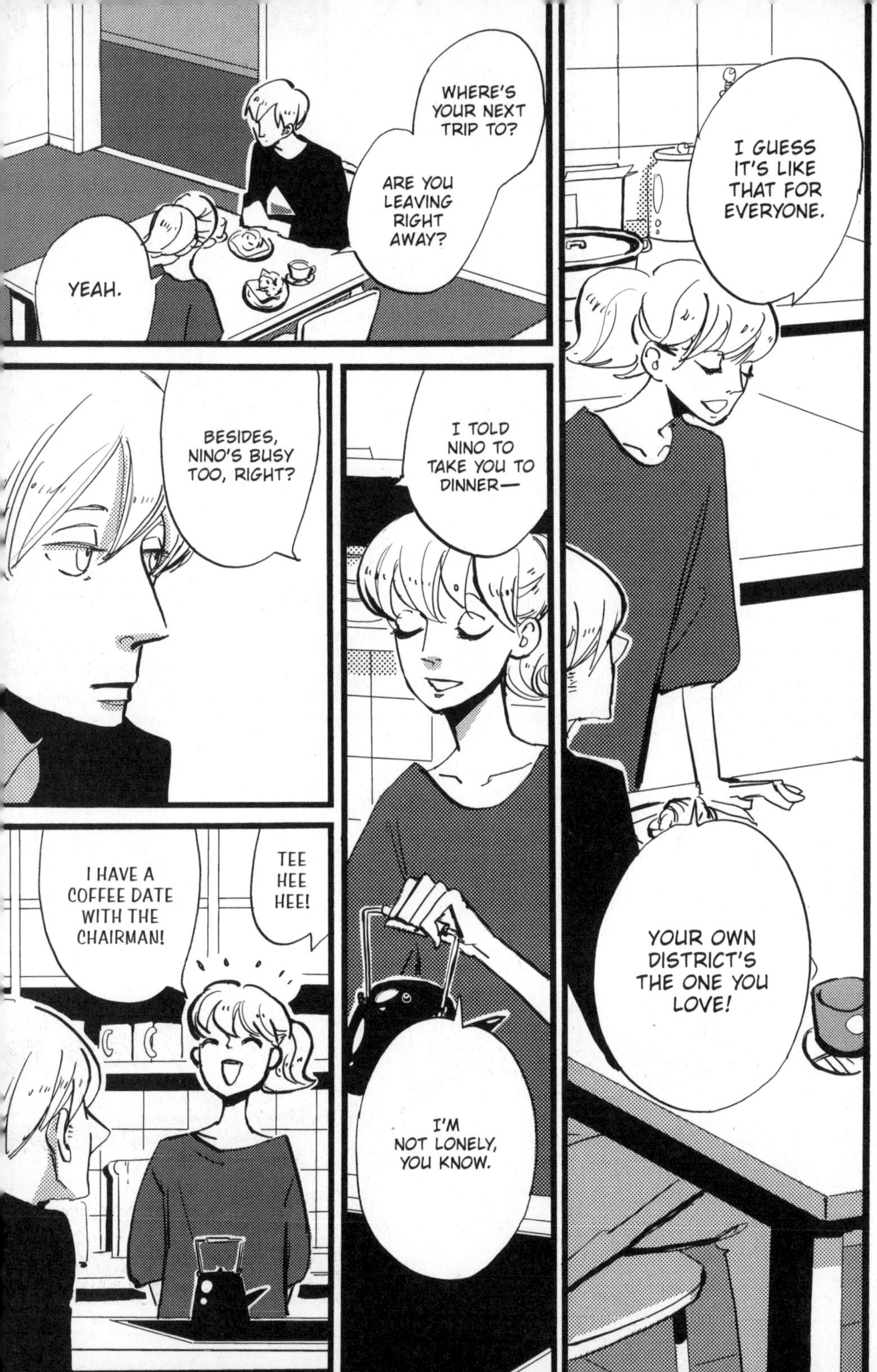
WHERE'S YOUR NEXT TRIP TO?
ARE YOU LEAVING RIGHT AWAY?
YEAH.
I GUESS IT'S LIKE THAT FOR EVERYONE.
YOUR OWN DISTRICT'S THE ONE YOU LOVE!
I TOLD NINO TO TAKE YOU TO DINNER—
I'M NOT LONELY, YOU KNOW.
BESIDES, NINO'S BUSY TOO, RIGHT?
TEE HEE HEE!
I HAVE A COFFEE DATE WITH THE CHAIRMAN!

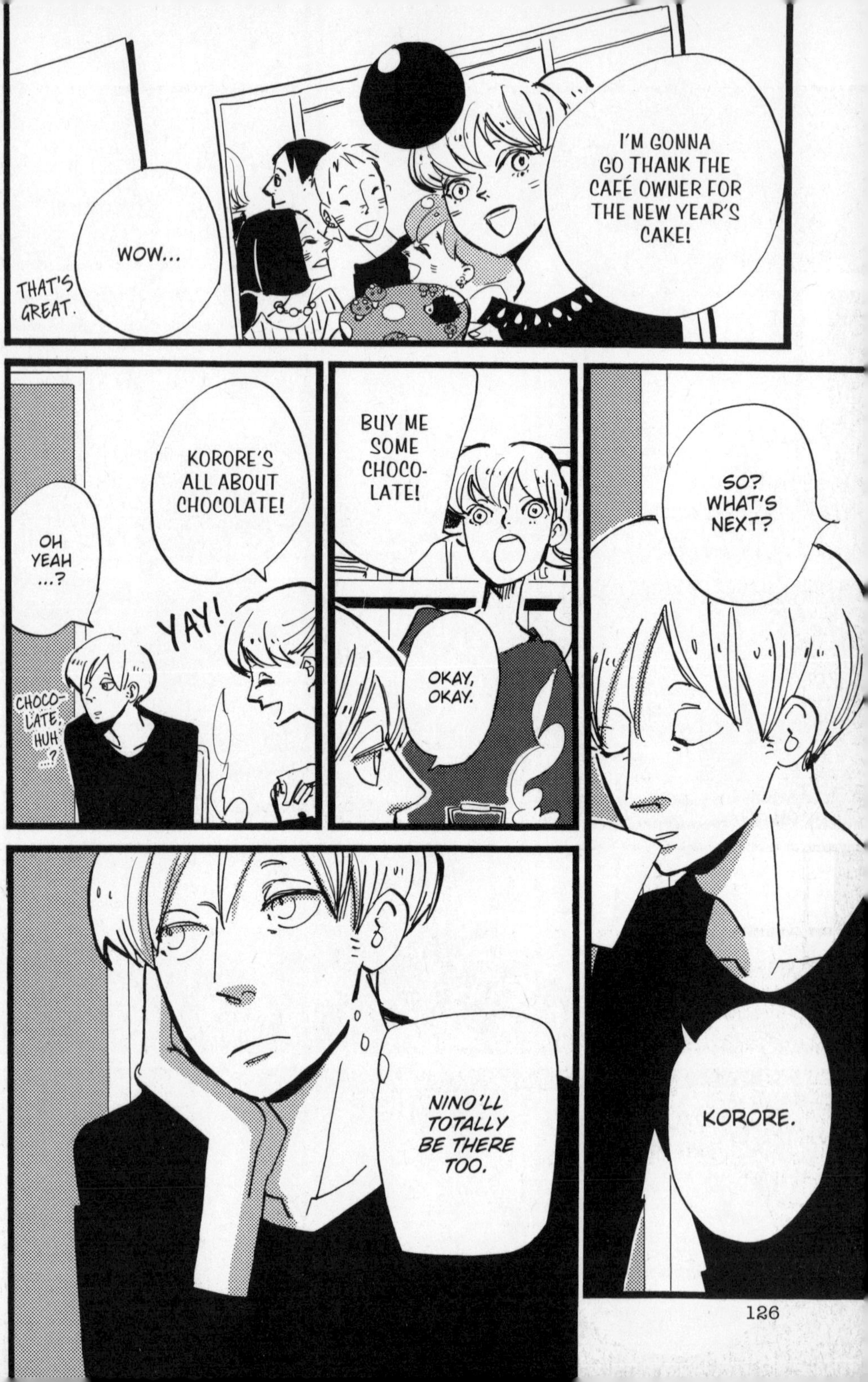
I'M GONNA GO THANK THE CAFÉ OWNER FOR THE NEW YEAR'S CAKE!
WOW...
THAT'S GREAT.
SO? WHAT'S NEXT?
KORORE.
BUY ME SOME CHOCO-LATE!
OKAY, OKAY.
KORORE'S ALL ABOUT CHOCOLATE!
YAY!
OH YEAH ...?
CHOCO-LATE, HUH ...?
NINO'LL TOTALLY BE THERE TOO.

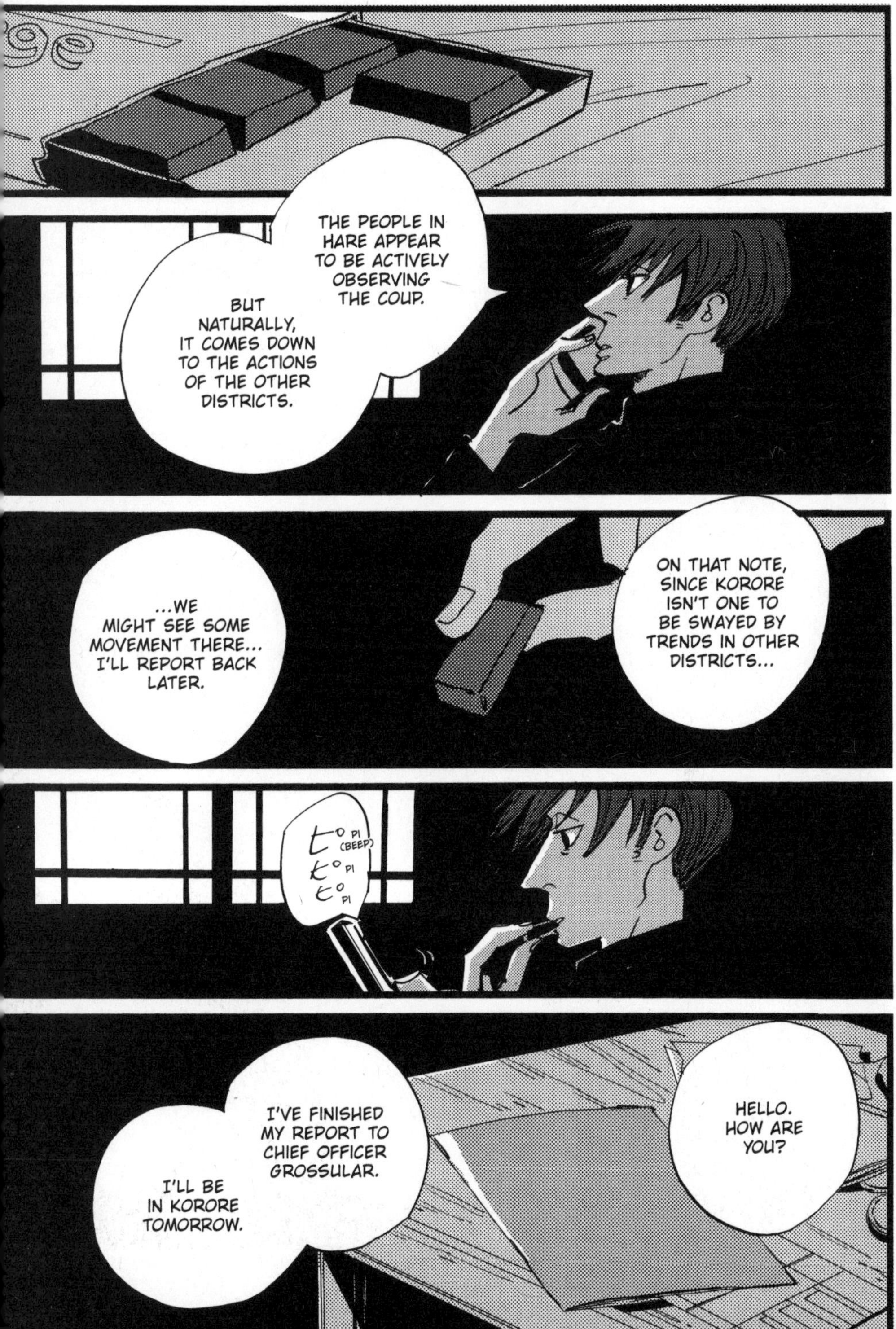
THE PEOPLE IN HARE APPEAR TO BE ACTIVELY OBSERVING THE COUP.
BUT NATURALLY, IT COMES DOWN TO THE ACTIONS OF THE OTHER DISTRICTS.
ON THAT NOTE, SINCE KORORE ISN'T ONE TO BE SWAYED BY TRENDS IN OTHER DISTRICTS...
...WE MIGHT SEE SOME MOVEMENT THERE... I'LL REPORT BACK LATER.
ピ PI (BEEP) ピ PI ピ PI
HELLO. HOW ARE YOU?
I'VE FINISHED MY REPORT TO CHIEF OFFICER GROSSULAR.
I'LL BE IN KORORE TOMORROW.

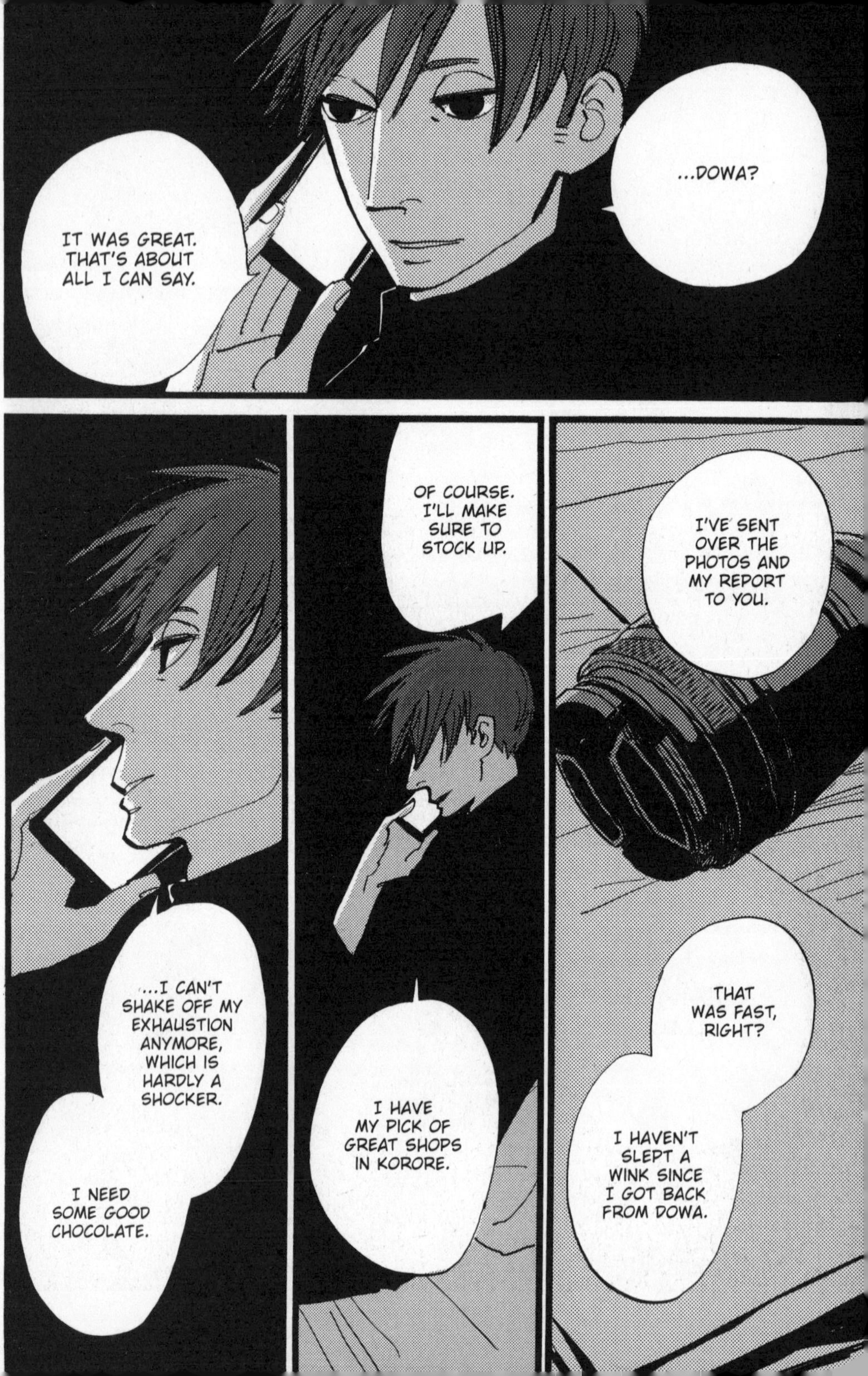
...DOWA?
IT WAS GREAT. THAT'S ABOUT ALL I CAN SAY.
I'VE SENT OVER THE PHOTOS AND MY REPORT TO YOU.
THAT WAS FAST, RIGHT?
I HAVEN'T SLEPT A WINK SINCE I GOT BACK FROM DOWA.
OF COURSE. I'LL MAKE SURE TO STOCK UP.
I HAVE MY PICK OF GREAT SHOPS IN KORORE.
...I CAN'T SHAKE OFF MY EXHAUSTION ANYMORE, WHICH IS HARDLY A SHOCKER.
I NEED SOME GOOD CHOCOLATE.

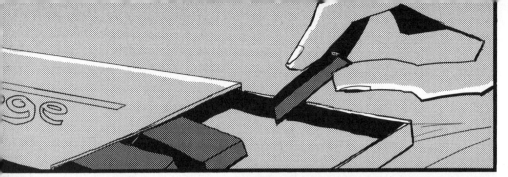

THIRTY YEARS, HUH...?

...I'VE GOTTEN OLD.

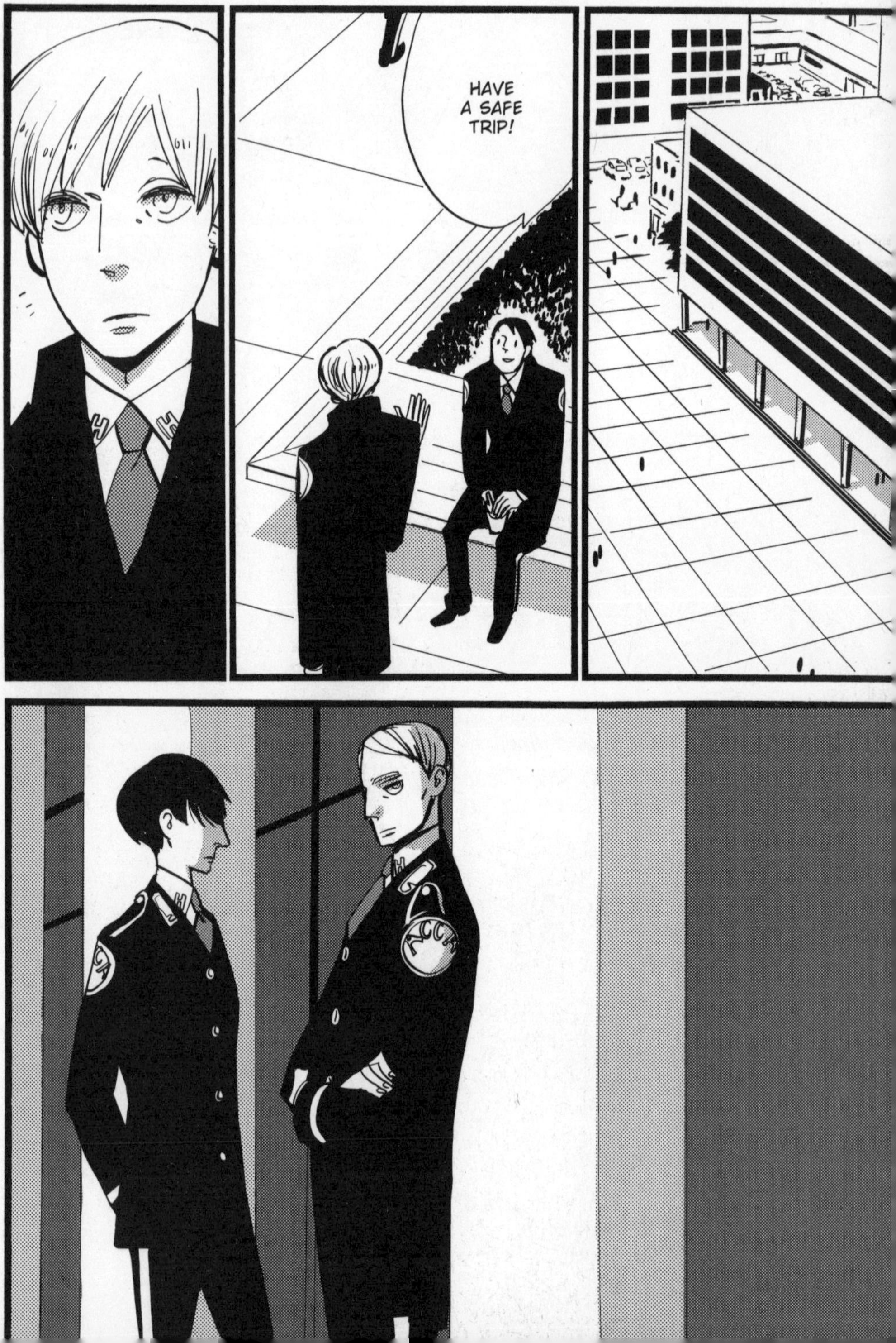
HAVE A SAFE TRIP!

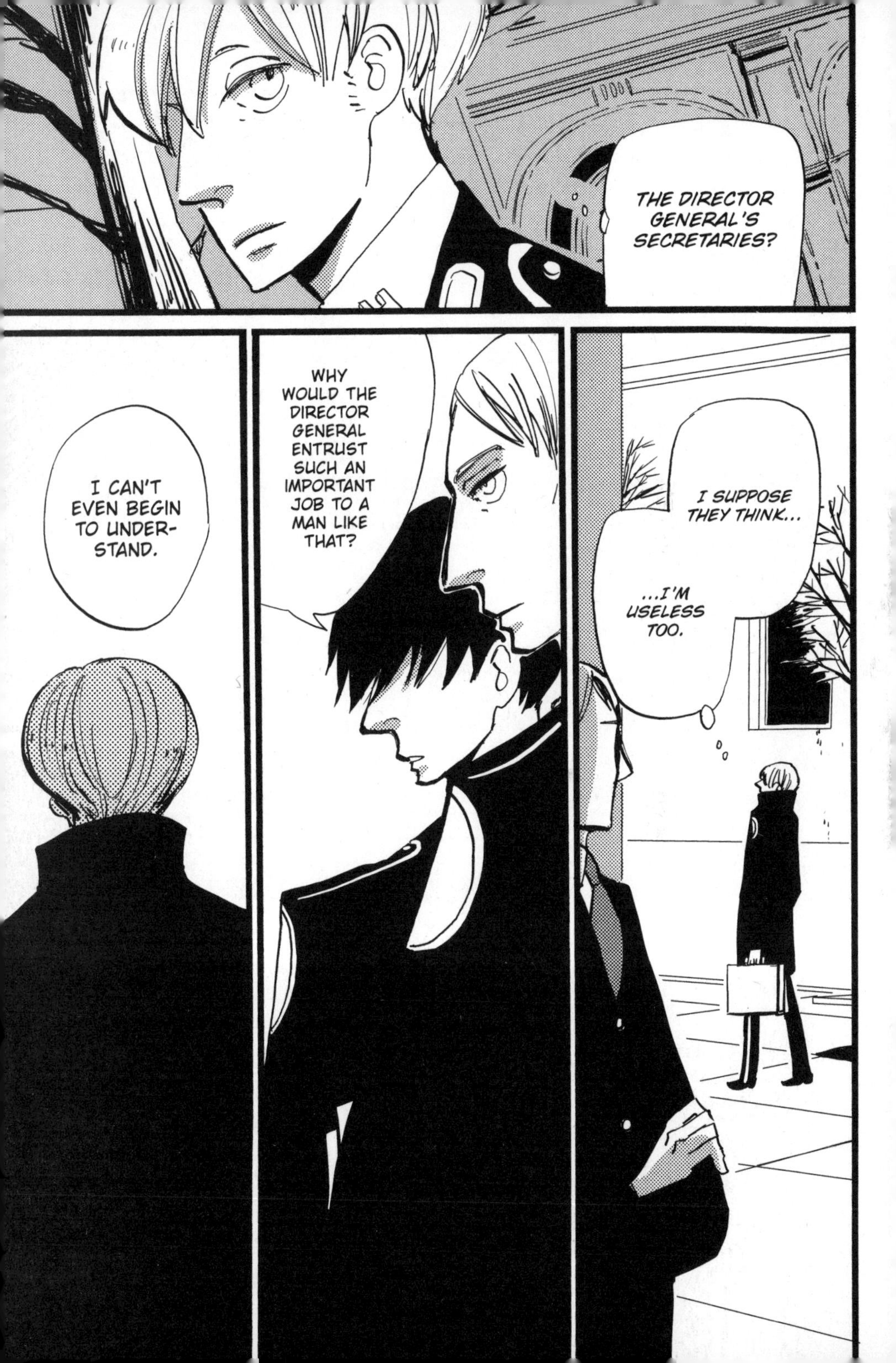
THE DIRECTOR GENERAL'S SECRETARIES?
I SUPPOSE THEY THINK...
...I'M USELESS TOO.
WHY WOULD THE DIRECTOR GENERAL ENTRUST SUCH AN IMPORTANT JOB TO A MAN LIKE THAT?
I CAN'T EVEN BEGIN TO UNDER-STAND.

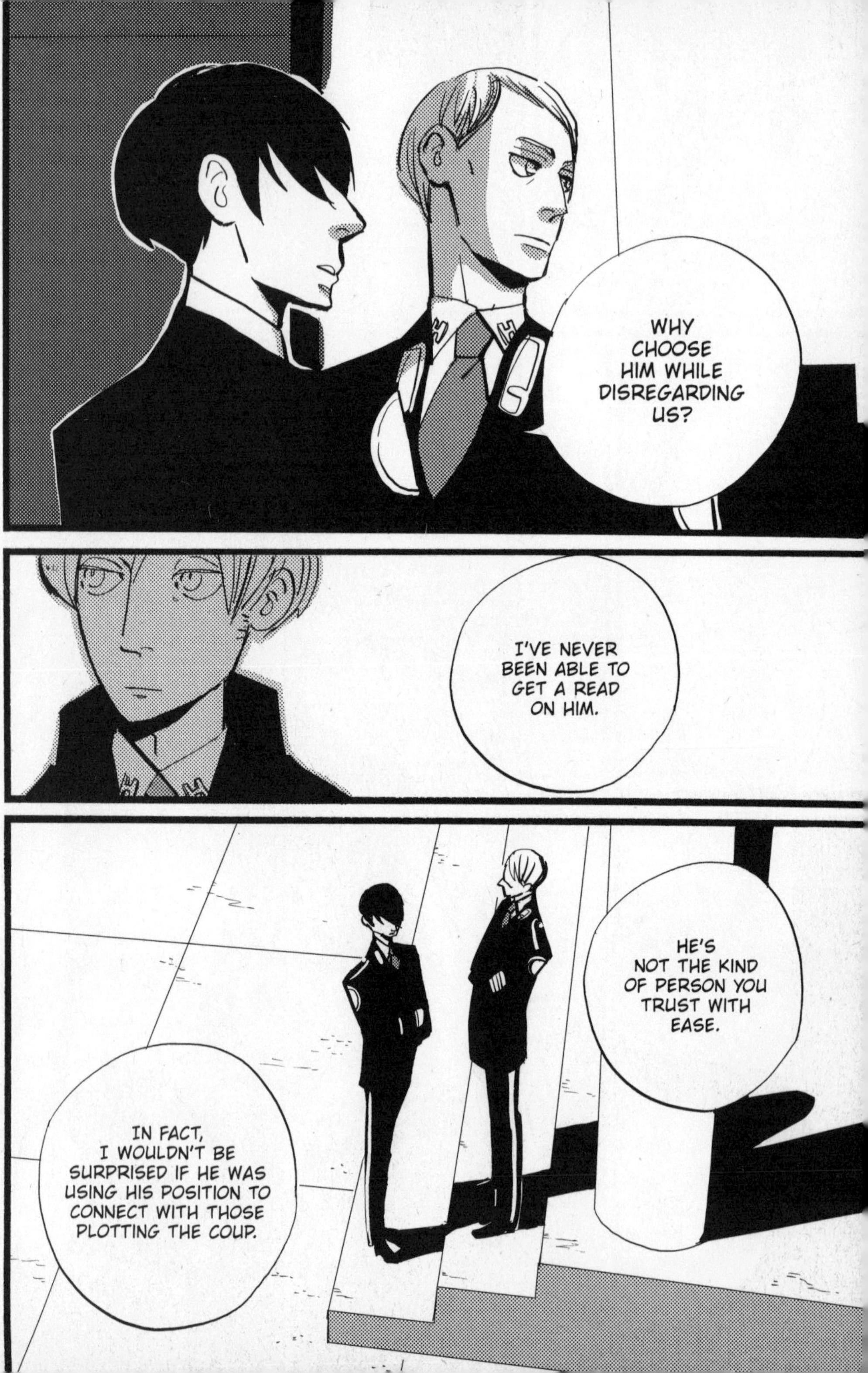
WHY CHOOSE HIM WHILE DISREGARDING US?
I'VE NEVER BEEN ABLE TO GET A READ ON HIM.
HE'S NOT THE KIND OF PERSON YOU TRUST WITH EASE.
IN FACT, I WOULDN'T BE SURPRISED IF HE WAS USING HIS POSITION TO CONNECT WITH THOSE PLOTTING THE COUP.

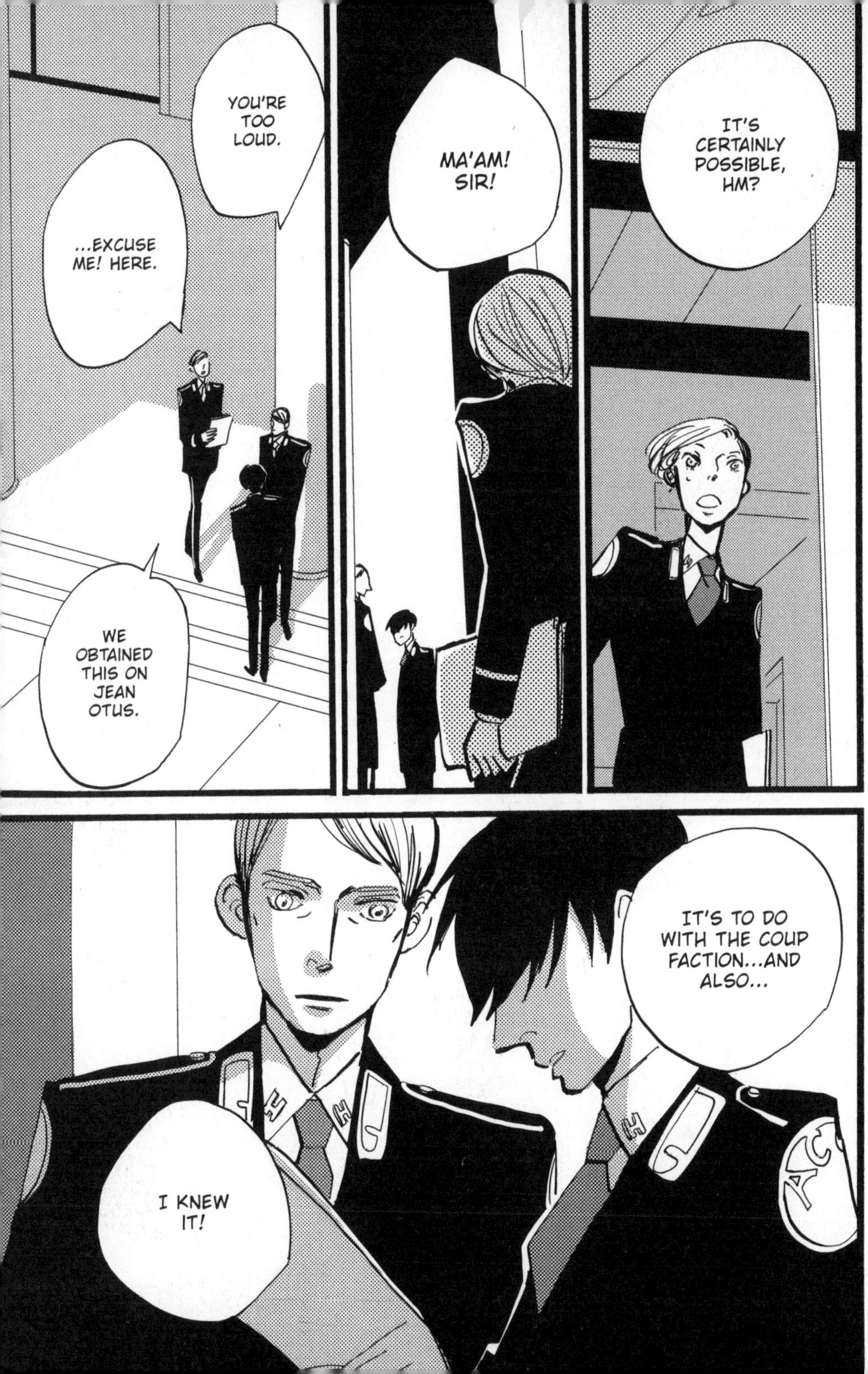
IT'S CERTAINLY POSSIBLE, HM?
MA'AM! SIR!
YOU'RE TOO LOUD.
...EXCUSE ME! HERE.
WE OBTAINED THIS ON JEAN OTUS.
IT'S TO DO WITH THE COUP FACTION...AND ALSO...
I KNEW IT!

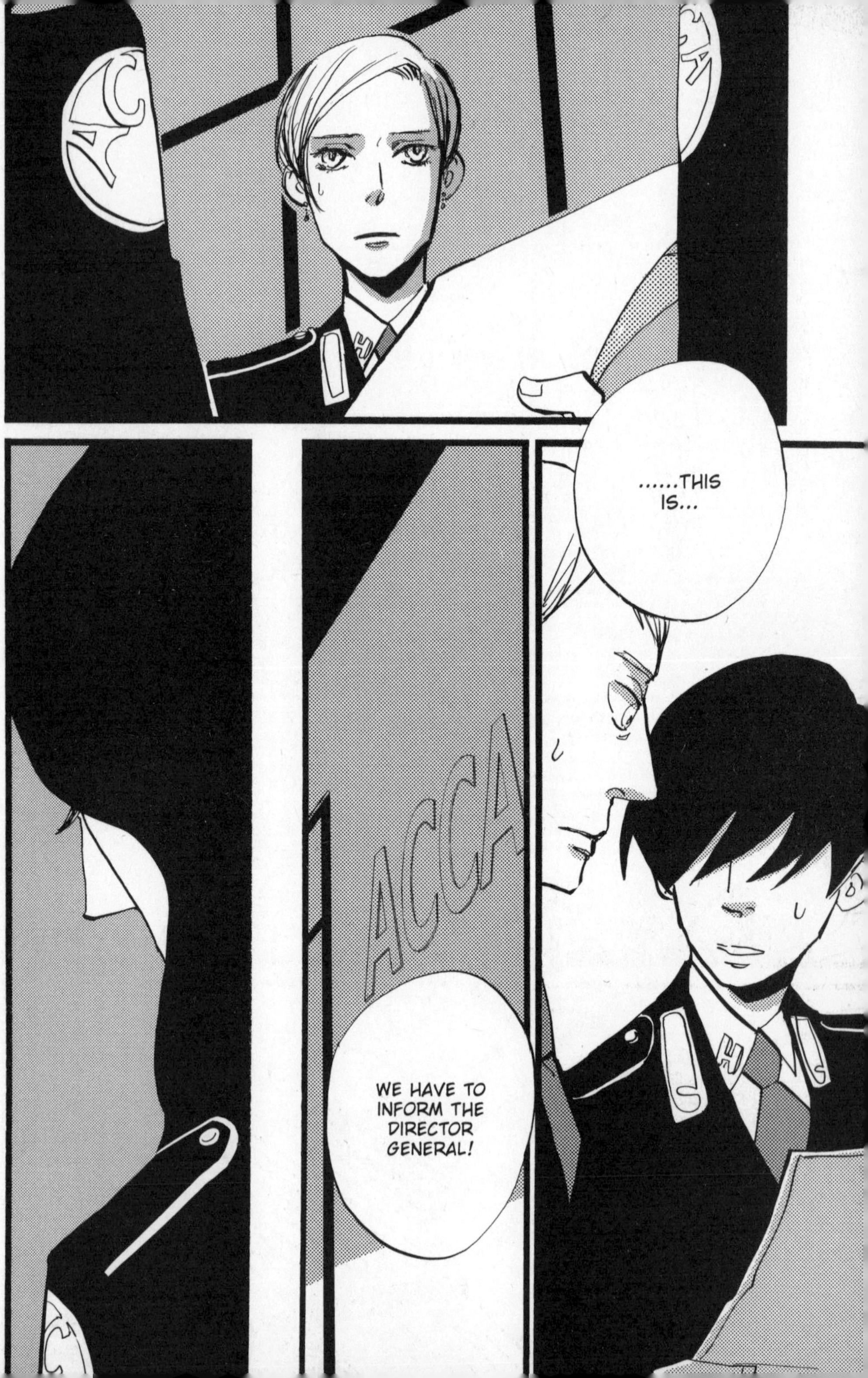
......THIS IS...
ACCA
WE HAVE TO INFORM THE DIRECTOR GENERAL!

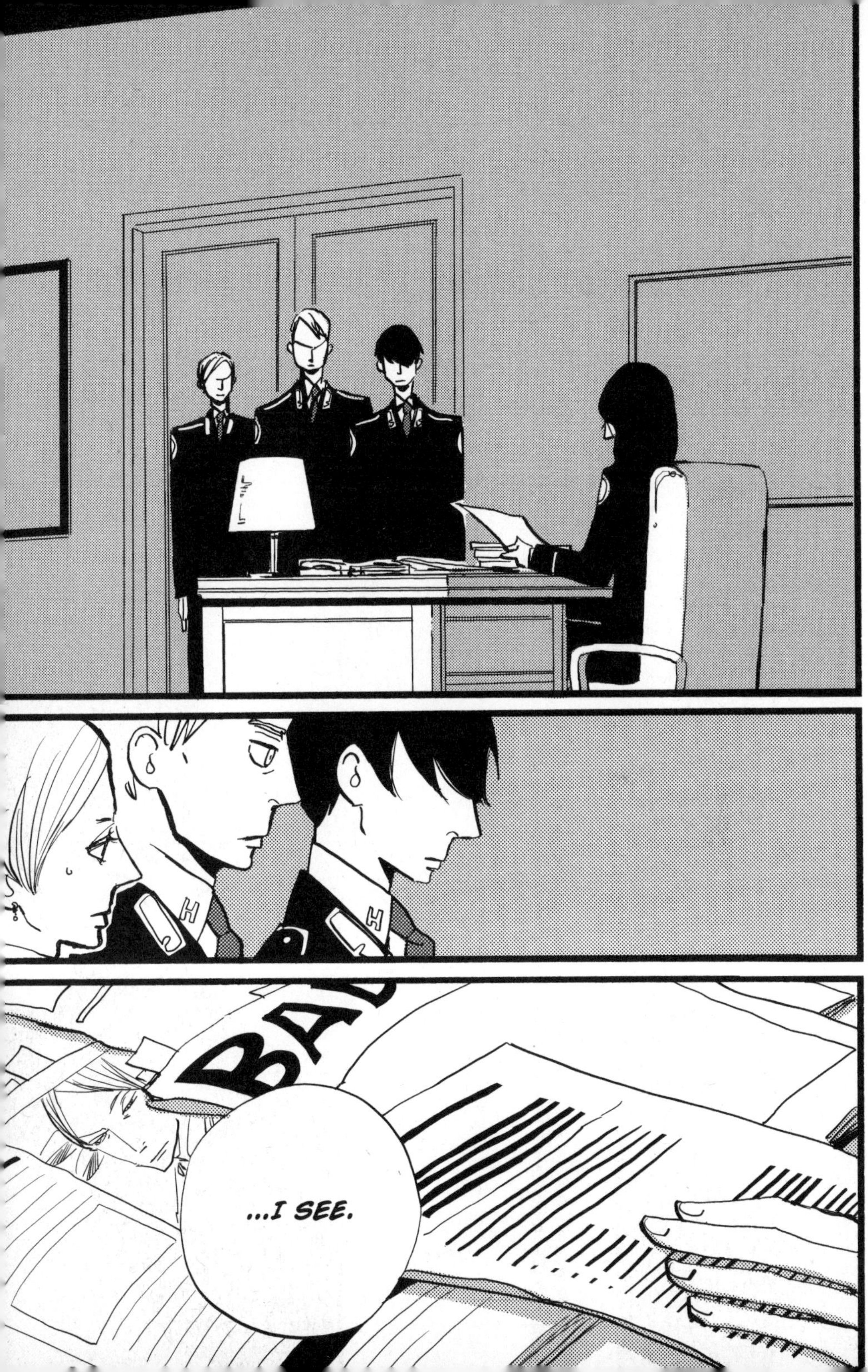
...I SEE.

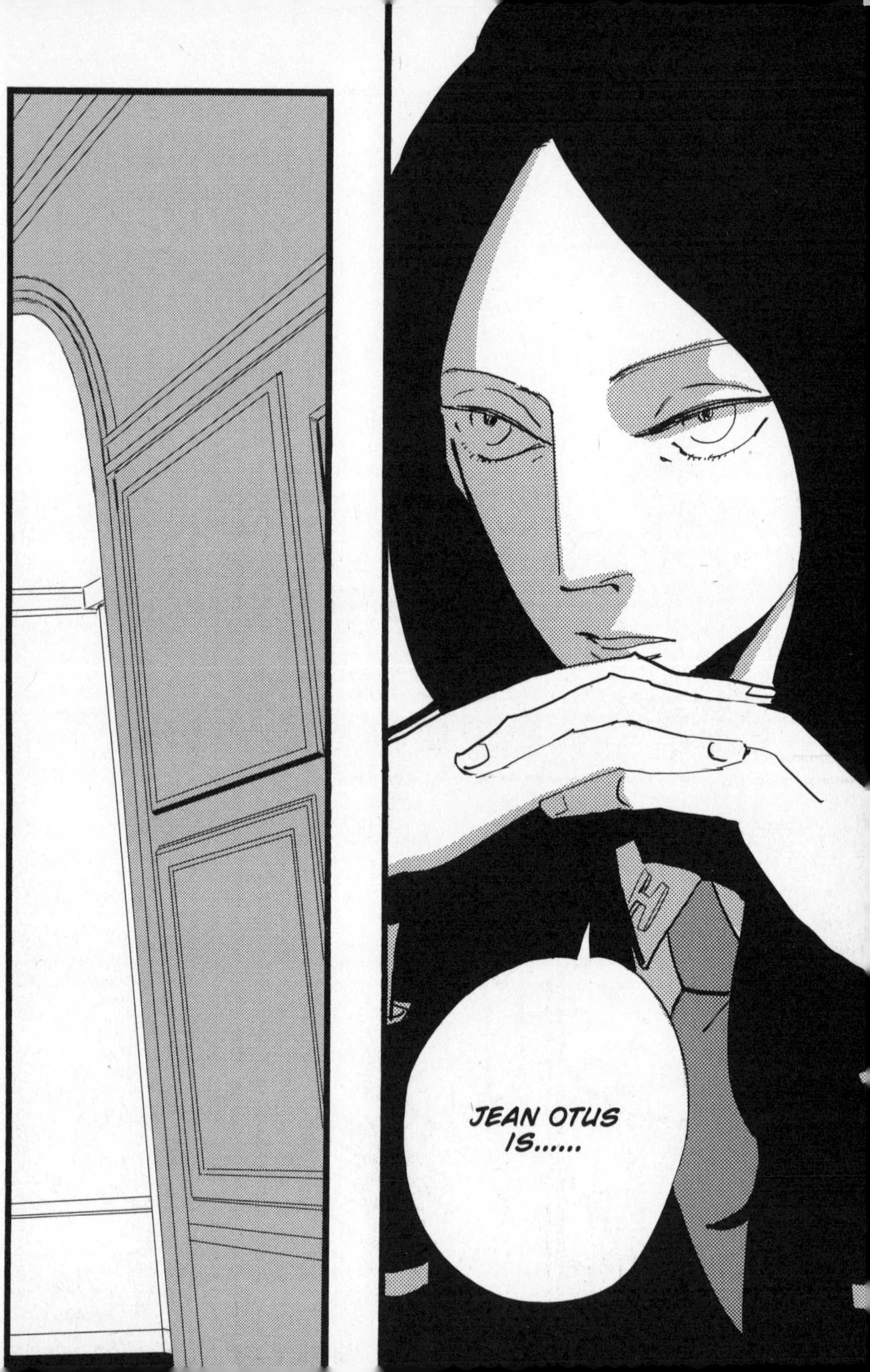
JEAN OTUS IS......

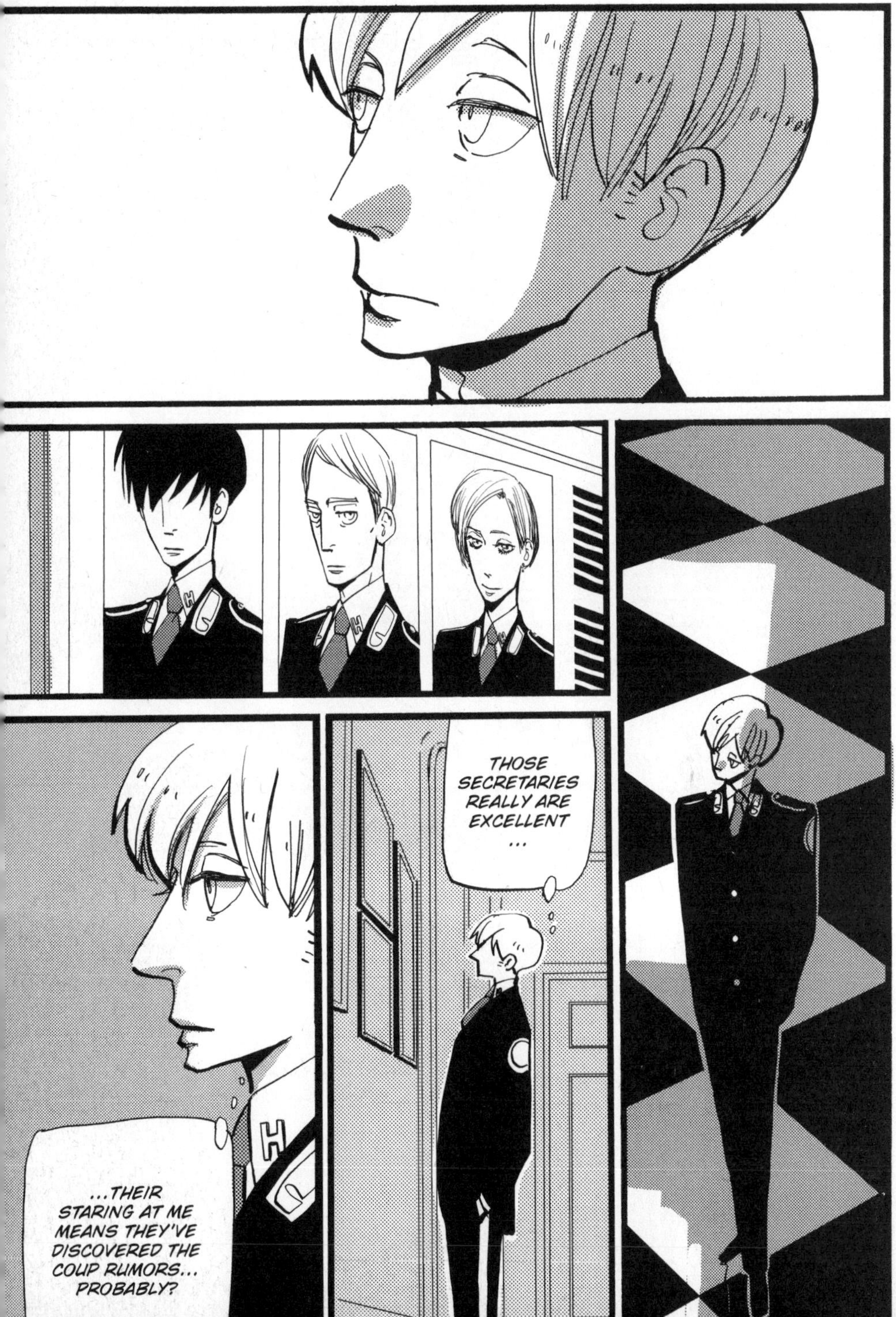
THOSE SECRETARIES REALLY ARE EXCELLENT ...
...THEIR STARING AT ME MEANS THEY'VE DISCOVERED THE COUP RUMORS... PROBABLY?

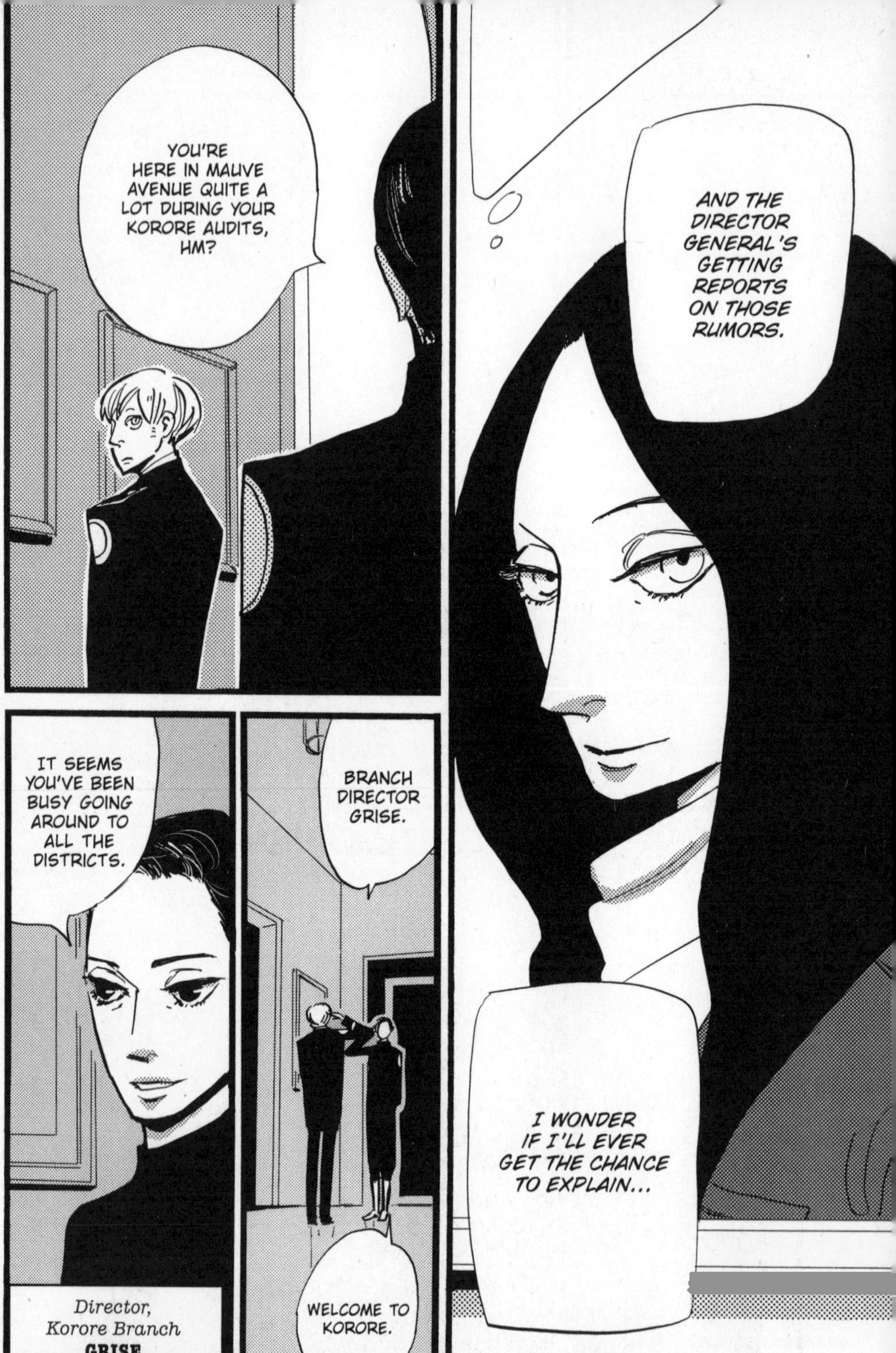
AND THE DIRECTOR GENERAL'S GETTING REPORTS ON THOSE RUMORS.
I WONDER IF I'LL EVER GET THE CHANCE TO EXPLAIN...
YOU'RE HERE IN MAUVE AVENUE QUITE A LOT DURING YOUR KORORE AUDITS, HM?
BRANCH DIRECTOR GRISE.
WELCOME TO KORORE.
IT SEEMS YOU'VE BEEN BUSY GOING AROUND TO ALL THE DISTRICTS.
Director, Korore Branch
GRISE

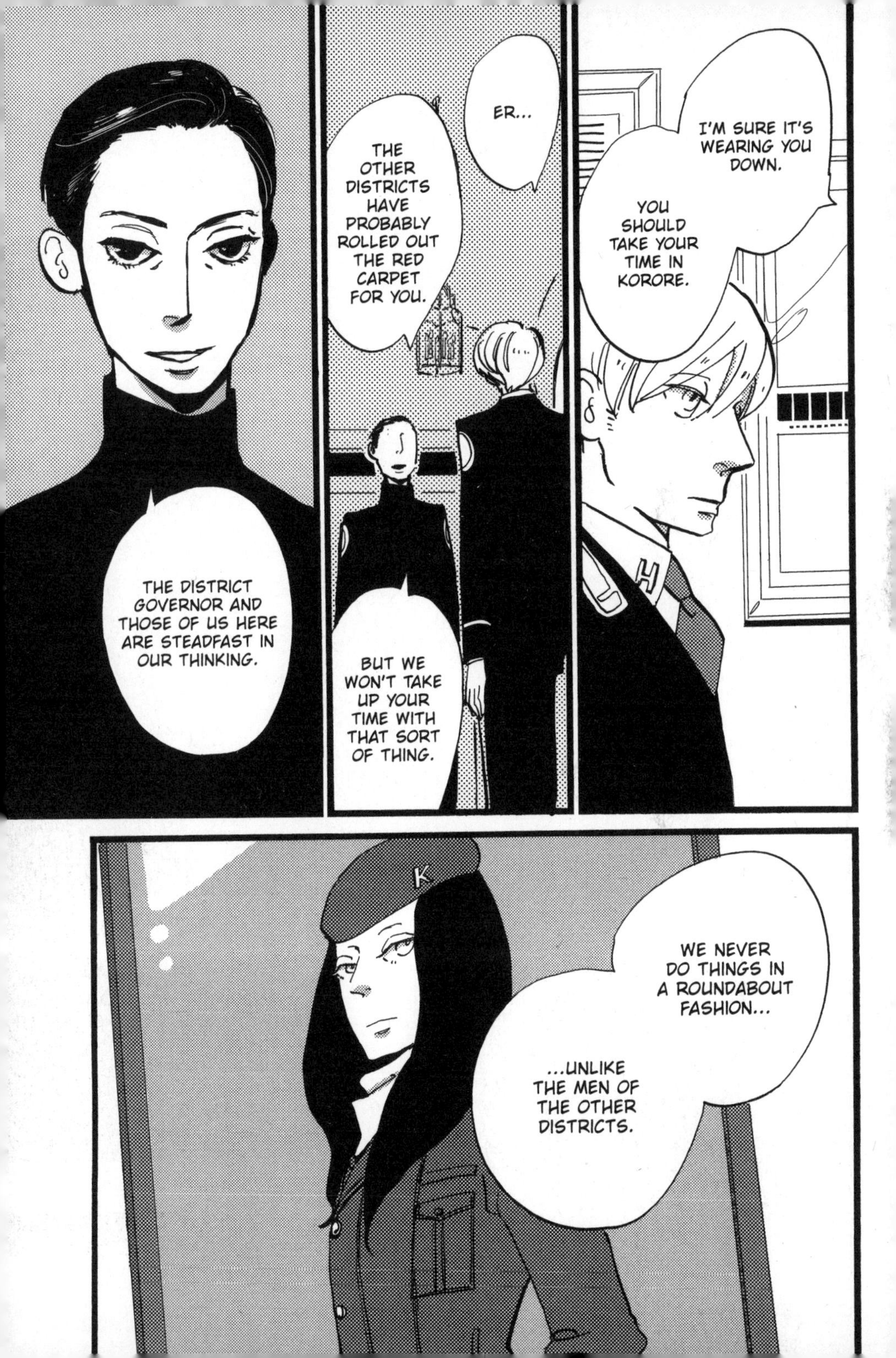
I'M SURE IT'S WEARING YOU DOWN.
YOU SHOULD TAKE YOUR TIME IN KORORE.
ER...
THE OTHER DISTRICTS HAVE PROBABLY ROLLED OUT THE RED CARPET FOR YOU.
...
BUT WE WON'T TAKE UP YOUR TIME WITH THAT SORT OF THING.
THE DISTRICT GOVERNOR AND THOSE OF US HERE ARE STEADFAST IN OUR THINKING.
WE NEVER DO THINGS IN A ROUNDABOUT FASHION...
...UNLIKE THE MEN OF THE OTHER DISTRICTS.

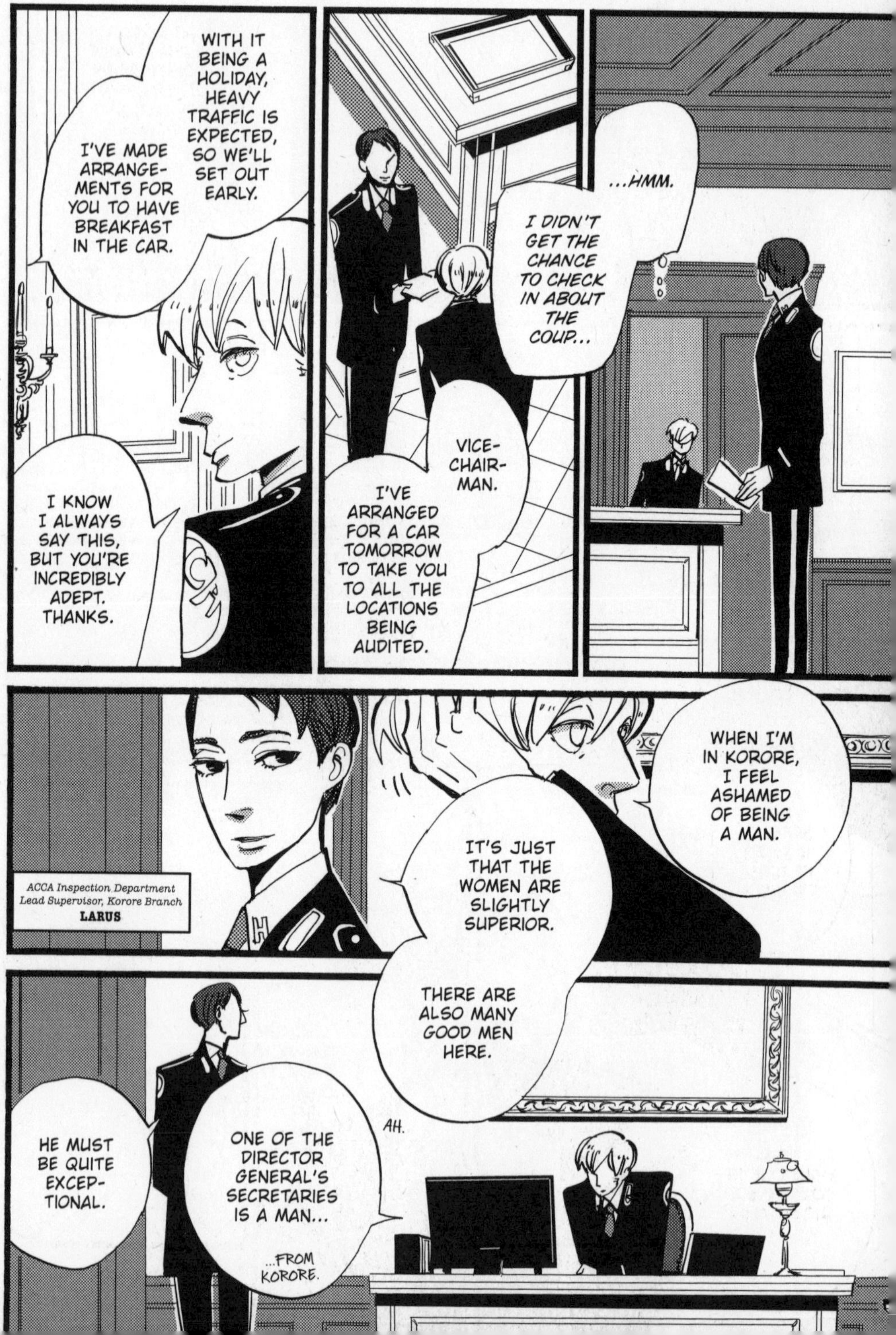
...HMM.
I DIDN'T GET THE CHANCE TO CHECK IN ABOUT THE COUP...
VICE-CHAIRMAN.
I'VE ARRANGED FOR A CAR TOMORROW TO TAKE YOU TO ALL THE LOCATIONS BEING AUDITED.
WITH IT BEING A HOLIDAY, HEAVY TRAFFIC IS EXPECTED, SO WE'LL SET OUT EARLY.
I'VE MADE ARRANGEMENTS FOR YOU TO HAVE BREAKFAST IN THE CAR.
I KNOW I ALWAYS SAY THIS, BUT YOU'RE INCREDIBLY ADEPT. THANKS.
WHEN I'M IN KORORE, I FEEL ASHAMED OF BEING A MAN.
IT'S JUST THAT THE WOMEN ARE SLIGHTLY SUPERIOR.
ACCA Inspection Department Lead Supervisor, Korore Branch LARUS
THERE ARE ALSO MANY GOOD MEN HERE.
AH.
ONE OF THE DIRECTOR GENERAL'S SECRETARIES IS A MAN...
...FROM KORORE.
HE MUST BE QUITE EXCEPTIONAL.

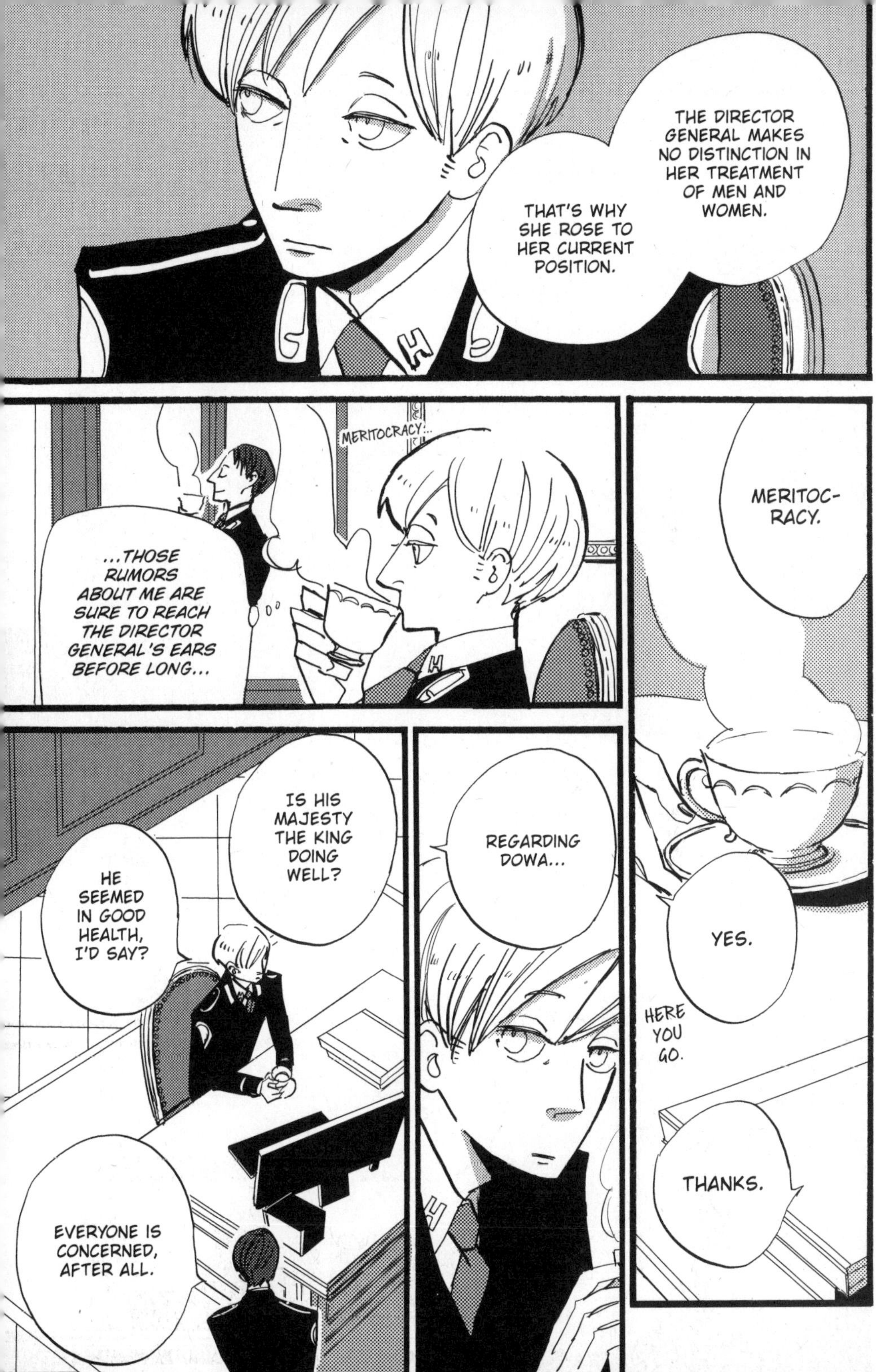
THE DIRECTOR GENERAL MAKES NO DISTINCTION IN HER TREATMENT OF MEN AND WOMEN.
THAT'S WHY SHE ROSE TO HER CURRENT POSITION.
MERITOC-RACY.
YES.
HERE YOU GO.
THANKS.
MERITOCRACY...
...THOSE RUMORS ABOUT ME ARE SURE TO REACH THE DIRECTOR GENERAL'S EARS BEFORE LONG...
REGARDING DOWA...
IS HIS MAJESTY THE KING DOING WELL?
HE SEEMED IN GOOD HEALTH, I'D SAY?
EVERYONE IS CONCERNED, AFTER ALL.

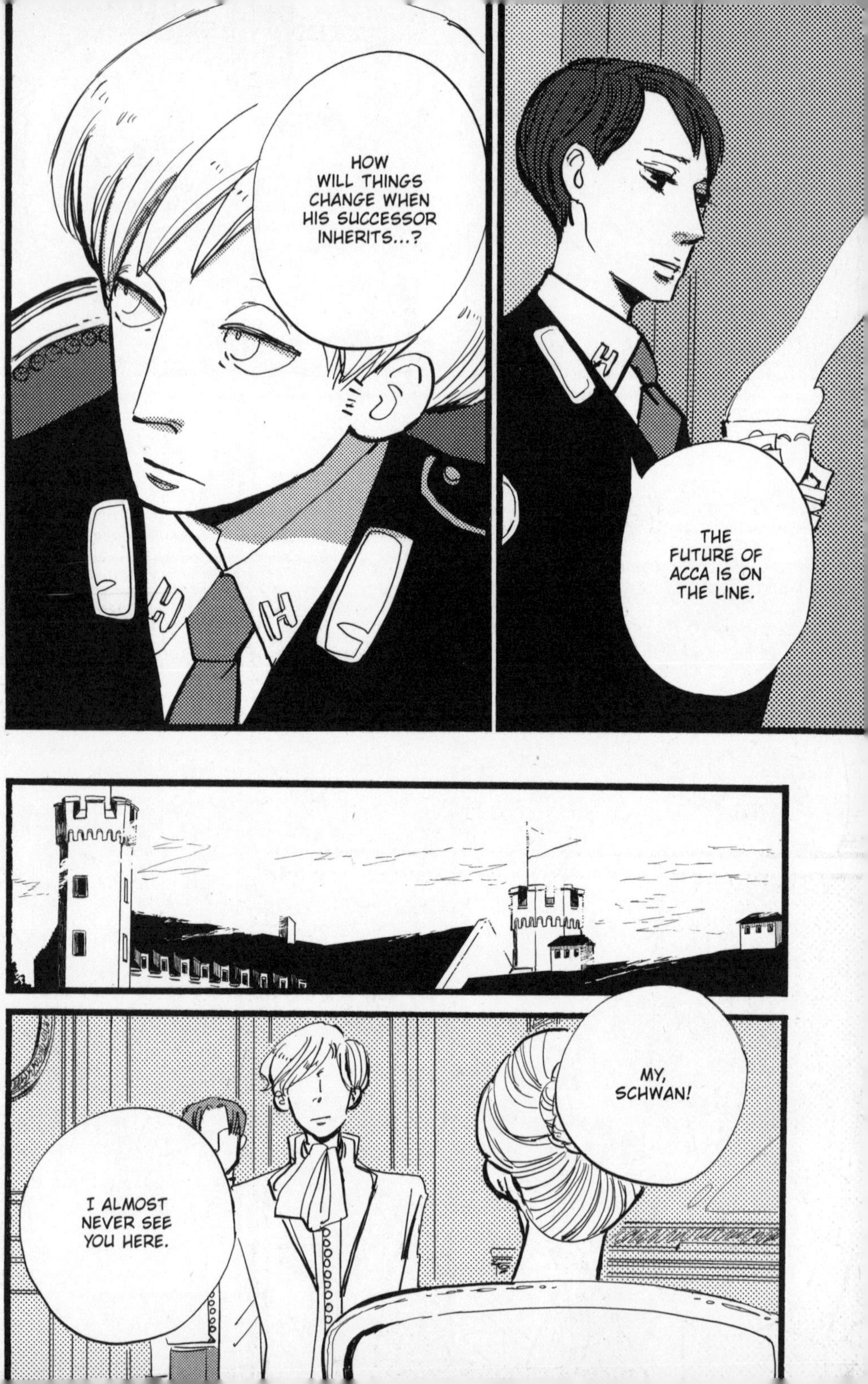
THE FUTURE OF ACCA IS ON THE LINE.
HOW WILL THINGS CHANGE WHEN HIS SUCCESSOR INHERITS...?
MY, SCHWAN!
I ALMOST NEVER SEE YOU HERE.

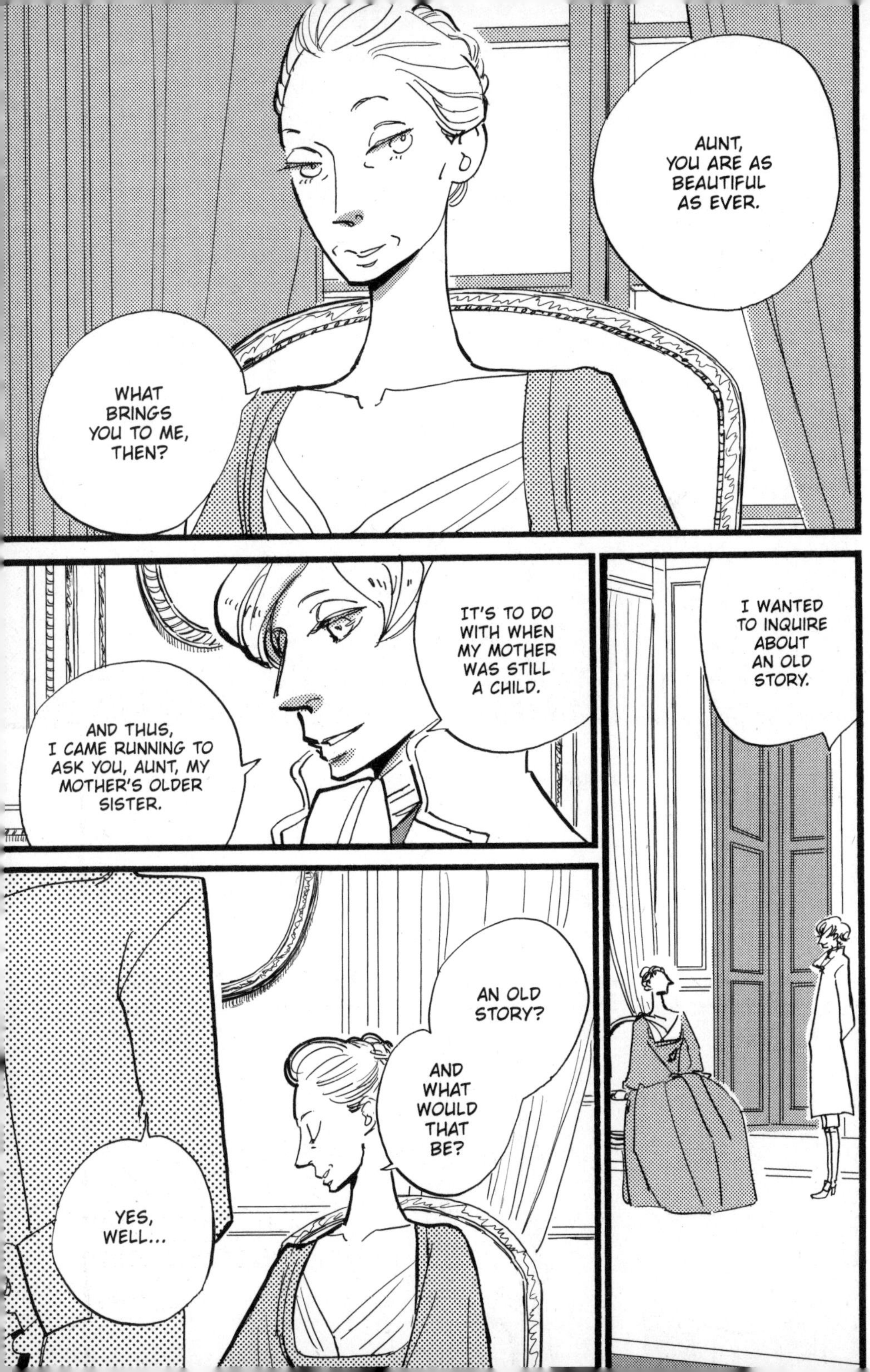
AUNT, YOU ARE AS BEAUTIFUL AS EVER.
WHAT BRINGS YOU TO ME, THEN?
I WANTED TO INQUIRE ABOUT AN OLD STORY.
IT'S TO DO WITH WHEN MY MOTHER WAS STILL A CHILD.
AND THUS, I CAME RUNNING TO ASK YOU, AUNT, MY MOTHER'S OLDER SISTER.
AN OLD STORY?
AND WHAT WOULD THAT BE?
YES, WELL...

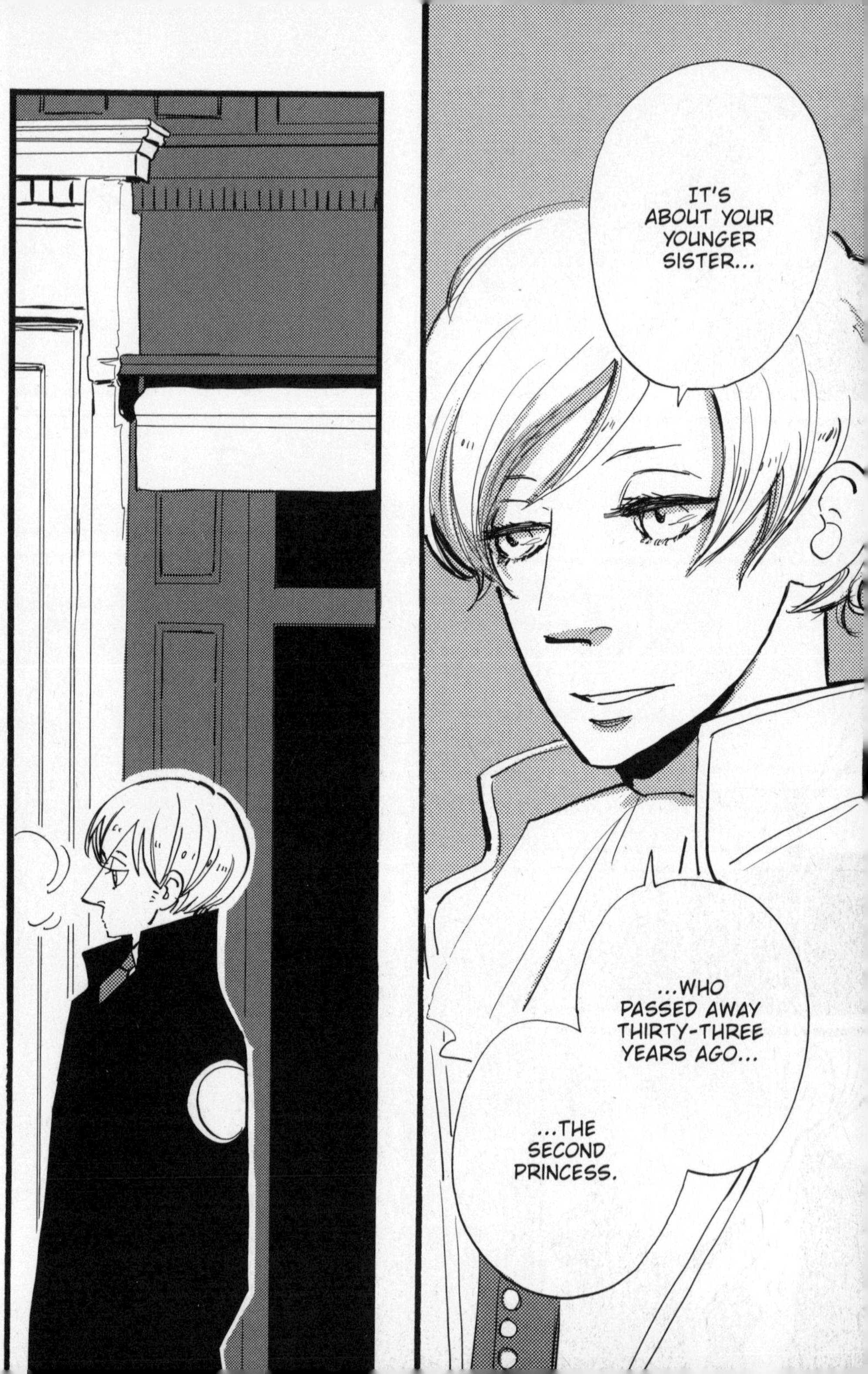
IT'S ABOUT YOUR YOUNGER SISTER...
...WHO PASSED AWAY THIRTY-THREE YEARS AGO...
...THE SECOND PRINCESS.

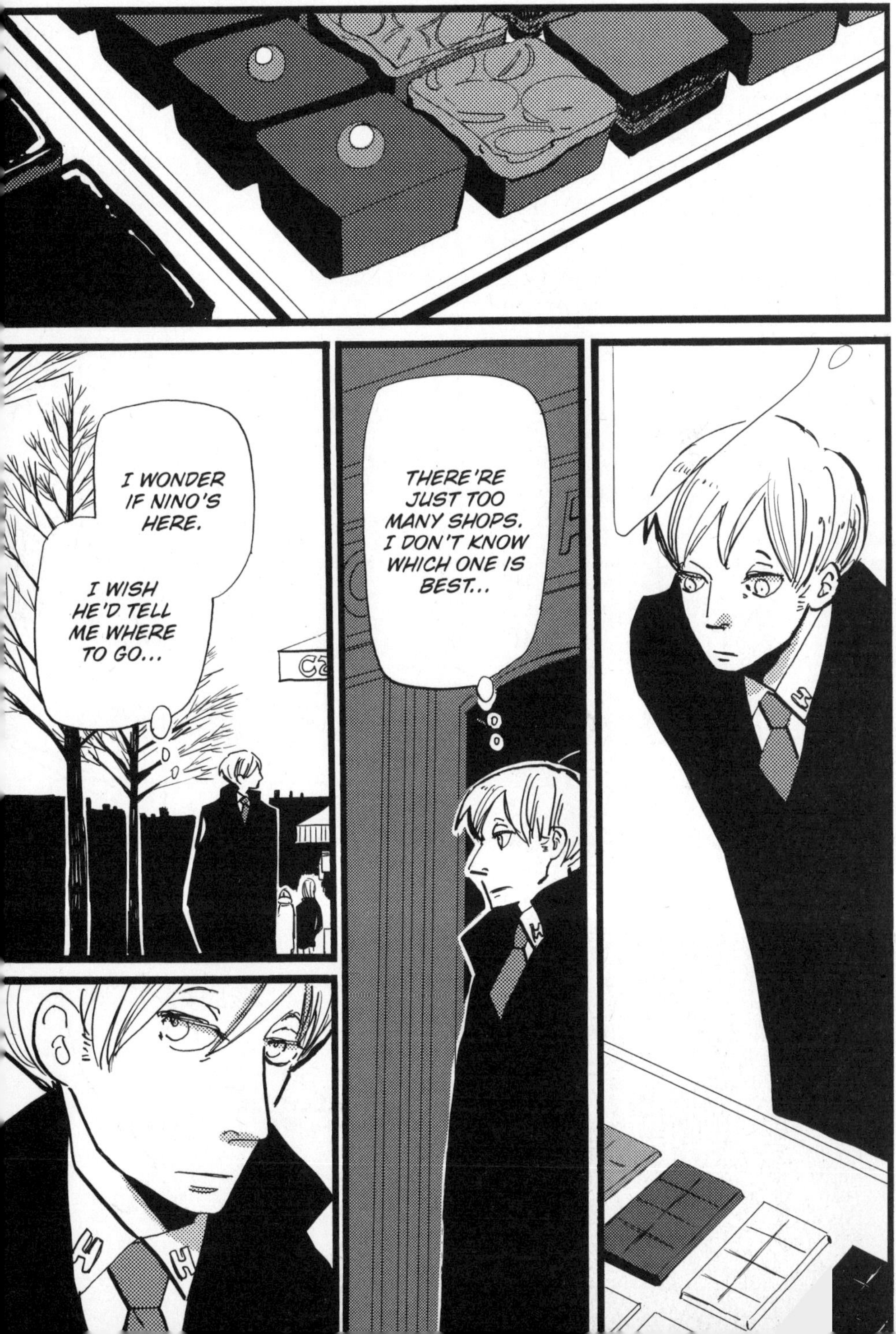
THERE'RE JUST TOO MANY SHOPS. I DON'T KNOW WHICH ONE IS BEST...
I WONDER IF NINO'S HERE.
I WISH HE'D TELL ME WHERE TO GO...

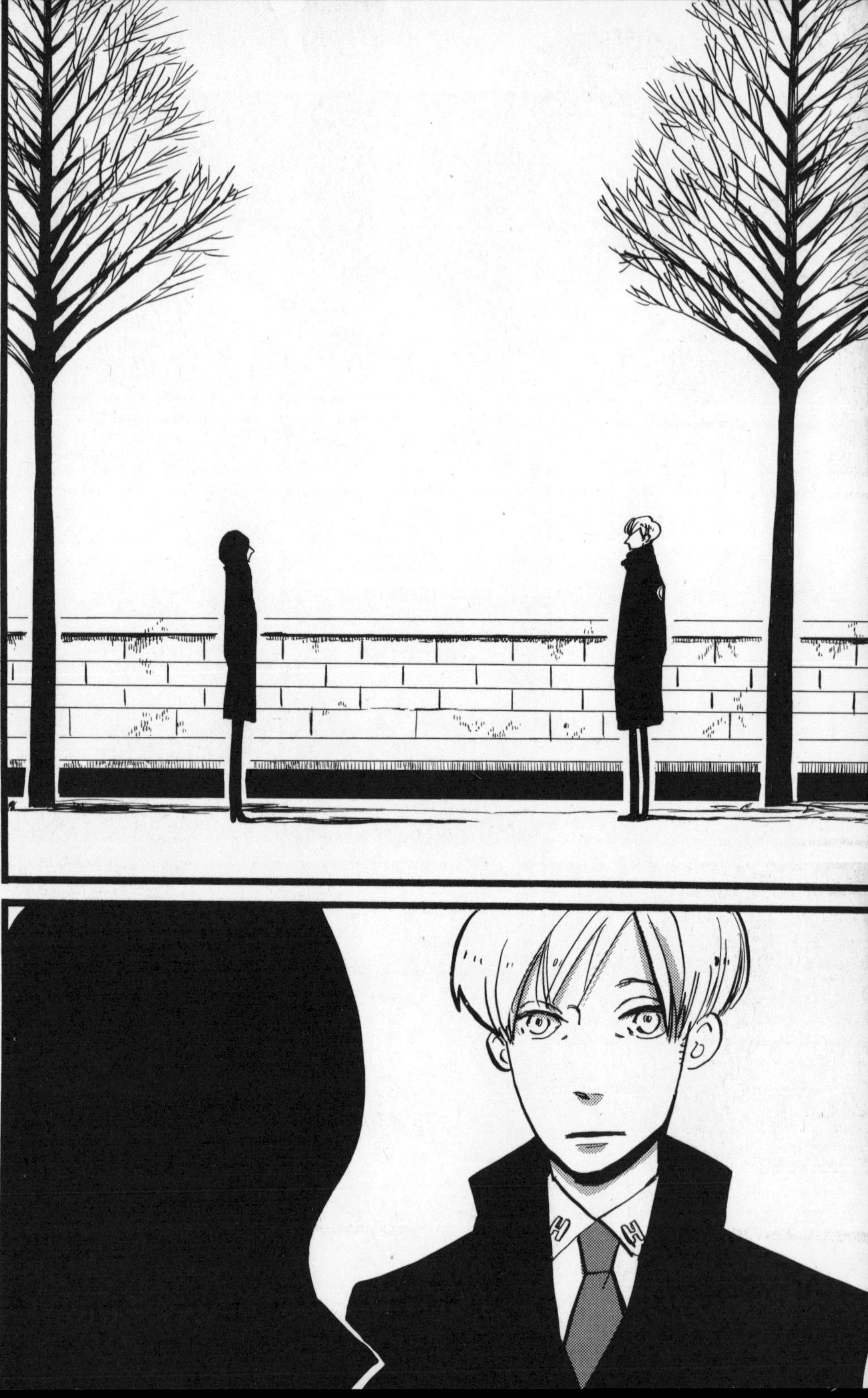

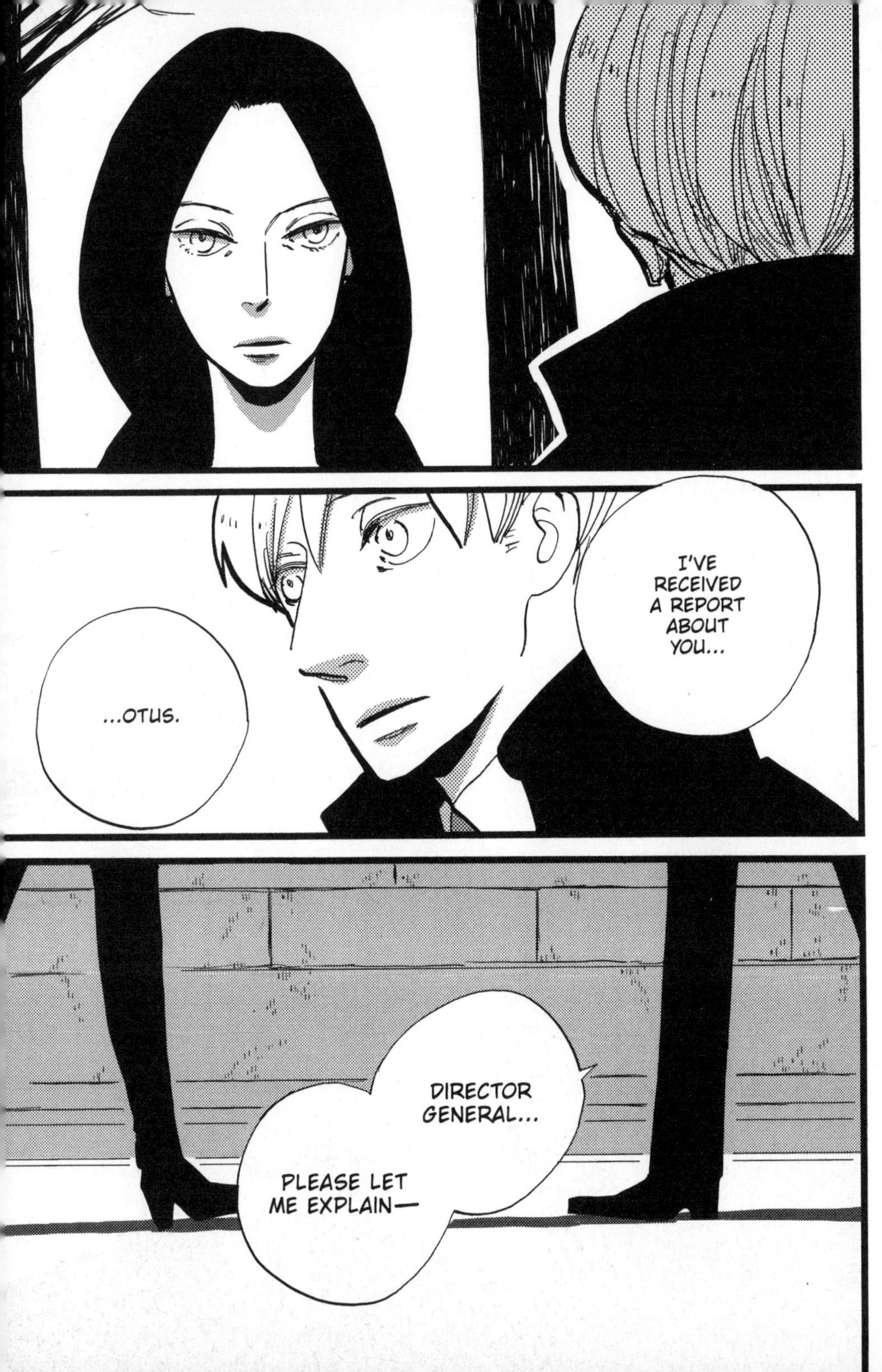
I'VE RECEIVED A REPORT ABOUT YOU...
...OTUS.
DIRECTOR GENERAL...
PLEASE LET ME EXPLAIN—

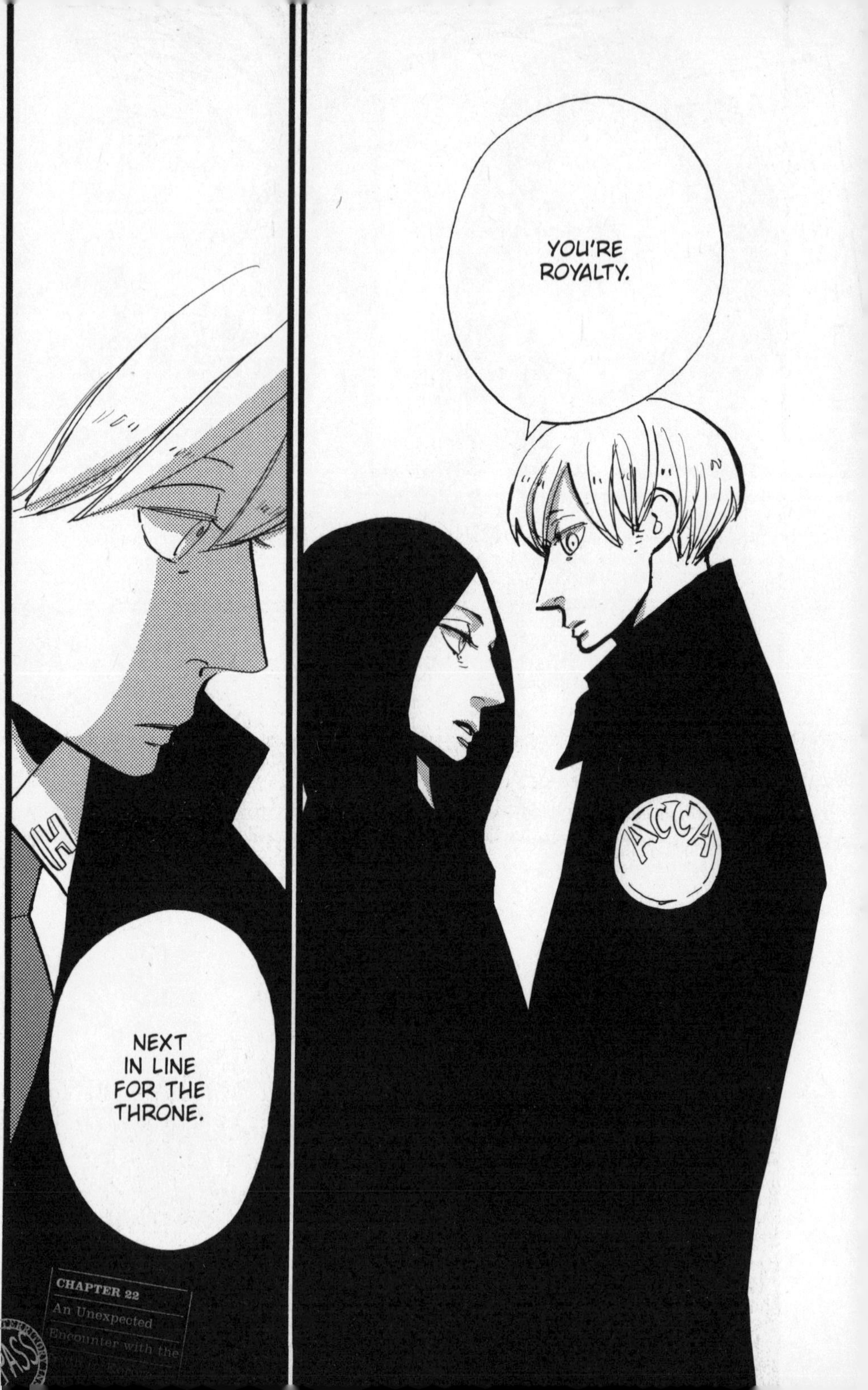
YOU'RE ROYALTY.
NEXT IN LINE FOR THE THRONE.
CHAPTER 22
An Unexpected
Encounter with the
PASS

CHAPTER 23
Two on the Bridge in Korore

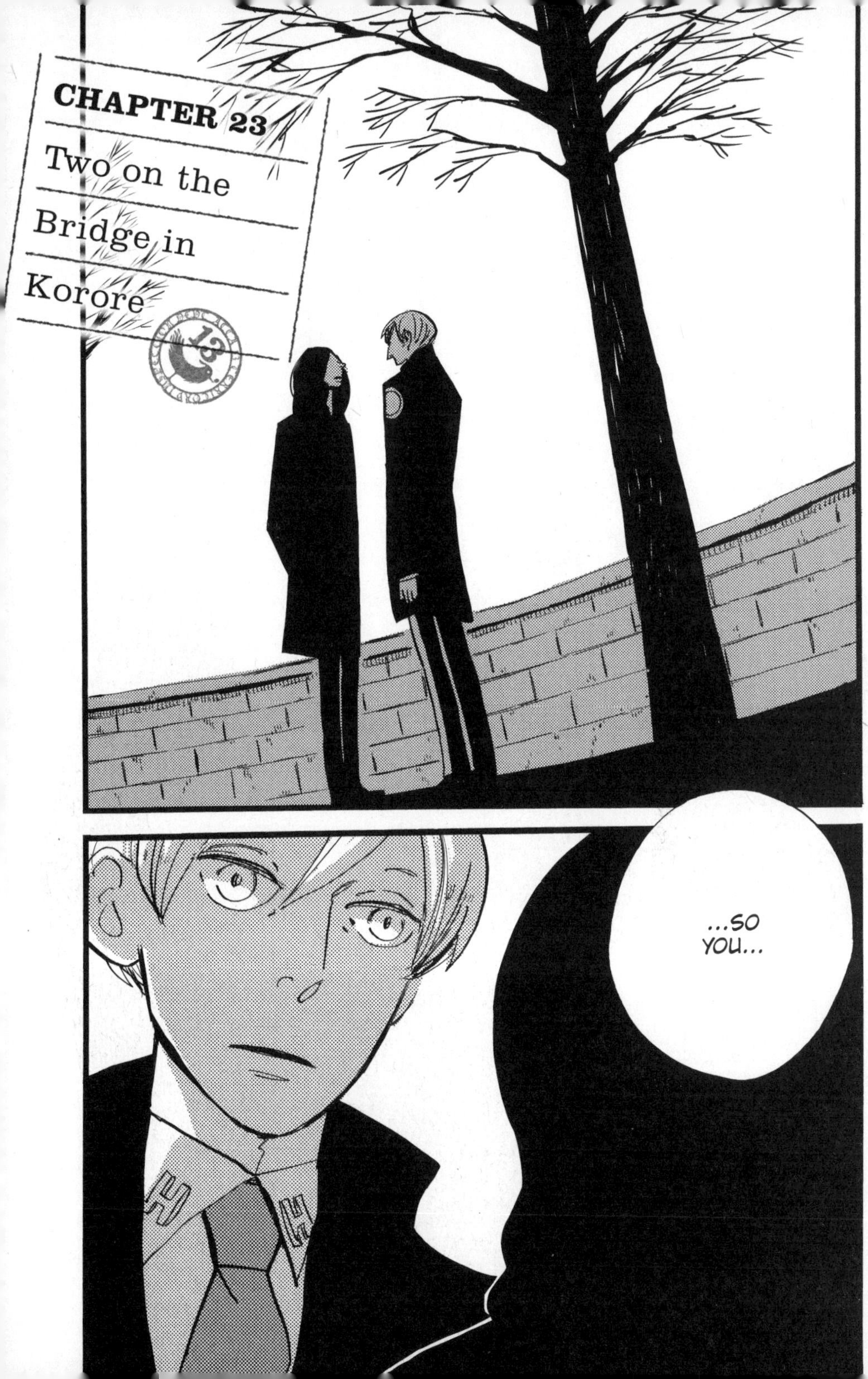
...SO YOU...

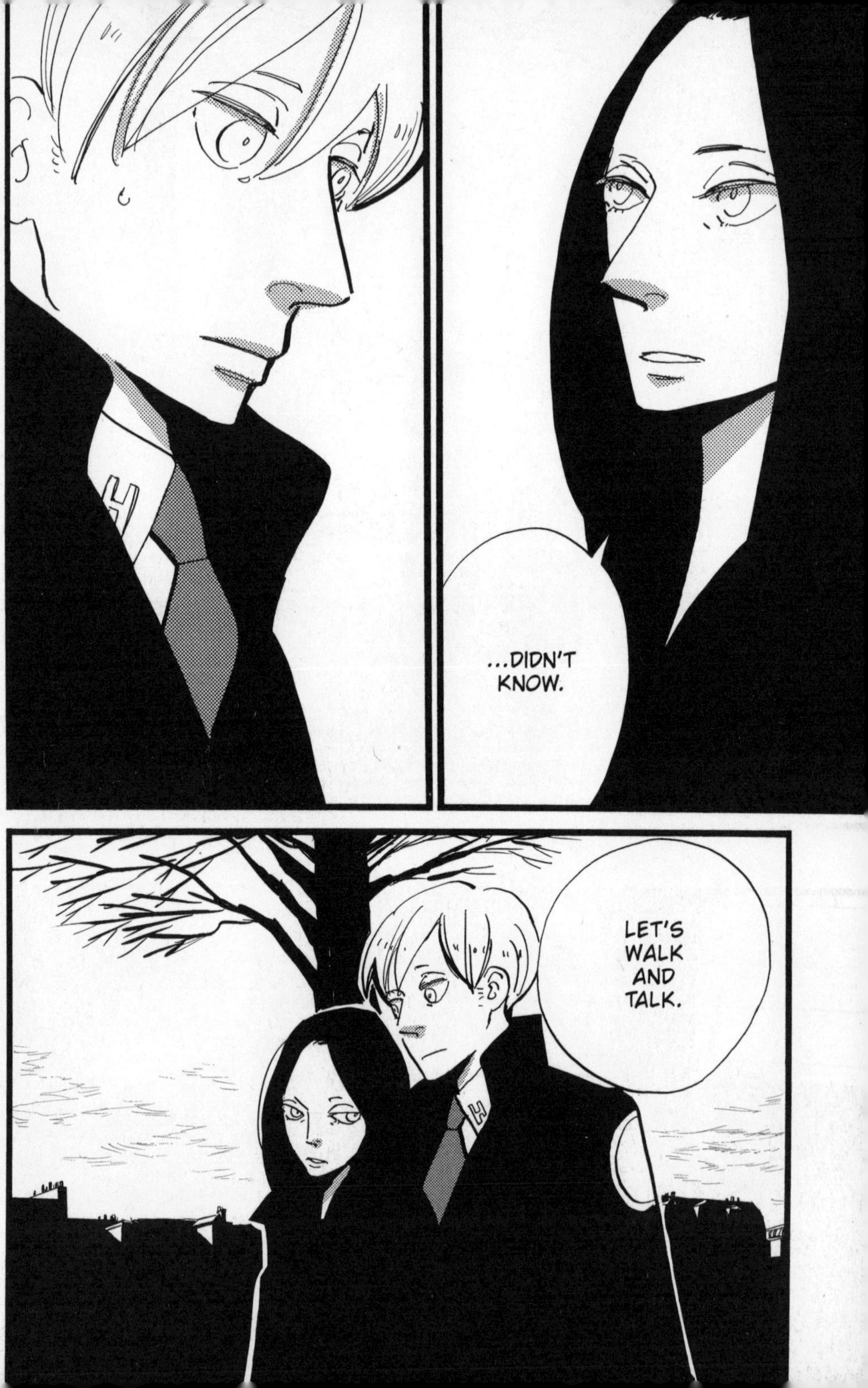
...DIDN'T KNOW.
LET'S WALK AND TALK.

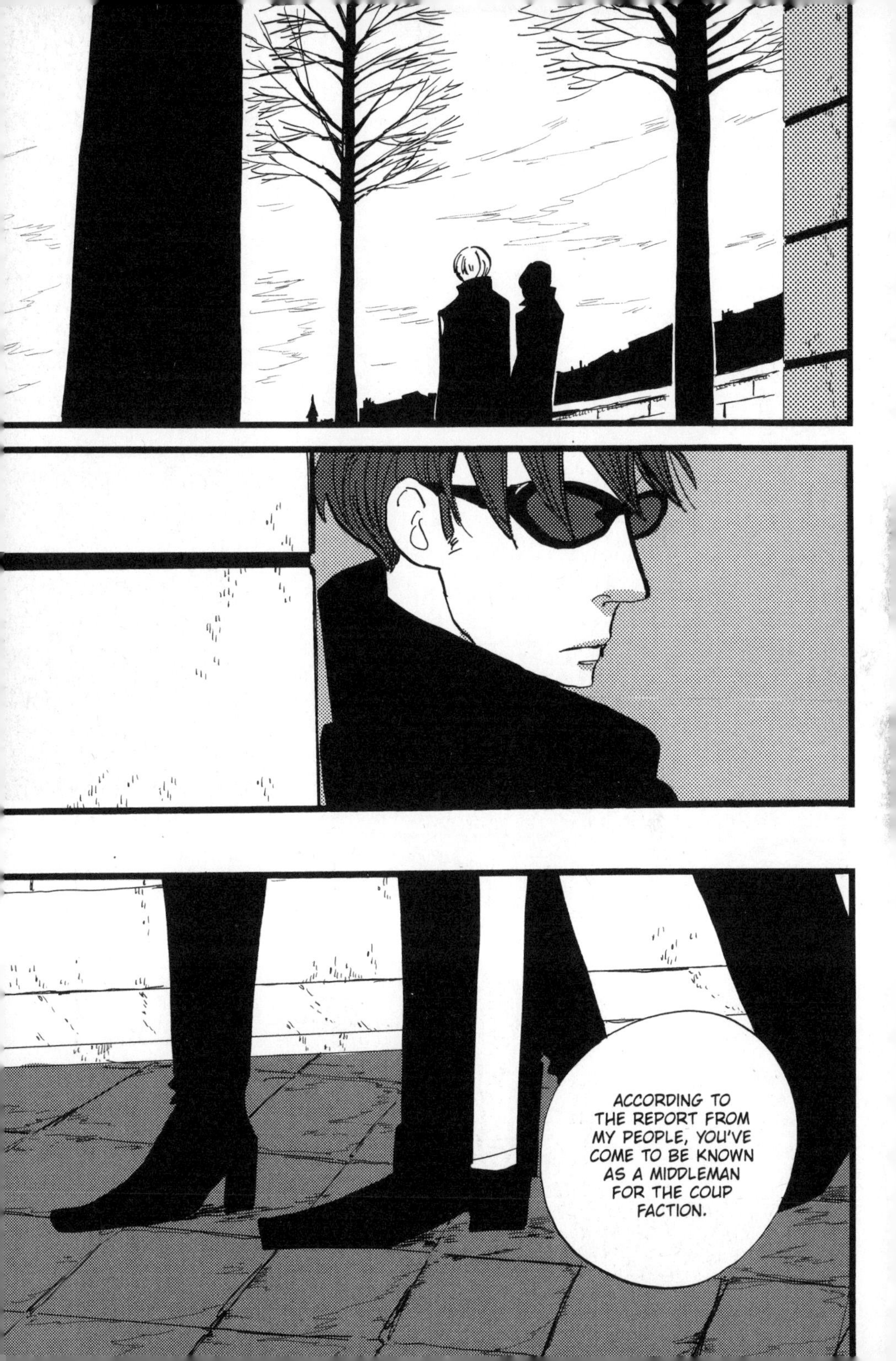
ACCORDING TO THE REPORT FROM MY PEOPLE, YOU'VE COME TO BE KNOWN AS A MIDDLEMAN FOR THE COUP FACTION.

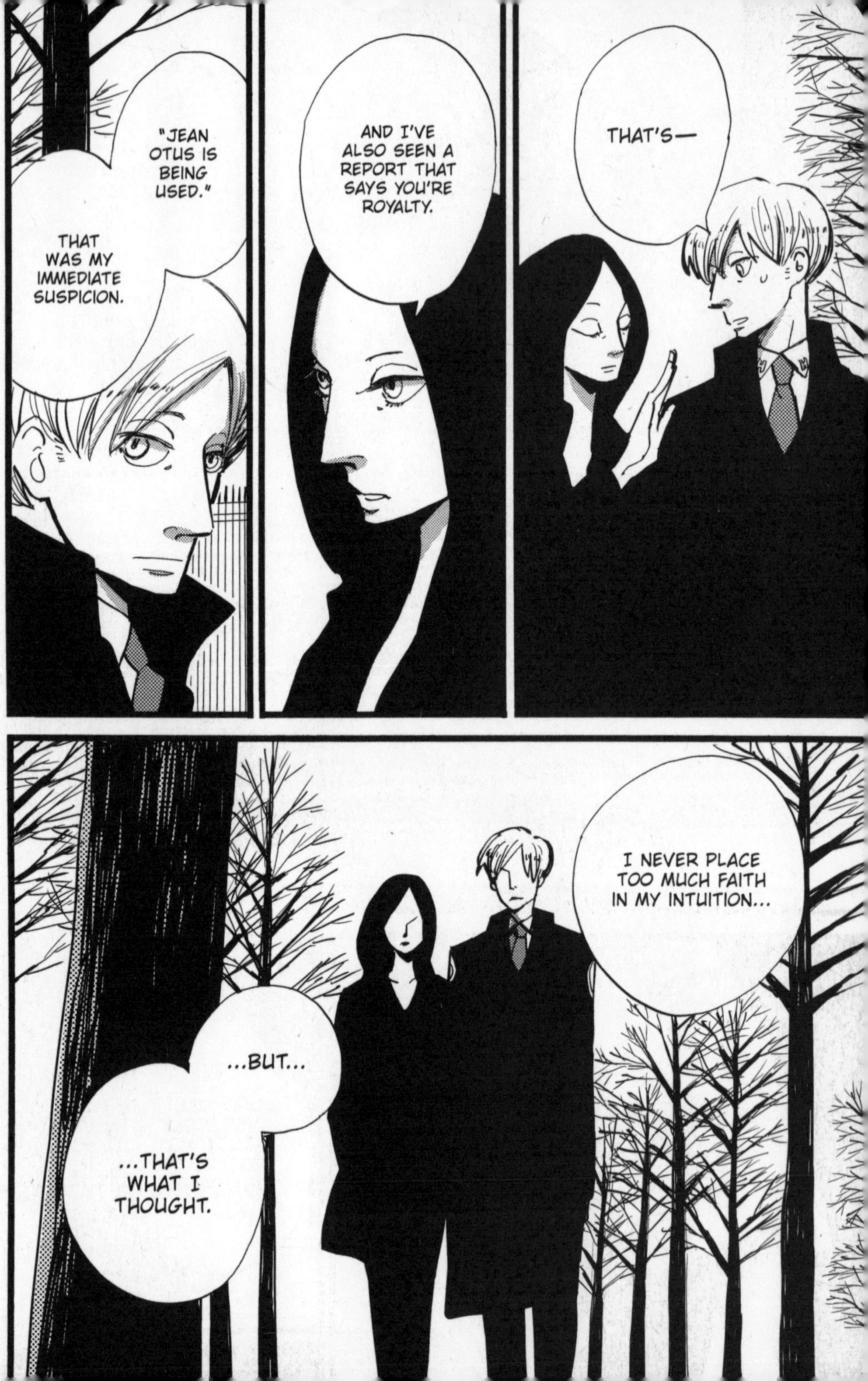
THAT'S—
AND I'VE ALSO SEEN A REPORT THAT SAYS YOU'RE ROYALTY.
"JEAN OTUS IS BEING USED."
THAT WAS MY IMMEDIATE SUSPICION.
I NEVER PLACE TOO MUCH FAITH IN MY INTUITION...
...BUT...
...THAT'S WHAT I THOUGHT.

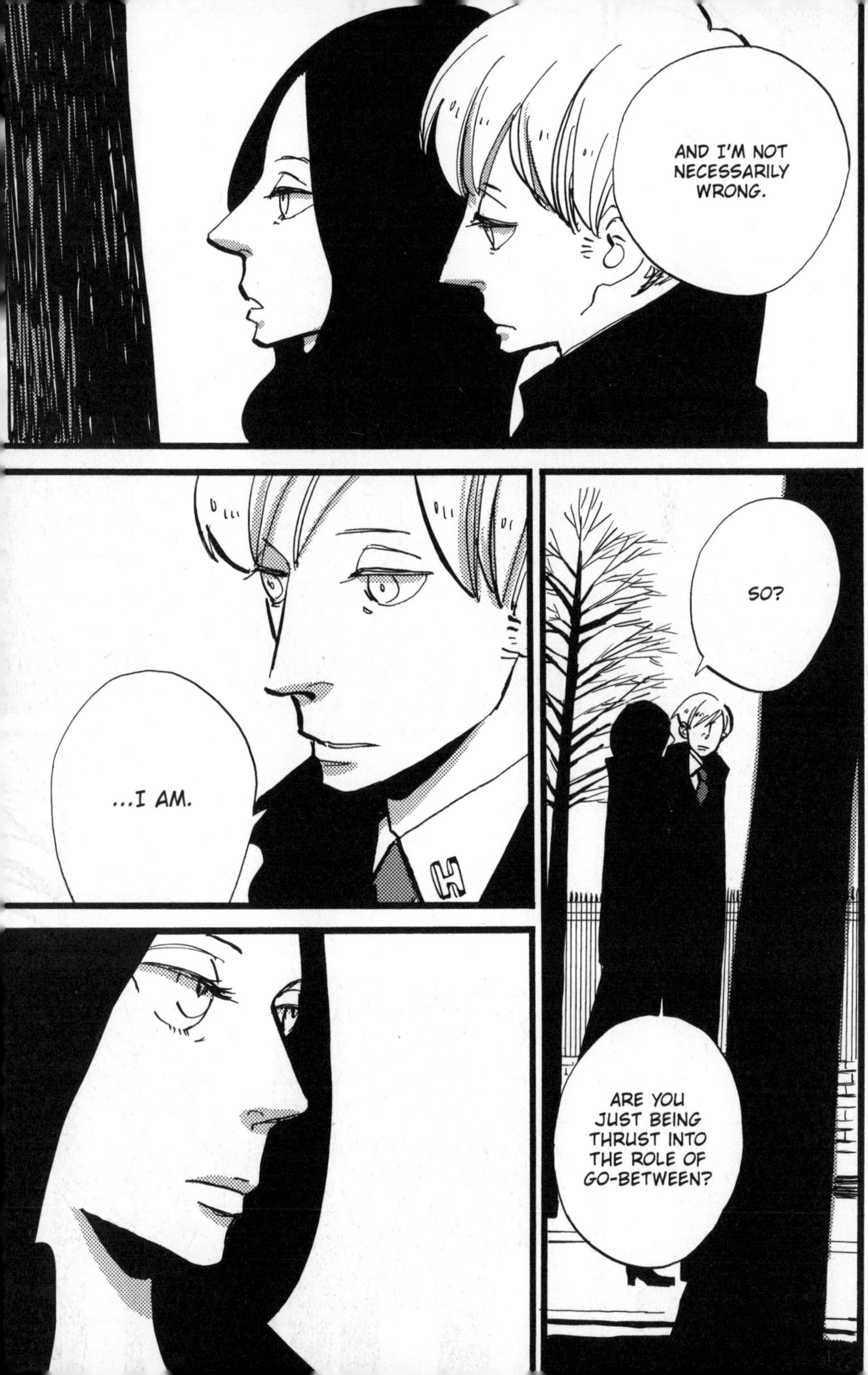
AND I'M NOT NECESSARILY WRONG.
SO?
ARE YOU JUST BEING THRUST INTO THE ROLE OF GO-BETWEEN?
...I AM.

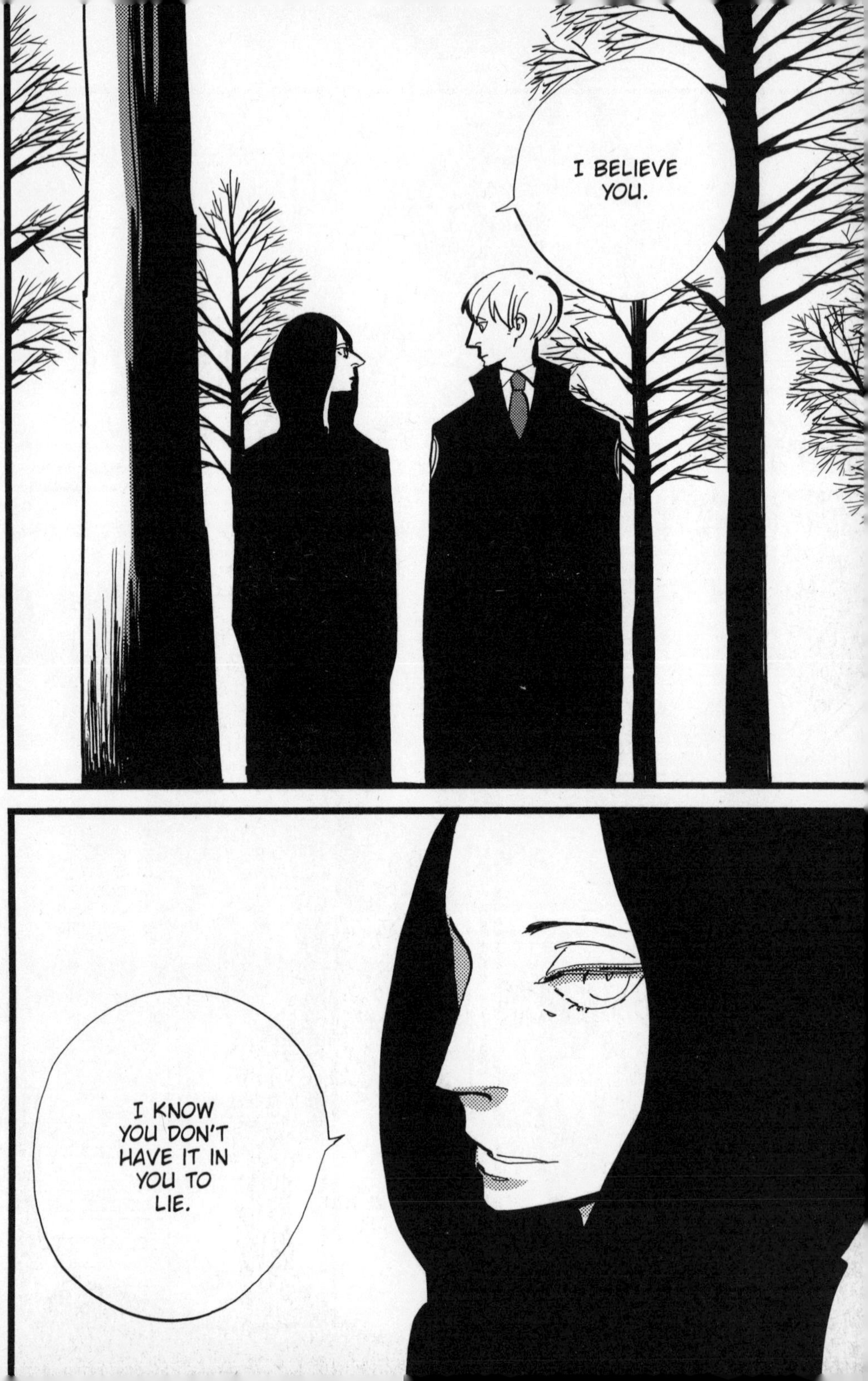
I BELIEVE YOU.
I KNOW YOU DON'T HAVE IT IN YOU TO LIE.

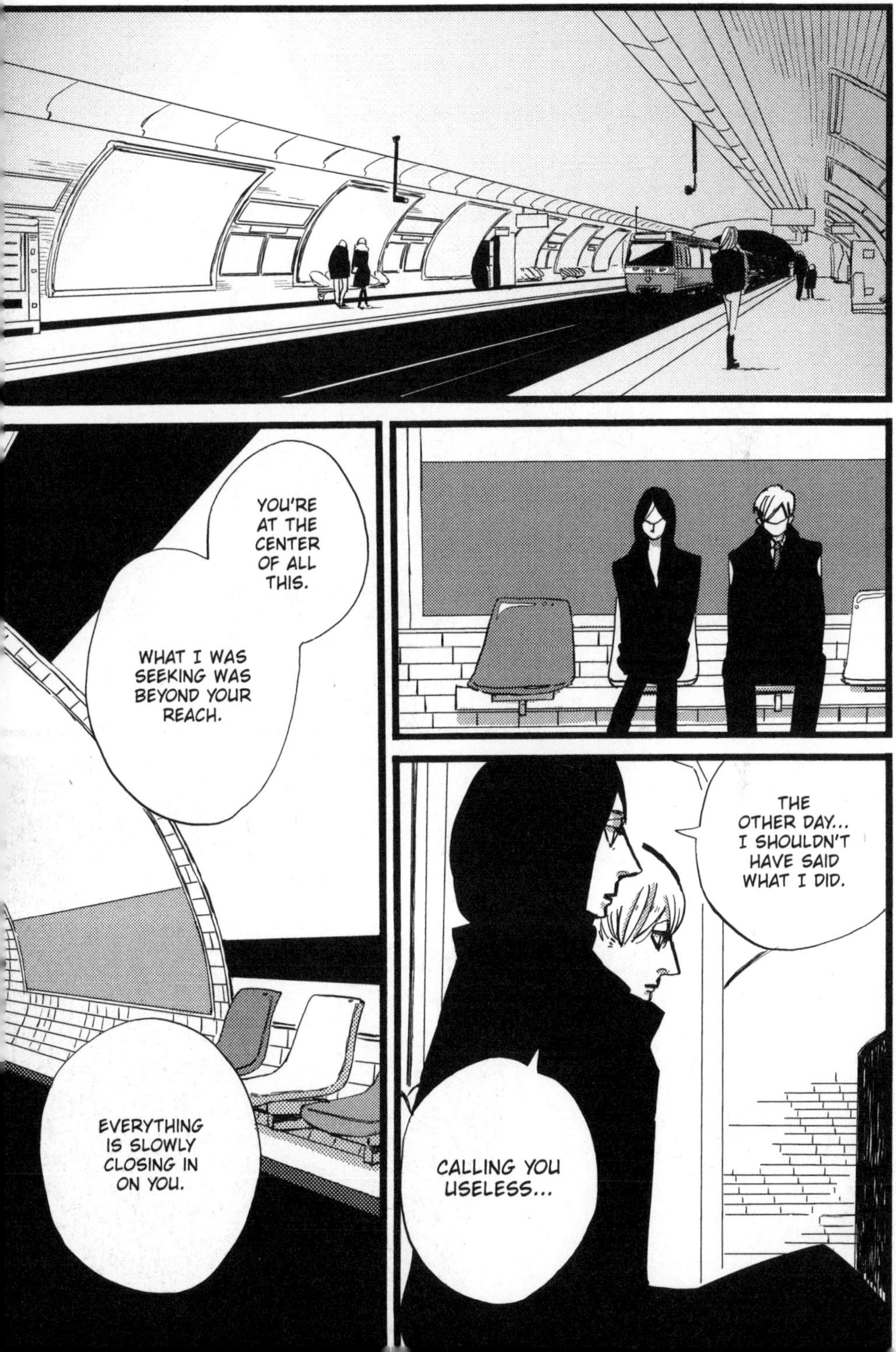
THE OTHER DAY... I SHOULDN'T HAVE SAID WHAT I DID.
CALLING YOU USELESS...
YOU'RE AT THE CENTER OF ALL THIS.
WHAT I WAS SEEKING WAS BEYOND YOUR REACH.
EVERYTHING IS SLOWLY CLOSING IN ON YOU.

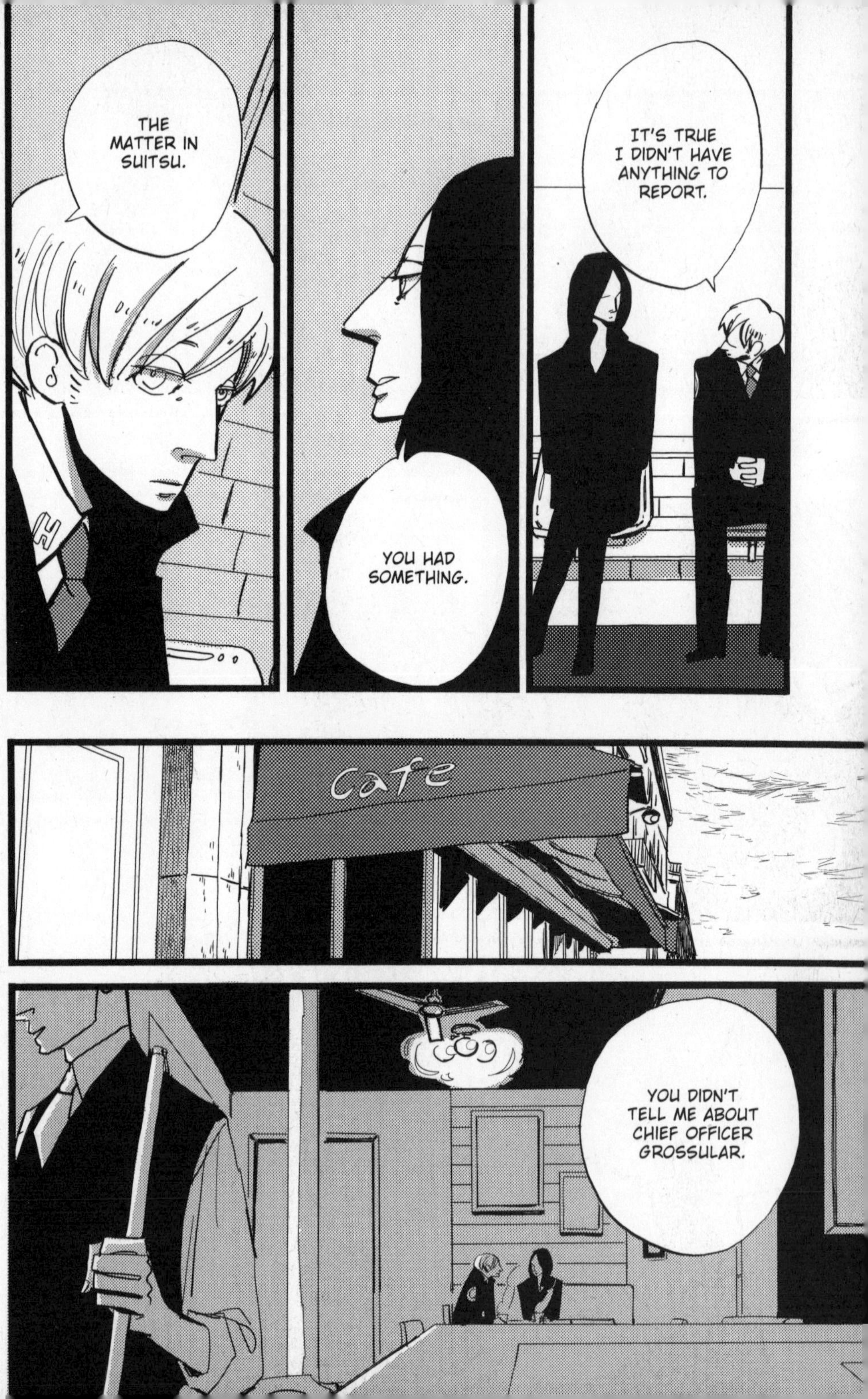
IT'S TRUE I DIDN'T HAVE ANYTHING TO REPORT.
YOU HAD SOMETHING.
THE MATTER IN SUITSU.
Cafe
YOU DIDN'T TELL ME ABOUT CHIEF OFFICER GROSSULAR.

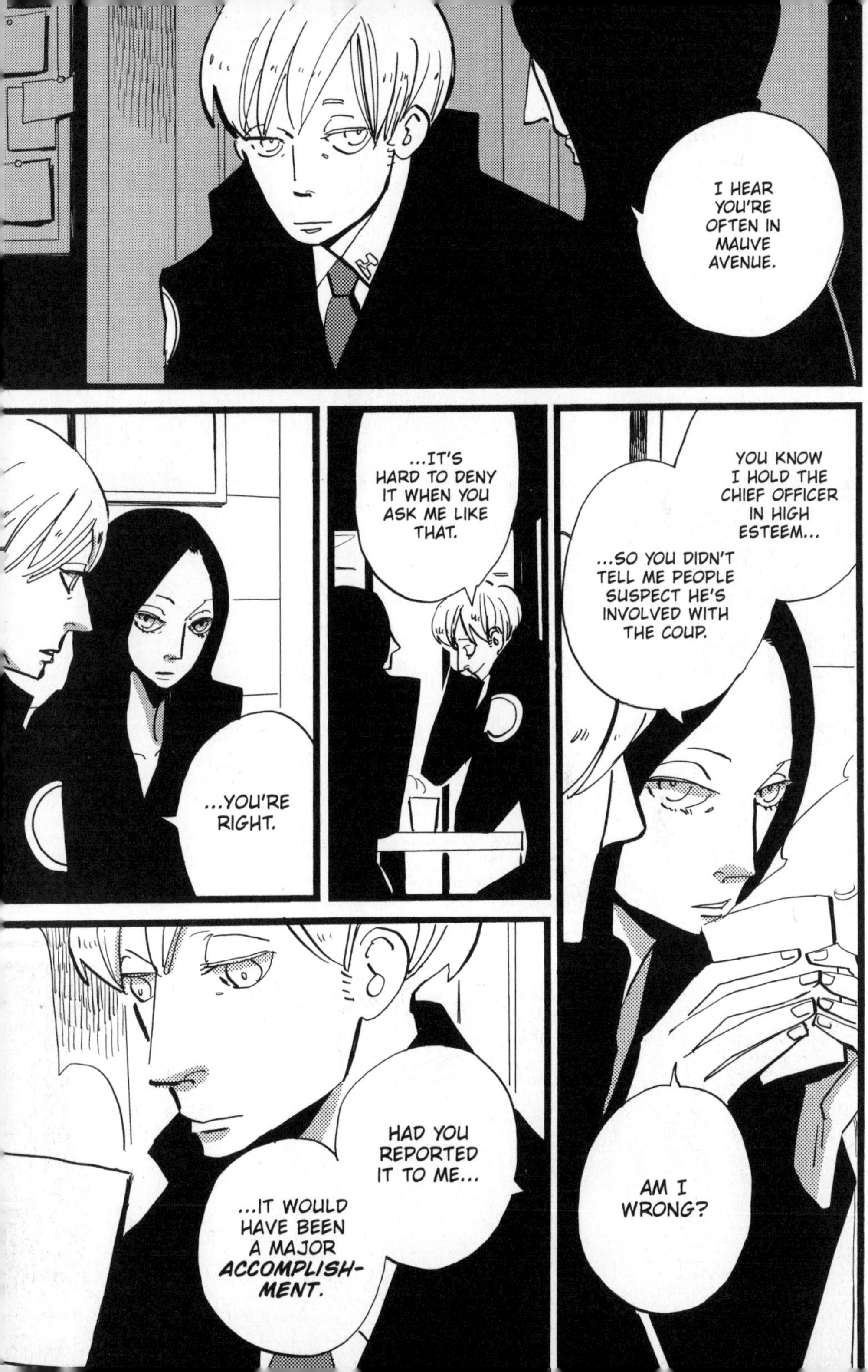
I HEAR YOU'RE OFTEN IN MAUVE AVENUE.
YOU KNOW I HOLD THE CHIEF OFFICER IN HIGH ESTEEM...
...SO YOU DIDN'T TELL ME PEOPLE SUSPECT HE'S INVOLVED WITH THE COUP.
AM I WRONG?
...IT'S HARD TO DENY IT WHEN YOU ASK ME LIKE THAT.
...YOU'RE RIGHT.
HAD YOU REPORTED IT TO ME...
...IT WOULD HAVE BEEN A MAJOR ACCOMPLISHMENT.

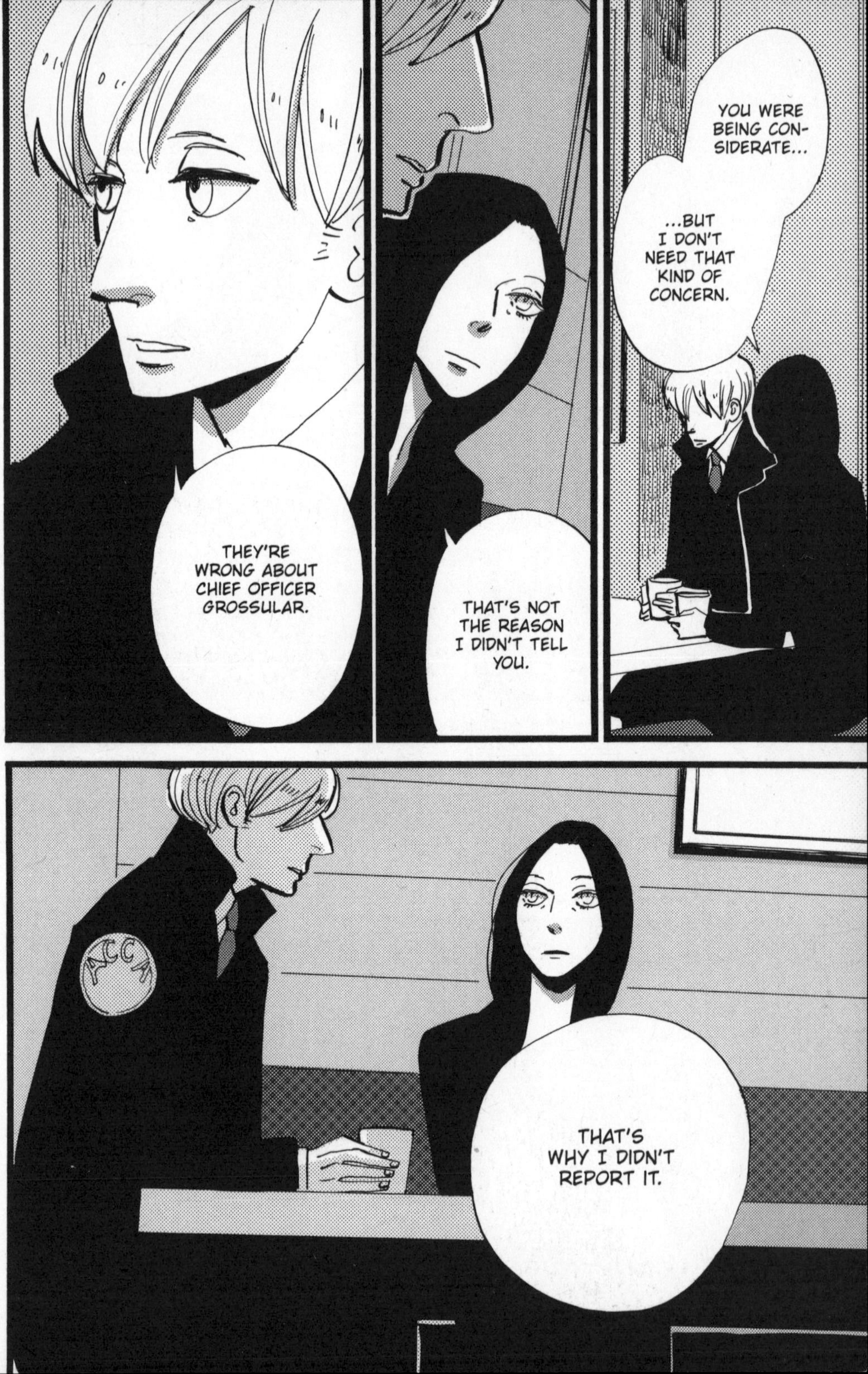
YOU WERE BEING CONSIDERATE...
...BUT I DON'T NEED THAT KIND OF CONCERN.
THAT'S NOT THE REASON I DIDN'T TELL YOU.
THEY'RE WRONG ABOUT CHIEF OFFICER GROSSULAR.
ACCA
THAT'S WHY I DIDN'T REPORT IT.

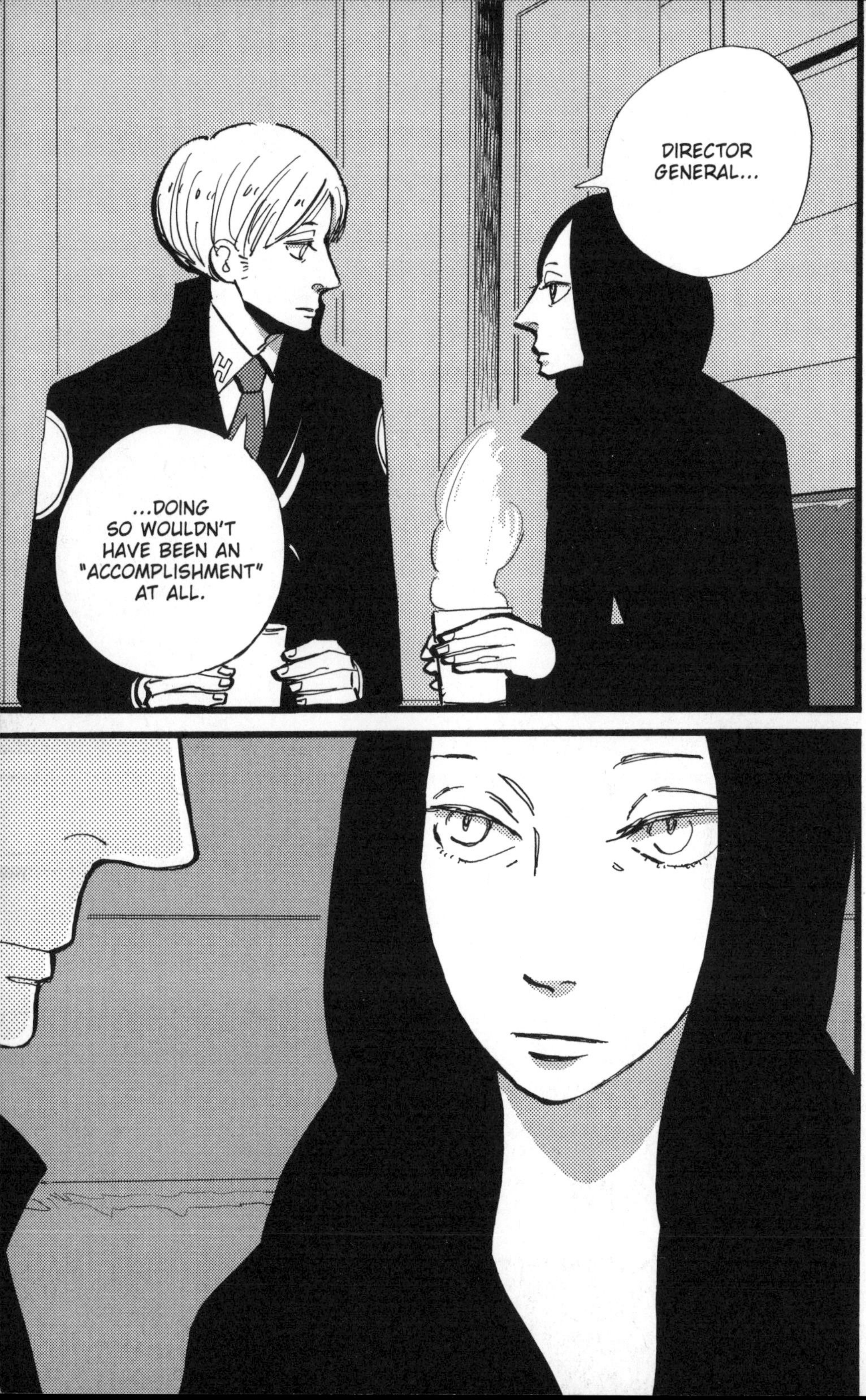
DIRECTOR GENERAL...
...DOING SO WOULDN'T HAVE BEEN AN "ACCOMPLISHMENT" AT ALL.

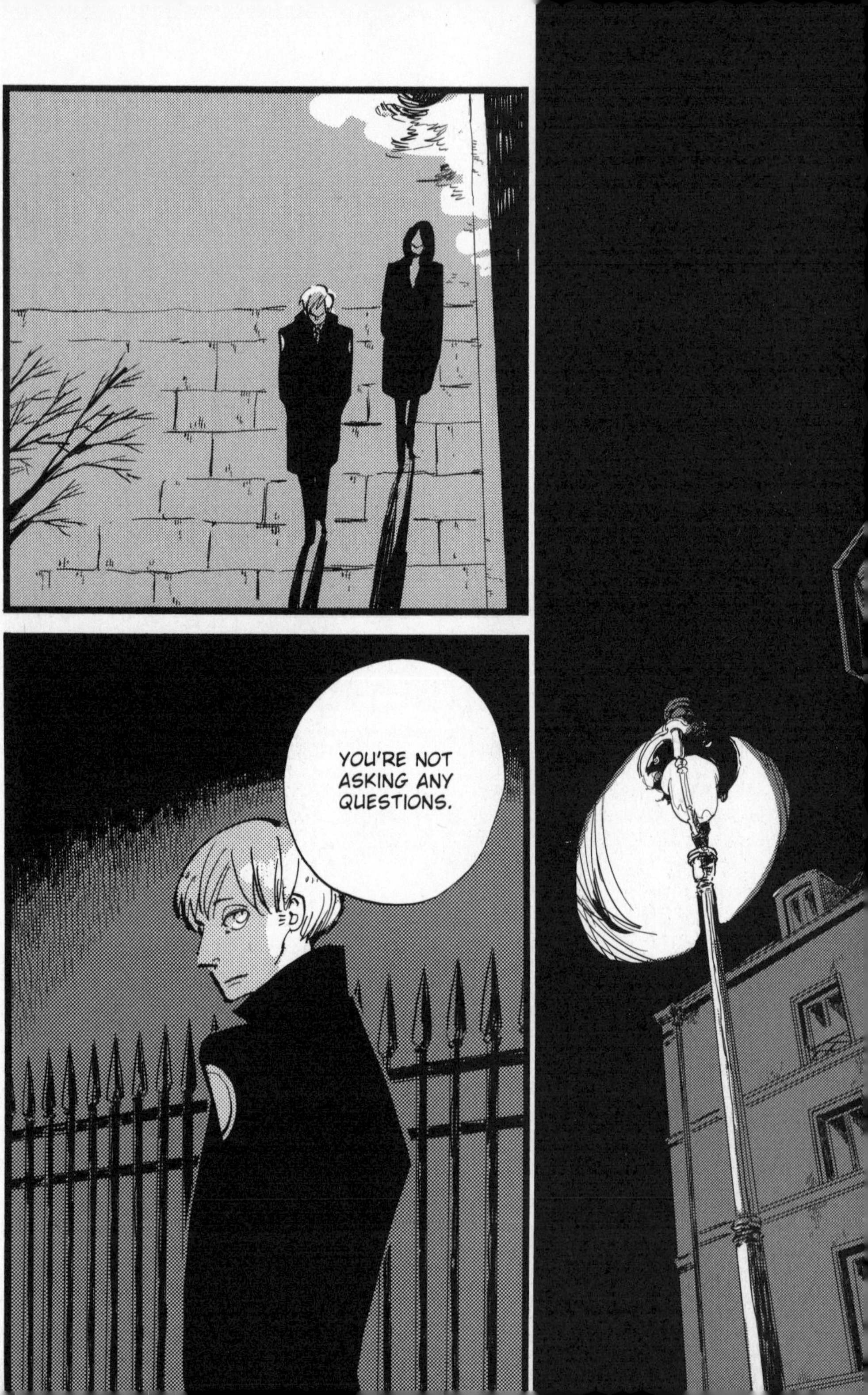
YOU'RE NOT ASKING ANY QUESTIONS.

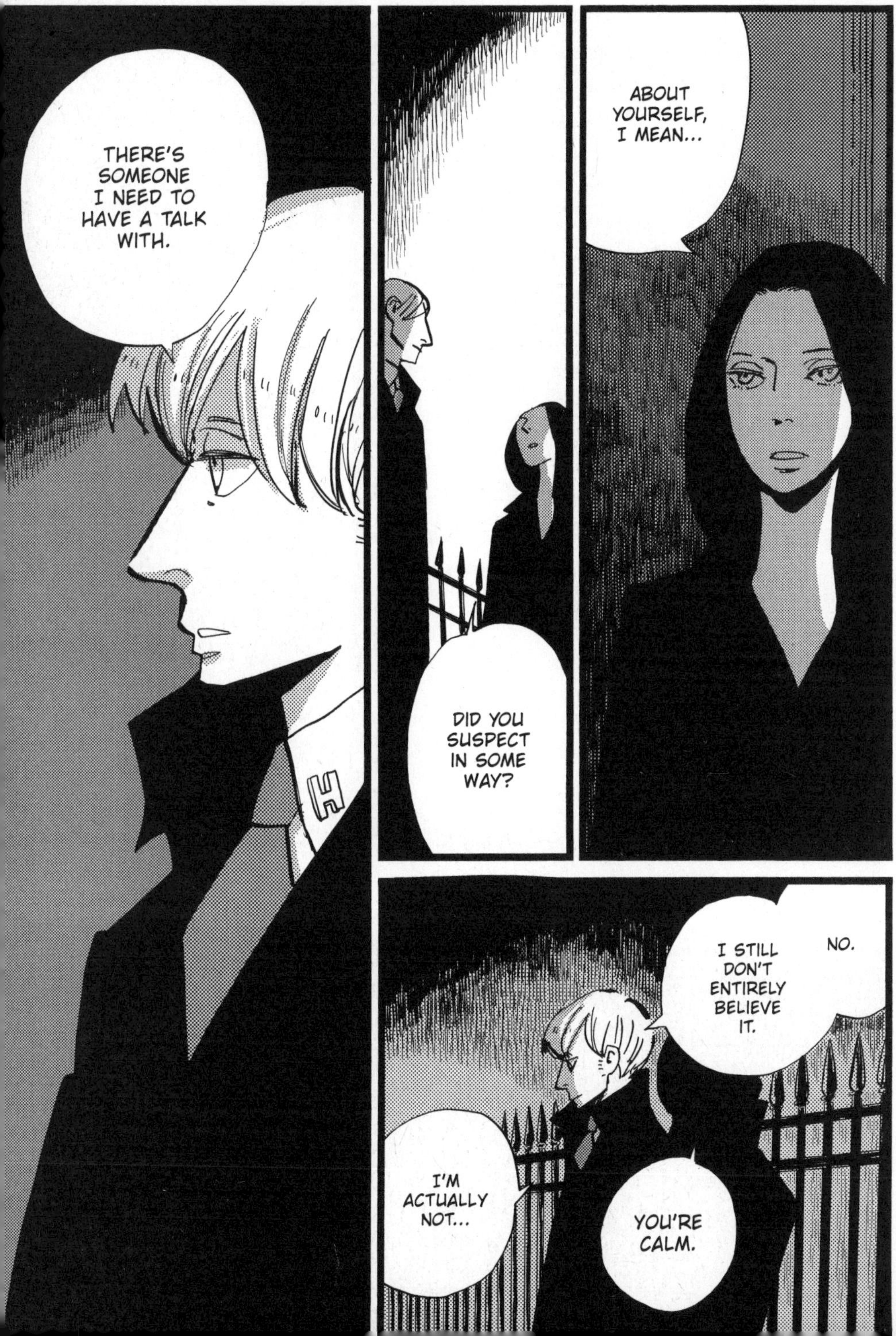
ABOUT YOURSELF, I MEAN...
DID YOU SUSPECT IN SOME WAY?
NO.
I STILL DON'T ENTIRELY BELIEVE IT.
YOU'RE CALM.
I'M ACTUALLY NOT...
THERE'S SOMEONE I NEED TO HAVE A TALK WITH.

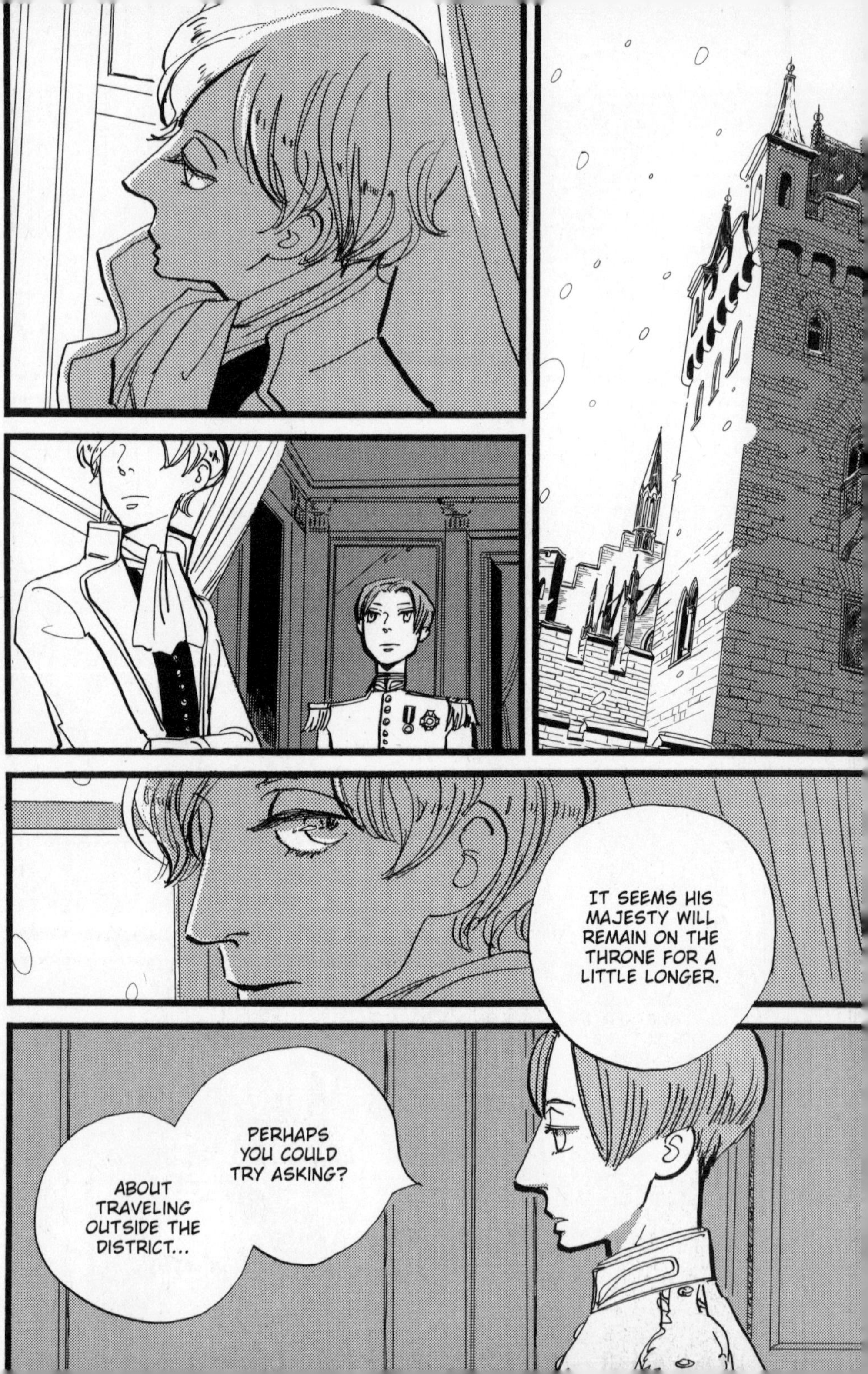
IT SEEMS HIS MAJESTY WILL REMAIN ON THE THRONE FOR A LITTLE LONGER.
PERHAPS YOU COULD TRY ASKING?
ABOUT TRAVELING OUTSIDE THE DISTRICT...

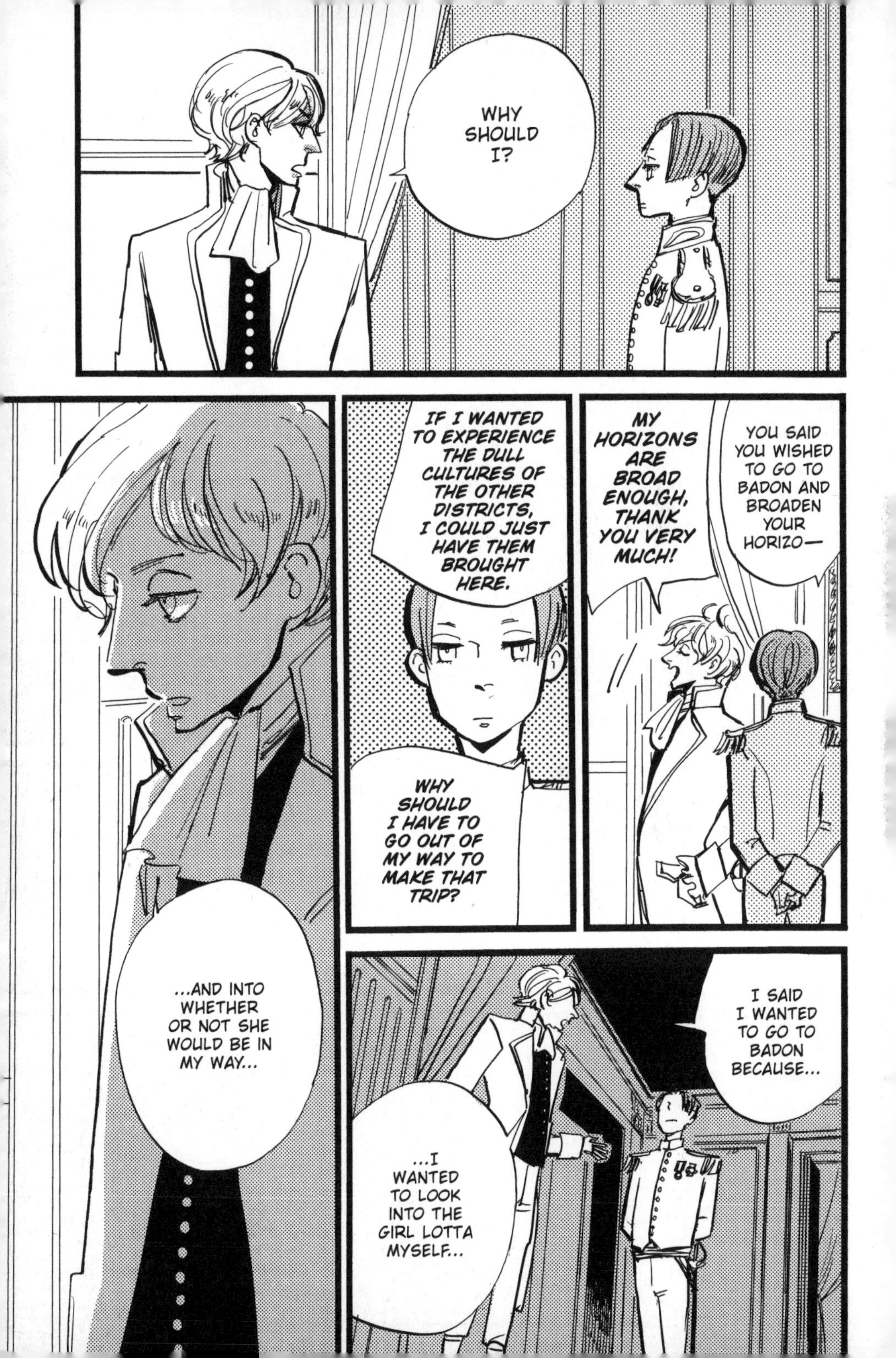
WHY SHOULD I?
YOU SAID YOU WISHED TO GO TO BADON AND BROADEN YOUR HORIZO—
MY HORIZONS ARE BROAD ENOUGH, THANK YOU VERY MUCH!
IF I WANTED TO EXPERIENCE THE DULL CULTURES OF THE OTHER DISTRICTS, I COULD JUST HAVE THEM BROUGHT HERE.
WHY SHOULD I HAVE TO GO OUT OF MY WAY TO MAKE THAT TRIP?
I SAID I WANTED TO GO TO BADON BECAUSE...
...I WANTED TO LOOK INTO THE GIRL LOTTA MYSELF...
...AND INTO WHETHER OR NOT SHE WOULD BE IN MY WAY...

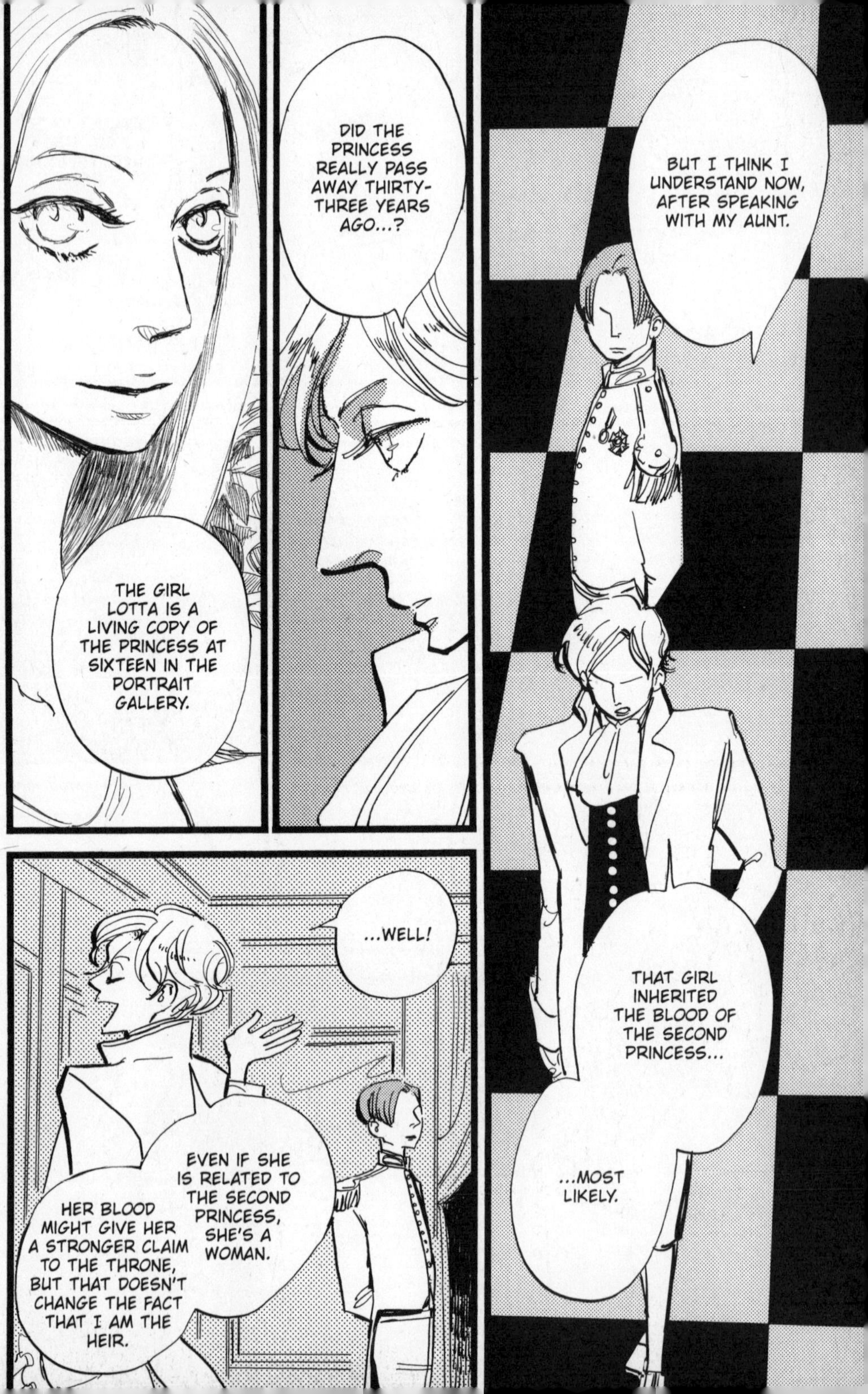
BUT I THINK I UNDERSTAND NOW, AFTER SPEAKING WITH MY AUNT.
THAT GIRL INHERITED THE BLOOD OF THE SECOND PRINCESS...
...MOST LIKELY.
DID THE PRINCESS REALLY PASS AWAY THIRTY-THREE YEARS AGO...?
THE GIRL LOTTA IS A LIVING COPY OF THE PRINCESS AT SIXTEEN IN THE PORTRAIT GALLERY.
...WELL!
EVEN IF SHE IS RELATED TO THE SECOND PRINCESS, SHE'S A WOMAN.
HER BLOOD MIGHT GIVE HER A STRONGER CLAIM TO THE THRONE, BUT THAT DOESN'T CHANGE THE FACT THAT I AM THE HEIR.

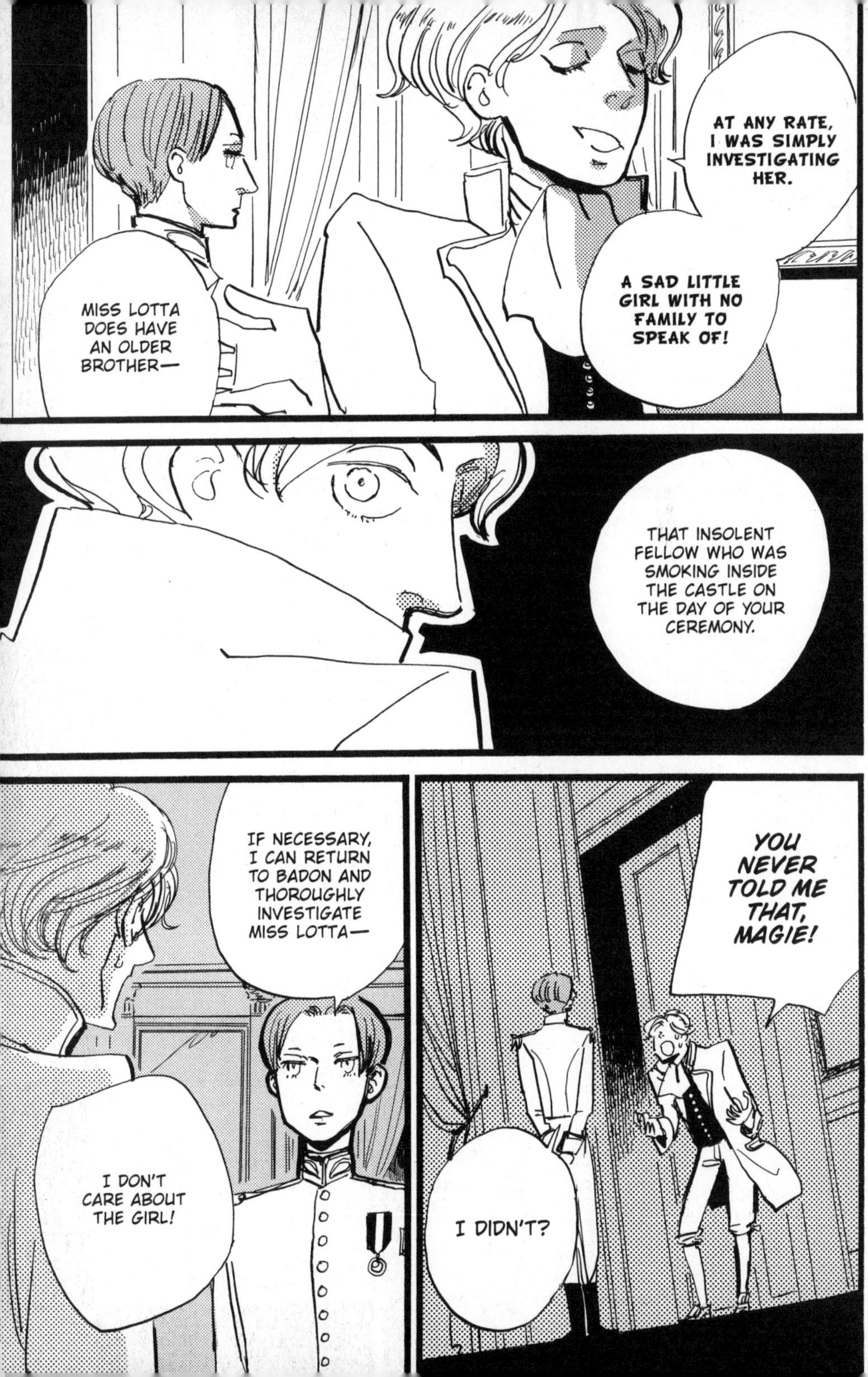
AT ANY RATE, I WAS SIMPLY INVESTIGATING HER.
A SAD LITTLE GIRL WITH NO FAMILY TO SPEAK OF!
MISS LOTTA DOES HAVE AN OLDER BROTHER—
THAT INSOLENT FELLOW WHO WAS SMOKING INSIDE THE CASTLE ON THE DAY OF YOUR CEREMONY.
YOU NEVER TOLD ME THAT, MAGIE!
I DIDN'T?
IF NECESSARY, I CAN RETURN TO BADON AND THOROUGHLY INVESTIGATE MISS LOTTA—
I DON'T CARE ABOUT THE GIRL!

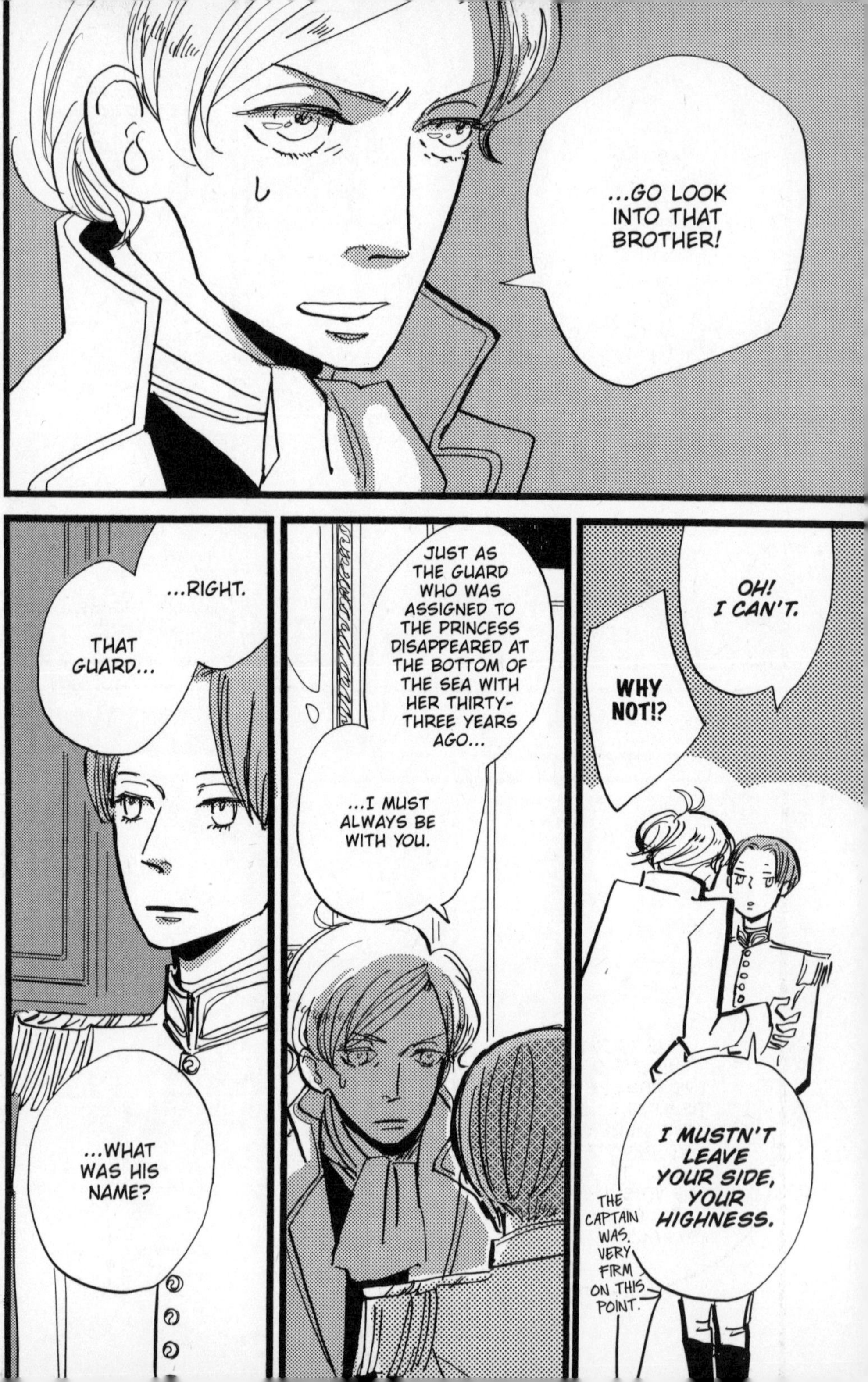
...GO LOOK INTO THAT BROTHER!
OH! I CAN'T.
WHY NOT!?
I MUSTN'T LEAVE YOUR SIDE, YOUR HIGHNESS.
THE CAPTAIN WAS VERY FIRM ON THIS POINT.
JUST AS THE GUARD WHO WAS ASSIGNED TO THE PRINCESS DISAPPEARED AT THE BOTTOM OF THE SEA WITH HER THIRTY-THREE YEARS AGO...
...I MUST ALWAYS BE WITH YOU.
...RIGHT.
THAT GUARD...
...WHAT WAS HIS NAME?

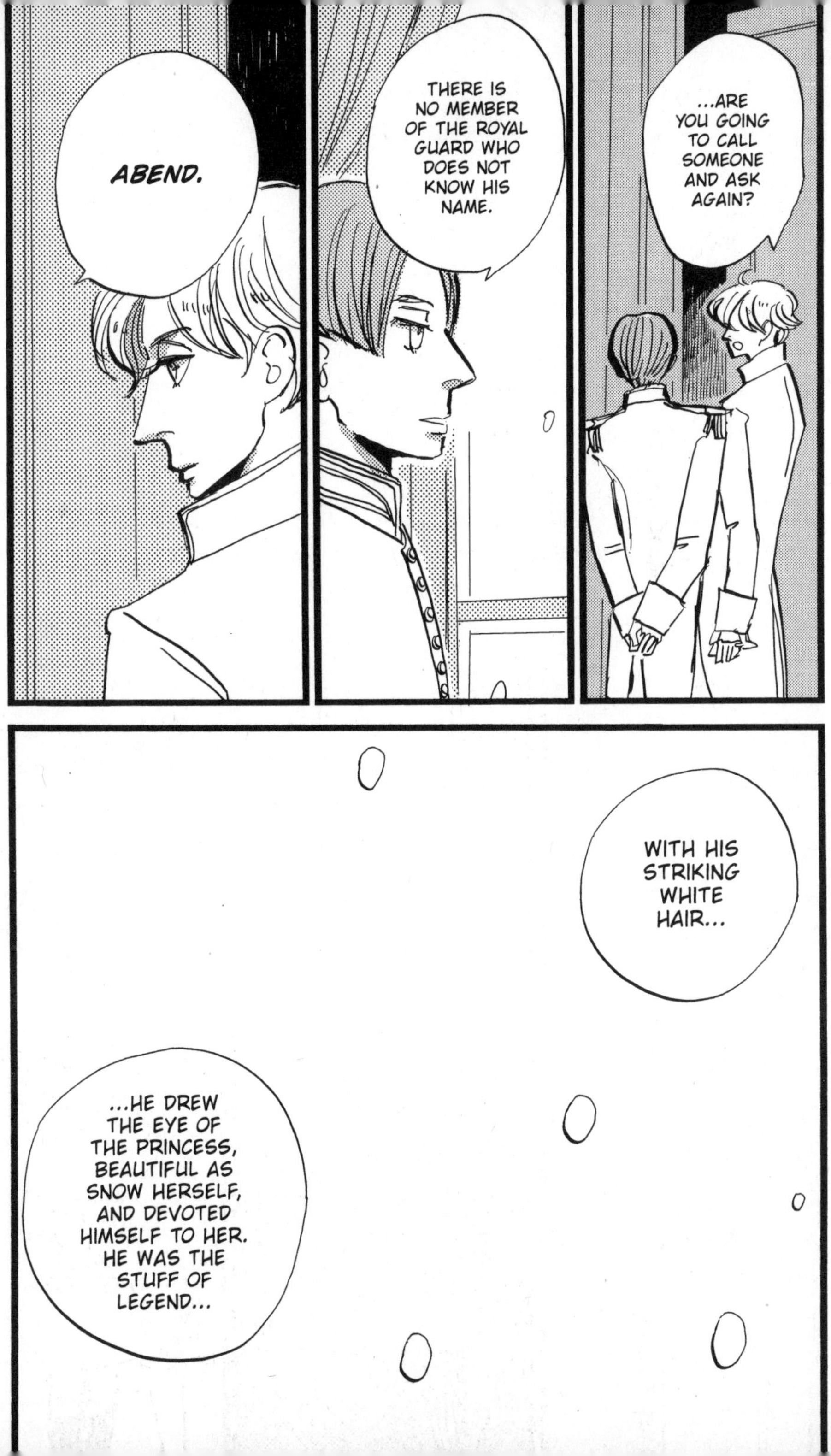
...ARE YOU GOING TO CALL SOMEONE AND ASK AGAIN?
THERE IS NO MEMBER OF THE ROYAL GUARD WHO DOES NOT KNOW HIS NAME.
ABEND.
WITH HIS STRIKING WHITE HAIR...
...HE DREW THE EYE OF THE PRINCESS, BEAUTIFUL AS SNOW HERSELF, AND DEVOTED HIMSELF TO HER. HE WAS THE STUFF OF LEGEND...

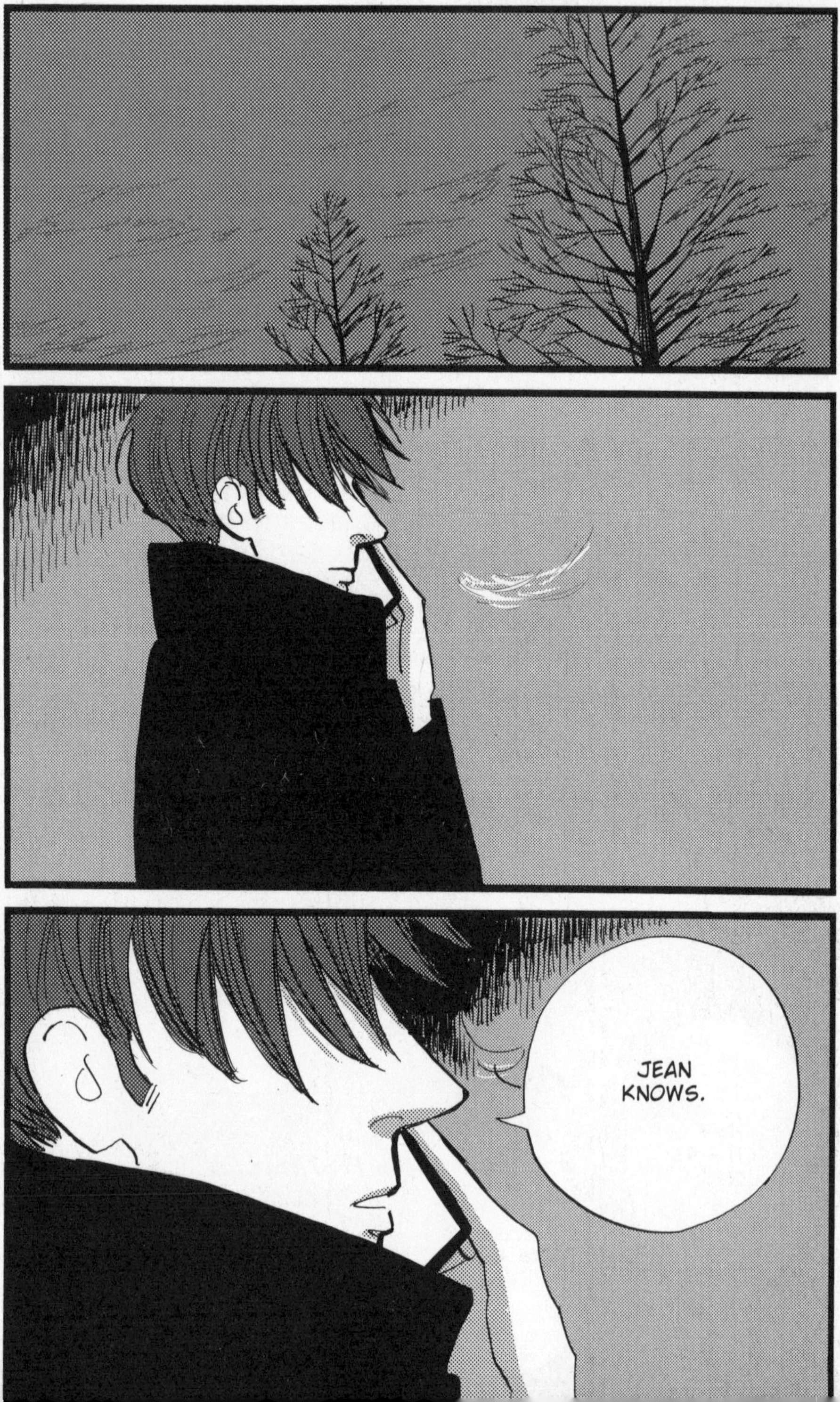
JEAN KNOWS.

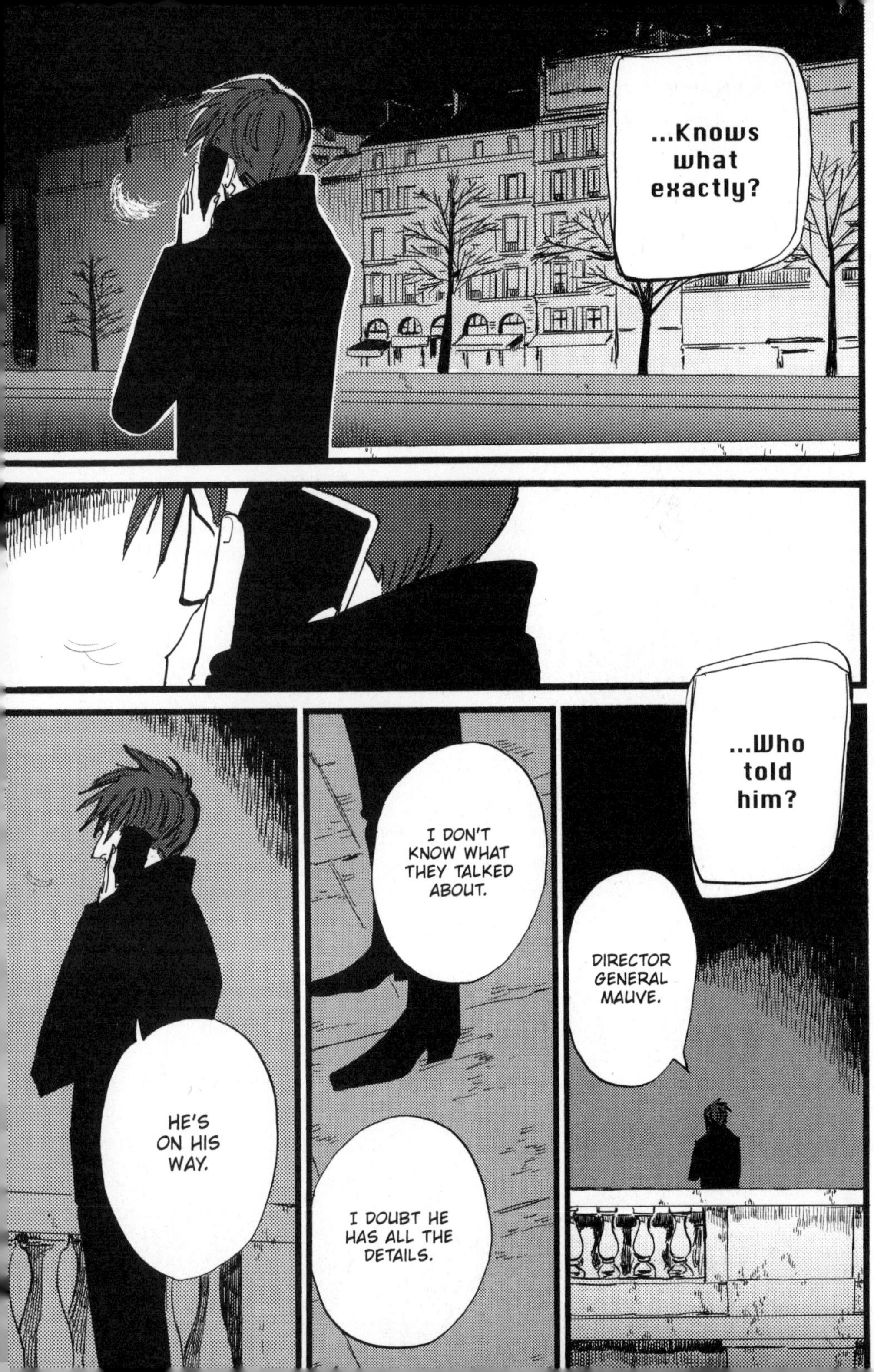
...Knows what exactly?
...Who told him?
DIRECTOR GENERAL MAUVE.
I DON'T KNOW WHAT THEY TALKED ABOUT.
I DOUBT HE HAS ALL THE DETAILS.
HE'S ON HIS WAY.

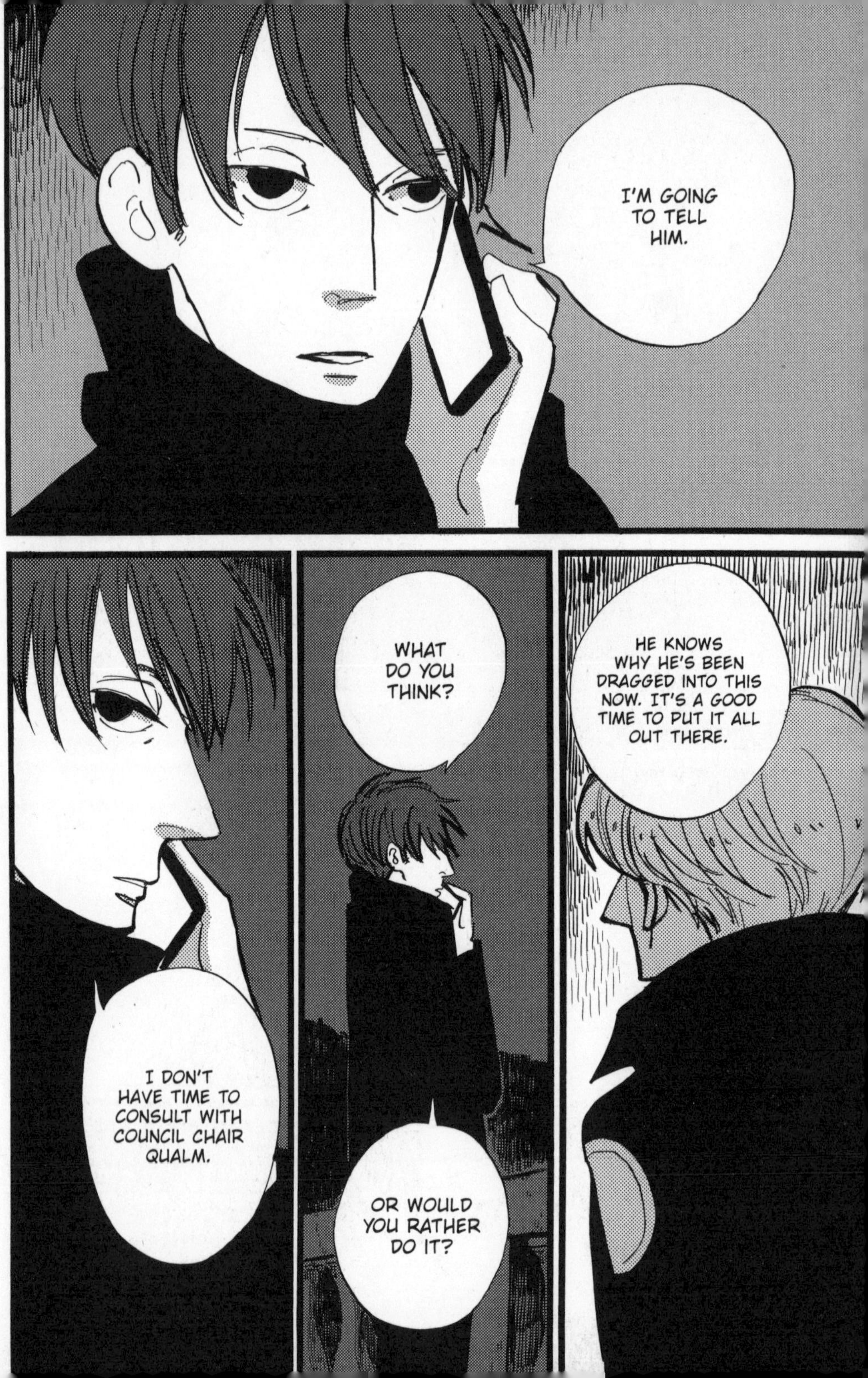
I'M GOING TO TELL HIM.
HE KNOWS WHY HE'S BEEN DRAGGED INTO THIS NOW. IT'S A GOOD TIME TO PUT IT ALL OUT THERE.
WHAT DO YOU THINK?
OR WOULD YOU RATHER DO IT?
I DON'T HAVE TIME TO CONSULT WITH COUNCIL CHAIR QUALM.

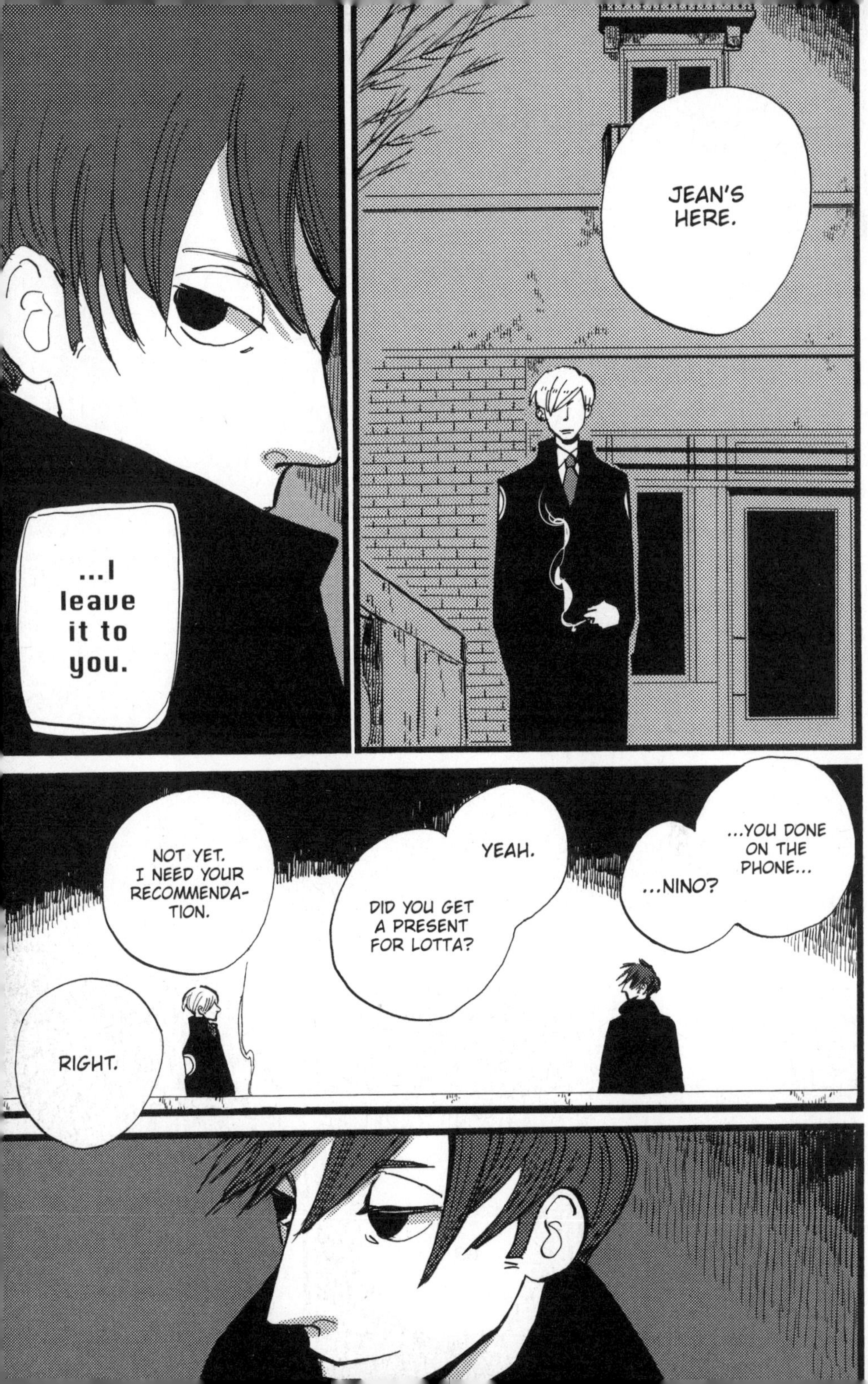
JEAN'S HERE.
...I leave it to you.
...YOU DONE ON THE PHONE... ...NINO?
YEAH.
DID YOU GET A PRESENT FOR LOTTA?
NOT YET. I NEED YOUR RECOMMENDATION.
RIGHT.

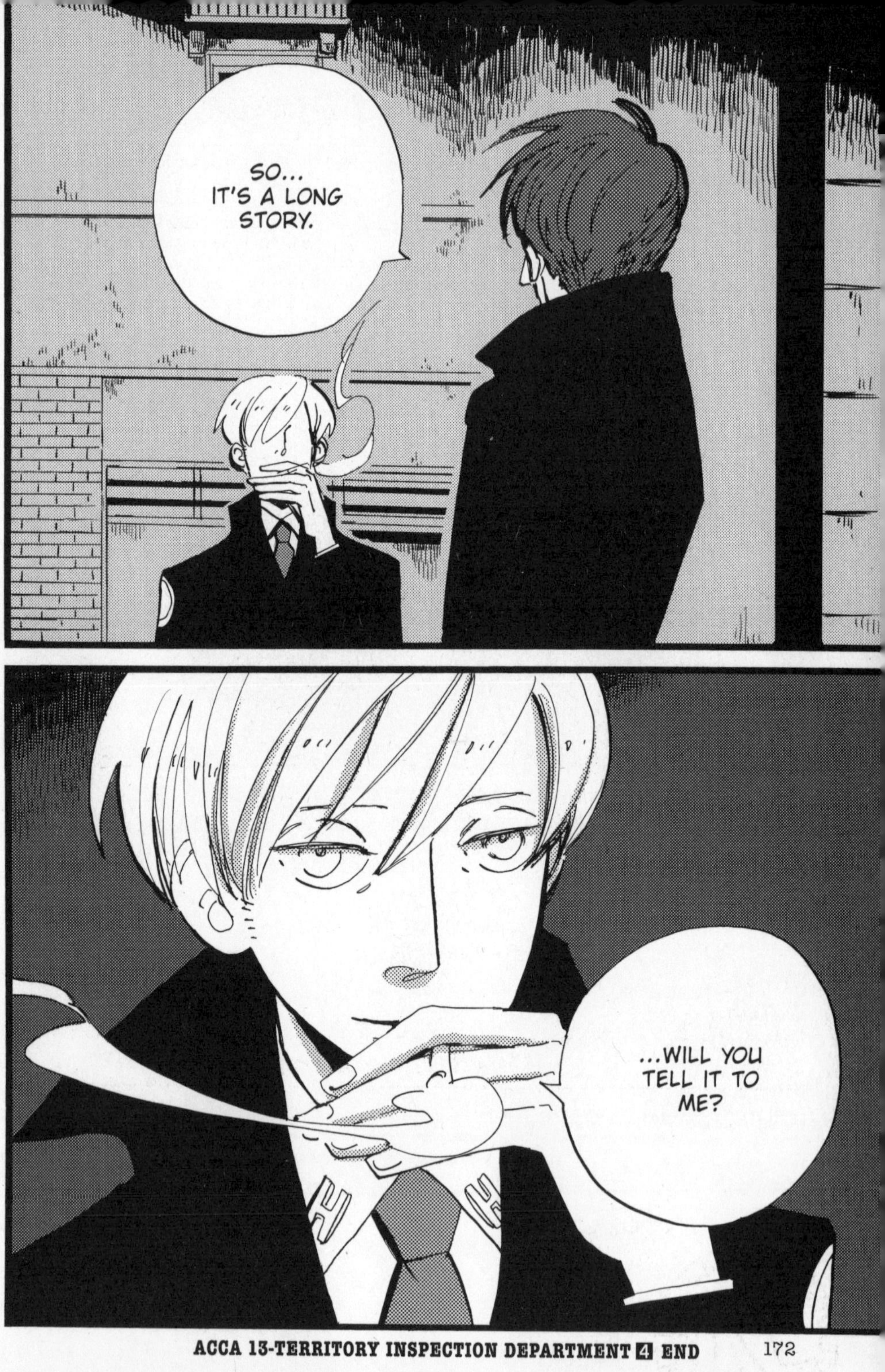
SO...
IT'S A LONG
STORY.
...WILL YOU
TELL IT TO
ME?

Kingdom of Dowa

Dowa, a kingdom with regional self-government, is divided into thirteen districts, with each district having its own unique culture.

ACCA is a massive unified organization, encompassing the police department, the fire department, and medical services, among others. The organization is managed by the branches in each district, with Headquarters in the capital performing the role of uniting the thirteen ACCA branches. The Inspection Department Jean belongs to has Headquarters agents stationed at each branch and also sends a supervisor to audit at irregular intervals in order to monitor the daily operations of the branches.

Birra
Badon
Korore
Dowa
Suitsu
Peshi
Rokkusu
Yakkara
Jumoku
Pranetta
Famasu
Furawau
N
Hare

※Darker areas on the map are districts where the audit has been completed.

Kingdom of Dowa

CHAPTER 23

Two on the Bridge in Korore

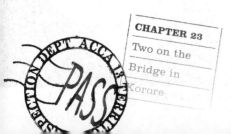

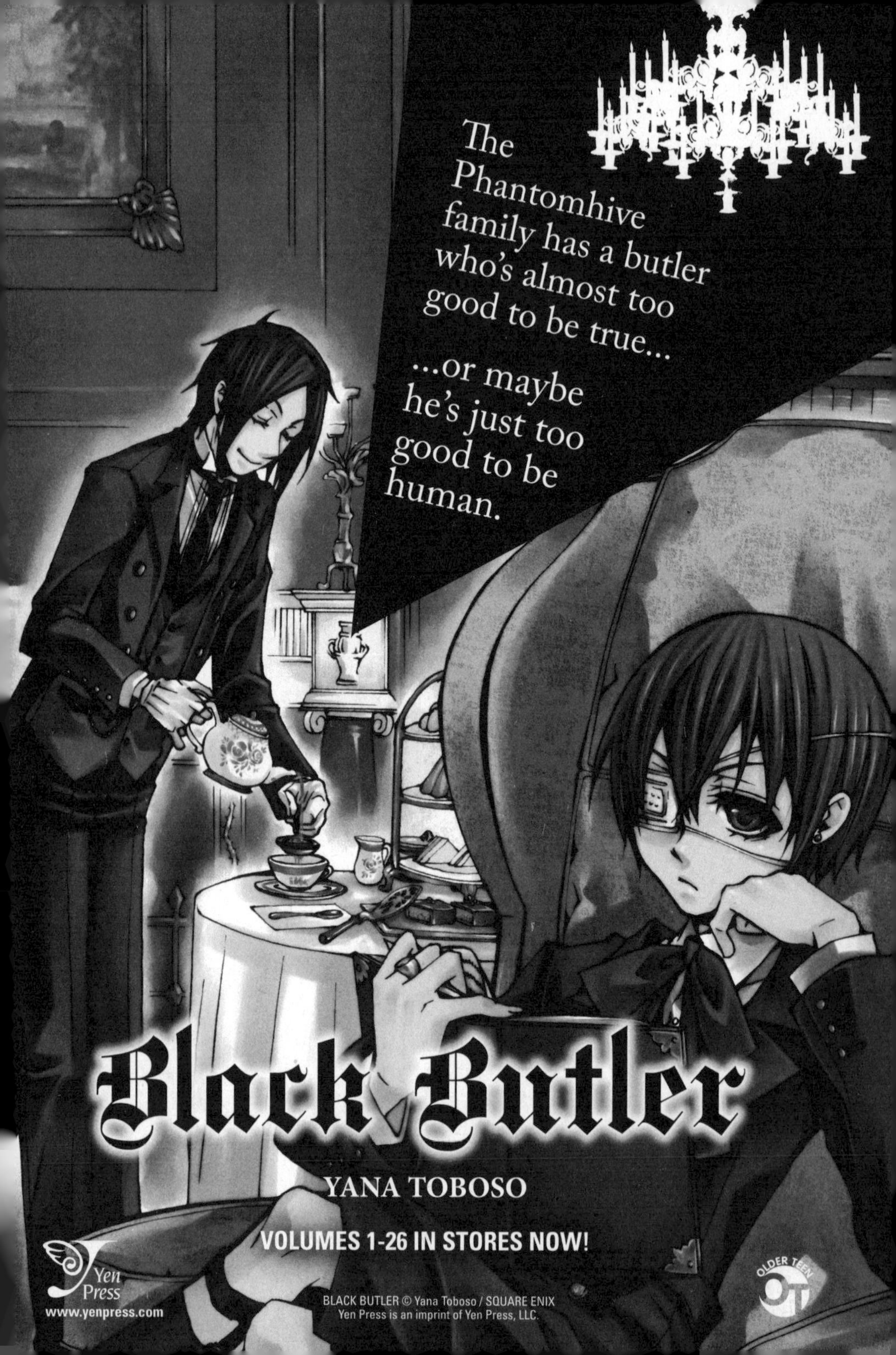
The Phantomhive family has a butler who's almost too good to be true...
...or maybe he's just too good to be human.
Black Butler
YANA TOBOSO
VOLUMES 1-26 IN STORES NOW!
Yen Press
www.yenpress.com
OLDER TEEN OT
BLACK BUTLER © Yana Toboso / SQUARE ENIX
Yen Press is an imprint of Yen Press, LLC.

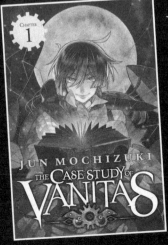

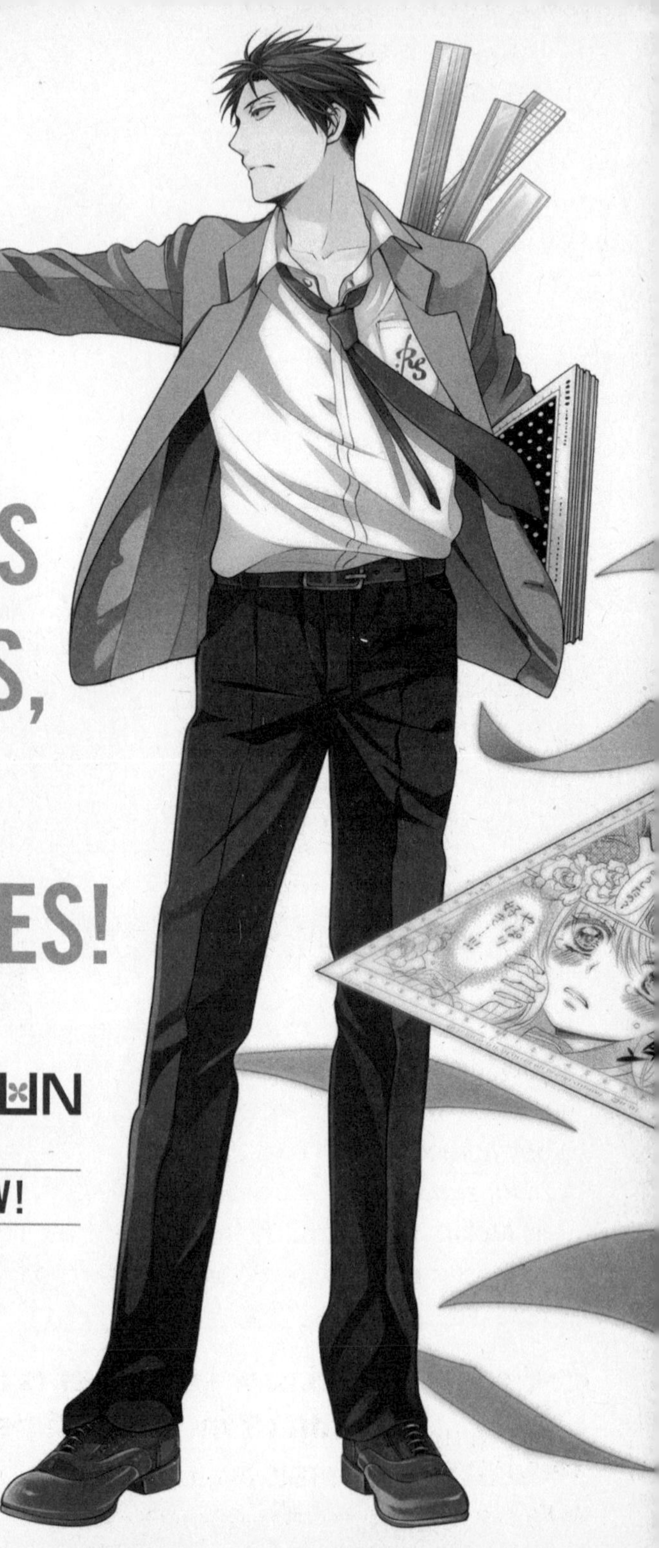

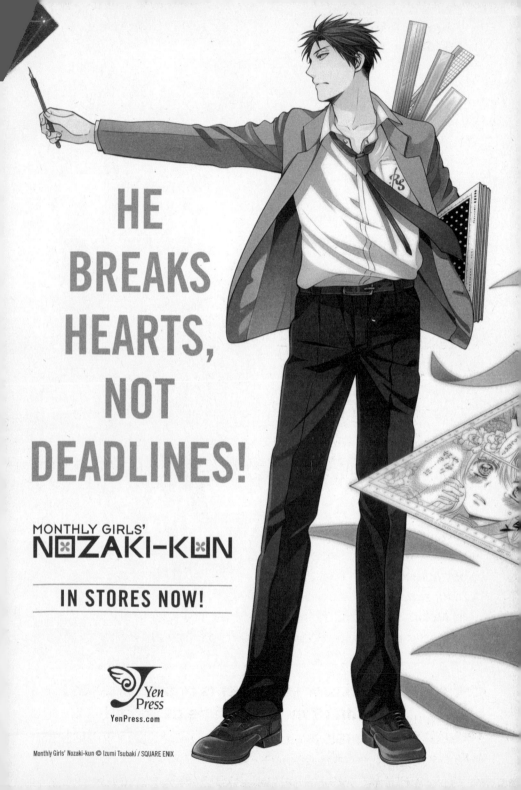

Karino Takatsu, creator of
SERVANT × SERVICE, presents:

My Monster Girl's Too Cool For You

Burning adoration melts her heart...literally!

In a world where *youkai* and humans attend school together, a boy named Atsushi Fukuzumi falls for snow *youkai* Muku Shiroishi. Fukuzumi's passionate feelings melt Muku's heart...and the rest of her?! The first volume of an interspecies romantic comedy you're sure to fall head over heels for is now available!!

YenPress.com

Read new installments of this series every month at the same time as Japan!

CHAPTERS AVAILABLE NOW AT E-TAILERS EVERYWHERE!

WELCOME TO IKEBUKURO, WHERE TOKYO'S WILDEST CHARACTERS GATHER!!

AS THEIR PATHS CROSS, THIS ECCENTRIC CAST WEAVES A TWISTED, CRACKED LOVE STORY...

AVAILABLE NOW!!

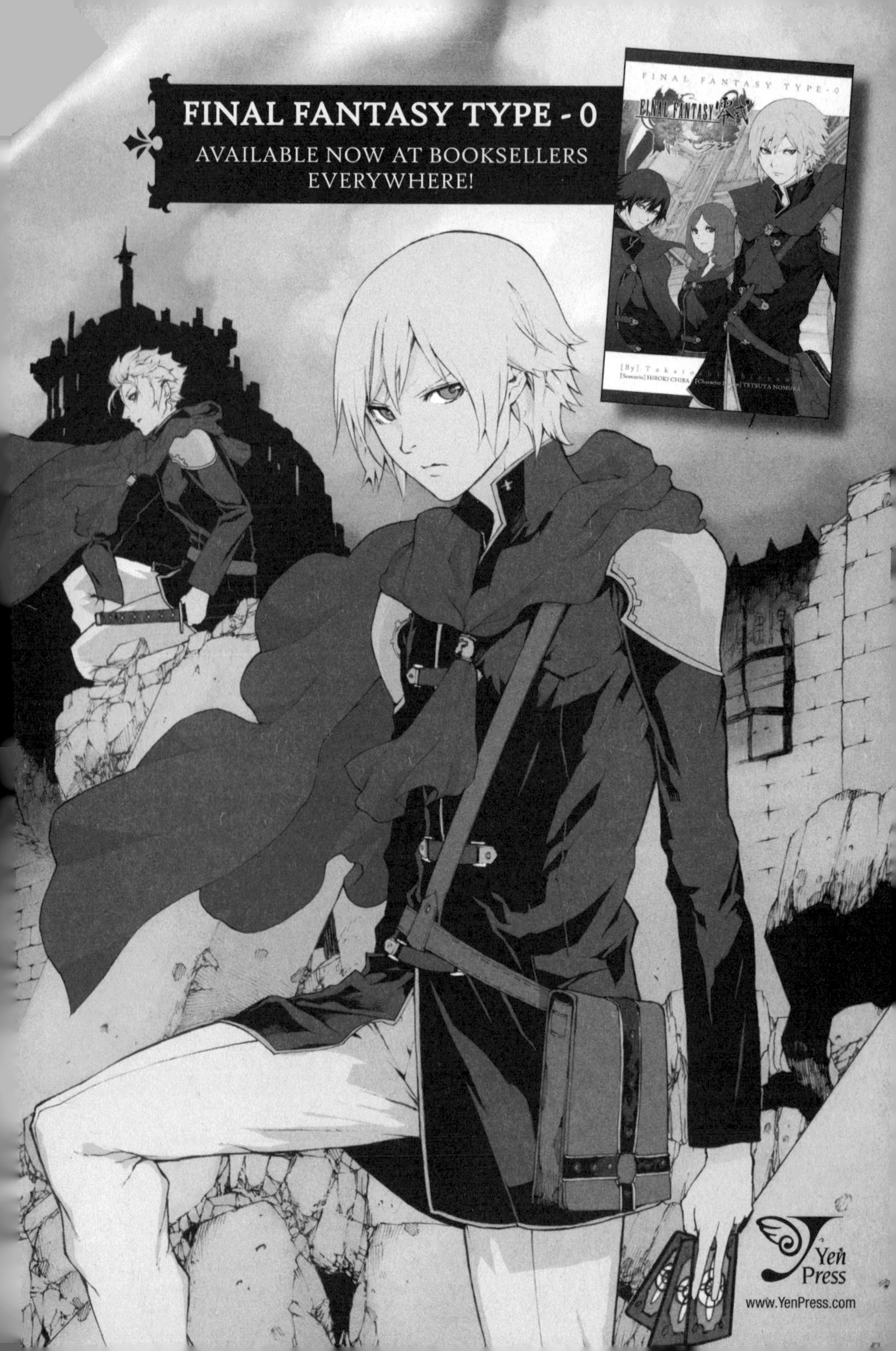
FINAL FANTASY TYPE - 0
AVAILABLE NOW AT BOOKSELLERS EVERYWHERE!
FINAL FANTASY TYPE-0
[Scenario] HIROKI CHIBA
TETSUYA NOMURA
Yen Press
www.YenPress.com

FINAL FANTASY 零式 TYPE-0

Art: TAKATOSHI SHIOZAWA
Character Design: TETSUYA NOMURA
Scenario: HIROKI CHIBA

The cadets of Akademeia's Class Zero are legends, with strength and magic unrivaled, and crimson capes symbolizing the great Vermilion Bird of the Dominion. But will their elite training be enough to keep them alive when a war breaks out and the Class Zero cadets find themselves at the front and center of a bloody political battlefield?!

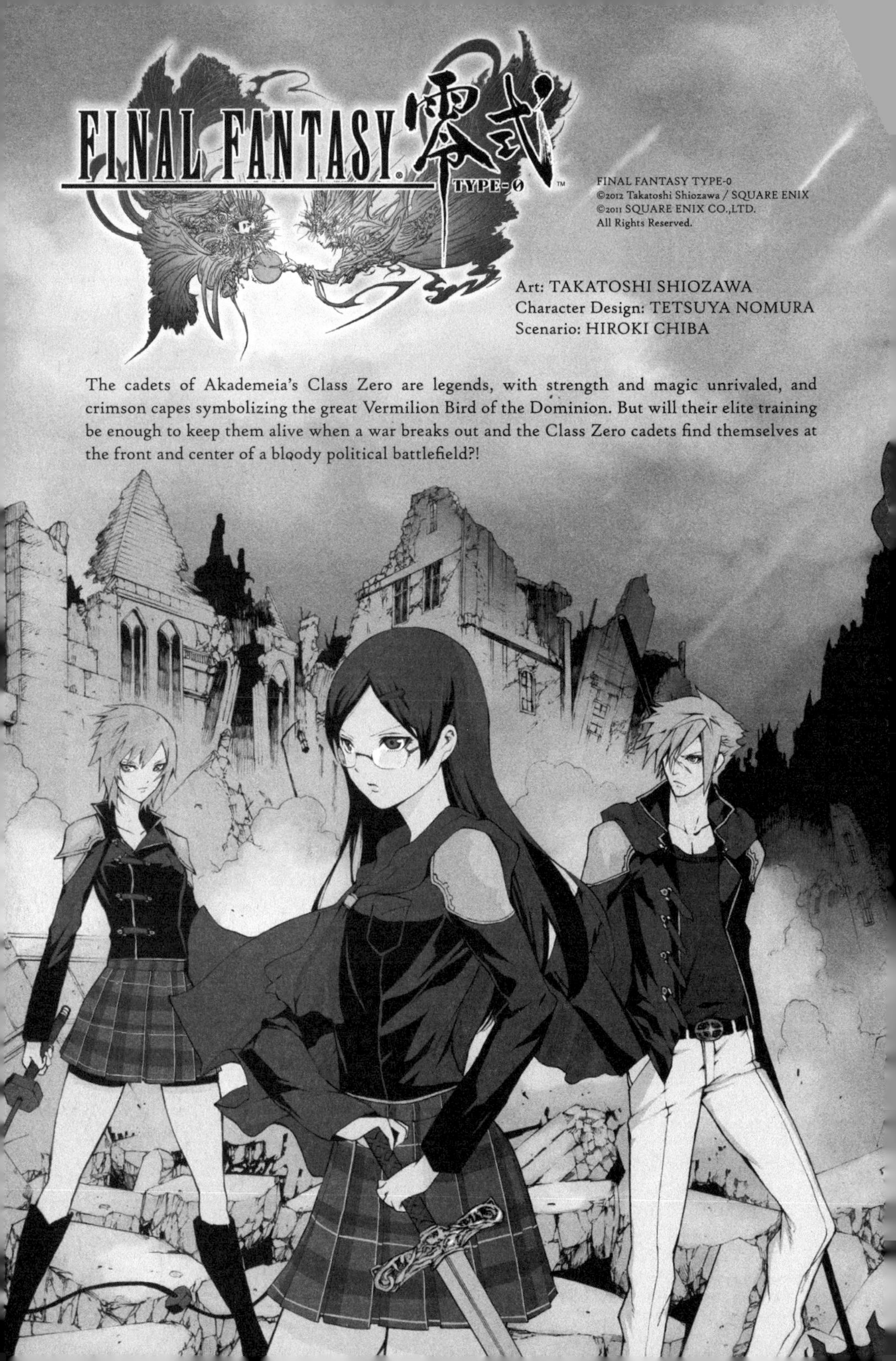

ACCA

13 TERRITORY INSPECTION DEPARTMENT

NATSUME ONO

Translation:
Jocelyne Allen

Lettering:
Lys Blakeslee

ACCA JUSAN-KU KANSATSU-KA Volume 4 ©2015 Natsume Ono/
Square Enix Co., Ltd. First published in Japan in 2015 by Square
Enix Co., Ltd. English translation rights arranged with Square
Enix Co., Ltd. and Yen Press, LLC through Tuttle-Mori Agency, Inc.

English translation ©2018 by Square Enix Co., Ltd.

Yen Press
1290 Avenue of the Americas
New York, NY 10104

Visit us at yenpress.com
facebook.com/yenpress
twitter.com/yenpress
yenpress.tumblr.com
instagram.com/yenpress

First Yen Press Edition: August 2018

Yen Press is an imprint of Yen Press, LLC.
The Yen Press name and logo are trademarks of
Yen Press, LLC.

The publisher is not responsible for websites (or their
content) that are not owned by the publisher.

Library of Congress Control Number: 2017949545

ISBNs: 978-0-316-44678-5 (paperback)
       978-0-316-44679-2 (ebook)

10 9 8 7 6 5 4 3 2 1

WOR

Printed in the United States of America